TWINMAKER

TWINMAKER

SEAN WILLIAMS

An Imprint of HarperCollins*Publishers*

HarperTeen is an imprint of HarperCollins Publishers.

Twinmaker
Copyright © 2013 by Sean Williams
All rights reserved. Printed in the United States of America.
No part of this book may be used or reproduced in any manner
whatsoever without written permission except in the case of brief
quotations embodied in critical articles and reviews. For information
address HarperCollins Children's Books, a division of HarperCollins
Publishers, 10 East 53rd Street, New York, NY 10022.
www.epicreads.com

Library of Congress Cataloging-in-Publication Data is available.
Williams, Sean.
    Twinmaker / Sean Williams. — First edition.
        pages   cm
    Summary: When her best friend, Libby, misuses instant transpor-
tation technology to alter her appearance, seventeeen-year-old Clair is
drawn into a shadowy world of conspiracies and cover-ups as she attempts
to save Libby from the hidden consequences of her actions.
    ISBN 978-0-06-220321-2 (hardcover bdg.)
    [1. Space and time—Fiction. 2. Conspiracies—Fiction. 3. Best
friends—Fiction. 4. Friendship—Fiction. 5. Science fiction.] I. Title.
PZ7.W6681739Tw   2013   2012043498
[Fic]—dc23   CIP
                                                                 AC

Typography by Erin Fitzsimmons
13 14 15 16 17   CG/RRDH   10 9 8 7 6 5 4 3 2 1
❖
First Edition

You are special.
You are unique.
And you have been selected.

Follow the instructions.
Don't tell anyone.
You are the lucky one.
You can be Improved.

The method is simple.
Improvement is certain.
You can change anything.
Change everything,
if you want to.

Keep this a secret.
You deserve it.

[1] ———————————————————

THE LUCKY JUMP was all the rage that year. Clair had tried it once but had become bored after arriving at a string of destinations that seemed anything but lucky. An empty field, a theater advertising a show in a language she didn't understand, an underwater viewing platform full of noisy kids, and somewhere so wet and hot she didn't even leave the booth. Clair could get better views from home, surfing media through her lenses, *and* be comfortable into the bargain.

It was Libby, of course, who convinced her to give it another try.

"Come on, it'll be jazzy."

"How exactly?"

"There's this clique—they call themselves crashlanders. Ever heard of them?"

Clair shook her head. Libby was into that kind of thing, not her.

"They're the coolest of the cool," Libby said. "You wouldn't believe how popular they are. Hardly anyone can join them, but we're going to."

"Just like that?"

"Trust me, Clair. Have I led you astray before?"

"Plenty of times."

"Come on! What about when we auditioned for the circus even though we couldn't even juggle? Or visited that hacked satellite and Ronnie threw up?"

"Yes, but then we got stuck at the South Pole—"

"You're the one who set the booth to Chinese."

"Only because you dared me to try!"

They laughed. That *was* a memorable moment. They had only gotten moving again when Clair found a friend of a friend who knew how to change the settings back.

"Where did you hear about the crashlanders?" Clair asked.

"Through Zep. He's not one of them, but he'd like to be."

Clair just nodded. Lately she clammed up when Zeppelin Barker, Libby's boyfriend, entered the conversation.

"Come on, Clair. Say yes. You always do in the end."

That was true, although she couldn't imagine it ever being jazzy to d-mat from place to place. There was no point resisting one of Libby's whims when she had her mind set on it.

"All right."

"Great! I'll come to your place after class. Be ready."

Clair lived in Windham, Maine, with her mother and stepfather. She and her best friend went to high school on the other side of the continent, near Sacramento Bay, California. Libby lived somewhere in Sweden—Clair always forgot the name, but that didn't matter. She just told the booth to take her to Libby's, and so it did.

Clair dialed a familiar outfit from the fabber's memory: navy plaid skirt and tank top, with black boots, bicycle shorts, and belt, and a navy headband in the vain hope of keeping her curly hair in line. She'd given up on ever having Libby's perfectly straight blond locks. Where she was dark, Libby was light; combine the two of them, she'd often thought, and you'd get someone of precisely average coloring.

Libby was running late. While she waited, Clair searched the Air for anything regarding the crashlanders. Apart from an old book with the same name, there were several peacekeeper reports concerning the new clique and its members. Founded by a woman called Alexandra Nantakarn, the clique held "crashlander balls" at different points around the world every night: in old missile silos, abandoned hospitals, and other ruins, often illegally. Exclusive parties in exotic locales sounded like the kind of thing Libby would be into, but there was no information on how the balls were organized or who was allowed to attend.

Before Clair could perform a more detailed search, Libby arrived, looking fashionable in white tights, silver A-line dress, bright-red leather retro Doc Martens with yellow laces, and a skull-hugging yarmulke that matched the boots but left her hair free to do what it did best. Her makeup was a wild contrast between white foundation and primary-colored lipstick and eyeliner designed to pull attention away from the brown birthmark that, despite numerous skin treatments, stretched from her left ear to her chin. Clair had given up trying to convince Libby that the mark was anything other than a minor imperfection—unlike, say, Clair's nose, which she had inherited from her birth father and hated with a blinding white-hot passion.

"Come on." Libby dragged Clair out of the apartment and up the hall. "It's starting."

"The ball?"

"Exactly!"

"What's the huge hurry?" asked Clair, messaging her stepfather to apologize for not saying good-bye in person. "We'll be there in a sec."

"No, we won't, because I don't know the way," Libby said, adding with an enigmatic grin: "But it's vitally important we get there first."

"What?"

"You'll see." Libby pulled a makeup applicator from her pocket and touched up the pancake over her birthmark. The booth's mirrored interior reflected and re-reflected thousands of Libbies and Clairs in all directions.

Libby said to the booth, "I want to get lucky."

Somewhere, a machine shuffled every possible public d-mat address and selected one by chance. Instead of taking them to a destination they specified, like home or school, the booth would take them to a random point anywhere on the Earth. People used Lucky Jumps to sightsee or while away an empty afternoon. Clair had never heard of anyone using them to actually get anywhere in particular.

Bright light flared from the booth's eight corners, and the air thinned around them. Clair opened her mouth from years of habit. Her sinuses strained.

sssssss—

She stuck a finger in her right ear, wiggled it—

—pop

The lights returned to normal and the door opened.

They were on a rugged coast, looking out over choppy water under skies as gray as granite. The northwest coast of England, her lenses told her. Nowhere.

"Well, this looks fun," said Clair.

"Better than that thing you took me to last month—the Morris Dance Festival, whatever it was."

"I was promised men in tights," conceded Clair.

"And if any of them had been under seventy, maybe it would have worked out. Again," Libby told the booth. "Lucky, lucky, lucky."

"We're not seriously going to randomly jump around until we find the ball, are we?"

"That's the plan."

"It's going to take us forever," said Clair. "We'll *literally* be in here forever."

"Don't be such a worrywart. Just wait and see."

sssssss-pop

Red Australian desert vanished at the horizon into the endless starscape above. A nocturnal lizard crouched in the light spilling from the booth, frozen by the sudden development.

"Crap," said Libby.

"You can say that again."

"All right, all right." Libby put her applicator in her pocket and embiggened Clair's hair with her fingers. "There, perfect. Third time *really* lucky, please."

The door slid shut on the sight of the lizard, stolidly chewing on an insect that had been attracted by the light.

sssssss-pop

The doors opened on an utterly ordinary, utterly un-interesting Ugandan d-mat station.

Clair folded her arms and raised an eyebrow.

Libby was starting to look a little impatient herself.

"Okay, I guess the surprise is ruined now. No one knows where the crashlander balls are until they happen, see? People Lucky Jump around until they find somewhere with potential and then they all converge."

"Anyone can do this?"

"Anyone can suggest venues on the crashlander forum, but they make the final decision. And they don't let any-one come to the ball who hasn't found a venue before. You get it?"

Clair did see. This wasn't just about a party. The ball was literally their ticket into the cool new clique, which in importance to Libby was right up there with the clothes she was wearing and the person she was dating. Schoolwork barely rated.

Clair piggybacked on Libby's feed from the crashlander forum and splashed its content across the infield of her lenses. Uganda vanished behind a wall of images, projected onto her retinas by contacts she had worn from birth. The forum was full of people exchanging images of suggested sites taken with their lenses. There were a *lot* of images.

Clair and Libby jumped twice more, without success.

"This is giving me a headache," said Libby despondently, brushing her bangs back into line after the doors closed and the gale outside ebbed to a muffled scream.

"Harder than you thought?" Clair tried not to sound smug.

"Much. Maybe we should pack it in."

"Why? We've only just started."

"I thought you'd be pleased."

"*Someone* has to find a venue. It could still be us."

"Not at the rate we're going."

This was the way it always went. Clair didn't like giving up on anything once she got into it, and Libby was easily bored. "We'll just have to go faster, then. Booth? Again, please."

sssssss-pop

Clair was seeing the fun of it, now. There was the challenge of finding the right place entirely by chance, combined with finding it before anyone else did. The odds for the former were low—there were tens of millions of d-mat booths in the world, after all, maybe hundreds of millions—but that made the odds of being the first to any one of them higher. Clair figured it canceled out.

And if they found the place, they would be crashlanders. *They* would be cool, and Zep would come to *them*, because he was as much a publicity hound as Libby. That incentive she kept carefully to herself.

Their seventeenth Lucky Jump put them in the middle of what looked like an abandoned industrial complex somewhere high up, judging by Clair's unpopped ear and the instant chill against her skin. She stepped out and looked around, skeptical.

"Booth's ancient," said Libby, circling it with a look of profound dissatisfaction. It was an outmoded model, square, with a single round-edged door opening out of each white face. Just four transits at a time. "It'd be a total bottleneck."

"Could work in our favor—you know, make it feel exclusive?" said Clair, gazing up at thick iron girders and bulging rivets, and beyond all that, a high, domed ceiling. The floor below was empty, because industry was a thing of the past. Anything except people could be fabricated at will, as long as it had been through a d-mat booth or a fabber at some point in its existence.

"It's freezing," said Libby, hugging herself, "and the air's thin."

"We can fab heaters," Clair said, peering through a window at the infinite quilt of mountains outside. "Oxygen, too, if people need it."

"Because passing out is a definite buzzkill."

"Doesn't it give you a high if you breathe it pure?"

Libby shrugged. "Don't forget the parkas,'" she said. "They're *always* sexy."

Clair checked the Air for details on their location. They were in Switzerland, it turned out, and the amazing building around them wasn't an old factory at all, but an abandoned astronomical research station, the Sphinx Observatory, just over two miles up on the top of a hollowed-out mountain, with an ice palace somewhere at the end of an old elevator shaft below and observation decks that had been sealed up for a decade. . . .

Clair read on with amazement. Was this place *real*?

"I'm getting a buzz," she said. "Quick, take my picture."

She opened her arms, and Libby stared hard for a second while her lenses worked.

"Got it, gorgeous girl. You want me to post it to the forum?"

"Worth a try."

"You really think they'll come?"

"Only one way to find out."

Libby's lenses flickered in the gloom, and when Clair checked the crashlander forum, she saw images of herself standing in the observatory spreading out into the world.

"How will we know if they like it?" Libby asked, worrying at her lip.

"They'll just come, I guess."

For five minutes, nothing happened. Libby kicked the floor in moody silence, hands plunged deep in the pockets of a thick woolen coat she had ordered through the booth, while Clair paced around the enormous space, refusing to give up hope. She was finding it harder, though, with every passing minute, as the cold seeped into her skin and she became aware of a faint dizziness from the thin air. Giving up, as Libby was clearly ready to do, would be a lot easier than persisting much longer. And the odds of talking to Zep were practically zero anyway, even if the party happened. . . .

The booth behind them clunked. They ran across the room to see. One of the four doors was closing. In quick succession, the remaining three closed too, and the echoing metal space was full of the hum of matter and energy spinning into new forms. Clair stopped pacing, barely able to breathe with anticipation. They were stranded, but only temporarily, and soon they wouldn't be alone. She saw the same eager alertness on Libby's face. Neither of them dared speak.

"Hey," said the first person out, a lanky man in his twenties with a British accent and a swoop of yellow hair that completely covered half his face. He stared around him with one green eye wide and gleaming, and shivered. "This is savage."

"You like it?" asked Libby.

"Maybe. Where's the telescope?"

"Don't know," said Clair. "We haven't looked yet."

He wandered off to explore. The door he had come through was already closing, processing someone else.

The second door opened, admitting another young man in a thick, furred overcoat, who simply ran across the room to the nearest window and gasped with something that might have been excitement or alarm. It was hard to tell. The view through the window went a *long* way down.

Libby looked at Clair, who shrugged.

The third potential partygoer was a girl with Thai features and a South American accent.

"Are you Liberty Zeist?" she asked Clair.

"No, I am," said Libby.

"And you want to be a crashlander."

"Uh, obviously. We both do."

"Haven't you heard that all the good sites have been taken?"

Libby looked at Clair in frustration. Clair's heart sank. All their jumping and standing around in the cold had been for nothing. If the crashlanders had already been here, that meant no ball and no Zep.

"Just messing with you," said the woman with a grin. "This is a great find. Congratulations."

She produced three beers from her backpack and tossed one each to Libby and Clair. The third she opened.

"What are you waiting for? It's time to party."

"But how do you know?" Libby asked. "Doesn't there have to be a vote or something?"

"Democracy is *so* twentieth century. Besides, the queue for the booth is thirty deep already. I'd say the decision's been made." The woman grinned and raised her can in salute. "Xandra Nantakarn. Welcome to the crashlanders."

Clair turned to Libby and saw the delight she felt mirrored on her best friend's face. They whooped and high-fived and toasted each other's brilliance with their gifted beers.

——————————————————[2]

ANYONE IN THE world over fifteen years of age could solo jump. Anyone over eighteen could consume alcohol. For the crashlanders, and for seventeen-year-olds like Clair and Libby, that was a winning combination.

For the next hour, people arrived singly or in pairs, four

times every three minutes—the fastest the old booth could cycle. Most brought supplies with them. Before long the cold metal space of the old observatory was transformed by inflatable couches, radiant heaters, multicolored spotlights, and even sparklers and other small fireworks. Food and drink flowed in ever-growing quantities. Eventually, someone brought a whole fabber through, so there was no more waiting for the old booth to cycle to see what came next.

Clair helped herself to a handful of warm roasted chickpeas and another beer and followed Libby through the crowd, syncing her lenses and ear-rings to the media enjoyed by whatever cluster she was closest to. Two separate dance parties were forming at opposite ends of the cavernous space, one swaying to cruise music with a syncopated Spanish beat, the other jerking and twitching to harsh, atonal synth. Libby migrated from one to the other with willful unpredictability, drawn by the attention of those around her.

"Super crashlanding, Libby."

"Outrageous space, Libby."

"Libby, how did you *find* it?"

Sometimes they thought Clair was Libby because of the photo Libby had posted to the forum. Libby corrected them, then accepted their admiration. Not once did she say that it was Clair who had made her post the picture. The beer in Clair's stomach soured slightly: Libby would have bailed on the site in a *second*. But what could Clair say? Besides, she wouldn't have been there at all but for Libby's insistence. They were both crashlanders now. It evened out, like their complexions.

There was no sign of Zep, even though Libby must have invited him: boyfriends or girlfriends were allowed, Clair had learned, whether they were officially crashlanders or not.

Then, ninety minutes into the ball, a metallic crash came from the booth. Both Libby and Clair spun around in alarm, fearing some kind of accident or breakdown that would bring the still-growing party to an end. The doors had opened on a delivery of oxygen canisters that went right up to the booth's ceiling. Canisters spilled out in a noisy silver flood across the floor, disgorging an achingly handsome young man from their midst.

Clair's breath hitched in her throat.

"Zep!" Libby rushed forward to help him to his feet. He was long, lean, and tanned, wearing a translucent red-check shirt with a white wifebeater underneath and holding an oxygen bottle in each hand. His grin was infectious. People cheered, whether they knew him or not.

"For medicinal purposes *only*, now," he said, taking a long pull on one of the bottles and handing the other to a random stranger. "If symptoms of altitude sickness persist, please see—oh, hey, Libs."

Clair was excited to see him, but she averted her eyes as

he and Libby locked lips. The way Libby pulled his blond head down to hers left no illusion as to who belonged to whom.

One of the bottles knocked against Clair's left boot. She raised it to her mouth to take a hit of cool clarity. It didn't help her light-headedness, though. It wasn't oxygen she craved, and it didn't ease the guilty ache in her heart at all. She turned her back on the tableau and moved away.

"Hey, Clair-bear," Zep called after her. "Wait up—"

She wandered on her own for a bit, not going so far as to deliberately avoid the happy couple but enjoying being among people she didn't know except as names and captions in her lenses. There were day-trippers in feathery cloaks and gothic moonwalkers in black and silver— two migratory groups who never normally met, since they occupied different hemispheres, day and night. The crashlanders had united them, as the ball united all races, types, and sexual orientations. Clair flirted a bit, flattered and embarrassed at the same time by the men and women who approached her, but her heart wasn't in it.

She moved on. It was getting crowded and increasingly hard to hear anything over the excited shouting and singing. There were a lot of nosebleeds from the altitude, but that didn't seem to dent anyone's desire to party. She wondered what would happen if someone got really hurt. Would the peacekeepers come to shut the ball down? Clair took some guilty comfort from the thought that if trouble *did* break out, Libby would get the blame, just like she took all the credit.

"Hey," said someone, "I think that Zep guy is looking for you."

"You mean Libby," she said, beginning to get a little tired of her perpetually mistaken identity. "I'm Clair, the other one."

"Oh, okay, sorry."

She headed for the nearest lookout, which was colder but had a spectacular view. A pair of unexpectedly familiar faces stood out from the crowd—fashionably bespectacled Ronnie and blue-haired Tash, friends from school. The girls drew her into their corner, where they hugged and kissed her and danced with her to a song they had been sharing. Clair felt her mood bounce back. The emotional knock of seeing Zep with Libby couldn't endure in the face of her friends' determined good cheer. They were at a crashlander ball! What wasn't exciting about that?

As the song wound down, Tash explained that they had scored invites when friends of friends responded sympathetically to their urgent need to attend. Libby's Air-wide announcement that she and Clair had made it in had prompted a rush of interest from their high school. Ronnie and Tash were the lucky ones.

Then Libby joined them, bursting out of the crowd with her hair plastered across her forehead, darkened with sweat.

"This was a great idea," Clair confessed to her, feeling

flushed and sticky. "I'm glad we did it."

"Told you I never let you down. Have you seen Zep?"

"No . . . but he's looking for you."

"Why don't you bump him?" asked Ronnie.

"The Air's so jammed in here," Libby said. "I can't get anyone."

"Well, he won't have gone home," said Clair. "He'd never leave a scene like this."

"Why would he?" Libby took a pull on Clair's beer. "Everyone's so totally gorgeous."

"That guy over there in the purple suit," said Tash, pointing surreptitiously, "he's *someone*, isn't he?"

"If he isn't, he should be." Ronnie pursed her lips in a silent whistle. "Oh, and look—he's with that amazing redhead we spotted earlier."

Clair glanced around and saw a couple leaning shoulder-to-shoulder in the nearest doorway. His eyes were perfect almonds, golden-irised like an owl's. Her hair swept up to golden points in a fiery wave. Clair's hands came up automatically to touch her thick curls.

"They're too fantastic to be real," she said. "Who are they?"

"Don't know," said Tash with yearning in her voice. "Their profiles are locked."

"I put a trawler on their images," said Ronnie, "but so far I'm just getting junk. Whoever they are, they're hiding deep in the noise."

"Who hides at a party like this?" asked Libby. Clair could only guess how often she'd checked her own popularity stats to see how high they'd risen.

"Spies?" suggested Tash.

"You've been watching old movies again," said Ronnie.

"Terrorists?" asked Clair. "Art prankers? Spammers?"

"How many beautiful criminals do you know?"

"Maybe they're advertising Improvement," said Tash.

Ronnie laughed. "Why not? That makes as much sense as anything else."

Clair didn't get the joke.

"What's Improvement?"

"A dumb new meme," said Ronnie. "I got an invite this morning and deleted it immediately."

"I got one this afternoon," said Tash. "Check your infield, Clair. You might have been 'selected' while you were here, you lucky thing, you."

Clair did check, and found the message exactly where Tash had suggested. It had come forty-five minutes earlier. She read the opening lines:

You are special.
You are unique.
And you have been selected.

"It does sound like spam," she said.

"Read it all," said Ronnie. "It's a classic."

Clair skimmed ahead. The idea was to write a series of code words on a piece of paper, of all things, with a description of what you wanted to change about yourself—height, intelligence, good looks, whatever; then you hid it under your clothes and took it with you through d-mat. Do this enough times, the invite said, and whatever you wish for will come true.

Keep this a secret.
You deserve it.

"Not even a sixth grader would fall for those last two lines, would they?" said Tash, adopting a fake voice. "'No one but *you* is special enough to receive this message, which we probably sent to everyone in the whole world.' Yeah, right."

"It can't be real," said Clair, approaching the issue from a more practical angle. "It'd be illegal, for starters."

"Absolutely," said Ronnie. "You just can't change patterns like that. But writing it down makes it seem real, like a spell from a fairy tale—something that *ought* to work, even though it's impossible."

"Nothing's impossible," said Libby. "Things go wrong. This afternoon my fabber mixed up my makeup—I asked for thirteen and it gave me a thirty-one. What's to stop a booth from mixing a person up as well?"

"Maybe you asked for the wrong skin tone," said Ronnie.

"I didn't. You think I haven't done this a thousand times before?"

"Let's not argue about some stupid meme," said Tash. "We're perfect as we are. Who'd want to change?"

"There's always something," said Ronnie.

"Like what?" Tash asked with a grin. "Being such a know-it-all?"

"Pfft. Legs and lungs so I could run a marathon. What about you?"

"Bikini line, no question. Clair?"

"Uh . . ." Clair would have chosen her nose, but she wasn't playing that game. Behind her sweat-thinned makeup, Libby's birthmark had turned a deeper shade, as though it was blushing on her behalf.

"My invite came yesterday," Libby said. "I did it. I used Improvement."

"Why the hell?" said Ronnie.

"Just in case, okay?" She looked sheepish but her jaw had a defiant set. "The note says it takes a while. Maybe I haven't d-matted enough yet for it to take effect."

"You could d-mat for a year and it wouldn't make a difference," said Ronnie. "Listen—"

Tash put a hand on Ronnie's arm, silencing her. Tash looked mortified, probably by the memory of her own "sixth grader" comment.

"No one even notices your birthmark," she said.

"It's true," said Clair. "You're the only one it bothers."

"*I* notice it," Libby said. "It *does* bother me."

"We love you no matter what," said Ronnie, "and you know Zep will, too."

Clair nodded a little too hard.

"I think Zep's seeing someone else," Libby said.

The resulting chorus of outrage drove all thoughts of Improvement from the conversation.

"Details!" Ronnie demanded, but there were none for Libby to relate, really, just a feeling of distance, of pulling back, that she was certain of but couldn't explain.

"Gut trumps heart," said Tash. "I always knew he was too good to be true."

"He wasn't good *enough*," said Ronnie.

"Agreed," said Clair. "Why would anyone cheat on you, Libby?"

Libby shot Clair a look that was unlike anything Clair had ever seen from her best friend before. It was challenging and vulnerable at the same time. This was a Libby Clair barely recognized.

She knows, Clair thought. *Oh God, she knows.*

But how could she? There wasn't really anything *to* know. That was the thought Clair had alternately reassured and tormented herself with since it had happened, or not happened, depending on how you looked at it. After an ordinary night hanging out and mucking around at Libby's place, wherever in Sweden, Zep had walked Clair to the booth on the ground floor and kissed her good night.

A simple good-night peck on the lips no different from any other in the past—except this time maybe it went on an instant longer than normal, and maybe something new crackled between them, and maybe Zep felt it too, whatever it was, because he hesitated before getting into the booth and zapping off to the Isle of Shanghai, leaving her reeling with the unprompted and unwanted thought that maybe he was dating the wrong girl.

It should be you, that thought said. Not Libby. Only it wasn't a thought. It was a feeling so deep in her gut, she couldn't fish it out. It was snagged in her, interfering with everything—school, her friendships, even her sleep.

Zep was fun, handsome, and her best friend's boyfriend. He wasn't an option. And she didn't know what was worse—the cliché or the strain of holding two equal and opposite feelings at once.

Nothing had changed since the kiss, of course. He had played typically hard to get ever since, and it didn't *look* like anything had changed between him and Libby.

But now this, and *this* only, made things worse. If Libby did break up with Zep, and if Clair and he did hook up, what would Libby think then? That Clair had been the other woman all the time?

As if, Clair told herself, unable to hold Libby's hot gaze any longer. Zep probably had girls mobbing him everywhere he went. Take that very night, the crashlander ball.

Who knew where he was right then? He wasn't with Libby, and he wasn't with Clair, either, and that spoke volumes.

"Sorry, guys." Libby's voice was barely audible over the racket of the party. "I think I'm going to go home. My head is pounding, and I'm not really up to this now."

Clair and her friends tried to talk Libby out of leaving, but she was adamant. Migraines were migraines, and the party bubble had popped, she said. It simply wasn't fun now that Zep was here; he was stressing her out too much. Yes, Libby would confront him about it, but not now. Tomorrow, maybe.

Clair trailed with Libby back to the booth, just the two of them, as the night had started.

One of the doors was open, its mirrored interior empty and waiting.

"You sure you'll be okay?" Clair asked.

Libby nodded, downcast. Clair impulsively took her hand and held her there for a moment. I love you, she wanted to say. I've known you nearly all my life, and you understand me better than anyone. You've fixed everything from grazed knees to panic attacks. I would never do anything to hurt you. When this stupid crush passes and you and Zep get married, I'll be your maid of honor, and no one will remember but me.

But the words wouldn't come. Clair could only hope that her eyes said everything she needed to express.

Libby let go and went into the booth.

"Stay beautiful," she said.

"Yeah . . . you too."

The door slid behind her, and the old booth whirred.

——————————————————————————[3]

CLAIR SAGGED, EXHAUSTED suddenly by conflicted emotions. She told herself to concentrate on the party. It was going well. People were enjoying themselves, so why shouldn't she? She would get herself another drink. She would find Tash and Ronnie and have another dance. She would—

"*There* you are, Clair-bear. Where've you been hiding?"

Zep was standing right behind her.

"Hey," she said, turning away from the door through which Libby had vanished. She couldn't just ignore him, could she? "Are you having a good time?"

"Spot-on. These guys are the coolest. Was that Libby I saw a second ago?"

Clair nodded. "She left. A headache."

"Her loss. A bunch of us cracked the lock on the old telescope hatch—whatever you call it. Come see. The view's amazing!"

She hesitated. Reason told her that he was only inviting her because Libby wasn't around and he wanted someone to show off to.

"All right," she heard herself saying. "Just let me get a coat."

They found a pile of parkas at the base of the ladder leading up to the walkway circling the base of the dome. The wide slit the telescope would once have peered through was indeed open, but the telescope itself was gone. Clair shrugged into a thick mountaineering jacket and zipped it up to her chin. The hood dampened some of the party's incessant racket. She put on gloves and followed Zep up the ladder and onto a narrow maintenance platform that circled the outside of the observatory. There was a rail, but it looked insubstantial against the black, mountainous space below. One misplaced step would lead to a sudden, stony death. Luckily, there were other things to think about.

"Amazing, isn't it?" said Zep from behind her. His face was barely visible inside his own hood. He had to stand close so she could hear him. "Head that way. There's another ladder around the bend that goes right to the top."

Clair followed his directions deeper into the night, everything bombarding her in sharp-edged focus. She no longer felt cramped and crowded as without realizing it she had inside. On the roof of the Sphinx Observatory, the night seemed almost mythic in its intensity.

When she reached the ladder, Zep said, "Here, let me give you a hand."

"No, I've got it." She hoisted herself onto the first rung and climbed carefully but surely upward. The first few steps were perfectly vertical, but slowly the angle lessened as she came over the bulge of the dome. When she was halfway, the circular observation platform at the very top came into view. It was ringed with another low metal rail and was full of people, some of them standing on the rail and pretending to fly.

One boy shouted, "I'm going to jump! No, really, I am. . . ." Judging by the way people ignored him, he had been saying it for a while.

Five yards from the top, there was a ledge protruding from the dome where some kind of rusted antenna installation jutted out into the night. The ladder went right past it.

"Let's stop at that ledge rather than go to the top." Clair didn't want to have to fight for a view, and the scenery was fantastic enough where she was.

"Sure. That's cool."

She climbed the rest of the way and stepped carefully onto the ledge. There was no rail, just the antenna to hang on to, and once they were off the ladder, the slope of the dome beneath them felt five times steeper. The metal looked slippery too, rimed with clear ice. She wondered if she'd done the right thing. Then she felt something pressing into her side and heard a distinct click. Zep had used a carabiner to attach her to a rope that looped around his waist. Another click and they were both safely attached to the antenna.

He grinned at her with something like relief, and she

laughed at the nervous moment she'd unknowingly shared with him.

They squatted down, then sat so their legs dangled off the ledge. Clair could feel the cold seeping into her backside, but for the moment it wasn't making her uncomfortable. The view seemed to go forever.

"It'll be light soon," Zep said.

She didn't check the clock in her lenses. Global time wouldn't tell her whether it was midnight or five minutes to sunrise in Switzerland, since it was the same time everywhere. Her eyes told her that the sky did look faintly lighter to the east. The highest peaks were dusted with faint haloes, like giant angels.

She pulled an oxygen bottle from her pocket and took a hit. The compressed gas actually felt warmer than the air biting at her cheeks.

"This is such an amazing place," Zep said.

"I know. We really did get lucky."

"Everyone's saying Libby found it, but you should get at least half the credit, I reckon. I bet she didn't like it at first, and you talked her into it."

She tilted her head and stared at him through narrowed eyes. "How do you know that?"

"Because you're Libby's finisher."

"Her what?"

"You finish what she starts, clean up her messes, right her wrongs, that kind of thing. You are, right?"

"I don't do that," she said, glancing out at the icy vista. "Not always."

"Yes, always," he said. "Sheesh. I know you two better than you know yourselves."

"Ha! You wish."

"Just try me."

"All right. What's my favorite kind of chocolate?"

"Dark."

"Yes . . . but I already knew that."

He grinned. "So give me something harder."

Clair thought for a second. "What's my least favorite city in the world?"

"Hmmm. Omsk."

"Is that a real place?"

"Of course it is. You'd never hate somewhere imaginary."

"But I've never been there."

"Doesn't matter. You'll go there one day, and you'll hate it. Take my word for it."

"Have *you* been there?"

"No."

"So how do you know?"

"I just know *you*, see? Want to go check it out? We can be there in thirty seconds."

"No thanks."

"Frightened I'll be right?"

She laughed and punched him on the arm. It was as solid as a rock, even through the parkas. He snatched the oxygen bottle from her and took a hit.

"I was beginning to wonder if you were avoiding me."

"What? No." Just you-and-Libby, she wanted to say.

"Good."

"Why?"

He sucked on the canister a second time, then gave it back to her. She resisted the urge to bring it immediately to her lips.

"Maybe it's the oh-two," he said, inching closer so they were pressed tightly against each other on the narrow ledge, "maybe it's this place . . . I don't know. But I've been wanting to get you alone all night. . . ."

Zep raised his right arm and put it around her shoulders while his other hand came across him to tip her hood back slightly. Her head tilted with it.

Every nerve cell in Clair's body came alive, and at the same time every neuron in her brain froze in shock. This wasn't happening, surely.

But it was. He leaned into her. She didn't pull away. His lips were parted. She could see his teeth. When he breathed out, the air misted between them, only there was hardly any *between* at all now. If he came any closer . . . all she had to do was . . .

"Wait, stop," she said, raising her left arm and pushing firmly against his chest with fingers splayed. "What are you doing?"

He blinked at her. "What am I what?"

"*Libby*, remember?"

"This isn't about Libby."

"But it *has* to be about Libby. You can't fool around with me while you're seeing her. You *can't. I* can't." She was talking to herself as much as him, and she didn't think she was doing a very convincing job. "Besides, she already thinks you're cheating on her with someone else. That's a clique I'm not eager to join."

"There's no clique," he said with a frown. "There's no one else. Is that who you think I am?"

Before Clair could answer, a boom of flesh on metal came from above and behind them, heavy enough to make their perch vibrate. Clair whipped around and saw someone skating down the slippery slope of the dome. It was the boy who had been threatening to jump earlier. He was waving his hands above his head to keep himself upright. His expression was one of shock, as though he couldn't believe what gravity was doing to him.

He tried to backpedal and fell with his legs in the air. It might have been funny except for his cry of absolute terror. He knew and everyone watching knew that if nothing arrested his fall, he would slide unchecked faster and faster to the edge of the dome. From there, there was nothing but down. To the icy rocks below.

People were shouting. Zep was moving. The ledge complained as he leaped to his feet and stepped over Clair. Two more steps gave him a short running jump off the ledge. Clair didn't have time even to think as he launched himself into space. Then the rope connecting him to the antenna snapped taut, and she clutched at it with both hands, fearing the carabiner giving way and him being swept off the dome.

Zep hit the dome spread-eagled and belly first, causing another hollow boom, louder than the first. He skidded down the icy slope and reached for the falling guy. They clutched at each other with graceless urgency, scrabbling for a grip on slippery parkas and gloves, and clung tight. The extra weight made the ledge under her groan alarmingly. Clair held on to the rope and leaned back as far as she dared.

The rope wrenched Zep and the guy along an arc, tumbling down over the bulge of the dome and out of sight. When the rope was pointing straight down over the dome, Clair felt some of the weight ease, as the falling guy was helped down from below, she hoped. She braced her feet against the antenna's base and kept pulling on the rope. Her breath came fast, rasping in her ears.

People were thundering down the ladder. Some of them shouted at her, but she couldn't make out what they were saying. The rope moved under hands again, and she leaned back as Zep rappelled up to the ledge. Her heart thudded extra hard on seeing him, and inside her gloves, her hands felt tremulous and sweaty. The world had narrowed down to just the two of them. She no longer saw the perilous view at all.

Zep looked like he might be feeling the same. His eyes were a bright, shining blue, and he was blinking a lot. Two red spots burned in his cheeks.

When he'd reached the ledge and had a good grip on the antenna, she let go and said, "Next time, just throw the *rope*, you idiot."

"Oh yeah," he said, his breath steaming, "I should've thought of that."

She grabbed his head with both hands and brought their lips together, hard. Not for long; he was breathing heavily, and it still wasn't right. But if the rope or antenna hadn't held, he would have fallen and Clair would have missed her one and only chance to do it properly. She had to make up for that now, while she could.

"Jesus," he said when she pulled away, "is this what I have to do get you to kiss me?"

She lowered her head so her face was buried in his chest. They both laughed, almost hysterical on adrenaline, and she clutched him as though she were the one falling.

—————————————————————— [4]

THE ACCIDENT DIDN'T kill the party, but it did have a decidedly sobering effect. Dawn did the rest. Within half an hour it all was over, and Clair was standing in line for the booth with Zep and Xandra Nantakarn and fifty other people, all shivering and awaiting their turns to go home. There was some disgruntled muttering about the delay. Clair hadn't considered that downside of the d-mat bottleneck.

"Don't feel bad," Xandra told Clair when her chance to leave came. "No one died, and the crashlander legend lives on. See you tomorrow night?"

"Uh . . . maybe." Clair wasn't thinking that far ahead. The electric bubble she had occupied earlier had popped. Now she just felt tired.

"Don't wait too long. One day we really will run out of venues."

Xandra winked as the door shut on her, leaving Clair and Zep alone in the restless crowd.

"Now what?" he asked her.

"Now what *what*?"

"The night doesn't have to end here. I have some scotch back at my dorm, and we could both use some warming up— Hey!"

She had kicked him. "Don't do that, Zep."

"Yeah, sorry." He retreated into himself a little. "I guess I should talk to her."

Clair hated pushing him away, but she knew it was the right thing to do.

"We were buzzing on adrenaline and too much beer. That's all."

The booth opened in front of them. Neither of them made a move.

"If I say 'after you,' will you kick me again?"

"No, because I'm tired and want to get home."

She stretched up to kiss him on the cheek and quickly slipped away.

The door slid shut. Clair was surrounded by reflections of herself. She looked completely washed out, something the bright, white light coming at her from all corners didn't help at all. She closed her eyes and wondered what she was feeling underneath that shade's pallid facade.

Zep liked her. What did that say about him? What did it say about her that she had really kissed him now, even if it was in a moment of weakness, just once? Where did that leave Libby? He clearly wasn't over her if he only "guessed" he should talk to her. Clair was an idiot for getting involved.

She felt as though her insides were being torn apart by invisible hands, which was a thousand times worse than how she had felt before.

It can't happen again, she told herself. Clair Larhonda Hill doesn't *do* things like this.

It would best for everyone, she decided, if Zep just got over whatever it was he felt for her and made things good with Libby. Clair could live with rejection if it meant keeping her best friend. There would be other boys. There would never be another Libby.

When she woke the next morning, there were over five hundred bumps in her infield. It was like on her birthday, only that was months ago, and there were no important holidays listed that she might have forgotten. She rolled onto her back with a groan, thinking, Who died?

The bumps appeared to float in the darkness above her, names in a soft Helvetica font against a minimalist, blocky background in burned oranges and yellows. The colors of sunrise, automatically selected by her lenses, probably by some algorithm that thought this would ease her into wakefulness rather than dump it on her like a bucket of cold water. If so, it wasn't working.

The alarm that had woken her came again. It was time to get ready for school. Why was she so tired? The party, right. The crashlanders. The kiss . . .

Her eyes flickered open. She felt faintly sick, and not just from the beers she had drunk. The list of bumps remained in her field of vision, as though demons had scribbled across the ceiling while she slept. The text slid from ceiling to drapes as she sat up with a jerk.

Zep's name was on the list of bumps—not as a recipient, but as a subject.

People were talking about him in the Air. And she was part of the conversation. Anxiously, she winked on one of the bumps and skimmed through a short vlog covering what had happened the previous night.

[37]

At first she was relieved. It was just a brief account of the ball, with emphasis on the incident of the boy who had almost died. There were interviews with people either praising Zep for his bravery or damning the entire clique. Xandra Nantakarn was unflustered in a brief clip doing the rounds. The Lucky Jump wasn't to blame, said a representative of VIA, the Virtual-transport Infrastructure Authority, whose job it was to make the rules about how d-mat was used. A peacekeeper spokesperson wasn't so sure.

It was news of a fairly minor sort. Clair supposed that she must have been mentioned somewhere in one of the posts, leading to the general topic's prominence in her infield. And it was pleasing in a way. Popularity in social media wasn't something she went out of her way to seek, like Libby did. She had never popped this way before.

Then she saw the phrase, "Zeppelin Barker and his girlfriend, crashlander Clair Hill . . ."

"Oh no," she said, skipping to the next bump and following its link.

This one came with a snapshot of her pulling on the rope, taken through the lenses of someone at the top of the dome. This time, they got the name of Zep's girlfriend right, but they had attached it to the wrong face. The caption on the picture of Clair read, "Liberty Zeist, discoverer of the latest crashlander ball that almost cost her boyfriend's life . . ."

"No, no, no!"

The mixed-up name wasn't going to save her. Clair's face was still there, recognized by the Air and sent to her as it would be to anyone interested in Clair Hill, crashlanders, or Zeppelin Barker. Among a multitude of correctly labeled pictures of Libby were enough of Clair to be certain that Libby would see them and ask the question: What had Clair done last night to make people *think* she was Zep's girlfriend?

Maybe Libby had already seen them.

Clair scrolled through the long list of bumps, looking for Libby's name. It wasn't there, but Tash and Ronnie's were.

"Thought you went home with Libby," Tash had sent earlier that morning. "Didn't know you were still there, being a hero!"

Ronnie's was more guarded. "Anything to this, or is it just another Airhead false positive?"

Clair didn't know how to respond. She hugged her knees and wished she could erase the bumps not just from her infield but from the Air itself. But the vast web of wireless connectivity covering the Earth tangled everyone in information. There was no escaping it or the myriad algorithms that guided data to its destination. It didn't matter if two or two hundred thousand people were following the story, Libby was absolutely, positively certain to notice.

How much worse would it look if Clair didn't say something to her right away?

When Clair checked Libby's public profile, she found a caption of an old woman on a swing with a shotgun on her lap and the words *Disturb at own risk*. Not encouraging.

Clair got out of bed, threw her clothes in the fabber for recycling, and dialed a set for school. While she was in the shower, she sent a message to Libby.

It's not what it seems. Really truly honestly. Can we talk?

She deleted everything from her infield so there'd be no mistaking a reply when it came.

Libby hadn't said anything by the time Clair got out of the shower and dressed in her freshly made clothes. The apartment was empty and tomb quiet around her. Clair's mother regularly started work in the middle of the night. Her stepfather lived in Munich most weekdays. Clair was an only child and heartily glad of it.

For breakfast she had perfectly scrambled eggs with freshly toasted bread, low-salt butter at room temperature, and the best black coffee a fabber could find. The coffee was the only thing she truly tasted.

"Libby," she sent, and was unable to stop once she had started this time, "did you get my message? Are you up yet? Are you feeling all right? Please call me back as soon as you can."

She desperately wished she could stay home with her head under the covers, but skipping school wouldn't solve anything. Being smart had gotten her parents' parents through the Water Wars, Allison Hill, Clair's mother, liked to say. That and never giving up. Allison claimed that Clair had inherited her maternal grandmother's stubbornness, and that even when they argued, it was something to be grateful for.

[5]

"WOODWARD AND MAIN, Manteca," she told the booth, avoiding the accusing stare of the reflection directly in front of her.

My nose is too big, she thought for the thousandth time.

A sneaky new voice internally riposted, *You could fix that.*

She scowled. That wasn't cool. Improvement couldn't be real, no matter what Libby thought, and even if it was, beauty was only skin-deep.

sssssss-pop

The door opened onto bright morning sunlight shining through dappled leaves, fresh sea air, and the sound of people arguing. Her booth was one of twenty in a line under the familiar d-mat sign of two overlapping circles in a chunky Venn diagram. There was a man in a green suit directly in front of her. She stepped out, and he stepped inside without acknowledging her. Woodward and Main was one of several hub stations servicing not just the Manteca New Campus High School but downtown tourism as well. Sacramento Bay was busy with amateur sailors day-tripping north to Yuba City or east to Rio Vista and the Joice Islands. The fishing was good, and so were the mangroves.

Clair hugged the strap of her backpack and pressed through the crowd. The station was even more congested than usual. Two UFO-like eye-in-the-sky (EITS) drones buzzed softly over the discontented crowd.

D-mat jumps took about two minutes, give or take thirty seconds, and this one had taken her just over two. Something other than unreasonable lag time was responsible for the disturbance, then. A blue peacekeeper's helmet stood out above a small knot of people three booths along. Clair rubbernecked to see what was going on but couldn't make out anything untoward, and couldn't justify standing where she was for long. People were pressing forward into the booths, anxious to be on their way, as she was.

School was crowded. A multilingual sea of kids navigated channels that curved organically between buildings four, five, and six stories high. Juniors, like Clair and Libby, were on the other side of the campus, near the gym. Clair leaned toward the practical arts—writing, music composition, and editing—with a smattering of history and soft sciences that most of her friends found boring. She didn't know what she would do with the combination, but she figured she had time to decide. It wasn't like money was an issue as it had been in her grandfather's day, when fabbers hadn't existed to make anything anyone wanted, and people had had to have jobs just to eat.

"You kids are getting smarter, younger every year," he liked to complain, "but you never actually do anything with those smarts of yours."

"That's not true," Clair's mother had responded the last time. "What about that kid who solved the Riemann hypothesis a month ago?"

"There you go, Clair," he had grumbled. "Why can't you be more like him?"

"*Her*, Grandpa," Clair had corrected him. "Anyway, I don't like math."

"Finding the right vocation is like finding the right spouse," Allison had said with a smile. "Better to have none than the wrong one."

Like friends, Clair thought now. *And boyfriends.*

Libby wasn't at the classroom when Clair arrived, didn't turn up with everyone else, and remained silent as they took their seats and the teacher started talking about survivor narratives of the Water Wars. When Clair checked Libby's public profile, it listed her location as school, but that was likely to be a fake for her parents' sake, the same as it was when she went out partying.

"She sent me something last night." Ronnie bumped Clair. "It was weird. Hang on—I'll show you."

A forwarded message appeared in Clair's infield, which had changed to greens and grays to match the New Manteca campus. Bumps kept coming in about the crashlander ball. Another time she might have been pleased by her newfound notoriety, but not today.

Clair fixed on the message from Ronnie and blinked her left eyelid.

"It worked" was all Libby had said, about two hours after the party. "Now I'm beautiful!"

"I think she was talking about Improvement," Ronnie said. "Check her transit data."

Like Ronnie and Tash, Clair had close-friend privileges to Libby's profile, which told her where Libby went and who with. Useful when Libby was running late, now it told Clair exactly where she had been the day before. There was a string of seventeen rapid jumps in the evening, when Clair and Libby had been looking for the crashlander ball, but there was also a long series of Lucky Jumps in the afternoon and another after Libby had said good night. Clair quickly tallied them up. Ninety jumps in one day. At two minutes a jump, that totaled around three hours' lag.

Tash whistled. "No wonder she had a migraine!"

"What did she mean about being beautiful?" Clair asked Ronnie. "It can't have worked, right?"

"Impossible," said Ronnie. "That's why she bumped me, I think."

"She wants you to believe because she really wants to believe . . . ?"

"Maybe she convinced herself the birthmark was actually fading," said Tash. "She must have been ultralagged."

"So then she crashes," said Clair. "And what does she wake up to . . . ?"

"Bumps about you and Zep," said Ronnie with characteristic bluntness.

"And of course the birthmark's still there, which makes her embarrassed as well as angry."

Clair was satisfied that they had her best friend's mood mapped out but decidedly unsatisfied by what that left her with. She was unable to *do* anything until Libby responded, and she found it impossible to concentrate as a result. Her right foot hooked around her left ankle and jiggled restlessly. Not turning up for school wasn't especially unusual; everyone skipped now and again, even Clair. But not like this, without an explanation, a single word . . . that wasn't Libby's style. She was a broadcaster, not a brooder.

"Clair? Clair, are you paying attention?"

She blinked and refocused. The teacher was talking to her, and the entire class was staring.

"I'm sorry," she said, gathering up her backpack and avoiding the eyes of her friends. "I'm not feeling well."

That was a lie, but staying would be a waste of time. There was no faking out a live teacher. That was the whole point of school, Clair's mom said. Anyone could cheat by copying answers from the Air; school was for learning how to cheat *people*.

[6]

Outside, Clair felt crushed by the silence. Ronnie and Tash sent bumps after her to see if she was okay. Had she heard something? Clair said she hadn't and that she'd be coming back to class soon. What else could she do? She wasn't sure that going anywhere would do any good. She just needed to *think*.

A chat request appeared in her infield.

Libby.

Before Clair could wink on it, the patch disappeared.

She thought, just for a second, about letting it go. Libby wasn't normally so hesitant. If she really wanted to talk to Clair, she'd call back when she was sure of it.

But that didn't fix anything now, Clair told herself. If best friends couldn't talk through their issues, who could?

She responded with a request of her own, and it sat there for thirty seconds before anything happened. Then a window opened onto Libby's bedroom. The shades were down, so if it was sunny outside in Sweden-somewhere,

Clair couldn't tell. Inside, the room was dark and grainy. Libby was a pale shape curled half beneath the covers. She was lying on her side with her head under a pillow.

"Why can't I see you?" Libby said in a gravelly voice.

"I'm walking outside at school. Why aren't you here?"

"Slept in. Mad headache."

"Why didn't you tell me? Why didn't you answer my bumps?"

"Turned everything off. It was all too much."

"What was?"

"Spam . . . strange messages . . ."

"What kind of messages? About the ball?"

"Just strange . . . Improvement stuff. I deleted everything."

"Oh," said Clair, feeling as though she'd dodged a bullet. If Libby had emptied her infield and switched off her feed, that meant she couldn't possibly have seen the news. But she would eventually. "Listen—"

"Can't talk long. Got to sleep some more." Libby rolled over, pushing the pillow to one side. "Don't want to waste this golden opportunity, before Mom gets home."

"I need to talk to you when you're feeling better."

"I am feeling better," Libby said with a sigh. "Slightly. Talk about what?"

"It's just . . . the party. It didn't end well. There was some confusion . . ."

"You're telling me. I think I drunk-bumped Zep at one

point when I got home. Did he say anything to you?"

"No. Why would he?" He had done the right thing and stayed away. Or was it the cowardly thing? Clair couldn't decide. "I hope you feel better about all that today. There's really no reason—"

"To worry about him being a cheating toad? Sure there is. He was cheating when he hitched up with me." She laughed, then clutched her head. "Ouch."

Clair chickened out. It felt almost cruel, raising the subject when Libby was feeling so bad. "I didn't think you drank that much last night."

"Neither did I. This is the worst migraine I've ever had. Comes and goes at weird times—just when I think it's done, it crashes back in. . . ."

"Do you need anything? I can probably get permission to come over—"

"You need to stay in school and study for both of us. I'll learn by osmosis. Maybe we could make it a permanent arrangement."

Libby grinned up at Clair via the camera pinned to the wall beside her bed. It was Clair's first good look at her. Libby's hair was pulled up in a nighttime knot. Her smile was wide and bright, but there were bags under her eyes, and her skin looked even whiter than usual—like the thin, fragile layer of ice riming the dome of the Sphinx Observatory.

"Stay beautiful," Clair said.

Libby raised herself onto one elbow, smile falling away. Her face ballooned bigger still in the window.

"You can *see* me, right?" She winced. "Ouch," she said again. "Crashing. Bye."

The window closed. Clair stared through the space it had been, not looking at the campus around her, not looking at anything, really, but the negative image of Libby as it faded from her retina.

Clair *had* seen Libby. What she hadn't seen was Libby's birthmark.

She bumped Ronnie. Clair knew what she would say but she needed to hear it again.

"Are you absolutely sure Improvement won't work?"

"Positive. Don't waste your time. And think of the Magic Mayflies. You don't want to piss them off, do you?"

Clair smiled despite herself. "The Magic Mayflies" referred to a story Ronnie's mom had told them when they were kids to explain how d-mat worked. You stepped into a booth and dissolved into a kind of pollen made entirely of light, which the Mayflies gathered and carried through the air to where you wanted to go. So if you used d-mat too much, the magic might run out, leaving you stranded.

But Ronnie's mom had come from a different generation—just one removed from the Water Wars, when power had been short and d-mat not something to be taken for granted, when the seas had been rising and fresh water becoming more scarce every year. Hundreds of millions of people had died of starvation and disease until d-mat had literally turned the tides, stripping the world of its poisons and feeding the billions by reorganizing the atoms, turning the bad into good. Now, with powersats high above the Earth beaming down limitless power and all the excess carbon dioxide sucked out of the air, there was no need for fairy stories. It wasn't Magic Mayflies at the heart of d-mat but everyday machines that analyzed travelers right down to the smallest particle, transmitting the data that made them *them* to their destination through the Air and rebuilding them exactly where they wanted to be, exactly as they had been before they left.

VIA existed to make sure that critical word *exactly* didn't go anywhere. The Virtual-transport Infrastructure Authority was a global body established to ensure the one hundred percent safe operation of d-mat. Two artificial intelligences oversaw VIA in turn, so no human errors could creep in. And it worked so comprehensively and constantly that the world's network of d-mat booths reported the lowest rate of data loss out of all of humanity's media. Everyone knew that the amount of *human* lost in a decade of d-mat was equivalent to a toenail clipping, total.

Of course, people told stories about criminals hacking the system. Dramas regularly featured duplicated jewels, disintegrated wills, cloned lovers, and the like. Every child listened breathlessly to tales about swapped bodies and shrunken heads, people flipped right-to-left or turned entirely inside out, scientists mixed up with insects, and worse. Clair herself had relished such stories even as she zigzagged across the globe, enjoying as everyone did the freedom to go anywhere she wanted at any time she wanted, safe in the knowledge that VIA and its AIs would simply never let anything bad happen to her. She would always *be* her at the other end.

So Improvement couldn't work, she told herself, just like Ronnie said. The image of Libby had been poor, and she had probably been wearing makeup from the night before—not unlikely, given she'd been lagged by ninety jumps on top of her migraine. Maybe Libby had been only half awake and had mistaken a darkened glimpse in a mirror for the reality she desired.

Improvement couldn't work. So why was Libby acting as though it had?

Let it go, Clair told herself as she walked to class. *You're worrying about the wrong thing. Libby may not be angry at you* now, *but she's obviously fragile, and her calm mood's not going to last forever. Like everything else, the Zep situation is bound never to improve on its own.*

But whether she was running from reality or not, the question wouldn't leave her. Instead of going back to her classroom, she went to the library. It wouldn't hurt to ask, would it? Just in case.

Calling up a query window in her lenses, she asked the Air, "Does Improvement work?"

"Yes" came the immediate reply, along with "No," "Maybe," and "Are you joking? This is what we use the sum of all human knowledge for?"

——————————————————————————[7]

CLAIR CLEARLY WASN'T the first to ask.

The library was noisy as always, full of students pretending to study. Clair had permission to enter the quieter rare editions wing, the only part of the library that held actual books. It was her favorite place at school, partly for the smell, mostly for the sense of isolation and peace. The rare editions wing was like a museum: outside normal time and private, best of all.

Putting on a live recording of her favorite Poulenc piano music, performed by her favorite pianist, Tilly Kozlova, Clair sent out crawlers and trawlers to scour the Air for more detailed answers to the Improvement question. Then she settled back to randomly skim the news reports, blogs, and media archives they found. There were countless discussions about what people *would* change given the chance, which only made her more certain that it couldn't possibly work, because if it did, why wasn't everyone impossibly tall, ripped, and well endowed?

The official word was that it was an urban myth, perpetuated by unknown pranksters through closely connected friendship networks. It didn't go everywhere at once, saturating the system with a flood of impossible wishes, but there was no rhyme or reason to the way it did spread either. It came and went with all the apparent randomness of something genuinely spontaneous. A fantasy from the collective unconscious, perhaps—or a warning from the superego of what might happen if VIA's safeguards were ever relaxed.

VIA dismissed it. Peacekeepers thought it harmless. Countless testimonies as to its lack of efficacy went a long way toward convincing Clair that Ronnie was right. Improvement simply didn't work.

Buried amid the torrent of information dredged up by her search, however, was one emphatic but mysterious dissenting voice.

The message was light on hyperbole and unfortunately light on details as well. It had been written three years earlier and consisted of a warning from a woman whose public profile had been defaced. Instead of name and contact details, the fields displayed a single word, repeated over and over again.

Stainer. Stainer. Stainer.

Abstainers were what the minority of people who didn't use d-mat called themselves. They didn't use d-mat because they thought it was immoral or something like that—Clair didn't know the details, but everyone she knew called them Stainers, after George Staines, their founder, and the idea that giving up d-mat would bring back all the pollution humanity had finally gotten rid of. They were regarded as crazy by pretty much everyone. Hence the defacement and worse.

Stainers didn't claim to be sane. They claimed to be right.

"Improvement killed my child" was all the woman's warning said.

Clair worried at her fingernail, thinking of Libby's ghostly image crashing to black.

Feeling faintly foolish but knowing her grandmother's genes wouldn't let the thought go until she had pursued it to the very end, she scoured her contacts until she found the name of the only Stainer in her grade and asked if they could talk.

Jesse Linwood was a junior like her, and they shared Modern History on Tuesdays, but that was where their similarities ended. Jesse's other subjects were focused on math and engineering. They never hung out.

It wasn't personal. Their paths simply never crossed. He didn't come on excursions if they involved d-mat—which they always did—or eat at the refectory, where the food was always fabbed. Libby called him the Lurker because he sometimes popped up in school social media but rarely said anything. That could have been the fault of his augs, which were embarrassingly ancient. His audio came through an actual earring clipped to his earlobe, instead of a tiny tube tucked neatly into the aural canal like everyone else had. He had only one visible contact lens, which he switched from eye to eye as though it irritated him. Clair took for granted the fact that she could type using menus in her lenses or just mouth the words she wanted to say, but Jesse audibly whispered when talking in a chat, and when he was bumping someone or accessing his menus, his fingers visibly twitched. Sometimes his augs broke down, leaving him deaf and dumb to the Air until he fixed them. It drove the teachers crazy.

He never proselytized like some Abstainers did, but people knew who he was all the same. His clothes were obviously not fabbed fresh each morning—sometimes they were patched or even dirty—and he carried a leather satchel that looked a hundred years old. He had other nicknames, some them undeserved. Clair was pretty sure he wasn't actually a terrorist, like the members of the World Holistic Leadership. WHOLE was always issuing manifestos and sending viruses through the d-mat network. Cold viruses, not computer ones.

After a delay of some minutes, Jesse replied, "I think you've got the wrong number."

"The wrong what?" she bumped back.

"Number. Address. Telephones, you know?"

She'd read of telephones in old stories but had never seen one.

"They used numbers, not names?"

There was another delay before he bumped back. She imagined his fingers twitching away, wherever he was, and was too impatient to wait for a reply.

"It's Clair Hill, from Modern History."

"I know who you are. You've never texted me before."

Another old word, but she knew what this one meant. "I want to ask you something about d-mat."

"I don't know anything about d-mat."

"What happens when d-mat goes wrong, I mean."

This time the pause was longer.

"I thought it might've been about this morning."

She frowned. "What about this morning?"

"You were at the station. I saw you."

"I didn't see you. What were you doing there?"

The pause dragged on so long, she thought he might not reply at all.

"Doesn't matter," he finally said. "What do you want to know?"

The delays between bumps were maddening.

"It would be easier to actually talk than do it like this."

"Sure, but not now. My audio's on the fritz, and I have a prac after lunch. Meet me at the gate after last period?"

Clair was reluctant. People might see.

Then she felt bad for feeling that way. So what if people

saw them together? Besides, there was a chance Libby would get better as the day progressed, and Clair wouldn't have to go through with it.

"All right," she bumped back. "Thanks."

"No probs. See you."

Clair leaned back in her chair and rubbed her eyes. She didn't want to leave the library, but she had done all she could, for now. And she had some explaining to do. Ronnie would tell her she was overreacting; Tash would go into a worry spiral. Both would make her feel worse. Neither would change her mind.

"Improvement killed my child," she thought, and then tried her best not to think it again.

"On my way," she bumped Tash.

"We were beginning to wonder what you were up to," Tash bumped back.

"And who with," Ronnie added.

Gathering up her backpack, Clair resigned herself to explanations on several fronts at once.

[8] ——————————————————————

MIDWAY THROUGH THE afternoon, Libby's caption changed from *Disturb at own risk* to *SiCkO*, with a crocodile biting a zebra on the rump. Clair took that as a clear sign that Libby wasn't feeling better, meaning that Clair had to go through with her meeting with Jesse Linwood. She was already regretting and feeling slightly embarrassed about contacting him. Jesse was so far out of her social circle, he might as well have come from another planet.

Ronnie and Tash waved her off at the end of school, peppering her with provocative bumps.

"Retro is in," said Tash, "but not *that* retro."

Clair walked on, telling herself to be glad they weren't giving her a hard time about Zep. She had been determinedly honest with them over what had happened at the party. She knew she had done the wrong thing. Forgiveness was optional. She would understand if they reserved their sympathy for Libby.

"I just want to know," Ronnie had said, "what're you doing poaching that slimeball when there are eligible bachelors all over campus. You know you can do better, right?"

"He may be a slimeball," said Tash, "but at least he has taste."

"I don't think Zep's really a slimeball," Clair started to say.

"Oh no!" cried Ronnie, putting the back of one hand to her forehead. "This can't be happening!"

". . . any more than I'm a poacher," Clair concluded firmly. "It just happened. It won't happen again."

They hadn't sounded convinced.

"Come lat-jumping with me this weekend," Tash said.

"We're taking the thirtieth. That'll give you something else to think about."

"Or come party with me," said Ronnie. "Plenty more slimeballs where he came from."

"Pass," Clair said. She wasn't interested in circumnavigating the globe latitude by latitude *or* in available men. "But thanks. I'm glad you're still talking to me."

"Just don't run off with the Stainer, or else we'll have to communicate by smoke signals. . . ."

Jesse Linwood was waiting for her by the gate, slouched in a way that belied his gangly height, with shaggy brown hair covering his eyes. He was wearing tatty blue jeans and a yellow T-shirt with a blocky logo she didn't recognize—it looked like an upside-down flowerpot, only bright red. The legendary satchel was on the ground at his feet, slumping listlessly like something melting in the sun. In one hand he held a paperback novel that was so dog-eared, it should probably have been in a museum.

She didn't catch the title. When he saw her, he put his weight on both feet and stood straighter, slipping the book into his back pocket.

"Hey, Clair," he said.

"Uh, hey." She wasn't quite sure what to say next. Already they'd spoken more words to each other in one day than they had in all their years at school together.

"Shall we go?" he asked her.

"Where?"

"I'll walk with you to the station. That's where you're headed, right?"

At her alarmed expression, he laughed.

"Okay, that sounded weird. I'm not stalking you or anything, honest. I just walk past the station on the way to school, and sometimes I see you."

"Me and lots of other people."

"I guess." He picked up his satchel and indicated the gate. "Yes?"

She shrugged. "Sure. Anywhere's fine."

Conscious of the occasional odd look from her fellow students, she set off with him down the road to the station. His legs were long, so his stride far outclassed hers, but he let her set the pace. They walked a dozen steps in silence, Clair feeling foolish but committed now, Jesse concentrating to all appearances on the tips of his sneakers. He was either growing a very slight goatee or he hadn't gotten around to shaving his chin for a few days. She tried not to stare at it, but with his eyes hidden behind his hair, it was hard to avoid.

"So . . . ," she said. "This is about a friend. I'm worried that . . . actually, I don't know what I'm worried about. There's this d-mat meme going around. Have you heard of Improvement?"

He shook his head. "I'm not really the target audience."

"Yeah, right. Anyway, my friend d-matted ninety times yesterday and she's convinced Improvement worked—changed her—although it can't possibly have, and I'm worried about her because she's behaving a little oddly."

"Oddly how?"

Clair shrugged, remembering the fleeting conversation that morning. "Mood swings, headache . . . I know it doesn't sound like much, but I can tell it's not normal."

"What's Improvement supposed to do?"

"It's like a chain letter. You receive a message. It tells you that you can be prettier, smarter, taller, whatever. You write a code on a piece of paper and list all the things you'd like to have changed. You take the note with you through d-mat, under your clothes, and supposedly it happens. Do it enough times, the meme says, and you'll be . . . Improved."

"Just like that?" he said.

She shared his skepticism. The idea was absurd, a fairy tale, just as Ronnie kept telling her. "I didn't say it was real. Just that this is why she did it."

"What's the code?"

She called up the original message and sent it to him.

Charlie X-ray Romeo Foxtrot
Whiskey Uniform Hotel Bravo
Oscar Echo
Tango Kilo
Alfa Papa Juliet Zulu

"Does it mean anything?" she asked.

"If I had to guess I'd say it's supposed to act as a kind of signal to the system, alerting it to the presence of someone who wants to be Improved. The system reads the note, takes on board what the bearer wants, and manipulates their pattern to make it happen."

"I thought that was impossible."

"If you believe VIA. But maybe if you fiddled the books bit by bit . . . tiny alterations that supposedly don't affect the hash sum of the entire transmission . . . maybe that's how you'd get away with it."

Clair nodded warily, even though she didn't know what a hash sum was. She was surprised he was taking it so seriously. "So it could actually work?"

"I don't know," he said. "I mean, the note isn't a *thing* once it enters the Air. It's just data, a string of ones and zeros like everything else. Sure, some patterns are scanned for explosives or specific DNA—but no one's looking for letters on a piece of paper. That'd be like trying to use a microscope to take a picture of the galaxy."

"So it *wouldn't* work?"

"Then there's the whole idea of Improvement itself. How does the system know what to change in order to make people the way they've asked to become? It's not a plastic surgeon or a genetic engineer. It's just a means of moving data around. It's not designed for anything else."

"So it's a scam after all."

"Can you imagine how illegal it would be if it wasn't? I mean, you'd have to get past both of VIA's AIs every time someone used it—and there's no program or anything to go with the note, so it'd have to be done manually. If you were caught, you'd be locked up for the rest of your life."

"Jesse, just tell me: *Will it work or not?*"

He shrugged. "Beats me. I'm not as good with this stuff as Dad is. He's the expert."

They walked in silence for a minute, Clair fighting a sense of disappointment and frustration. All she wanted was to know for certain, either way.

"It was Libby, wasn't it?" Jesse said out of nowhere. "Liberty Zeist?"

"What, you stalk her, too?" Clair said a little more sharply than she intended.

"No. I just guessed. She wasn't at school today." He shrugged, making his satchel bounce against his shoulder. "Besides, the only people who would consider using Improvement are those who are already beautiful but don't appreciate it. Chasing the impossible dream, you know? Libby's one of those."

Clair couldn't tell if he was insulting Libby or just trying to be weird now.

"Don't tell me you're not tempted," she said.

"Me? Hardly. Have you forgotten what I am?"

"An Abstainer, yeah . . . so what were you doing at the station this morning?"

He glanced at her sideways.

"Being hassled by the PKs. For no reason. You really didn't see me?"

She remembered a disturbance and seeing a peace-keeper's helmet above the crowd.

"That was you?"

"A return performance in Civil Harassment 101. The starring role, in fact. It was written for me."

"You must have been doing *something*."

"Don't you start," he said, brushing his hair off his face and staring at her with a resentful expression. "You think I was trying to plant a bomb? For my friends in WHOLE? Because all Stainers are terrorists? That's right, I keep forgetting. If you're not with the herd, then you're against it."

His hot gaze returned to his sneakers.

"I was just curious," he said in a cooler tone. "There's no law against that, is there?"

"So you really have never—"

"No, not ever. I suggested it once, and my dad threatened to kick me out on the street. Said he didn't want what I'd come back as rattling around the house—because it wouldn't be me, not in his eyes."

"What do you mean?"

"He thinks anyone who uses d-mat dies inside. You know, it takes you apart, destroys you, and what it rebuilds is just a good copy, not the real thing. Soulless. Empty. Hollow."

"For real?"

"Yes. He calls people like you *zombies*."

That was a horrible thought—someone thinking she wasn't real when she knew without question that she absolutely was.

"Do you call us that too?"

"I think the soul question is one thing d-mat has finally put to rest. Thank God."

A softer glance accompanied this small joke, as though he was embarrassed for his snappy tone a moment ago. Or embarrassed for his father. She couldn't tell.

The double-circles sign for the station was coming into view through the palms ahead. Her window of opportunity was about to close, and she hadn't really learned anything.

"You said your dad knows more about 'this stuff' than you do."

He nodded. "He lives to pick holes in it."

"Maybe I should talk to him."

"You don't really want to do that."

"Why not?"

"He's . . . difficult."

"I don't mind."

She didn't know if Jesse had heard anything about the Zep crisis and wasn't about to explain her fear that Improvement might be making Libby's emotional state worse.

"All right," he said, "but don't tell me I didn't warn you."

"Thanks. So . . . will you introduce me so we can chat?"

"He doesn't do that. You'll have to come home with me. That's where he works. We live just around the corner."

"Oh," she said, realizing only then what she'd gotten herself into. "Of course. You'd have to." How else would he get to school—fly?

Jesse picked up his pace. They passed the station and turned left up Main Street, into unknown territory.

—————————————————————[9]

JESSE LIVED IN a terrace apartment on a broad and over-grown thoroughfare with well-worn sidewalks and bike paths shaded by eucalyptus branches and clumps of sighing bamboo. Unlike many of the developments around Sacramento Bay, it looked lived-in. Someone had planted daisies that bobbed and winked in the pale November sun. There were dog turds on the path. Clair could hear kids calling a couple of houses along.

"Have you been here long?" Clair asked Jesse, thinking of her sterile apartment block and the empty sidewalks below.

"I've lived here all my life."

"Really?"

"Kinda hard to move around if you don't use d-mat."

"Yeah, I guess." Clair had moved more times than she could count. Each time her family had relocated, they had recycled almost everything they owned and fabbed replacements at the other end. Friends were equally easy to visit from anywhere.

"Abstainers tend to stick together," he said, turning an old-fashioned key in the lock and kicking the stiff door open with the side of one foot. "It's us against the world, 24-7."

His satchel dropped with a thud in the hallway as he waved her ahead of him into a house like no other she had seen before.

The ground floor was one unbroken space, with living area and kitchen overlapping in a series of worn couches, scratched tables, and scuffed counter surfaces. Two ceiling fans swirled lazily overhead, circulating the warm air. Clair took it in, feeling as though her eyes were bugging out of her head. There was a stove, a fridge, and a trash can. There were framed sketches that showed signs of fading next to real bookcases holding antique photos and dusty trinkets. The rugs beneath her feet were tatty around the edges. Through the wall-to-wall windows at the far end of the space, she saw vegetable gardens neatly arranged in rows and a big green shed.

"That's where Dad works," said Jesse, indicating the shed. "I'll take you out there in a sec. Let me just get this going first."

The surprises kept on coming. Clair watched in amazement as Jesse chopped leaves of some kind, grated a carrot, sliced an onion and three large, dark mushrooms, and mixed it all into a bowl with five broken eggs and some grated cheese. Actual ingredients, not something built in a fabber. She dreaded to think how much they cost. For most people, physical goods were free, like access to the Air, but for Abstainers like Jesse and his father, that wouldn't be the case. Time cost money, and vegetables took time to grow. Weeks, even.

Jesse added green herbs and ground pepper, then poured the mixture out into a low transparent dish. He opened the oven, releasing a blast of dry heat, and slid the dish inside.

"What?" he said. "Never seen anyone cook before?"

She shook her head. "Only in old movies or for fun."

"It's not hard," he said. "That'll be ready in forty-five minutes or so. You're welcome to stay for dinner, if you like."

She shook her head again, but there was no denying her curiosity. "You don't eat meat?"

"No, and you've probably never met any vegetarians before either. Not now that eating meat is a victimless crime, right?"

He grinned at her discomfort, and she sensed that he was enjoying her awkwardness.

"Well, my mother won't eat chicken," she said. "There

was a corrupt pattern once, or perhaps a copy of meat that had gone off. Either way, I got really sick, and she's never recovered from it. Telling her I've eaten some is a sure way to make her freak."

"Same with Dad, but with a whole lot more than chicken."

"Has he always been a Stainer?" Clair asked him.

"Body and soul. Look." He pointed at one corner of the living room, where hung a photo of a jowly, gray-haired man standing proudly against a white marble background. "Good old George has been watching over me as long as I can remember."

Clair didn't know much about the founder of the Abstainer movement. George Staines' unassuming features hadn't earned him a following during his lifetime. That had been the product of his political writings, his philosophies, and his death from a rare form of cancer caused, some claimed, by the technology he despised.

"We have meetings here once a week," Jesse was saying as he chopped more vegetables into a salad. "I tend to stay upstairs in my room for those. After the hundredth time, 'We Shall Not Be Moved' stops being ironic."

She laughed, but he didn't, and then she felt embarrassed. Maybe he hadn't meant it as a joke.

She looked around for something else to talk about. The only thing remotely normal was a Psychotic Ultramine poster in the stairwell, cycling through recent images of the band.

"You live here alone with your dad?"

"Yes."

"What happened to your mom?"

"She died," he said. "When I was very young, so I barely remember her now. When I picture her, it's from photos and old video files."

There were no safe topics of conversation.

"There." Jesse finished laying out two settings on the dining table. Blue Willow patterned plates came from a cupboard, utensils from a drawer, chipped and scuffed by long use. He wiped his hands on his jeans and brushed his bangs back from his eyes. They immediately fell back down again.

"Come on," he said. "I'll take you to the workshop and introduce you to the man himself . . . if you're sure that's what you want."

She nodded. "What does he do out there?"

"He's an artist," Jesse said, opening the back door and waving her through. "His medium is transport old and new. Electrobikes and sunboards—anything other than d-mat. He sells them as fast as he can make them, and they keep the idea of alternative transport alive in people's minds. That's the plan, anyway. . . . You've really never heard of him?"

"No. Sorry."

"Well, don't tell him that, whatever you do."

[10]

THE SHED WAS larger than it had looked from the apartment. At some point, the Linwoods had absorbed the backyards of both their neighbors, creating a spacious environment for Jesse's father to work and store materials. Jesse knocked on the door and opened it without waiting for a reply. It was dark inside. Clair's eyes took a moment to adjust. The shed was crammed to the ceiling with tools and equipment: antique 3D printers, skeletal landsurfer frames, Air-free processor cores, and other shapes Clair couldn't identify. Cogs and chains hung from nails everywhere she looked, as though she were inside a giant clock. If there was any order to the maelstrom of parts, it was invisible to her.

Jesse's father occupied a relatively clear space in the center, surrounded by a cone of yellow light projecting down from the ceiling. He wore a jeweler's glass over one eye, a red-check shirt, canvas shorts, and open-toed sandals. Through the glass he peered at an angular chip extracted from a mess of wires and circuit boards to his left.

"This is Clair Hill from school," Jesse said, approaching via a zigzag path through the clutter.

"What does she want?" Jesse's father glanced up at them. His magnified eye seemed impossibly blue.

"I'd like to ask you a question, Mr. Linwood," she said,

stepping gingerly for fear of knocking something over. "I'm sorry to interrupt your work."

"Call me Dylan." He reached up and took the eyepiece away. "Go on."

"I'm worried about a friend of mine," she said. "She's been using Improvement."

"She has, has she? And did it work?"

"No. . . . I mean, it wasn't clear."

"Well, I don't see what I can do about that."

"You can tell me not to worry about her. You can tell me it can't possibly be real."

He stood up, revealing himself to be much shorter than Jesse. Dylan Linwood was lean, with wild gray hair and deep facial lines. He too hadn't shaved for several days. His skin was spotted with grease. He looked like an ordinary man concentrated into a much smaller space.

"The system is governed by AIs," he said in a lecturing tone, "and the AIs are governed by protocols. Who writes the protocols? People do. So if the Improvement code causes a shift in the protocols . . . . well, a thing imagined is a thing halfway done. What's to stop someone trying to make it work? Nothing. So the very existence of Improvement proves that someone, somewhere, at least thought about it, and that thought alone is dangerous, in the memetic sense."

"The what sense?" asked Clair.

"You know, memes—things that reproduce ideas, like

genes reproduce traits. A new idea is a mutant meme, and the idea spread by Improvement is that people deserve to be Improved by means other than hard work and merit. By just clicking their fingers and wishing. These are dangerous thoughts if sufficient people share them."

"Memes come and go," said Jesse. He was slouched against a bench with his arms folded, closely observing the conversation. "Won't this one do the same?"

"Don't underestimate the power of a seductive idea, son. Bad enough that people are using d-mat to get around. What happens if their patterns start being interfered with en masse? That'd be a monstrous crime perpetrated on the entire human race."

"Yes, but it's *not* happening, is it?"

"Libby thinks it is," said Clair.

The way Dylan looked at her made her feel as though she was still under the magnifying stare of his eyepiece.

"Do you have a copy of this particular message?" he asked Clair.

"Give me your address and I'll send it to you."

"Send it to Jesse, and he can send it to me. I like to keep my connections to a minimum."

Jesse's father sat back in front of his 3D monitor and began typing hard on a manual keyboard.

"You were right to come here," he told her as the message flashed up in front of him. "I'm sure the truth's out

there, but it'll be buried under a snow job of misinformation and noise. Fortunately for you, I have colleagues who
track this kind of thing. We share information in a private
database. I'm looking into that right now."

Clair wondered who exactly "we" were. Ordinary
Abstainers or someone more organized and active in their
opposition to d-mat?

"If there is something to Improvement," he said, skimming through data too quickly to follow, "it's not what it's
advertised to be. No one believes it's making people taller
or more beautiful or whatever. What I can tell you is that
there are different strains of the letter, as with viruses.
Some are the real thing, some are bad copies, and some
are fakes. Apparently, this is one of the real ones. You can
tell by the irregular number of lines in each stanza of the
message: three-four-five-two."

"What do you it mean that it's 'real'?" asked Jesse. "If
it doesn't do anything, what difference does that make?"

"I didn't say it didn't do anything. I said it didn't work
as advertised. My best theory is that someone tried to get
it to work but succeeded only in interfering with the system, causing random errors to people's patterns."

Clair nodded. That made a scary kind of sense. "What
could we do about that?"

"Well, first we need evidence of anything at all out of
the ordinary, something that will prove the need to take
action. Evidence of real harm, not just vague concerns."

"Libby said she's received some weird messages."

"Do you have copies of them?"

Clair shook her head. "She deleted them."

Dylan looked up at her, then back at the screen. With a flick of one fingertip, he cleared the data and turned to face Clair.

"Of course she did. So at the moment we have nothing— just a theory and a note that according to the Air and the peacekeepers doesn't mean a thing."

"You could ask Libby to save any other messages she gets," Jesse suggested. "If we had them, maybe the peacekeepers would listen."

Dylan dismissed that thought as casually as he had dismissed the data on the screen,

"The peacekeepers take VIA's so-called safeguards for granted. They can't afford to do otherwise. If they thought for a second that someone had made d-mat unsafe, the world would come crumbling down around them. It would take something definite, something completely undeniable, to bring that about."

Clair studied him, beginning to suspect that his motives weren't at all the same as hers. "When you talked about taking action—"

"I wasn't talking about peacekeepers."

"So—"

"People should stop using d-mat, Clair. Errors caused by this kind of interference are nothing compared to the many accidental errors that go unnoticed every day. Have you ever worried about that?"

He had taken a step closer. She backed the same distance away. "I'm not here to talk about me. I came to you for Libby's sake."

"What do I care about another zombie girl? Her fate was sealed the moment she first stepped through a d-mat booth. Nothing you can do now will bring her back."

Clair didn't know how to respond to that, short of being unspeakably rude. If Libby was dead to him, so was Clair, and no amount of arguing would change that.

"Dad—" said Jesse.

"It's all right," Clair said. "I'll go now. It's getting late, and this . . . isn't helping."

She turned and headed for the garden, not caring that she knocked over a stack of cogs and gears as she went. Dylan watched her go with a cold expression.

The aroma of baking food hit her as she entered the apartment. Clair concentrated on finding her bag and getting out of there.

Jesse followed, his face a mask of anxiety.

"I'm sorry, Clair," he said at the door.

"Don't be. It's not your fault." Clair had invaded Jesse's world in search of answers, and now her head was full of Stainers and dead mothers and d-mat conspiracies.

"You remember the way to the station? It's a safe neighborhood, but I'm happy to walk you if you feel uncomfortable."

"No need for that."

"Hey," he said as she headed for the road, "next time bring Libby along. Dad can browbeat her in person. He might even convert her. That'd look great for him at the meetings."

Clair glanced back at him and was brought up momentarily by the stricken expression on his face. She wondered how many kids from school ever came to visit him. She might have been the first in years. How, in his mind, had he imagined it playing out?

He looked *lonely*.

"Miracles happen," Clair said, not stopping, "but not that big a miracle."

[II]

CLAIR WENT HOME, angry at Dylan Linwood and at herself for imagining that he would help her. He didn't owe her anything. He and Jesse might as well really exist in a different world from her. By refusing to use d-mat and fabbers, Jesse Linwood existed farther away than Libby, who lived thousands of miles around the bulge of the Earth.

She could see it from their eyes now, and she was embarrassed on her own behalf. To them it must have seemed deeply patronizing, the way she had barged into their lives, seeking answers to questions that didn't matter to them in the slightest. She lived in a world of instantaneous plenty, and she was worried about a friend's *bad mood*? No wonder Dylan Linwood had responded by trying to prop himself up as someone with secret knowledge and influence far beyond her own. His theory about Improvement causing random errors was imaginary, no doubt, but it was all he had to retaliate with. That and feeding her anxieties. She had enough of those without him adding to them.

When she reached the station, she gave the booth directions and closed her eyes, grateful for her ordinary life. One moment Manteca, the next Maine. Hissing, the door opened on cooler air and a barrage of silence.

Her mother was in the living room. She nabbed Clair before she could escape to her room.

"Come sit with me awhile," Allison said. "I feel I haven't seen you in person for ages. How's school? What's the latest gossip?"

The crisis among Clair, Libby, and Zep surely counted as gossip, but Clair was loath to go into that with her mother.

"School is the same," she said, stretching out on her back along the couch. "There's this new clique . . . the crashlanders. Libby and I got in."

"Well, that's great." Allison didn't ask for details. "As long as it doesn't interfere with your study . . ."

"It won't, Mom. What about you? Where have you been working this week?"

"Northern Australia. We've got two self-sufficient herds now, and we're working on a third."

"Still elephants?"

"Still elephants. The tweaks we made to the clones seem to be holding. No sign of inbreeding yet."

Allison was a veterinarian specializing in the restoration of animals to their natural environment, or the closest available. For community service, she was employed by ERA, the Environment Reclamation Agency. For fun and popularity, she played with ancient DNA in the hope of bringing back woolly mammoths.

Clair didn't understand every aspect of her work, but she knew one thing for certain. Allison changed the molecular coding of her animal clones using d-mat.

"How does it work?" Clair had never before had cause to ask her mother that question. "Does VIA give you permission to break the law?"

"No one can do that. VIA won't allow any pattern changes in the global system at all—not to living things and especially not to people. We use our own private network instead. We can do whatever we want in there."

"What would happen if someone hacked VIA . . . you know, if they wanted to make those kinds of changes in the global system . . . for whatever reason?"

"It happens every now and again," said Allison. "Young

idiots wanting to show off their skills and bad taste in body sculpting." She flashed a quick grin. "The peacekeepers pounce on them within minutes. There's no error too small to spot; that's how the system works. Really, if you wanted to do something illegal like that, you wouldn't do it in public. Like most crime, home is where the harm is."

"So someone *could* do it with a private network," Clair said.

"They would need resources that are tightly controlled, and access to the powersats as well. It's not the sort of thing you can just fab up in your basement." The smile lines around her eyes creased. "What's brought this on?"

Clair shook her head, wondering how Dylan Linwood would respond to this. Would it reassure him or make him more paranoid than ever? Would he find a way to make his *theory* work despite everything Allison said? "Nothing. Just something going around. A meme."

"Is it the one about how the government installs tracking devices in all of us so they can monitor our movements? I remember that from when I was your age. Somehow my generation managed to avoid being crushed under a totalitarian boot heel, and we'll avoid whatever it is you're worried about too, I'm sure."

She reached out and entwined her fingers in Clair's heavy curls. Apart from several streaks of gray at her temples, Allison had exactly the same hair as her daughter.

Their brown eyes were the same too, but there the similarity ended. Allison was fortunate to have her mother's nose, unlike her daughter.

"Oz will be back in the morning," Allison said. "Would you like to do something together?"

Oscar Kempe—Clair's stepfather—had been the third in their family unit since her second birthday, and he fulfilled the role of father in all but genes.

"Sure," she said warily. "Depending on homework."

"And the crashlanders." Allison smiled again. "I understand. Let's talk tomorrow."

Her warm fingers released Clair's hair, allowing Clair to retreat to her room.

"Good night, Mom."

"Sleep tight."

Clair posted a good-night caption (a house slowly overtaken by sand dunes) but was in no mood for sleeping.

She had bumped Libby on the way home, but Libby hadn't replied. Ronnie and Tash hadn't heard from her either. In desperation, she called Zep.

"Has she called you?" she asked, cutting through his usual chitchat.

"No, but she's home," he said. "I spoke to Freda. She said that Libby hasn't left her room all day."

Freda, originally Freedom, was Liberty's only sibling. Often annoying and frequently in the way, she was occasionally good for dishing the dirt on her older sister.

"Has she seen a doctor?" Clair said.

"Freda didn't know. Maybe not. She's only been out of school for a day."

And that, Clair told herself, was where she could leave it. Libby had a headache caused by transit lag and nothing more. Improvement had nothing to do with it. It was just a passing thing, an empty meme, a symptom of Libby's insecurity, not the cause of anything sinister or dangerous.

Maybe, Clair thought, she just wanted Libby to be sicker than she was so Libby would be out of the picture for a while. Was Clair's self-absorption really so profound? She hated that thought. But here she was talking to Zep and feeling the same hateful ache as ever. She could see him in a window superimposed on her ceiling as though he were floating or lying over her. It was all too easy to imagine reaching out and touching him.

"There'll be another ball tonight," said Zep, as though he could read her mind. "If you go, you could take me along."

"Your real date isn't feeling well," she said, forcing herself to say the words. "Do I have to remind you of that?"

"Well, exactly. She's out of action. The night is young. What do you think?"

"I think I've had enough of the crashlanders for one week," she said. "And gossip, too. We should probably take a break from hanging out until Libby is feeling better."

He frowned. "You mean I can't see you at all?"

"That's for the best. Don't you think?"

"Hell no. It's not our fault Libby can't or won't talk to us. She's the one who's making us do this."

"What difference would it make if she did talk? What would you tell her?"

"That we're going to the ball without her. That's all."

"What about what happened? What about you and her . . . ?"

Breaking up, she wanted to say, but she wasn't going to put the words in his mouth.

"Not yet. I mean, how could I? She's sick. It wouldn't be fair."

"But it's fair to kiss her best friend and then try to cover it up?"

He had the humanity to blush. "I feel bad about that . . . not the actual kissing part, though. I guess I could bump her, but that would be as bad as waiting, wouldn't it? It's not something you'd want to hear in a message. Right, Clair?"

"I guess so."

"What about you—have you told her?"

He had a point there. She *had* had the chance to tell Libby, but she had shied away from doing so. It wasn't something she was proud of.

"I don't know what to tell her," Clair said. "That's why I'm not coming out tonight. I don't want to get into something I'm not sure about. Not when it could cost me so much."

"Sometimes you don't know until you give it a try, Clair."

"Sometimes . . . but not this time."

He nodded without meeting her eyes. "Okay, Clair-bear. If that's how you want it to be, that's how it'll be. I promise not to be a dick about it."

"Do you really think you can manage that?"

"Oh, it'll be tough, I know, but for you . . . anything."

She managed a smile, although it hurt her to pretend to be anything other than torn up and miserable.

"Call me if she calls you," Clair said.

"I will."

He signed off, and she was alone.

Tomorrow, she told herself, everything would be different. Zep would talk to Libby, and Improvement would be revealed as nothing at all. The emotional storm would be rough, but she would weather it as she always did. And when life returned to normal, maybe she would let Ronnie take her out partying. She was sure there were guys out there who weren't slimeballs or taken.

——————————————————— [12]

ZEP WAS HUGE, a giant monster smashing the dikes of Tokyo. Libby and Clair were the pilots of a massive robot sent to stop him, except they couldn't agree on which way to go. The robot began to tear itself to pieces while the sea rushed in to engulf the city. instead of foam, the waves were topped with thousands of handwritten notes, all saying the same thing: *Charlie X-ray Romeo Foxtrot . . .*

Clair rarely dreamed, but when she did, it was memorable.

Her sleep was interrupted by a nagging flash that brought her out of deep unconsciousness in stages. Only slowly did she become aware that someone was calling her and that they were doing so through her most intimate and private channel, reserved solely for Libby.

"What?" she said, fumbling with her night-darkened lens interfaces. Behind the dark shutters of her eyelids, she imagined crises unnumbered. "Libby, what is it?"

"You called me," came the reply. Libby sounded shockingly bright and breezy. There was no sign in her voice of migraine or fatigue. "I'm calling you back. There's no drama."

"Are you sure?" She checked the time. "It's the middle of the night. I was asleep."

"Well, I've been sleeping all day, and I'm tired of doing nothing. Lying around is a waste of the New Improved Me, right?"

"Let me see you," said Clair, pulling herself up in bed onto her elbows and blinking the sleep from her eyes.

"Why?"

"Because I want to." The last dregs of the dream disappeared, leaving a lingering sense of alarm.

"You want proof. That's what you mean," said Libby in

a sharp tone. "Life is good, Clair. I'm beautiful. You're not going to make me feel bad, no matter what you say."

Libby appeared in a window in Clair's vision like a translucent ghost. She was dressed in a tight-fitting white top and had styled her blond hair in a wave. Her complexion was impeccable. Clair could see nothing but clear white skin from hairline to jaw and a smile that was as sharp as her tone.

The birthmark certainly *appeared* to be gone . . . but appearances could be deceiving. Libby was touching up her lips in pink, and her eyeliner was blue, so there was definitely makeup in play. Could she have found a new shade that did the job more effectively than the last one? Would she really lie about such a thing just to save face?

"I don't want to make you feel bad," Clair said, wondering why Libby would even suggest such a thing.

"You may not want to, but that's what you do. You talk about me behind my back, you think I'm crazy—"

"That's not what I think—"

"You want to swoop in and solve all my problems. Well, I'm not your *project*, Clair. I have everything under control. It's time you realized it and let me be who I am."

Clair blinked back a sudden sting of tears. Was that really how Libby saw her? Interfering and controlling? Not helping or *finishing*, as Zep had put it? Libby had never said anything to indicate that she thought this way, not in all their long years together.

"That's not what I mean to do, Libby. Honest. I love who you are. You don't need to change anything or do anything for me to think you're the best."

"But you won't let me change. That's the problem." Libby was fussing with her appearance as she talked, either ignoring or not noticing Clair's attempts to make her look back at her. "You don't believe in Improvement."

"Well . . . it is a little hard to accept. . . ."

"Basically, you're calling me a liar."

"I'm not calling you anything, Libby!" Clair's sense of hurt flared into frustration. Why was Libby trying to pick a fight with her in the middle of the night? Was it the Zep situation or another weird mood? "I'm just . . . just worried about you, that's all."

"Don't be. I feel fine. Just look at me. I *look* fine, right?"

She pirouetted for Clair's benefit, and Clair agreed that she did look good. It was hard to equate this Libby with the grainy figure she had glimpsed that morning. But what did that mean? Improvement either worked as promised or it was dangerous: those were the two choices Libby and Dylan Linwood were forcing on her. That it did nothing at all was a possibility that seemed to have evaporated over the course of the day, leaving her feeling stranded in the middle.

"Are you going to the ball?" Clair asked, trying to change the subject.

"That ended ages ago. No, I'm going to Zep's."

[87]

Clair made her face a mask, feeling as though she'd been punched in the guts. *He was supposed to call*, she thought.

"Well, have fun," she managed to get out, although it felt like hauling heavy rocks out of her chest.

"Oh, I will. And I'll think of you while I'm doing it."

"What?"

"You could use a little fun in your life, Clair. Maybe you should try it. See what happens. You might be pleasantly surprised."

"Are we still talking about . . . ?"

"Improvement, of course. Look what it's done for me. Instead of lying there being critical, why not do something to better yourself? What are you afraid of?"

"I'm not afraid," Clair said.

"Yes, you are. You're afraid of being beautiful like me. You think I did the wrong thing, and now you're trying to steal what belongs to me."

Libby's pale face stared directly at Clair, just for an instant, in naked challenge.

"That's not what I'm doing," Clair said. "That's not what I think. . . . It's confusing. . . ."

"I bet it is," said Libby. "Instead of trying to fix *my* life, why don't you concentrate on the mess you call your own?"

The window closed while Clair floundered, lost for something to say. For a moment, there were no words at all, just a seething roar in her ears. She could only stare into space while she tried to decide what she felt most: anger, guilt, jealousy, or grief. Was this the end of her friendship with Libby?

She fell onto the bed and ground the heels of her hands into her eyes, willing herself not to cry. She wanted to call back right away and apologize—but what for, exactly? For having a connection with Zep that didn't include Libby? For not believing in Improvement? For trying to *help*?

She wasn't going to apologize, she promised herself. And it wasn't about Zep or anything obviously superficial and in the moment. If it had really been about a single kiss, maybe Clair would have let Libby have her time in the crisis spotlight, safe in the knowledge that it would blow over soon enough. She could live with that for the sake of eventual peace. It was what Libby had said about being Clair's *project* that stung the most. Like it wasn't just as often the other way around—Libby trying to drag her off to things Clair wasn't interested in, safe in the knowledge that Clair would either enjoy it or make things work out when they didn't. That was why they worked as friends when they were so patently different from each other— and now Libby didn't want it to be that way anymore. She wanted to break the central dynamic of their friendship, which was that it went both ways.

Clair could hear her own breathing echoing back to her from the confines of her room. It was fast, as though she had been running.

The story Clair had told Jesse earlier that day came back to her now. Food poisoning thanks to bad chicken had kept her out of school for a week. Her friends had sent her get-well messages through the Air, but that hadn't been enough for Libby. She had brought around a pot of congee that she said was an old family recipe—fabbed a generation ago and perfect, Libby said, for settling a bad stomach. It *had* made Clair feel better, but not just because of the rice broth. Because Libby had known that Clair felt in need of more comfort than the Air could provide, and Libby had been there for her. She had felt, in that moment, that Libby would always be there, whenever Clair needed her.

It goes both ways, she thought again.

Libby might be acting hatefully toward her at the moment, but that didn't mean they weren't still friends. What if she was still looking out for Clair now? What if Libby, in her own way, genuinely thought she was giving Clair good advice?

————————————————————— [13]

CLAIR SAT UP and flicked her bedside lamp on. The light made her blink, but it echoed the sudden feeling in her mind that she was seeing the situation in an entirely new and important light.

Libby was one hundred percent certain that Improvement worked.

Dylan Linwood was one hundred and *ten* percent certain that anything to do with d-mat was evil and that Improvement was just one example of the system causing errors.

Both were asking Clair to believe them.

Who would Clair rather was right? Whom did she trust?

She didn't even have to think about it. Not the madman who built bikes for a living and ate plants he grew in the dirt. Not the conspiracy nut who wished there was something seriously wrong with Libby so he could use her for evidence against the system he hated. Not the insecure father who put Clair down in order to look tall in front of his son.

There were two possibilities: Improvement was all in Libby's mind, or the global network was broken.

Clair would rather discover that all of VIA's safeguards were useless than that a man like Dylan Linwood was right.

It was the middle of the night in Maine, but that didn't matter. It was day for half the world. Clair got out of bed, got dressed in yesterday's clothes, and moved quietly through the apartment to the dining room, where she fabbed notepaper and a pen. *Gone out*, she wrote for her mother's benefit. *Will call.* That way there was no chance of being talked out of it, should a bump wake Allison up.

On a second piece of paper she wrote, *My nose is too big. Like, HUGE. Help!* Then she added the code words and folded the piece of paper in four and slipped it under the elastic of her underwear, so it pressed against her hip.

She was going to make things right between her and Libby by proving Dylan Linwood wrong.

Clair left the apartment and headed up the hall. Clair had never had d-mat at home. She counted herself lucky that the apartment building she lived in had a booth on each level, opposite the fire stairs that led down to the sidewalks, which no one ever used. That meant she only had to worry about the weather at the other end of her journey.

For the immediate future, there would be no *other end* to worry about.

"Lucky Jump," Clair told the booth as the door slid shut.

The lights flared. The air thinned.

sssssss-pop

Her face in the mirror was unchanged. Of course.

She didn't wait for the door to open.

"Again."

sssssss-pop

"Again."

sssssss-pop

"Again . . . no, wait."

The booth was still and silent around her. An infinite

number of Clair Hills stood motionlessly, wondering if her haste was a little ill-considered.

There were in fact *three* possibilities she needed to think about. One, Improvement was Libby's fantasy; two, Improvement was a global hack; or three, Improvement happened in a private network.

Everything everyone had told Clair constantly reinforced the certainty that Improvement, if it worked, couldn't operate in the public domain. VIA's network was absolutely secure. She could jump the normal way a million times without changing the polish on her toenails one iota.

So for Improvement to work, it had to be as Clair's mother had said: it had to be by the third option. That meant the note would have to operate as a signal to someone watching, someone who would reroute her from the public network to another place entirely—kidnapping her, in effect, if only temporarily, before returning her to the public network. That could happen to her on the very next trip or on the hundredth. Maybe it had already happened without her noticing.

Her lenses instantly put *that* fear to rest. She was on Rhodes, not far from the rebuilt Colossus.

"Woodward and Main, Manteca," she instructed the booth.

sssssss-pop

She checked her coordinates, as she should have been doing from the start. No deviation.

"Now back home, please."

sssssss-pop

She checked again. No deviation.

She repeated the cycle three times without deviation.

That would do it, she decided. Bouncing back and forth between the two, checking every time, would ensure she was only ever where she expected to be.

And if she did deviate, she would know there was something to Improvement—the meme, if not the actual process of changing someone into a better person. Proof wouldn't necessarily require any physical changes to her nose. If she wasn't at either the Manteca station or Maine, she would know that someone had read her note and diverted her—proving Libby right and Dylan Linwood wrong. The existence of a private network meant only that VIA had made a mistake, not that the entire system was at fault.

Or nothing at all would happen, in which case she would know that Libby was going through a bad patch that time, honesty, and a lot of patience would heal.

The eleven jumps had passed quickly, but just shy of half an hour had passed in the real world. Another eighty jumps to go before she equaled Libby's marathon effort. As a young girl, Clair had imagined what it would be like to spend all day jumping. If her parents had let her use a booth without them, she would have danced across the world as though wearing twelve-league boots. Once she had her solo license, the impulse had worn off. Transit lag was a pain. It made her feel tired in advance just thinking about it.

Squatting with her back against the mirrored wall, she instructed the booth to return her to Manteca. Some people talked about losing their train of thought when they jumped, seeing wild flashes of color or even experiencing vivid microdreams. She, however, felt nothing as the machines cycled around her, sucking up enough power to run an old-time country for a year.

Ten more cycles, which made over thirty jumps. No deviations, no change. Clair was getting bored. Using d-mat never really felt like going anywhere, but at least there was a change of scenery to look forward to. This was worse than running in circles. This was just an endless cycling of air in a human-sized vacuum flask. She and her reflections went back and forth, back and forth, with only the Air for company, and that was poor fodder.

Libby had cut Clair's close-friend privileges, so Clair couldn't tell where she was. Ronnie and Tash were asleep. Zep wasn't an option. No one else knew what was going on except Jesse, and he was a total dead end.

She thought about leaving Ronnie and Tash a message: *If you never hear from me again, you'll know I've turned into a turnip or something.* But this was between her and Libby; it wasn't for anyone else to know about. And it certainly wasn't a joke.

Ten more cycles and her ears were starting to hurt. After her fortieth jump, her right eardrum didn't unpop, so she spent an awkward ten minutes walking around the booth in Manteca, waiting for her sinuses to clear. A sharp pain shot through that side of her head, and she stood still for a moment, waiting anxiously for it to go away.

It did, along with the blockage in her ear. She performed one more lap of the booth, for luck, and to prepare herself for resuming the tedious confinement within. How long until she decided that her theory about private networks was wrong? Part of her hoped that her nose *would* change, just to liven things up.

——————————————————— [14]

SSSSSSS-POP

After her seventieth jump, a new message appeared in her infield. Thinking it might be Ronnie or Tash saying good morning, she opened it without thinking.

It said: "'Woman, I behold thee, flippant, vain, and full of fancies.'"

The words hung in bold sans serif over her on the reflecting surfaces of the booth. The message was unsigned, but there was a winking reply patch associated with the text. The address was hidden by some kind of anonymizing protocol. The name was simply a long string of lowercase *q*'s with an ellipsis in the middle, which indicated that the full text exceeded the field's maximum character length.

qqqqq · · · qqqqq

If someone she knew had sent the message, they were going out of their way to keep their identity a secret. But the text resonated with her. It was something she had read recently in school. The lines were from a poem, but they had been misquoted.

Clair could have ignored it and taken the next jump, back to Manteca for what felt like the thousandth time.

Instead she sent a reply. She was bored and restless and wondering if she had done enough to prove that Libby was right yet. What did it hurt to send a few words through the Air?

"If you're going to quote Keats," she bumped back, "at least do it properly."

Nothing happened for a while, and she began to wonder if it ever would.

Then a new bump appeared from the same address.

"I *Improved* it."

Clair felt gooseflesh rise up on her forearms. She folded her arms tightly across her chest.

There was no way anyone could see her in the booth, but she knew, suddenly, that she was being watched.

"Who are you?" she sent. "What do you want?"

The reply came in the form of another misquote.

"'Your eyes are drunk with beauty your heart will never see.'"

Clair searched the Air for the source. It was from some-one called George W. Russell. She didn't know him from her writing class, but someone remembered him—or misremembered him, rather. The original line ran, "Our hearts are drunk with a beauty our eyes could never see."

Whatever was going on, Clair decided to fight fire with fire.

"'No object is so beautiful that, under certain condi-tions, it will not look ugly,'" she sent. "That's Oscar Wilde, and I didn't need to twist his words to make my point. It's all about beholding, right, so why does anything need to be changed at all?"

Another bump arrived.

"'That which does not change is not alive.'" Clair didn't realize it was another quote until the source of the words added, "Sturgeon, exactly. The irony is mine."

Clair was determined not to let her uneasiness show, whether she was talking to some random troll who had spotted her movements or a creep connected to Improve-ment somehow. If he wanted to chat, why not let him? Words couldn't hurt anyone.

"Are we going to talk properly," she bumped back, "or just sit here all day slinging quotes at each other?"

An incoming call patch began to flash.

She took a deep breath. This was it.

"Who are you, and what do you want?"

But the voice at the other end of the call was a familiar one.

"Clair?" said Zep. "Quit screwing around. I need you."

[15]

CLAIR'S INFIELD SHOWED no return bumps, just Zep's anxious face staring at hers.

"What is it?" she asked. "What's going on?"

"It's Libby. You have to get here, fast."

"Where are you?"

"My dorm. Quick, she's leaving."

"I'm on my way."

Clair hesitated just for a second. If someone was tracking her, this was exactly the wrong time to go anywhere.

But what else could she do?

She told the booth to take her to Zep's and hoped for the best.

He lived in a cheap all-male dorm on the Isle of Shanghai. It was an open community, not sealed off from the outside world like a lot of natural-sports frats. Its gaggle of young men came from widely scattered regions, united only by the willingness to put their bodies through hell in exchange for a shot at fame.

The booth finished its work. Her nose was unchanged. The moment the doors opened, Clair knew she was in the right place.

The street outside was filled with the constant ding-dinging of bicycles in vigorous use, decorated with multicolored flags and ribbons. From every fabber streamed the aroma of spices. Shanghai was not so much a city as an inextricable tangle of numerous cultures and times, with traditions that stretched back centuries before d-mat.

Lines of market stalls stretched into the hazy distance, with hundreds of hawkers competing for the attention of passersby. The trade was in original goods—handmade, hand grown, freshly killed, or wrenched from the sea—but convincing customers that something was unique and not built from a fabber's memory could be very difficult. Claims and counterclaims were being made in loud voices. The racket hurt Clair's ears.

She hurried toward Zep's quarters, bumping him to let her know she was on her way. The ground-floor entrance led to an elevator and a flight of stairs. She took the former to the third floor.

"Clair, through here," Zep called when its doors opened.

She looked up, saw him waving, beyond a bunch of young men playing a haptic MMORPG in a communal hall. They jumped and tumbled like spastic acrobats, laughing and calling in a patois she didn't understand.

Someone whistled at her. She ignored him.

Zep's room was no cleaner than usual. It was small, cluttered with trophies, and filled almost entirely with bed. There was a fabber in one corner. A pile of clothes lay next to it, awaiting recycling. There was an overwhelming scent of him, with a faint hint of familiar perfume around the edges.

"Where is she?"

"Gone." Zep came around behind her and shut the door. "Libby's out of control, Clair."

"Out of control how?"

"Like crazy how. She came over last night—"

"I know she did. I spoke to her."

"How did she seem to you?" If he noticed her accusatory tone, he didn't say anything.

"We argued. She knows about us, I'm sure of it. Did you tell her?"

He shook his head. "She didn't say anything to me about it."

"Were you going to?"

"I don't know. I couldn't get a word in. She came out of nowhere. I had no warning at all." He collapsed back onto the bed. It *skreek*ed under his weight. "The very second she got here, we had to go out again. She had this terrible headache, she said. I can't get meds from my fabber—doping regulations, you know—so we went to a friend of mine who gave her something really strong, something I'd never heard of before. Then she wanted a drink, and it didn't mix so well. I tried to get her to cool down, but she wouldn't listen. She was going on and on about awful stuff—things I'd never heard before about her family. If half of it is true, no wonder she's such a mess."

"What about her family?"

"How her grandmother was murdered in a death camp, and she was raped as a child. You must know all about this. You've been her friend forever."

Clair rubbed at her temple with the ball of her right thumb. "She wasn't raped as a child, and both her grandmothers are alive. I've met them."

"So why would she tell me that?"

"I don't know. Maybe she's trying to get your attention."

"Well, it's working. But why she'd want this kind of attention is beyond me."

Clair sat on the edge of the bed, feeling exhausted and confused. Libby had taken drugs and gone a little wild. Nothing unheard of for a girl in high school, and there were campus counselors trained to deal with things like that.

"Did Libby say anything to you about strange messages?" Clair asked him.

"What kind of messages?"

"Like someone was watching her," she said, extrapolating from her own experience, "judging her, even."

"No. Did she tell you about them?"

Clair debated with herself for a second, then showed him the bumps she had received.

"When I spoke to her yesterday, the first time, Libby mentioned weird messages," Clair said. "I used Improvement to prove that I trust her. . . ."

He scooched down the bed so he was sitting behind her.

"You used Improvement?" he asked. "Seriously?"

"Why not? It didn't do anything—nothing I can see, anyway. But now these messages have come, and I don't know what to think."

He touched her shoulder, and she shrugged him off. "Don't."

"I'm not trying anything," he said, backing away with his hands raised. "Honest."

"I believe you, but . . ." Clair clenched her fists and pressed them into her thighs. She found it hard to think with him so close. "If someone's bugging her, too, maybe that's helped push her over the edge. On top of what you and I did, I mean." She turned on him. "Zep, how could you let her leave like that?"

"I didn't have a choice. She slipped me one of the pain-killers before we went to bed. I was groggy. Still am."

He did look washed-out and pale, a far cry from his usual confident, unstoppable self.

"I'm going to try calling her," she said. "Maybe she'll talk to me."

"Brace yourself," he said. "It's like she's an entirely different person."

"Don't say that. She's just going through a rough patch."

To Clair's amazement, Libby answered immediately.

"I'm beautiful, Clair." She sounded stoned. "I'm *beautiful*."

"Of course you are—you always have been, right? Tell me what's going on. Let's talk."

"What's there to talk about?" Her voice hardened. "He only wants you because you're *different*."

"Libby, listen to me." Clair did her best to ignore the attempt to wound her. "I tried Improvement, and it didn't work—"

"I'm in heaven, and I'm so beautiful," Libby chanted, marshmallow-soft again. "You're not and never will be."

Libby ended the call, and she wouldn't answer when Clair tried again.

"What did she say?" asked Zep.

"She . . . hang on."

A call patch appeared in her infield, its source the string of *q*'s.

Clair turned to face Zep.

"He's back."

"Who?"

"The creep . . . stalker, whatever he is."

"What are you going to do? Are you going to talk to him?"

"He's the only lead we've got."

She reached out and took Zep's hand. His strong fingers gripped hers as she winked the patch on.

Before she could utter a single word, an unexpected voice spoke to her. It didn't sound like a stalker. It sounded like a child, but that could have been a filter designed to disguise the speaker's true identity, Clair supposed.

"How do you know Liberty Zeist?"

With the voice came a streaming video, not of the person who was talking but of Libby pacing back and forth in an empty marble foyer, biting her fingernails. It looked real-time but didn't have any map data or date stamp. The picture was greenish and grainy. Libby was wearing a clingy jumpsuit that Clair had never seen before. Her white hair was tied back in a severe ponytail that made her look somehow older and younger at the same time. There was no sign of the birthmark. Was that makeup or something real? It had to be makeup, surely.

"How do I know Libby?" Clair said. "She's my best friend, and I'm not going to let you hurt her."

"I have not hurt her. She is beautiful."

"Yes, she is, and that's the way she's going to stay, buddy."

"All things change."

"Not if I can help it."

"What's he saying?" whispered Zep. "I can only hear your side."

Clair shook her head. The voice was still talking.

"You say that she is your friend. You are trying to help her. Is that correct?"

"Of course it's correct," she said. "Tell me why you sent me those messages."

"Change and beauty are the heart of Improvement. I thought you would understand."

"Understand what?"

"It puzzles me that you do not understand. I don't understand you in return."

"Did you message Libby as well?"

"Yes, but she didn't answer as you did."

"Is that disappointing? Would you rather Libby had been talkative than silent? Is that how you prefer your . . . your victims?"

She was being deliberately provocative, trying to get a rise out of him.

"I don't understand what you mean by 'victims.' I have hurt no one."

"So you say, pal."

"I am merely talking. We are exchanging information and learning from each other. Is that not stimulating for you?"

Clair made a disgusted sound that echoed flatly off the dorm's walls. She didn't really want to think about what the person she was talking to found *stimulating*.

"If you've hurt Libby in any way at all—"

"I would never hurt her. She is beautiful."

"She is, and I'm going to do everything I can to make sure she's safe."

"Because she is your friend," said the voice in its too-innocent way. "If I helped her, would that make me her friend, as you are?"

"What?"

"I said: if I helped her, would that make me her friend—"

"I heard what you said. I just . . . I don't believe this. You're screwing with my head. Is this what you do to people? Is this how you get your kicks? You reel people in with false promises. You find out who they are and toy with them. Maybe you drive some of them out of their minds. Is that what's happened to Libby? Did you get inside her head and have a little fun?"

There was silence at the other end for a long time.

"Tell me I'm wrong," she said.

"I do not understand," said the voice. "I am not in your head. I do not understand your motivation at all."

"Oh . . ."

Clair bit down on a frustrated retort. This wasn't helping.

"Clair?" said Zep, squeezing her hand. "What's going on?"

She shook her head. There was only silence on the other end of the line. No breathing, even. It was almost as though there was no one there at all.

"Hello?"

"Hello, Clair Hill," said the voice. "It is nice to meet you."

That was the first time her name had been used. It frightened and alarmed her. Of course the caller knew who she was—otherwise they wouldn't be talking—but to hear her name when she didn't know the stalker's in return made her feel vulnerable and exposed.

She ended the chat immediately. The video of Libby closed with it. A new call patch started flashing in her lenses, regular and relentless, like the ticking of an electronic heartbeat.

qqqqq . . . qqqqq

---

[16]

"CLAIR, ARE YOU all right?"

Zep's hand was still gripping hers. She didn't want to let go, but she forced herself to.

"I'm definitely okay," she said, thinking through a fog of confusion and exhaustion. "I used Improvement seventy times, and I feel perfectly fine. Do I look fine to you?"

"Your usual excellent self."

"So Libby being such a mess can't have anything to do with Improvement . . . right?"

"Maybe she was a mess to start with."

Clair glared at him, and he looked away with a shrug.

"What did the stalker say? Did he give you any clues?"

"Nothing. It was weird. I'm not even sure he was a he. . . ."

She trailed off because another call patch was coming through, and this time it had an ID. She stared at it, puzzled. Why was Jesse Linwood contacting her now?

Curious, she took the call.

"Are you at school?" he asked, sounding breathless.

"Why?"

"It's Dad. I hassled him to keep looking into Improvement, and he found something."

"What is it?"

"He wouldn't tell me. Then he left on the electrobike without telling me where he was going."

"So he went for a ride. So what?"

"This just came." Jesse sent her a link to a streaming video. "You need to see it."

She followed the link and saw Dylan sitting in the principal's office of Manteca New Campus High School.

"Always a pleasure," said Principal Gordon, a tall, smartly dressed woman with tightly wound auburn hair. Her nickname was Gordon the Gorgon. There was a sour cast to her lips that expressed anything other than pleasure. "What is this regarding?"

"It's a matter of life and death," Dylan told her. "One of your students is already at risk."

"Oh no," said Clair, standing. There was only one thing Dylan could be talking about. "How long has this been running?"

"It just started. I called you right away."

"Has he mentioned anyone by name?"

"Not yet, but he might," he said. "Maybe I can stop him. I'll come as fast as I can."

"All right." She was already on her feet. "I'm on my way too."

Zep had risen to his feet when she did, and when she went to leave, he pulled her back.

"What now?" he asked. "Where are you going?"

"I'll tell you on the way," she said, tugging free.

"Wait. I'll lock up."

"No time!"

She was out of his room and running across the dorm, sending him the link as she went. The facts would have to speak for themselves.

Libby's popularity was higher than it had ever been, thanks to the crashlanders. But how long would that last if Dylan used Libby's name? Her closest friends had refused to believe that Improvement was anything other than spam targeting the gullible. Even if it worked, the fact that she had used it would undermine Libby's carefully maintained facade of cool. When Libby learned that Clair had passed on something that she had revealed only to her innermost circle, she was bound to feel embarrassed, betrayed, undermined . . . and in her current state, that might be the straw that broke their friendship's back. It would certainly undo all the effort Clair was making to prove to Libby that she trusted her.

"A matter of life and death, you say, Mr. Linwood?"

Principal Gordon was saying in the video. "Do explain."

The principal's office was furnished in mid-twentieth-century style, with wood paneling, leather armchairs, and a low desk that was pure ornamental ostentation. She had taken the seat farthest from the door, a magisterial perch with a coffee table beside it. Facing her were three less-imposing pieces. Dylan was in the center chair, scruffy but straight-backed in his work clothes. The video was being taken from a position high up on the wall opposite them, where a clock or bookcase concealed a camera. Hacking into its feed and releasing the data into the Air didn't seem beyond Dylan's capabilities, based on the little Clair knew about him.

"There's a dangerous meme, called Improvement, and it's here on your campus," he said. "You need to stamp it out before it claims another victim."

"Really, Mr. Linwood." Principal Gordon arched an eyebrow. "I believe that once again you are overstating the case."

"But you are aware of the phenomenon?"

"I have heard rumors."

"Have you taken any provisions against it?"

"Not specifically."

"So you admit that you allow your students to fend for themselves as an insidious threat spreads among them."

"Please. We're not talking about some deadly new virus—"

"In a very real sense, we might be. Improvement spreads in exactly the same fashion as a virulent disease. Outbreaks flare up and fade away, apparently at random. Each time, it disappears, only to reappear later and wreak further havoc."

Clair reached the street and hurried for a d-mat booth.

"We're talking about a meme much more sinister than any mere disease," Dylan was saying, "and I'm not leaving until I am certain that this institution is capable of providing its students with the protection they deserve."

Clair was at the booth. She dived in and called out the name of her usual station. The video feed died as the lights in the booth flared. She forced herself to stand still and not fidget too much—not that it made any difference to her or the way d-mat worked. The flight of a bullet fired across the booth at the exact moment of transit would have been unaltered in any way. That was the VIA guarantee.

The doors opened in Manteca and Clair began to run.

"Mr. Linwood," Principal Gordon was saying over the video stream, "I completely agree with you that Manteca New Campus is obliged to protect its students to the fullest extent possible, but we cannot protect them from imaginary threats. I thought I had made this absolutely clear the last time you—"

"If there were evidence of harm, would you act?"

"Of course we would."

From under his jacket, Dylan pulled a slim document folder.

"I have here pathology reports on the deaths of nine girls who, according to family testimonies, all used Improvement within six months of one another." He proffered the folder to Principal Gordon. "Go on, take a look."

The principal took the folder, opened it, and flipped through the pages with a tightening frown.

Clair wished she could see what the folder contained— a wish that was almost immediately answered. Appended to the video feed was a second stream of images and data that she glanced at but couldn't interpret.

"When you're done," Dylan said, "we can discuss what measures you will introduce to protect the students of this school from the malevolent influences they have been exposed to via d-mat."

The school gates were in view. Anger and the first hint of anxiety made Clair run faster. Was this really pure bluff on Dylan's part, or was there something truly to worry about?

The principal abruptly closed the folder and placed it in her lap.

"I fail to see how these cases are related, to each other or to Improvement," she said. "These poor young women committed suicide."

"The manner of their deaths is irrelevant," Dylan insisted. "Look at the brain scans. There's clear evidence of damage to the prefrontal cortex, temporal lobes, and hippocampus. Such damage is not related to their medical histories."

"So?"

"The only thing these poor girls had in common was Improvement. The connection cannot be disputed."

"Where did you obtain these records, Mr. Linwood?" the principal asked. "If this data is real, why has it not come to light before now?"

"It's very real," he said, "and readily available to anyone who looks hard enough. Buried in the Air under a mountain of irrelevant information, as all important things are. Nothing is hidden, and everything is ignored. The surveillance state doesn't need violence to perpetrate injustice. All it needs is our indifference."

"Mr. Linwood, please, can we stick to the topic?"

Clair was on campus. A crowd had gathered in front of the principal's office, watched over by a UFO-shaped eye-in-the-sky drone. Students in turn were staring at a two-wheeled silver electrobike parked on the slate quadrangle, all sweeping planes and fragile-looking lines. It listed slightly from vertical, supported by a kickstand protruding from its left-hand side. The engine was ticking like an old-fashioned clock. "I think that's a Linwood," Clair heard someone breathe in awe. "One of a kind—I mean *literally*!"

She hurried through the crowd, grateful for all the

jogging Libby had made her do that summer. Her lungs were burning, but she would be able to talk when she got inside.

"Are you calling me a liar?" Dylan was saying.

"Nothing of the sort. Misled by your prejudices, possibly. I can't conclude anything until you tell us more."

"The onus is on you to ensure the safety of your students. I've given you cause to look deeper. Now I expect you to do it."

"I see no cause at all. Just rumors and pictures." Principal Gordon tossed the folder lightly in her hand as though to demonstrate how little it weighed, physically and symbolically. "These documents could easily have been falsified."

Outside the office, the principal's assistant, a slender young man with flickering lenses, tried to stop Clair from going inside.

"I'm sorry," he said, "but Principal Gordon is engaged at the moment."

"I know," she said. "The world knows it. Get out of my way."

She feinted left and slipped past him to the right, driven by a mixture of indignation and fear.

Both Dylan Linwood and Principal Gordon stood as she burst into the room. Clair came to a halt between them, struck by the sudden vertigo of seeing herself in the streaming video. Her skin was shining and sweaty. Her hair was wild. She looked as crazy as Dylan did.

"What are you doing here, Clair?"

The principal's eyes were very hard. All Clair's personal information had probably been uploaded into her lenses the moment Clair entered the room.

"I'm the one who told him about Improvement," she said, choosing her words with care. Only now did it occur to her to wonder what she was going to do to make Dylan shut up and go home. "I went to Mr. Linwood for advice. I didn't want him to do anything like this . . . not at all."

"Did you really think I'd sit back and do nothing?" Jesse's father asked her.

The principal waved him silent.

"Clair, do you know someone who has used Improvement?"

She hesitated, then nodded. "Do I have to say who she is?"

"Not unless you want to or you think she is in any danger. Do you think she would submit to a physical examination to see if she has suffered any ill effects?"

Clair thought about Libby's headache and mood swings. These weren't certain evidence of anything—although she was sure Dylan would claim they were. Clair might have been willing to put the suggestion to Libby but for one critical detail.

No one apart from Zep and her knew about the drugs Libby had taken the night before. Whatever they were, they obviously weren't legal, or else she could have fabbed them herself. An examination would undoubtedly include a drug test.

"No," she said, afraid now of damaging more than just Libby's reputation. "It's no one's business but her own."

She glanced at Jesse's father. He was glaring at her. What had he expected—that she would sit back while he destroyed her best friend's life?

"This speaks volumes to me, Mr. Linwood," said the principal. "Clair's friend could come forward if she wanted to, but she hasn't. Surely she would if there was something wrong with her. Improvement is a meaningless prank. Unless I have hard evidence to back up your allegations, Mr. Linwood, I can only, once again, follow the health and safety guidelines issued by the appropriate authorities—"

"That's not good enough," said Dylan, stepping forward. "This is about more than just Improvement, and you know it. The whole deadly system is what we should be railing against. How many students of yours come to campus by d-mat every day? Do you know or care what dangers they're exposing themselves to each time they use this technology? Don't you think it's irresponsible to encourage them to take such risks when telepresence alternatives exist?"

Gordon the Gorgon didn't back down. "Every class is already posted to the Air for anyone who wants to use their lenses. How my students choose to engage with the educational resources we offer is entirely up to them."

"That's a coward's answer, Principal Gordon." Dylan's face was red, his voice too loud. "You sit here in your comfortable chair while your students are fried up and scrambled and scattered in pieces across the planet. How many deaths would it take to spur you into action? How many kids could you bear to lose? Perhaps you're so jaded already, so inured to this cult of disintegration, that you would cheerfully herd your wards into a slaughterhouse without losing a minute's sleep. You monster, you murderer—"

The door to the office burst in behind them again, revealing Jesse and the principal's flustered assistant.

"Stop it, Dad. You're embarrassing yourself!"

"I'm embarrassing *you*, you mean." His father rounded on him. "Why does it matter what these people think?" He waved an arm in front of him, as though sweeping the entire world away. "Let them burn. Let them die if they want to. What do I care?"

He pushed past Jesse into the antechamber and stalked off through the crowd.

——————————————————————————[17]

JESSE CHASED AFTER his father. With a screech of tires, Dylan Linwood sped away on the electrobike, leaving his son behind.

"Is that all, Ms. Hill?" asked the principal, dragging Clair's attention back to the office.

Clair hesitated. The video stream had ended with Dylan Linwood's departure. There were no public eyes on her now.

"What if I said that I had used Improvement and was willing to take the test?"

"Then I'd say you've wasted time and energy better spent doing your homework. You look perfectly fine to me. And if you're thinking of killing yourself, I strongly urge you to talk to a counselor. That's why we provide them."

Principal Gordon opened the folder Dylan Linwood had given her, removed the pages, and ripped them in half.

"I have better ways to spend my mornings than with scaremongering students and difficult parents. It's time for class, Clair. Go."

Clair did as she was told, her face burning. The principal's assistant ushered her outside, and she was happy enough to go. That scene couldn't have gone much worse for her.

The crowd was dispersing, staring at but not talking to her. Jesse was standing, looking lost, next to his own bicycle—a human-powered one, with pedals at the front and a horizontal seating position. He was wearing the same jeans as yesterday but with an orange T-shirt this time. Maybe the yellow one was in the wash, Clair thought, distantly wondering how that worked.

"I'm sorry," he said to her. "This is his way of helping, believe it or not."

"Well, he's not. Was any of that real, or did he fake the whole thing?"

"He thinks it's real, for what that's worth."

Clair didn't know what to do. She didn't really think that Improvement was causing anyone brain damage, but the thought was out there now. Who knew how Libby would react? She was bound to get wind of it. Would she understand that Clair had been trying to protect her? Would she see that Clair had put her own reputation at risk in order to undo the damage she had already done to their friendship?

"I want to talk to him again," she said, coming to an instant decision. "I want your father to tell me everything he thinks he knows."

"Uh . . . I don't think he's going to like that idea—"

"I don't care. Can you call him?"

"I tried. He's not responding."

"Try again. If he's lying, he needs to take it back. And if he's right, against all the odds, Libby might be in real danger."

"I know," said Jesse, "Libby and everyone else who used Improvement, but what can I do? What can *you* do? It was her choice to do it. Whether it works the way it's supposed to or not, it's on her, right?"

Clair was about to deny that she would *ever* abandon Libby like that when it truly struck her that she, too, was one of Improvement's potential victims. If Dylan Linwood was right, she and Libby were in exactly the same boat.

"You look like hell, Clarabelle," said Zep from behind her. "And no wonder."

She turned, wondering if he was reading her mind. "What?"

"The video. I saw all of it except for when I was in transit. Fifty people have sent me the link since then. That's the most popular Gordon the Gorgon has ever been. You too. It's popping in the wake of the crashlander thing."

"Oh, great," said Clair.

"Soon you'll be famouser than famous—until some cat meme takes your place, anyway." He actually looked jealous.

"Don't. It's not helping." She pressed her palms hard into her temples, wishing she could squeeze out a solution. Her infield was full of bumps, distracting her.

"Do you think it's real?" Zep asked in quieter tones. "Nine girls in six months?"

"It can't be, can it?" said Jesse. "There'd be no missing that kind of correlation."

"Not if no one's looking. . . . Hey, you're the Stainer kid. Son of the lunatic himself."

Zep held out his hand, and Jesse warily shook it.

"Nice entrance back there, by the way," Zep said. "Bet you're looking forward to going home and facing the music."

"I'm going there now," said Jesse. He was speaking more to Clair than Zep. "I'm really sorry it went like this."

"It's not over yet," she said. "I'm going with you."

"What?" Zep looked from Clair to Jesse and back again. "Are you crazy?"

"Maybe, and maybe he is too. But I can't leave it here." Fury and frustration were making her hands shake. "He's going to talk to me properly, and I'm not leaving until he does."

"All right," said Jesse, looking resigned to an awkward replay of the previous night's confrontation. "I'll leave the bike here. We'll walk together."

"You don't have to do that," said Clair.

"Don't worry about the bike," he said, misunderstanding her concern. "I've got a spare if this is stolen. That's the trouble with Dad's plan to reeducate the world. He can only make so many things, which makes them valuable, which makes people copy and fab them so anyone can have their own. It's stupid. *He's* stupid."

Jesse stopped himself. He had wrapped a chain through the front wheel and fastened it to a water fountain.

"Screw school," said Zep. "I'm going too. This is for Libby, right?"

Relieved, Clair could only nod.

———————————————————— [18]

SHE SCANNED HER infield as they headed for the school gate. The small crowd had completely dispersed, and the drone had gone with it. There was no physical sign that anything untoward had happened at school that day. The aftershocks were all semantic, with Clair's lenses still full of strangers bumping her, her news grabs filling up with related topics and caption updates, and nags from both of her parents. They had seen the video, like everyone else. She expected another nag the moment they noticed her leaving school.

She sent them a quick note telling them she was all right and would explain later. She said the same thing to Ronnie and Tash and deleted everything else, including the blinking call path from her string-of-q's stalker. She concentrated on matching Jesse long pace for long pace as they left school and headed up Woodward. His head was down, so she couldn't see his eyes through his hair, just his mouth and the unhappy shape it made.

"You think Dad is some kind of mad bigot," Jesse said, "but he wasn't always that way. Mom used d-mat, and they were married for ages before they had me. She came from Australia. Her family still lives there, but we don't have anything to do with them now."

"So he used to be cool," said Zep. "That doesn't help us now, does it?"

"I just mean there's a reason why he's the way he is. One night when I was very young, there was an outage all down the west coast, as far inland as Utah. It was the tail end of a run of errors that stretched from the superconductor grid right back to a particular powersat, where some astronaut had messed up the routine maintenance a week earlier. There are safeguards against this kind of thing, of course, buffers, backups, blah-blah, but in this case they all failed. Tens of thousands of transits were interrupted. I have the exact number somewhere. The outage lasted less than a second, but that was long enough."

"Long enough for what?" asked Zep.

"Nineteen people died that night," Jesse said. "My mother was one of them."

"Dude, that sucks."

"It does," Clair agreed, feeling a modicum of understanding, then, perhaps even sympathy for Jesse's father. But the bulk of her feelings were for Jesse. She couldn't begin to imagine what it would be like to lose her mother that way, literally in the blink of an eye.

"I'm sorry," she said.

"You don't have to be sorry." Jesse was emerging from his shell of hair as he talked, first his nose, then his eyes, which gleamed in the afternoon light. "You just have to understand. VIA was keen to pin the blame on someone else. It was a terrorist action, they said. WHOLE, specifically. They never revealed how WHOLE had done it—for fear of copycats, they said. It didn't change what happened, and that's why Dad would say that d-mat can never be trusted. Because you can't trust the people who are supposed to make it safe."

"You might think he's nothing but an asshole," Jesse concluded, "but Mom's death is at the heart of everything he does. All he really wants is for everyone to be safe. He wants to protect me like he couldn't protect her."

"You make him sound like a saint," said Zep.

"Oh, he's definitely not one of those. You saw the video, right?"

Clair's attention was tugged away by two new notifications that had appeared in her infield. One was the q's again. The other was a bump from Libby.

"You just can't help yourself, can you?" the latter said. "You just won't leave well enough alone."

So, thought Clair, she had seen the video too.

"I'm sorry," Clair sent back. "I was worried."

The return bump was almost instantaneous. "You don't trust me."

"I do, I swear. I tried Improvement like you told me to, but it didn't do anything."

"I don't believe you. You're jealous. You want to ruin it for everyone, just like Dylan Linwood."

"What if he's right?" Clair bumped back, acknowledging the risk she was taking by even raising the possibility with Libby. "What if Improvement has hurt you somehow?"

"You're the one who's brain damaged. Improvement is a good thing. Why would anyone want to hurt me? Apart from you and Zep, I mean."

"We don't want to hurt you, I swear. We're trying to help."

"Who says I need your help?"

"We just want to do what's right."

"Too late for that."

Clair wrote half a reply, then deleted it. She would get nowhere by responding to Libby's barbs. Instead, she thought through everything she had learned in the previous twenty-four hours in the hope of finding another tack.

"What if someone's hacking the system, and that's interfering with d-mat somehow? Changing people's patterns by accident. What harm is there in having yourself checked out, just in case? I'll do it too. We'll do it together when the drugs have cleared your system. You and me."

"What happened to keeping Improvement a secret, like the note says?"

Before Clair could reply, she was blinded by a bright emergency flash, the kind she only ever saw in stories, never in real life. Only peacekeepers had the authority to override someone's vision. She stopped momentarily, stood blinking until her lenses cleared. When they did, a single red patch was glowing like an afterimage of the sun in the center of her vision.

qqqqq · · · qqqqq

Furious, she hurried to catch up with Zep and Jesse and took the call.

"That flash was you, wasn't it?" she said, mouthing the

words so she wouldn't interrupt Jesse's story. "How the hell did you hack my lenses?"

"That is what I'm good at," said the eerily childlike voice. "There is nothing I can't get into. Nothing I have come across yet, anyway."

"Why won't you leave me alone?"

"I just want to clarify the connection between you and Dylan Linwood. This is something else I don't understand."

"He's nothing to me. A pain in the neck. I thought he might help *me* understand something, but he's only made everything worse."

"He broadcast you against your will," the voice said. "Is that correct?"

"Of course it is. Why are you so interested?"

"I could help you, if you wanted."

"Like you helped Libby? No thanks. I want you to leave me alone."

"But—"

"I mean it. If you're not going to tell me what's going on, stay away from me and stay away from my friends."

There was another empty silence, until finally the voice said, in a tone that was almost reproachful, "'Beauty is a terrible and awful thing where boundaries meet and all contradictions exist side by side.'"

Another quote, one Clair recognized. It was Dostoevsky this time, but there was a missing piece: "God sets us nothing but riddles," something like that.

She agreed wholeheartedly.

The call closed from the other end, and Clair's infield returned to normal. The last message from Libby was still in view. Clair felt no loyalty to the secrecy Improvement demanded of its users, only to Libby's privacy and well-being.

Zep was saying, "I've heard that Stainer meetings are where WHOLE recruits hard-liners. Is that true?"

"I don't know, Zep. No one's ever tried to recruit me."

"What about your father?"

"He never came out and said he was in WHOLE."

"But he never said he wasn't, either."

Jesse nodded. "He and I argued all the time. When I was a kid, I used to talk about turning fifteen and getting into a booth and visiting my grandmother in Melbourne. Dad had cut me off from her, pretty much. He didn't want me *influenced* by her. So it was exciting to imagine—because it was a little bit terrifying, too. My mother died in one of those things. Who's to say it wasn't going to kill me, too? When it came down to it, though, I couldn't make myself go through."

"That's what you were doing yesterday," Clair said. "When the PKs hassled you."

He looked surprised that she was listening. "Yes. Thinking about it but never *doing* anything about it. The story of my life."

A new bump from Libby appeared in Clair's infield. She opened it, hoping.

"You can't stand that I'm perfect," Libby said. "Get over it or stay away from me forever."

[19]

CLAIR DIDN'T HEAR much of the conversation between Zep and Jesse after that. They passed the station, and Jesse led them onto the side streets of the suburb he lived in. All Clair could think about was the people stepping into and out of the rows of shining booths, remembering games she and Libby had played when they were younger. "Guess" involved one taking the other blindfolded to a destination that they then had to determine without using the Air. "Cram or Crap" scoured the strangest corners of a fabber's memory to find the most revolting food officially designated as edible. They had attended performances advertised in the Air just moments before the acts went onstage, braving traffic jams and instant crowds just to be there in that moment.

Libby had always been the one to push Clair into something new, and Clair the one to pick up the pieces afterward. Now, it looked like there would be no putting the pieces back together, no matter what Clair did. It wasn't even about Zep and Improvement anymore. Clair was caught between the uncompromising extremes of competing with Libby or trying to unravel her new sense of self-worth. It was a lose-lose situation.

Clair felt a terrible hollowness in her chest, as though Libby had already vacated from her life, leaving nothing behind but the echoing sense that it was all her fault.

"If Libby *would* only come forward," Jesse was saying, "if we could prove that her birthmark has really gone, then we'd have all the evidence we need to make someone act."

"If it really has," Zep said.

"Don't talk about her like that," Clair said. "Libby's not a courtroom exhibit. She's a person."

Jesse's face disappeared behind his bangs again.

"I'm sorry—I know that."

They turned onto Jesse's friendly neighborhood street and walked along the opposite side, sticking to the shade. No sign of the kids, but the dog droppings were still there, turning white in the heat.

"That's my place," said Jesse to Zep, pointing two houses along. "Don't expect much—oh, hey, there's Dad."

Dylan Linwood walked through the front door of his house and stood there with his hands on his hips. He had changed since Clair had seen him. He was wearing a shirt that was even more crumpled than the one before, and there was a bruise on his forehead. One of his eyes, the left, was red where it should have been white. He looked as though he had been beaten up. But he didn't look beaten. His expression was anything other than cowed.

Jesse raised his hand in greeting.

Dylan Linwood vanished into a giant ball of flame.

The flash, the bang, and the physical impact of the explosion weren't simultaneous. They came in that order, spaced out over tiny slices of time that the human mind couldn't individually distinguish. All of them outraced alarm. The electrical impulses in Clair's nerves might have traveled much faster than the ball of flame radiating outward from the structure that had once been Jesse's home, but the shocked tissues of her brain needed time to catch up. A second wasn't long enough. Two seconds wasn't long enough.

After three seconds, she found herself on her hands and knees in some bushes, coughing her lungs out. The air was full of soot and smoke. There was ash in her eyes, making her lenses sting. Her ears were ringing so loudly she could barely think, and her skin felt hot and raw, as though she had been rubbed all over with sandpaper. Her headband had come off, and she had no idea where it was. Next to her right knee, a tiny flame burned a black hole into the grass.

Rough hands grabbed her around the waist and pulled her upright. She lurched to her feet and threw up. The bile was acid and foul and seared her already aching throat.

Distantly, through the whining in her ears, she heard a voice urging her to hurry. She didn't recognize it, but she did her best to obey, fleeing the fire.

The street was transformed. Where Jesse's home had been was now a shattered, skeletal frame issuing thick black gouts of smoke. There was almost nothing left. The apartments on either side were burning too, along with the gardens and trees lining the sidewalk. Broken glass crunched underfoot. There was debris everywhere. Bits of Jesse's life. Bits of his dad, too, probably.

That made Clair feel sick again, but this time she kept her gorge down.

Clair blinked grit from her eyes and discovered that the hands tugging her away from the blast zone belonged to a solid woman with close-cut brown curls. She was wearing a dark-purple sweater and black jeans that, like everything around them, were now gray with ash. Her eyes were noticeably out of alignment, giving her face a lopsided cast.

Clair could see the woman's mouth moving, but her words were indistinct. "Take your own weight. I can't carry you."

Clair felt light-headed, but she found the strength to stand on her own. The four of them—Clair, Zep, Jesse, and the woman who had pulled them from the blast site—staggered to the nearest corner. Clair felt bruised all over, as though she had been hit by a giant fist. The woman urged them to go faster, but Zep was falling back, limping, his face contorted in pain. Blood flowed in a steady stream from his right thigh. Clair took Zep's right arm and put it over her shoulder in order to bear as much of his weight as she could.

Jesse trailed them, looking stunned. The right sleeve of his orange T-shirt was burned black. His jeans were filthy. Multiple tear tracks carved lighter lines down the dust on his face, and he kept glancing behind him as though to check the veracity of what had happened. The columns of belching black smoke left little doubt of anything.

Through her shock, Clair noticed a couple of drones swooping in from the north, smoke swirling like translucent wings around them as the woman hurried Clair and the others down another side street. The effects of the blast were minimal there, just a light rain of ash settling on the roofs and grass. People were issuing from their houses in ones and twos, some of them heading to the blast scene, most standing about uneasily, uncertain of what they should do. Someone offered help. The mystery woman waved them away.

The fog Clair had been operating under began to lift, and it occurred to her to wonder what was going on.

"Wait," she said. Her voice echoed in her ears as though it came from the bottom of a very deep well. "Who are you? Where are you taking us?"

"I'm a friend of Jesse's," the woman said. "We have to get off the streets."

"Why?" asked Zep through gritted teeth.

"You're injured, for one."

Jesse didn't say anything. He didn't seem to be hearing or seeing anything at all.

"What happened back there?" Clair pressed. "Who did this?"

"Later. Come on."

She pulled Jesse up the path to a simple single-story house behind a stand of drooping palms. Clair, unsure of her options, followed. Blood continued to flow from the wound on Zep's leg, and even through the ringing in her ears she could hear him gasp with every step. Whoever she was, the woman leading them seemed to know what she was doing.

The door opened before they reached it, and two men urged Clair and her bedraggled entourage inside.

"Get that door shut," said the woman to the smaller of the two men, who was wiry, flat faced, bald, with ears like jug handles. "Go on in, you three."

"Did anyone see you?" The second man followed them up the hallway. He was long and overstrung like a fencing wire, a head taller than Zep.

"Just drones, and they were focused on the house. We got past them okay."

Clair wondered why that was necessary. Any disturbances the drones spotted drew PKs to the scene like red blood cells to a cut—and that was a good thing, right?

They entered a boxy sitting room, lit only by what natural light came through the loose-shuttered windows. The walls were uniformly cream-colored, the floors carpeted in flecked gray. The woman led Zep to a low couch, and he fell awkwardly onto it, crying out with pain.

"Easy," she said, crouching down to inspect the source of the blood. A small cross swung from a silver chain around her neck, and she tucked it down into her sweater, out of the way. "You've taken some shrapnel, but it can't be too serious or you wouldn't be here to complain. Jesse?"

Jesse was still in shock, staring at nothing in the real world.

"Jesse, listen to me."

The bark of command in the woman's voice snapped him out of it. "Gemma?"

"What were you doing back there? You're supposed to be at school."

"We came . . . we came to talk to . . ." He stopped, Adam's apple bobbing. "Dad stirred up something serious this time."

"He did. I tried to talk him out of it, but he wouldn't listen." Her uneven eyes were watching Clair. "You're the girl from the video."

"And you're Abstainers," Clair said, beginning to piece it together. "Like Jesse."

"Congratulations." Jesse had called the woman Gemma.

"You win a prize. How about you tell me what you're doing here?"

"She wanted to ask Dad about the data," Jesse said. "Where he got it from . . . what it means . . . if it's real."

"Of course it's real," Gemma said. "You really know someone who's had a problem with Improvement?"

"Maybe," said Clair. "My best friend."

Zep groaned again. Gemma had found a rip in Zep's track pants and torn it wider. His leg was slick with red. Something was sticking out of his thigh. Something metal, like a shuriken. Gemma wiped the blood away, revealing one of the metal cogs from Dylan Linwood's workshop.

Jesse turned even paler under the ash and grime.

"All right," Gemma said. "Jesse, take her to see Dancer, in back. I need to deal with this. Ray." The tall man looked up. "Get me the med kit. Watch the door. Tell me if anyone comes."

[20]

THE TWO MEN jumped at Gemma's command. Clair did too, because it was only beginning to sink in that they had just seen someone die. Dylan Linwood had been standing in front of her one second, gone the next. How was that possible?

Jesse took her arm and guided her through the house.

After the sitting room was a flight of stairs leading down to a cellar shrouded in gloom. There was an old-fashioned wall telephone anchored to one wall, then a dining room and a Stainer kitchen, complete with stovetop and sink and cupboards for preparing the ingredients that would become actual food. The air smelled stale, though.

"In here," called a voice from the kitchen. "Come clean yourself up and let me take a look at you."

Silhouetted against the rear window was a figure in an electric wheelchair. A woman in her seventies with a halo of gray hair, spine straight not slumped, wearing a comfortable pantsuit in peach. Her hands were long boned and thickly veined, and her nails neatly trimmed. She was watching them with keen attention.

"Aunt Arabelle?" said Jesse in a cracked voice.

She nodded. "Wash your hands in the sink. There's a towel for your faces. Then come and sit with me."

Jesse nodded and used the tap first. While she waited, Clair felt the bright gaze of the old woman studying her closely.

"Are you Dancer?" Clair asked.

"That's what they call me," the woman said. "My real name is Arabelle. Are you a friend of Jesse's?"

"Uh . . . kind of. I'm Clair, Clair Hill. I don't think Zep and I are supposed to be here."

"None of us are, Clair. Wash up and I'll explain."

It was Clair's turn to use the tap, and she felt relief that the woman's gaze was temporarily off her. Her hands shook as she splashed cold water onto her face. In her mind she saw the fireball over and over again, Dylan Linwood's compact figure vanishing into it, lifted momentarily off his feet as though about to take flight.

He hadn't even had time to look surprised.

She leaned her elbows on the sink and let the trembling spread from her hands, up her arms, and into the rest of her body. It was okay to feel shock, she told herself. No one was hurrying her anymore. She could take all the time in the world if it made her feel better.

It did.

When the shakes passed and she was done with the towel, she found Jesse kneeling and weeping into the old woman's shoulder. Arabelle—Aunt Arabelle—Dancer . . . Clair hadn't decided yet how to think of her . . . *Arabelle* put an arm around him and patted his back.

"Shhh," she said softly, as though to a child. "I know what happened, and I'm very sorry. We all are, Jesse. You have to be brave. Those psychopaths in VIA have been up to no good again."

"VIA blew up Dylan Linwood?" asked Clair in disbelief. "Who says it wasn't an accident?"

"I do." Gently but firmly, Arabelle pushed Jesse from her. "Take off my shoes, dear boy. She needs to understand what she's gotten herself into."

I haven't gotten myself into anything, Clair wanted to

say. Then she wondered if that was entirely true. It had all started with Zep and Libby and led via Improvement to Dylan Linwood's door. Maybe she could have walked away, but she hadn't. And here she was, watching Jesse crouch down, tug the old woman's traditional paraplegic blanket aside, and expose a pair of brown slip-ons.

Jesse pulled the left one off first, revealing a thin but perfectly ordinary foot. The right shoe was next.

When he had finished, he sat back and stared resentfully at Clair, as though daring her to argue with what she saw.

Clair saw a thin but perfectly ordinary left foot. A second one. She clenched her fists to stop them shaking again.

"I wasn't born with two left feet, believe me," said Arabelle. "In fact, I used to be a very good dancer. But I can't walk on it now, thanks to d-mat. The entire leg is out, and my hip, too. I tell myself I'm lucky a blood clot didn't kill me the very moment it happened. But I don't *feel* lucky. I feel trapped and ignored by a system that doesn't like to acknowledge its failures. It prefers to sweep them under the rug like they never existed. Well, Clair, some of us won't be swept away so easily. Jesse's father wasn't one of them, God take his precious soul. None of us will be."

"WHOLE," said Clair again, feeling as though she had fallen down Alice's rabbit hole and landed in a nest of vipers. "That's who you are. You're terrorists."

"Jesse, you can put my shoes back on. My toes are getting cold."

Jesse wiped his nose on his sleeve, smudging his face with ash anew. Clair was relieved when the feet were hidden. They made her feel queasy—not in a getting-sick way, but as though the world had just shifted underneath her in a subtle and utterly disconcerting way.

Gemma came into the kitchen to wash her hands. Her curly hair was full of scraps of plaster and plants, like urban camouflage. Tiny drops of blood matted the front of her shirt.

"Your boyfriend will be all right," she said. "Just a scratch."

"He's not my boyfriend," said Clair emphatically. "Why are we here and not in a hospital?"

"We're avoiding the peacekeepers."

"Why?"

"They're nothing but glorified security guards in the service of the OneEarth government. And what does One-Earth rely on to keep the peace? D-mat. If you think they'll have our best interests at heart, you're living in a dream."

"You think VIA killed Jesse's dad because he said bad things about d-mat?" Clair said. "That doesn't make any sense. He was paranoid but he wasn't dangerous."

"You're not the only one who thinks we're terrorists," said Arabelle. "That gives the PKs carte blanche to do whatever they like to us."

Clair refused to let the matter go just because someone told her to.

"So what happens now? Do you expect me and Zep to hide in here with you?"

"It makes sense to sit tight until the cleanup's over," Gemma said in a businesslike fashion, as though people being blown up was all in a day's work. "When we can, we'll move out in ones and twos. Hopefully, there'll be no reprisals."

Arabelle leaned forward and touched Clair lightly on the shoulder. "You go see to your friend. I need to talk with Gemma alone. Jesse, don't worry. You'll be looked after, I promise. We won't abandon you."

He nodded and walked like a robot out of the kitchen. Clair hesitated, then followed. The way the two women from WHOLE were looking at her, it was clear they wanted her gone so she wouldn't overhear. *Zombie girl*, she thought. They obviously weren't telling her the entire truth, but that look was hard to contend with.

[21]

CLAIR AND JESSE walked back through the dining room, past the stairs and the old telephone, into the living room. Zep was sprawled uncomfortably on the couch with his legs stretched out before him. His right thigh was bandaged tightly. There was blood all over what remained of his pants. He was staring at the man with the big ears, who stood in a corner of the room, watching him back. There was no sign of the taller man. They both looked up as Jesse and Clair entered.

"I was beginning to wonder if you were ever coming back," Zep said. He looked wan and weak.

"Whoever Gemma is, she says you'll be okay," said Clair, coming to sit at his side. *Not my boyfriend.* "How are you feeling?"

"I'll be a lot better when the painkillers kick in." He sketched a rough smile. "Now I'm wishing Libby's drugs hadn't worn off so fast."

Clair didn't laugh. Neither did Jesse. He collapsed into a chair and retreated into himself, as though he hoped everything would disappear if he ignored it hard enough.

Clair turned to the man with the big ears. Her hands were shaking again, and her mouth was desperately dry.

"I could really use a drink," she said. "We all could. Is that possible?"

"Sure," Big-Ears said, but not before glancing up the hallway to the front of the house. Clair knew then that his tall companion was watching the front door. Was he a sentry or a jailer?

Big-Ears headed into the back of the house. His feet beat a tattoo down the stairs to the lower floor.

"Have you tried your lenses?" Zep whispered when

they were alone. "Mine are dead, and every time I access the Air, I get an error message."

Clair discovered that she had the same problem. Every field of view was clear of patches, even from the creepy "q." She'd lost access to her family and friends, her blogs and grabs, her media and shows, her wardrobe and meals. Every pattern she had ever saved was cut off from her. Her whole life. God, her books! Her Tilly Kozlova recordings! She had never once been deliberately disconnected from them.

Jesse spoke from deep in his funk. "The house is a big Faraday shield."

"Which means what?" Zep prompted.

"Nothing electromagnetic can get in or out. No one can spy on what goes on in here. I think we're in some kind of safe house."

"Safe from who?" asked Clair. "Have these guys done something we should be concerned about?"

"If you're in WHOLE, you're automatically on the PKs' watch list," said Jesse.

"Yes, but we're not in WHOLE. Why are *we* hiding?"

"They're WHOLE?" Zep asked, eyes wide.

Big-Ears came back with bottles of water for the four of them, and a fifth for Ray, who appeared from the front of the house to give a status report.

"Drones still flying," Ray said. "The fire's out, though. So that's something."

"My father is dead," said Jesse. "*That's* something."

There was a moment's awkward silence.

An image struck Clair out of nowhere, perhaps inspired by Arabelle's crippled feet. It was from a cheap-scare story Clair had been told when she was younger, about a girl who'd gone into a booth but not arrived at her destination. Her pattern had gotten hung up in the back end of a file system and wasn't discovered until someone stumbled across it during a routine cleanup twenty-five years later. VIA brought her back perfectly well and whole, but by then her parents had died and all her friends had young families of their own. The girl found herself in an entirely new world, cut off from her life like a time traveler. So the story went.

Clair was beginning to feel that way. This shadow world of broken families, sabotage, and conspiracy wasn't the world she wanted to live in. It wasn't even supposed to exist. The world she knew had regulations and AIs to make sure of that. Billions of people traveled by d-mat every day without evidence of harm. Arabelle's feet were horrible to look at, and it made Clair shudder now to think of them, but they weren't evidence of anything, really. Maybe she had been conceived near one of the old radioactive waste dumps before they were cleaned out. Maybe the feet were fakes.

WHOLE was the one with the track record of social disruption and violence, not VIA. *And now we've seen their faces*, added the part of Clair that enjoyed too many bad horror movies.

But it didn't make sense. Why would WHOLE blow up Dylan Linwood when he had gone to such efforts to expose Improvement? If anything he had said was true, it actually made more sense, crazy though it seemed, that VIA might have been behind his death.

Clair wasn't willing to go that far. She had enough to trouble her as it was. If improvement *was* hurting people, and someone was trying to cover it up . . . and if Dylan *had* been targeted by this someone because of his stunt . . . why hadn't Clair been too?

The question rocked her. Dylan Linwood might have masterminded the stunt in the principal's office, but *she* had been part of it as well. She had been asking questions. Was there a bomb waiting at her house too?

Not since childhood had she felt such an intense yearning to see her parents. It was like an adrenaline hit times ten.

She drank heavily from the bottle and swished the water around her mouth to get rid of the taste of vomit and ash. Ray resumed his watch at the front door. No one seemed in a hurry to go anywhere, except Clair.

She wanted to find out more about Improvement, but that wasn't worth anyone else getting killed or hurt. Looking after herself and Zep had to be her first priority now. *She* would decide what happened to them, not Gemma and Arabelle.

"How are you feeling, Zep?" she asked. "Up for a walk?"

"I can't feel my leg at all now, so I guess that's a yes."

"Good." She stood up and held out her hand.

"About time," he said.

[22]

"YOU'RE LEAVING?" ASKED Jesse, blinking at her in surprise.

"Come if you want to," said Zep. "But we're not sticking around any longer. You're not going to stop us, are you?"

Big-Ears looked up at Zep, who was easily a foot taller and wider than him.

"Uh . . . wait."

Clair and Zep were already on their way to the front door, where Ray barred their way with his arms outspread.

"Come on," said Zep. "You're not doing your reputation any favors."

"We are the good guys. You don't want to meet the bad guys."

From behind them, deeper in the house, came a shrill, electric tone. Ray turned to stare up the hallway, eyebrows bunching in puzzlement.

"It's too early," he said.

Clair understood. That sound came from a telephone. The antique landline she had seen earlier was probably the only way to get signals in and out of the Faraday shield.

But that wasn't her concern. While Ray was distracted, she ducked under his arm and lunged for the door. It opened smoothly.

"Hey—"

Zep pushed him to one side and followed Clair out into the light. The smoke-dimmed sun was bright. Daylight hues stirred in her lenses: greens, blues, and whites. Patches winked and flashed as she reconnected to the Air. Out of the Faraday cage, into the fire.

"Which way?" asked Zep.

"We came from the left," she said, leading him up the path and onto the street. Ray didn't follow, and neither did Gemma and Big-Ears, who had joined him. Jesse craned past all of them, curious or concerned enough to come see what was going on.

"You're making a mistake," Gemma called.

"I really don't think so," Clair said.

Gemma stayed just inside the door, where the sun barely touched her, and where, presumably, there was no possibility of a drone seeing her. There was a pistol in her hand, held close to her chest. It wasn't pointed at Clair, but there was no mistaking its meaning.

It's just a bluff, Clair told herself, even as she wondered why Gemma *needed* to bluff. What did it matter to WHOLE if she and Zep left right then?

"Let's split up," said Zep. "I'll go that way."

"Clair!"

She hesitated. That was Jesse's voice.

"The phone call was for you!" he shouted.

"So take a message!"

Zep was already limping away from her, raising his middle finger to Gemma as he went.

Gemma raised the gun. She didn't fire, but now Jesse had seen it. He stared at the gun in shock and horror, which reassured Clair that Gemma had to be bluffing. The gun was out of character, or at least something Jesse had never seen before.

"Go after them," said Gemma to Ray and Big-Ears. "Don't let them do something stupid."

Clair ran. Away from WHOLE and away from Zep.

Something whined in the sky far above. Clair glanced up and saw an eye-in-the-sky drone hanging in the air above her. Drones ran on crowd sourcing, directed from place to place by community service volunteers who tapped into EITS feeds as the whim took them. Events of interest, criminal or not, drew in watchers until a threshold was reached and peacekeepers were summoned.

Clair waved her hands above her head to attract the

attention of the drone. It noticed her but didn't raise any audible alarms. Someone running along a straight road was much less interesting than the fire burning a couple of blocks over. Lots of people waved at drones.

Clair turned right instead of left on Jesse's street and ran away from the smoldering wreckage as quickly as she could. Her second sprint for the day was taking its toll, thanks in part to all the soot in her lungs. She threw a quick glance over her shoulder to check if anyone was following her and saw Big-Ears take the corner behind her, head down, eyes glaring under furious brows at her.

Why? she asked herself, even as she somehow found the energy for a new burst of speed.

There was a peacekeeper patch in her infield. Her parents had insisted she install it, but she had never had to use it before. She winked on it now and was put straight through to an operator.

"Hello, Clair," said a broad-faced woman with short blond hair, identified as PK Anastas. "How can I assist you?"

"I'm being chased," she said.

"Have you been physically threatened? I can send a Rapid Response team if you feel you are in immediate danger."

"Just tell me how to get away from him."

"May I access your location?"

"Yes, of course."

The woman examined the information scrolling down her lenses.

"You are approaching a d-mat station, Clair. Any destination you choose will be untraceable."

Clair knew that. She also knew that Big-Ears wouldn't follow even if he did know where she was going, since using d-mat wasn't an option for him or any Abstainer.

She pushed people out of her way and threw herself bodily into the first open booth. There she turned, put her back against the mirrored wall, and saw Big-Ears just four yards behind her. He was shouting something—a warning, perhaps—but she couldn't tell if it was intended for her or the crowd of people milling in his way.

"Home!" she ordered the booth.

The door hissed shut on Big-Ears' scarlet face.

Clair slumped forward against the mirrored surface, forehead-to-forehead with her own reflection. She looked awful, a mad thing running wild in the ordinary world. She barely recognized herself.

The sound of her breathing was loud in the booth. Big-Ears couldn't follow her now. The only way he could get to her was by physically crossing the continent from California to Maine, and without d-mat, that could take *days*.

sssssss—

Her lenses lit up with another emergency flash, exactly the same as the one her mysterious caller had sent her at school.

—*pop.*

The flash was still there when she arrived, and so was the window to PK Anastas, which she closed now that she was safe in the gloom of her Maine apartment block. Cool East Coast air was a blessing against her overheated skin. She was almost home.

Clair walked up the familiar corridor, with its wood-paneled walls and hideous green carpet, finally able to bump Zep as she went. Hopefully he had made it to a booth as well.

A second emergency flash joined the first, then another, and another, until her entire vision was strobing so violently, she could barely see.

She stopped and put her hand against the nearest wall to steady herself.

From somewhere nearby came the sound of raised voices.

More flashes. She clicked on the *qqqqq* link accompanying them. It was either that or stand where she was, blind, until they went away.

"Leave me alone," she said, "or I'm calling the peacekeepers again."

"That is an excellent idea," said the young-sounding voice. "There is a man in your apartment holding your parents hostage. I believe he intends to do them harm."

"What?"

"I said, there is a man in your apartment holding—"

"I heard you the first time. Are you serious?"

"I would not lie about such a thing, Clair. I want you to trust me. I am providing you with a reason to trust me."

A cold feeling swept through her. What new trick was this? "You leave my family alone, whoever you are."

"It is not I who threaten them. That responsibility falls on the man WHOLE is trying to kill. I believe it is his intention to harm you in turn."

"Okay, I'm calling the peacekeepers."

"Please do. And do not enter your home until they arrive. It is far too dangerous."

Clair's lenses cleared. She hit the peacekeeper patch again, even as she approached the door to her apartment. The sound of raised voices was getting louder. Someone was shouting over a babble of protest.

"Hello, Clair," said another peacekeeper, a man. "How can we assist you this time?"

"Hang on," she said.

She was close enough to the door to her apartment to hear what the voices inside were saying. The Thanksgiving wreath she had made in junior school was still hanging under the peephole, looking dustier than ever.

"I said *call her*. Tell her to come home now and make her listen to you. If she doesn't, there will be consequences."

"Don't hurt her . . . please don't hurt her."

Clair stiffened at the sound of her mother's voice. Her heart swelled up inside her, threatening to burst inside her chest like the bomb that had killed Dylan Linwood.

"We've been nagging her all day." That was Oz, her step-father. "What makes you think she'll answer us now?"

There was the sound of flesh hitting flesh.

"You figure it out."

Clair's fingernails dug into her palms as she fought a powerful urge to burst in and hurl herself at the man in her apartment, armed with nothing but teeth and nails. The voice behind the emergency patch was right. That would be the action of someone with a death wish.

She backed up a step, feeling shaky in the knees, and spoke silently to the peacekeeper.

"I need a . . ." What had PK Anastas called it? ". . . a Rapid Response team at my home in Maine. Quickly!"

"What is the situation, Clair?"

"My parents are in trouble. They're being threatened. Send someone, now!"

"All right, Clair," said the peacekeeper. "We'll have a team there shortly. Keep this window open and don't go anywhere."

Behind her, the door to the d-mat booth slid shut.

A new bump flashed in her lenses: it was a nag from her stepfather, flagged as urgent.

Clair highlighted the bump and without reading it sent him a quick message.

"Stall. Help's coming."

"!!" he shot back immediately. "Stay away! Not safe!"

The apartment went quiet. Even her mother was silent. Clair held her breath, wondering what had changed.

When the voice of the man in the apartment came again,

she was struck by a feeling of impossible recognition. She couldn't know who he was. No one in her world was capable of something like this.

The man WHOLE is trying to kill, as the mysterious "q" voice had called him, spoke in response to something only he could hear.

"What?" he said. "She's here? *Now?*"

Clair backed away from the door. He couldn't be talking about her, could he?

Footfalls hurried to the other side of the door.

The booth behind her was still closed, processing the data that comprised the Rapid Response team.

The locks clicked and clunked on the door to her apartment. He was coming out to get her. But who had told him? How had he *known*?

"Run, Clair, run!" said the childlike voice in her ear.

—————————————————————————— $[23]$

THERE WAS A door marked FIRE at the end of the corridor. Clair burst through it, onto a steep flight of concrete stairs that wound down to the ground floor below.

"Clair! Hold it!"

She *definitely* knew that voice from somewhere but didn't stop to see who it belonged to. She ran down the stairs three at a time.

"What's happening, Clair?" asked the peacekeeper.

"You told him," she said. "You told him where I was!"

"Told who, Clair? I'm afraid I don't know—"

She closed the window. The door leading into the stairwell burst open above her, sending echoes flying like startled birds all around her. The man was close. She ran flattened against the wall as best she could, minimizing the likelihood that he would see her.

She ducked through the next exit and closed it quietly behind her. Feet thundered down the stairs. She ran for that floor's booth, threw herself inside, said the first address that came to her.

"Woodward and Main, Manteca."

The stairwell entrance burst open just as the booth door started sliding shut. Framed at the other end of the hallway was the man chasing her. He didn't look like an assassin. He was scruffily dressed, with gray hair, a bruise on his forehead, and a glaring, blood-filled eye. He was Dylan Linwood, and he was holding a sleek black pistol in his right hand.

Clair couldn't move. The end of the barrel was like a black hole, growing larger with every degree it rose. Behind it, Jesse's father aimed the pistol with both hands and squeezed the trigger twice.

Two bullets slammed in quick succession into the closed booth door, *bang-bang*.

Clair dropped to the floor with her hands over her ears.

sssssss—

She glanced up fearfully. The mirrored inside of the door showed no damage. It wasn't even warped.

—pop

Her legs had no strength beneath her. She wasn't sure she could stand. But she was instantly on her feet, thinking: *Manteca? What the hell am I doing?* Crazy to go back to where she'd come from, where Big-Ears might still be looking for her.

A stunned part of her was thinking: *Dylan Linwood?*

The door hissed open. She ignored the people waiting and leaned out, searching for any familiar faces.

Isn't he dead?

Outside the booth there was no sign of anyone she recognized. No Big-Ears. Zep hadn't responded to her bump. Maybe he was in transit.

Drones were whining overhead. She breathed out through pursed lips and moved to step from the booth. Then Dylan Linwood burst into view three doors along, and she threw herself back inside.

Very much alive, apparently. *And using d-mat!*

People complained in the queue outside her booth.

"Clair? I know you're here," Dylan Linwood called.

"Take me to the Isle of Shanghai," Clair said in a quiet, fast voice. If Zep *had* gotten away, he might have gone to his dorm. "Ju Long Hostel."

"You can't run, Clair, and you can forget about calling for help."

He walked into view. They stared at each other for a split second. His pistol was hidden from the drones as Gemma's had been. He moved toward her just as the door closed.

"Shi—!" she heard him say.

sssssss-pop

She came out of the booth at a run, not sticking around to see if he had followed her a second time. Hurrying toward Zep's dorm, she opened the *qqqqq* patch in her infield.

"You were right," she said. "How did you know?"

"I told you, Clair," said the voice. "There is very little I cannot access."

"Was it you who rang the safe house?"

"Yes. The landline was the only way I could contact you while you were inside the Faraday shield. Unfortunately, you had left by the time I got through."

"Why are you doing this? What's in it for you?"

"I just want to help you, Clair. I am on your side. You can trust me."

Clair wasn't certain about that. "Who *are* you?"

"Does that matter? Can't I just help you?"

Clair screwed up her face. It was like she was talking to a kid of some kind—a hacker prodigy sticking her nose in for kicks. There were isolationist communities that lived in a state of passive-aggressive antagonism with the world around them, governed by peculiar notions of society and morality. She could accept that one of their offspring might have developed an unhealthy curiosity regarding Improvement and its victims. Was that what was going on?

If it was, would Clair be crazy not to take advantage of it?

Zep wasn't in his room, but there was another huddle of young men in the common area. They all looked the same to her. One of them called something, a slightly more verbal version of a wolf whistle. This time she didn't ignore it.

"There's a guy following me, trying to hurt me," she said. *A dead man.* "Please don't let him come through here, will you?"

The huddle broke apart, puzzled and territorial in equal measures, as Dylan Linwood burst into the common area behind her.

"That's him!" she cried. "Stop him!"

The huddle swarmed forward.

She grabbed the nearest guy before he could run into the fray.

"Is there a back way out of here?"

He nodded and hurried her to the far side of the room. A single shot sounded behind them, and her guide turned back to see what was going on. She kept running, hoping it was just a warning round, that none of Zep's friends had been hurt.

She took the stairs all the way to the bottom and burst out into the busy Shanghai street. It was full of pedestrians and bicyclists, conveniently rowdy with music and calling voices. She pushed her way through the crowd, putting as much distance and confusion between her and the hostel as she could. There was a d-mat station at the next junction. She headed for it.

As she fled, she sent a call request to "q," who answered immediately.

"Okay," Clair said. "I'm really out of options here. If you can tell me why Dylan Linwood is back from the dead and what I have to do to shake him, then maybe I'll start trusting you."

"I cannot help you with the first part at the moment, but I might be able to do something about the second. The first thing to do is find out exactly how he is tracking you. He is clearly not accessing friend privileges, since he is not your friend. I doubt he hacked into VIA or the peacekeepers. He could be monitoring surveillance cameras and EITS data like the peacekeepers do—"

"I don't need a list. I just need to get rid of him!"

"Take the next left," said the voice.

"But the station—"

"It is too obvious. And you do not have enough time. He is behind you."

Clair glanced over her shoulder. There he was, shouldering his way through the crowd with a determined expression on his face. Again she felt a moment of fundamental *wrongness* about his existence. *You're dead*, she wanted to yell at him. *Lie down and leave me alone!*

"Next left it is," she said, renewing her efforts to press through the throng and into a crowded market stall.

"Go straight ahead. Take the second lane on your right."

Clair did as she was told, the skin between her shoulder blades burning with an ancient sense of danger. Dylan Linwood could see her, but at least he couldn't fire at her, not without risking hitting someone else. That helped a bit.

She ducked into the lane when she reached it and snatched a brightly colored shawl from a stand. She slipped it over her head and ducked lower, easing through the crowd as quickly as she could.

"Is he far behind me?" She didn't dare look.

"Keep going straight. I will tell you when to deviate from this course."

"But you'll warn me if he's about to catch me, won't you?"

"Yes, Clair. I will not let that happen."

She squeezed past a woman pushing a small child in a stroller. "Have you worked out how to stop him from tracking me yet?"

"I believe I have. Do you still have your Improvement note on your person?"

[24]

CLAIR'S MIND WENT blank for a moment, then filled with alarm and self-recrimination. Of course she still had the note on her. She'd slipped it under the elastic of her underpants the previous night, and she was wearing the same underpants now.

"Yes, I do," she said, slipping her index finger around her waist until she found the note. It was creased and softened by sweat, a piece of paper made far from ordinary by the words written on it—a "signal to the system," as Jesse had called it. Could his father be using that very signal to track her now?

"What do I do? Tear it up?"

"No. Turn left here."

Clair ducked into another lane lined with market stalls. At the far end was an exit. Next to the exit was the sign for a d-mat station, and on seeing it she understood.

"A wild-goose chase," she said. "That would work, I guess."

"Not this jump," said the voice, "but the next one. Clair, do you trust me?"

"Uh." That was a difficult question. "How far, exactly?"

"I can program the booth for you, if you will permit me. That will save time."

"Can't I do it myself?"

"You can. But in that case I must ask you to give me the list of destinations in advance so I can prepare the way. And you will need to speak without hesitation."

"How many?"

"Four should be sufficient."

The impossibility of her situation made it hard to think of anything other than putting one foot in front of the other. The resort in Switzerland she'd stayed in with her parents as a kid. The dig in South America she and her friends had visited last year as part of their Lost Civilizations elective.

Somewhere random? *That would be good,* she thought. And somewhere she'd never been before.

Not Omsk. Cape Town. And the Tuvalu memorial in the Pacific.

"Perhaps we should we send it to the moon," she said. "That'd really throw him off."

"All lunar installations are restricted while the OneMoon embargo is in place."

Clair had been joking, never dreaming that accessing somewhere off-Earth was remotely an option.

She forced her way through a tangle of people at the market's exit, into the relatively free space of the street outside. She ran the last dozen yards to the station.

"Take the note with you to your first destination," said the voice. "You will dispose of it before the transmission after that."

Clair shouldered her way into the nearest booth and

cried out the Swiss address. Dylan Linwood burst out of the market and moved sharklike in her wake. Not firing, not shouting, just moving quickly, confident she wouldn't get away from him. The gun wasn't visible.

That it would reappear when she was caught, she had no doubt.

The door shut. Her ears popped. The door opened.

It was cold and dark in Switzerland. Heavy snow was falling outside the station. She wrapped the shawl tightly around her neck and shoulders and hugged herself.

"Put the note in the next booth over and use your second destination," the voice told her.

She did so, giving the booth the South American address and requesting an unaccompanied freight transfer. She ducked out before the door shut on her and went to the third booth.

The doors closed and opened again a moment later in Cape Town, her third destination. She stepped out of the booth and warily looked around. It was nighttime there too, but the air was warm and humid. The station was deserted. A sign in her lenses welcomed her to the Devil's Peak lookout. Below her was the university, on the edge of a moon-shaped bay. Across the bay was Ndabeni, lit up by a ghostly spear of light fired at a slant from a powersat above the equator.

Clair unwound the shawl and threw it away.

"Why are you doing this for me?"

"I have been following Improvement, Clair. That is what I do. Now I am involved, and it is very exciting."

"Is this some kind of game to you?"

"No, Clair. I am not playing a game. I am very serious. I want to be your friend. Like Libby. Like the two of you are friends."

"You can't just *become* my friend. Friendship has to be earned. And besides, who knows what Libby thinks of me now . . . ?"

"Her profile declares your relationship to be unchanged."

Clair checked her lenses. Libby's most recent caption simply said "I'm beautiful!" with a rapid-fire sequence of women's faces, all of them blondes like her. She was in the Manhattan Isles, not at school, but she didn't say why.

"I can't find Zep," Clair said when she looked for him.

"He cannot be located."

"What does that mean?" Her heart skipped a beat. "He's dead?"

"No. He is disconnected from the Air."

Recaptured, she thought. *Back inside WHOLE's Faraday cage.* Every instinct in her railed at the thought.

"I have to go back for him," she said. "I can't just leave him behind."

Before "q" could offer a reply, the booth behind her came to life. Its door closed, and the machines within busily whirred, processing new data and spinning pure energy into matter. Someone was coming.

"Is that . . . him?"

"Yes."

"But it can't be," she said in disbelief. "We got rid of the note."

"This proves that your location is being tracked by means other than the note."

"What do I do now?"

"You must disconnect from the Air and go to your fourth destination."

She balked at that. Disconnecting from the Air would be like locking herself in a coffin and nailing it shut.

"Think of something else," she said.

"I cannot. This is now the most likely method your pursuers have used."

"But if I leave the Air, no one will know where I am."

"Including the man following you."

"Yes, but . . . oh, damn it."

She opened another booth, didn't enter.

"What if I disconnect now and then reconnect when I arrive?"

"Any direct connection is undesirable."

"Is there any way just to *hide* my connection?"

"Not in the time remaining, Clair."

"All right, but first I need to bump Mom and Dad—"

"You have five seconds precisely, Clair."

The whirring of the active booth reached a crescendo. It was going to open any moment.

She shot into her booth and asked for the Tuvalu monument. As the door shut, she called up menus and options in her lenses. *Disconnect. Sever. Disallow. Isolate.* Interface by interface, she plucked at the ties connecting her to the rest of the world. Her augmented senses, her sunburn epidermals, even the pedometers built into the soles of her shoes—everything.

sssssss—

One by one, the patches in her lenses went dark.

"Wait," she said as the air thinned around her. "If I do this, how will I talk to you?"

—*pop*

[25]

IT WAS SUNNY in the Pacific. There was nothing but ocean in all directions. A full circle of booths opened up on a broad viewing platform with unobtrusive holographic displays showing where the islands had once been. The tiny former nation had a special place in the history of the twenty-first century as the first country destroyed in the Water Wars. Where some had fallen in armed conflicts and others had crumbled from within, Tuvalu had simply vanished beneath rising seas. Clair had learned about it in high school but couldn't care less now.

For the first time in her life, she was truly alone.

There were people around her, presumably tourists and perhaps some grandchildren of the now-stateless Tuvaluans as well, but she couldn't discover anything about them by reading their public profiles, just as she couldn't access the platform's multimedia options, metadata tags, or even Muzak. She couldn't talk to her parents, her friends, anyone. She couldn't caption the experience (a snapshot of the endless ocean: *Not a drop to drink!*). The world was entirely cut off from her, and she from it.

It was unendurable.

Don't do it, she told herself. *Don't give in and reconnect. You can stay offline for a few minutes, if that's what it takes to shake him. Give it ten, and then move on, reconnect somewhere else. Maybe fifteen. See what happens. It won't kill you, whereas Dylan Linwood very well might.*

Her stomach felt sick and watery. She picked a spot at random and tried to look inconspicuous. It wasn't hard, and that was a relief. She wished she could roll back the days to the crashlander ball and leave when Libby had. That way she wouldn't have kissed Zep, and the wedge of Improvement wouldn't have been driven between her and her best friend.

Except Libby had been using Improvement already, and Clair had already had feelings for Zep. A crisis had been coming all along.

You want to swoop in and solve all my problems.

You just can't help yourself, can you? You just won't leave well enough alone.

Libby's accusations stung because there was some truth to them. Clair wasn't naturally gregarious and might have languished in bookish obscurity had it not been for Libby's efforts to bring her out of her shell. To Libby, it came easily. Noticed everywhere she went, she was spontaneous, provocative, and charming. In that sense she made a perfect match for Zep—and Clair had wondered if that lay at the heart of Clair's attraction to both of them. They opened up her world while at the same time allowing her to be herself. She had never once felt that she had to change who she was in order to fit in, and for that, Clair knew, she would always be grateful.

But social life wasn't everything, and it had always been clear that Clair had had an advantage over Libby in other areas. A teacher had once supported her mother's belief by telling Clair that she was more stubborn than smart. It was probably the most honest thing any teacher had ever told her. Not everyone was born a genius, like Tilly Kozlova had been. The concert pianist was barely five years older than Clair, and for a while Clair had had an obsession with the rising star that had only passed when Clair's mom had started using her as a goad for working harder at piano lessons. For all Clair's fantasies of growing up to be like her—or even just Libby, funny and outgoing and loved by everyone—Clair knew she wasn't the same as either of them. She was good at most things but not a genius at anything, and so she had to be determined most of all. When Clair wanted to understand something, she worried at it until the veils fell away, like the literary puzzles of James Joyce or the art mazes of Esther Azikiwe.

Hours ago Dylan Linwood had been foaming at the mouth about d-mat in the principal's office. Now he had not only apparently faked his own death but was threatening her parents and following her all over the world. How did that work? Whose side was he really on? What did that side *want*?

There were few things she had resigned herself to never understanding, and she swore this whole thing—this *WHOLE* thing—wasn't going to be one of them.

"Is there a Clair here?"

Clair jerked out of her thoughts at the unfamiliar voice. It came from a large woman in a floral dress and matching lenses. A complete stranger.

"Maybe. Why do you want to know?"

"Your friend asked me to tell you that he is still coming," the woman said.

"What?"

"That's what your friend says: 'He is still coming.' Do you know what she means?"

Clair cupped the base of her skull with one hand and bunched up her greasy hair. She nodded.

"Does she . . . my friend . . . say where to go?"

The woman shook her head. Her florid eyes tracked up and then to the left, checking a menu. "She's gone. I'm sorry, dear. Are you all right?"

"I . . . thanks."

She had to move on or Dylan Linwood would find her. Whatever he wanted, she wasn't going to stand here and let him get it.

Picking a booth at random, she stepped inside and asked for Melbourne, where Jesse had dreamed of going to see his grandfather. She had never been there and figured she might as well go now, even if she would see no more of it than a d-mat station.

sssssss-pop

Clair blinked. Her eyes felt weird. Her hand flew to her right ear. There was something clinging to it that hadn't been there before. In her reflection, she saw a wiry clasp that pressed against the skin of her skull. An old-fashioned headset.

The ear-rings in her auditory canals were gone. She wasn't wearing her contact lenses.

The door opened, revealing an empty plain in the middle of nowhere.

Not Melbourne. And her pattern had been *changed*.

"No," she said, backing as far as she could into the booth. "This can't be happening. . . ."

"Don't say or do anything," said a now-familiar childish voice through the tinny headset.

"What's going on?" she cried. "What have you done to me?"

"I am changing your public identity so someone searching for 'Clair Hill' won't find her here. According to the Air, your name is Pallas Diana Hughes."

"What does that mean?" she asked, touching her nose. It was the same as ever. Her face looked frightened in the mirrors surrounding her but hadn't changed an iota.

"I am saving you."

The door to the d-mat booth closed before she could slip through it. She hammered at it, but it wouldn't open.

sssssss-pop

This time the door stayed shut.

"Saving me from what? From Improvement?"

"Your name is Rebecca Watts-Veldhoen," was all the voice said.

sssssss-pop

"Your name is Shun Fay Anderson Wong."

Clair's reflection looked bloodless and desperate—the same hair, the same nose, but the fright in her eyes was new.

sssssss-pop

Claire could be anywhere. Would she step out of the booth twenty-five years later with two left feet and her heart on the wrong side of her chest? Would she lose her name and be stuck, unable to convince anyone of who she really was? Would she end up like Libby, beautiful, with a new nose and proud of it . . . or brain damaged and delusional?

Clair wished she could sit down with her best friend and find out was really going on. One proper conversation would be enough. At the very least, one good look at her cheek. . . .

sssssss-pop

The earpiece was gone. Her lenses and ear-rings were back. She winked on the call patch blinking in her infield.

"Your name is Clair Hill, and you are safe."

---[26]

THE DOOR OPENED. Clair stepped shakily from the booth and looked around. Dusk was thickening in the California sky. She smelled the sea. Definitely Manteca again. There was the same mix of tourists and commuters. The same summery twilight sky, even in November. She had come full circle.

There was no Dylan Linwood, and no one from WHOLE, either.

She thought she might weep with relief. But she couldn't afford to let herself. It wasn't over yet.

"What did you do to me?" she asked over the open call to "q."

"I cut all the connections between you and the rest of

the world. Then I made you look like someone else—not physically but semantically, so anyone searching for you through the Air wouldn't see you. Now I've built you a mask to hide behind. All your identifiers are temporarily scrambled—name, address, preferences, history—everything that makes you look like you. The disguise will allow you to interface with the Air without being discovered, but I advise against contacting anyone you are closely associated with. That may draw attention to the mask, and therefore to who you really are."

There were five benches arranged in a pentagon around the base of a broad-trunked tree. She took a seat, bouncing her right leg compulsively up and down as she tried to watch every direction at once, half expecting Dylan Linwood to leap out of a booth and attack her again, no matter what "q" said.

"Are you saying I can't call my parents? Or Zep? Or anyone?"

"No, Clair. You can, but I *strongly* advise against it. I can tell you that your parents are in no danger, if that helps. Their injuries are superficial. They are of no value to your enemies now that you have escaped the trap they set for you."

"Did the peacekeepers come?"

"Yes."

"Does that mean they're *not* my enemies?"

"I do not know, Clair."

"Can I at least go see Mom and Oz?"

"You should avoid using d-mat for the foreseeable future."

"What?"

"A search is currently under way for you. I can hide your identity from the Air, but there's no hiding your DNA from VIA. All transits will be red flagged."

Clair wiped sweaty palms on her skirt. Slowly it was sinking in that "q" had indeed gotten Dylan Linwood off her tail. But at what cost? By isolating her from everything and everyone she knew. And only by *changing* her pattern . . . reaching into it and editing out her lenses and ear-rings . . . in a way that was supposed to be utterly impossible.

Whoever "q" was, she had just done everything Improvement said it did. The implications were immense. On top of the possibilities that Improvement might be causing brain damage and Dylan Linwood was trying to kill her, it was too much. Clair wanted nothing more than to bury her head in the sand until it all went away. Clearly that wasn't possible. The best she could do was hope to understand it one piece at a time. Starting with the piece that had nothing to do with murder or anyone apparently coming back from the dead. . . .

"You changed my pattern," she said. "How did you do that?"

"As long as I maintain parity and don't hurt anyone," the voice said, "I can do a lot of things."

"I don't know what you mean by 'parity.' Doesn't changing someone set off an alarm?"

"Material objects come under far less scrutiny than people, which makes them much easier to reroute or create from scratch. That's all a fabber does, after all, and fabbers are allowed to do it as often as you ask them to, because you only ever use them to make *things*. The difference is a legal one: People are alive and shouldn't be duplicated or altered like hats or chocolate bars can be. The trick I used was to change a person's tag from *alive* to *material* so I could alter your pattern—your lenses and your ear-rings, specifically—and then change it back before anyone spotted it happening."

"Like you did with my name?"

"Something like that," "q" said. "When a pattern is taken by a d-mat booth, two very important things happen. First, it's checked against databases containing prohibited compounds, genetic records, and so on. Most people are licensed to carry most things through d-mat, but suicide bombers shouldn't be allowed to, and neither should young kids trying to run away from home. If the database doesn't reveal anything like that, the transfer is given a conditional green light. This phase of the process is handled by one of the two AIs VIA uses to keep the system running safely.

"Now, if you think of the first AI as the conductor of a bus—"

"A what?"

"An outmoded mass-transport vehicle."

"Like a train?"

"Kind of. If the first AI, the conductor, is the one that checks your ticket as you get on and off the bus, then that makes the second AI the driver of the bus. Its job is to get you safely to your destination without being duplicated or erased or sent to a booth that doesn't exist.

"These two AIs, conductor and driver, are bound by a principle similar to the laws of physics: that in a d-mat booth, unlike a fabber, matter can neither be created nor destroyed. Even though both happen at opposite ends during the jump, it has to *look* as though it didn't."

Clair was about as vague regarding physics as she was buses. It was a struggle to keep up with what "q" was telling her.

"What happens when it doesn't?"

"That's called a *parity violation*, Clair. Equilibrium hasn't been maintained, and an alarm does sound. It's the number one alarm in VIA. It can't be ignored, and you can't turn it off, because it means that at least one of the AIs is broken. The only way to fix things quickly is to crash the entire system, reboot it again, and hope the break isn't permanent."

"Which obviously hasn't happened, or we'd have noticed," Clair said. "How did you work this out?"

"It's right there in the algorithms, if you know where to look."

"Do you know who else might be doing it?"

"No, Clair. I'm sorry."

"Don't apologize. If anything, I should thank you for what you did back there. I was completely out of ideas. It was clever of you to figure it out." She paused before adding, with all the parental firmness she could muster, just in case the owner of the voice *was* a child, "But please don't spring something like that on me again. If you're going to muck around with my pattern, you have to warn me in advance. You have to ask my *permission*."

"I promise I will, Clair. I'm sorry."

"No, really, don't apologize. Just, well . . . I don't know. Hopefully there won't ever be a next time."

Her mind reeled at the implications of what "q" had told her, but there were greater issues calling for her attention. She looked around, still worried about people creeping up on her while she was distracted. She knew this station. It was four blocks away from school, putting her northwest of the WHOLE safe house.

"Why did you bring me here?" she asked. "You could have sent me anywhere you wanted. What's so special about Manteca?"

"You have to go back for your friend Zeppelin Barker: that is what you said in South Africa. You can't just leave him behind. And this is where he is."

Clair almost laughed even as she was reminded of the predicament Zep was in. "You know who those people are, right? The ones who are holding him prisoner?"

"I do not. Their identities are obscured, even when they are connected to the Air."

"That's because they're WHOLE, and they eat people like me and Zep for breakfast. At the very least, you could've given me a gun before sending me back in there."

"I could if you wanted me to."

Clair rubbed her brow with the knuckles of both hands. She had been joking about the gun, but not about Zep. Rescuing him was critical, if she could only find the energy to get moving again. She felt like every vein in her body was full of mud.

"What I'd like more than anything is a cup of coffee."

"Go to the third booth on the right."

She forced her weary legs into motion and jumped to the front of the queue.

"Sorry," she said to the commuters whose journeys she was briefly interrupting. "I'm expecting something."

The door opened, revealing a plastic box big enough to hold a large melon. It had an identity patch addressed to Carolyn Edge. Clair pressed her right palm against the patch until it flashed green and unsealed. Then she took the box back to the bench and eased the lid open.

The first thing that hit her was the scent of fresh coffee. It was like a shot of energy straight to the brain. The insulated mug it came in wasn't drawn from her private pattern catalog, and the brew, she suspected, wasn't her favorite, but that was okay. It was still caffeine—and if someone *was* looking for her, the less evidence she left of her presence, the better.

Next to the mug was a bundle of fresh clothes and a pair of sneakers. Again, not her favorites—lightweight travel gear in grays and blacks, anonymous and easy to layer— but at least they looked to be her size. The new clothes went with her new identity or mask or whatever it was, she assumed. There was a new backpack, too, the same nondescript color scheme as the clothes.

Inside the backpack was an automatic pistol.

She touched the cold metal with the tip of one finger.

No, she told herself, *this is crazy.*

Or was it?

In all her life, she'd never fired a gun. Her parents had never owned one. But when people started pointing them at her, didn't it make a kind of sense to point one back? It wasn't as if she had to actually *fire* it or anything.

Clair shoved the pistol under the clothes, well out of sight, and stuffed it all into the pack.

She wanted nothing more than to shower and drink her coffee in peace. A headache was throbbing behind her right eye.

Reprisals, she thought, remembering something Gemma had said in the safe house. *The man WHOLE is trying to kill . . .* That was what "q" had called the person holding her parents hostage. That person had turned out to be Dylan Linwood.

Distant pieces of the puzzle were slowly starting to come together, but what good did that do her? She couldn't call Libby. She couldn't call her parents. She couldn't call her friends. She couldn't call the peacekeepers without giving her location away. Clair had escaped from one cage only to find herself caught securely in another.

"One piece at a time," she reminded herself. If she could get Zep out of the safe house, that would be a start. At least she wouldn't be alone in the cage then.

"Can I call up a map?" she asked "q."

"Yes, Clair. I will advise you if you are about to do anything dangerous."

There was a public bathroom one block to the north, worth going out of her way for. She didn't want to arrive anywhere looking like a refugee.

She slung the pack over her shoulder, threw the empty mug and box into a bin, took one last look around her to make sure Dylan Linwood really wasn't still following her, and set off.

——————————————————[27]

ONE HOUR LATER, after a lonely walk under stars as crisp and cool as a cosmic chandelier, Clair strode up to the safe house door and waited. She didn't need to knock. She knew Ray or someone else would be watching.

The door opened after thirty seconds. Gemma stepped out. The door closed behind her and clicked shut.

"We didn't expect to see you again," Gemma said. Her face was unreadable in the darkness. There was no porch light.

"I didn't expect to see you, either." Clair held the pistol at her side, not hidden but not aimed at anyone either. A bluff like Gemma's had been. This time, Gemma appeared to be unarmed.

"You should have told me," Clair said.

"About what?"

"About Dylan Linwood."

Gemma looked surprised but unrepentant. "You've seen him, then?"

"He tried to kill me."

Gemma nodded and said, "We couldn't tell you about that. You wouldn't have believed us."

"How long have you known he was a traitor? And how on earth did he survive that explosion?"

That earned her a long, measuring stare.

"You'd better come inside. Your boyfriend is making my life a living hell."

"He's not my boyfriend," she said again.

Gemma knocked on the door, a quick rat-a-tat, and it opened. Clair's eyes had adjusted to the darkness. Ray looked pissed off. Clair didn't care.

"I'll be out of touch for a bit," Clair told "q." She squeezed the pistol grip tightly, feeling as though she were leaping off a high dive. Gemma followed her into the house, too close for comfort, but no one tried to search or disarm her. No one said anything. All the menus in her night-darkened lenses were dead.

She found Zep in the living room, sitting on the couch, with wrists and ankles secured by plastic ties. Jesse sat next to him, not tied but not exactly one with his cap-tors, either. Big-Ears stood over them both with his arms folded. Arabelle, in her wheelchair, blocked the door to the back of the house, long-fingered hands resting loosely in her lap.

"Clair!" Zep tried to get up, but his bindings prevented him. Seeping blood had stained the bandage around his thigh bright red. "What are you doing here? You shouldn't have come back."

"I didn't have to," she said. "I'm here of my own free will, and I'm not making any demands, either. That counts for something, doesn't it?" She said that to the woman in the wheelchair.

"Perhaps it does," said Arabelle.

"Why *are* you here?" asked Jesse, looking up at her with eyes wide through his thick hair.

"I haven't worked everything out, but I know one thing," she said, figuring there was nothing to be gained by prevaricating. "Neither VIA nor the peacekeepers blew up your house. It was these guys. That's why Gemma appeared so soon after the explosion. That's why she was surprised to see you. Your father was the target, and we were almost collateral damage."

Jesse looked at Gemma and Arabelle in turn, then back at Clair. His expression was furious.

"It's not true," he said to her. "Why are you lying to me? Haven't you done enough damage?"

"What Clair says is true, Jesse," Arabelle said. "I'm sorry."

"When your father didn't call in on schedule," Gemma said, "we knew he'd been compromised, and we acted immediately to neutralize the threat."

"Compromised?" Jesse's head swung back and forth. Clair wanted to grab him and make him be still. "You blew up our *house!*"

"The charges were laid years ago," said Ray. "I helped Dylan put them in place myself, but we never thought we'd need them."

"He would never have done anything to hurt you," said Jesse, face turning pink. "You murdered him."

"If we were murderers," said Arabelle, "you would already be dead."

Zep was nodding grimly. "Yeah, right. We're witnesses. So why are you sitting around talking to us?"

"They don't know what to do with us," said Clair.

"That's true," said Arabelle. "We can't let you go without exposing you to grave danger."

"She's already run into him," Gemma said.

The members of WHOLE shifted uneasily.

"Run into who?" asked Jesse.

"Let's talk about that later," said Arabelle firmly. She was probably thinking the same thing as Clair. Was it better for Jesse to know that his father wasn't the man he believed in or to remember a lie?

"For now, why don't you tell us what you want, Clair?" Arabelle said.

This was it. Everything she had pondered in the long walk to the safe house came down to this moment. They were seven people lumped together in a way none of them would have chosen. But that was the way it was, and she had to work with it.

"We need to leave," Clair told them. "It's not safe here."

Gemma shook her head. "The Faraday cage—"

"Is part of the problem. When enough people disappear into a blank spot, you know something secret's going on in there. Remember the phone call before? That was from someone who worked it out. Someone I know. If she can do it, so can the bad guys."

"I don't believe you," said Ray. "You're trying to flush us into the open."

"Really?" she said. "Well, feel free to sit here and see what happens. I'm leaving now, and I'm taking Zep with me. Come along if you want. It's your decision."

"You want them to come with us now?" asked Zep in

disbelief. His wounded leg was jiggling as though his muscular tension simply couldn't be contained.

"Yes," she said. "Improvement has to be more than just sucking in people like Libby, or else why would someone kill to keep it a secret? I want to know everything. These guys can help. No one else can."

"Peacekeepers—"

"I tried calling them before." She outlined what had happened to her in Maine, carefully avoiding naming Dylan Linwood to spare them getting mired down in Jesse's protests again. "If it was just one crazy guy with a gun, maybe they could help, but we don't really know what happened back there. He definitely talked to someone else. Maybe my call was intercepted; maybe the PKs set me up. Until we know exactly what we're dealing with, we can't risk talking to anyone."

Clair tried to radiate self-assurance, but the pistol was heavy in her hand, and she was afraid everyone could tell it was only for show. Who was she to tell a bunch of adults what to do?

"She's right," said Arabelle, easing her wheelchair through the doorway. "You need us, and we need you. If you can bring your friend Libby around, Clair . . . if we can prove that she's been altered illegally, particularly in the wake of that video stream . . . then that's a big step forward."

"But we don't have forever to get her on board," said Gemma. "The clock is ticking."

"What do you mean?" asked Zep.

"People affected by Improvement rarely live longer than a week."

Clair stared at her, struck to the pit of her stomach with a new fear.

"What do you mean?" she asked.

"Improvement doesn't affect everyone, otherwise there'd be dead kids everywhere. Those who do show the symptoms last seven days, maybe eight. Never nine."

"What are the symptoms?"

"Headache, erratic behavior . . . I'm guessing you already know, otherwise why would you be so worried about your friend?"

"Shit," said Zep, looking as aghast as Clair felt.

Libby had used Improvement two days ago. How many days did that leave her? Five or six?

"Cut the boy's feet free," said Arabelle. "Raymond, call and give the code to move out. Clair and the others will come with us."

Ray vanished into the hallway while Big-Ears sliced Zep's ties with a pocket blade and helped him to his feet.

"I'm not going anywhere with you," said Jesse, red-faced and teary eyed. He was obviously struggling to take it all in. "You killed my father."

"Do you really want to stay here and take your chances with the PKs?" asked Gemma. "You'll be guilty by association."

"I didn't *do* anything!"

"That doesn't matter. You're one of us now."

"I'm not going anywhere unless you tell us where," Clair said.

"Escalon. We have a cache there. Once we're away from here, we'll have more options."

"Like what?" asked Clair.

"I'll tell you," Gemma said, "if you tell me who your hacker friend is."

"Uh, that's harder than you think."

"Well, the same goes for us."

Clair looked at Zep, who shrugged.

"All right," she said. "That far. Then we talk again."

"Agreed," said Arabelle.

"I haven't agreed to anything," said Jesse.

"You're not staying behind." There was steel in the crippled woman's voice. "I won't let you."

"Why not?" he asked her, fists balling in frustration. "Why won't you tell me what's going on?"

The phone's shrill ring cut the argument short. Ray called Clair's name from the hallway in puzzlement.

"It's that friend of yours again. Says it's urgent."

Clair squeezed past Arabelle and took the phone from him while everyone watched her. "Hello?"

"Surveillance has changed in your vicinity," said the voice of "q," sounding faintly tinny.

"What kind of change?"

"All EITS drones within camera range have been detoured along alternate routes. Not only that, but crowd-sourcing allocations for the surrounding area have been reduced to zero, so the drones are flying on internal reckoning only."

"What does that mean?"

"It means that the Manteca Municipal Authority is effectively unmonitored for two blocks around you, and the blind spot is widening."

Clair bit her lip. "Someone's up to something, and they don't want to be seen doing it. Any sign of *him*?"

"None, but I too am blinded by the lack of data. I can't tell you anything until I can hack into a satellite or something."

"Okay. Thanks for letting us know. We're heading out now."

"Be careful, Clair."

"I will."

[28]

CLAIR PUT THE handset back in its cradle and hurried back to the living room. Zep was waiting for her, looking rumpled and rubbing his chafed wrists, but at least he was free. Jesse had gone reluctantly with Gemma, Big-Ears, and Arabelle to the back of the house. Only Ray remained, back at his post by the front door.

Zep limped across the room and took Clair into his arms.

"My hero," he said.

"I'm glad you're okay."

"Me too, frankly."

Her laugh was choked, but she told herself that was because he stank of stale sweat and tension. She leaned into him, grateful for his solidity and unafraid for once if anyone saw it. *What happens behind a Faraday shield*, she thought, *stays behind a Faraday shield.*

"You haven't hit on me once today," she said.

"I'm not the one with the gun in my pocket, in case you'd forgotten."

She laughed and held him more tightly still.

"Don't tell me you're disappointed," he said.

"Can I be honest?" she said. "I've been chased around the world and shot at. My parents were threatened. Libby might have brain damage. You're hurt. I can't even think about anything else at the moment."

"Maybe when this is over—"

"Don't say it."

"Why not? I mean it."

He brushed an errant curl from her forehead. She kept her cheek pressed against his chest, suppressing a sudden gulp of emotion.

"I just don't get you, Zep. Why would you *ever* choose me over Libby?"

"Are you really asking that?"

She shrugged, not sure what she wanted him to say.

"Libby could never do what you just did," he said. "You faced up to a pack of terrorists and got them to do what you wanted. You know how to figure things out. You can handle yourself. And you know what's right, too, or else we'd have had this conversation weeks ago."

She looked up at him, not sure she'd heard him correctly. "Really?"

He rolled his eyes. "Hell yes. You're fine as limes, girl. Too good for me, if you really want to know the truth. Look at how I sat there like a useless lump while you did all the negotiating."

"Don't," she said, not wanting to hear him put himself down.

"See? You're always saying that."

She pulled out of his arms, although doing so betrayed every muscle in her body.

The phone shrilled once more, then went silent.

"That's the signal," said Ray, joining them. "Come on."

They followed him up the hallway.

"Just tell me," said Zep, "who *is* this friend of yours who keeps on calling? None of your usual troop could hack their way out of a paper bag. Well, maybe Ronnie, but—"

"Quiet," said Gemma. She was peering through the curtains at the rear of the house.

Big-Ears had his hand on the latch of the door that led out into the yard.

"I'll tell you later, Zep," Clair whispered to him. Of the rest, she asked, "What are you waiting for?"

"Our ride," Gemma said.

Clair couldn't see anything remotely mobile past Gemma's head. The yard was long and narrow. It was crowded with ornamental fruit trees and flower beds, creating an irregular canopy through which a redbrick path meandered. The path terminated in a gate. Beyond the gate was a lane of some kind—a relic of the original urban layout, back when there were roads for cars to drive on.

The phone rang a second time, and Big-Ears opened the door.

Now Clair could see it, after a fashion. There was something in the lane, hulking low and silent. Whatever it was, the starlight didn't seem to touch it. It had edges but no visible sides, just an outline. It wasn't even a silhouette. On the other side of the lane was a tree, and Clair could clearly see its trunk though the thing that stood between it and her.

Big-Ears edged out into the yard, followed by Gemma. Ray indicated that Clair, Zep, and Jesse should go next, with him and Arabelle bringing up the rear. Clair lined up with the rest, glad that someone else was making the decisions. Jesse didn't protest, perhaps feeling the same way.

The air was fresh and lively, scented with the sea and

late-flowering plants. The only sound was the whining of Arabelle's chair and the rustling of leaves. It was so dark under the arbor that Clair could barely see Gemma's back. Patches winked to life in her lenses, but she had more important things to concentrate on just then, such as putting one foot in front of the other and not tripping over the edge of a loose brick.

The shots took her completely by surprise.

The first dropped Big-Ears like something had reached up from the shadowy ground and pulled him down. One moment he was in the lead, waving with a cupped hand for them to hurry, the next he was gone.

The second shot might have been an echo but for the way Gemma jerked. The bullet struck her right shoulder and buried deep, gifting her with all its considerable momentum. She spun 180 degrees to face Clair, fumbled for something at her waist, and then she, too, fell to the ground.

Clair was already ducking into the shadows and raising the pistol she didn't know how to use. People were shouting. She didn't hear the words. Two more shots cracked the night, and this time she saw the muzzle flashes, bright-yellow flames that came and went faster than lightning. The shooter was on the roof of the safe house, aiming down along the yard. A bullet whizzed over her head; then Zep was on her, pushing her down, under cover.

Ray was returning fire from her right. Clair rolled over under Zep's protective weight, planted her elbows on the ground, and braced the pistol in both hands. She had seen plenty of movies. Aim and pull the trigger—what could be easier?

Chances were, she told herself, that she wouldn't hit anyone anyway. But she had to try before someone else was shot.

More muzzle flashes from above. The shooter had moved. She adjusted her aim and pulled the trigger. The pistol boomed much louder than she had expected, and the kick was like catching a ball from a great height, hard on both her wrists. She fired a second time, and then red crosshairs appeared in her vision with an arrow pointing left. She shifted the pistol and the arrow shifted with it. When it was centered on the crosshairs, she fired again and kept firing until the magazine was exhausted and her hands had lost all feeling.

Ringing silence fell. Ray darted out of the shadows and scrambled onto the fence and from there to the roof. No one fired at him. A spotlight flared behind her, casting the scene into crisp black-and-white relief.

There was a body sprawled against the gutter; it had slid there and gotten stuck, leaving a red smear in its wake. Ray approached warily and shoved it with the sole of his boot.

The body tumbled off the roof, hit the ground, and sprawled faceup in the glare. The shooter had been hit in the stomach and throat. His flesh was ripped and bruised.

Did I do that? It seemed incredible to Clair. Out of panic and darkness had come this unexpected reality, sickening her to the stomach.

There was worse to come. It was Dylan Linwood's battered face that stared back at her, a single bloodred eye gaping like something from an Edgar Allan Poe story. She knew that it would haunt her dreams forever.

The cry Jesse emitted was all pain and surprise. Even through Clair's gunshot-deadened ears, she could hear the depths of his hurt. Ray dropped down next to the body and did his best to keep him away.

"We have to move," Arabelle was saying. "Clair, you have to get up. Don't freeze on us now."

Why would she freeze on them? Because she might have killed Dylan Linwood? Clair didn't know who should take credit for that—"q" most likely had guided her hand, via the gun's sights. Anyway, the reason she wasn't moving had nothing to do with Dylan Linwood.

"Move, you big lug," she said to Zep, elbowing him in the belly. "It's over."

He didn't move. She rolled half over and looked away too late.

The bullet that had narrowly missed her had caught him under the left ear, entering just behind his jaw and tearing a violent path through the base of his skull, destroying the top of his spinal column and sending fragments of bone and metal all through his brain. His right eye bulged as though someone had pushed at it from behind. His expression was one of absolute bewilderment.

Clair was covered in his blood and hadn't even noticed.

"Come on," said Gemma over the roaring in her ears, "or we're leaving you behind."

[29]

"NO," SHE SAID. Her voice sounded like something ripped from the depths of her chest. She was moving without thinking, slithering out from under Zep's body and brushing herself down, feeling his blood on her hands and hating herself for the instinctive revulsion she felt.

"That's it. Come on."

Gemma pulled at her, forced her to her feet for the second time that day. Clair fought her, not wanting to accept anything that was happening to her. She had seen Gemma fall to the ground, but now she was upright, bleeding from her shoulder, and very much alive. Why was she standing when Zep was not? Why was Clair?

"We can't leave him," she said, wrenching herself free.

"You really want to stay here and wait for the PKs? Two guns, two dead bodies, one murderer. That'll wrap things up nicely for them. Couldn't be simpler."

Clair stood over Zep and told herself to do as the

woman said. Her legs felt as unreliable as saplings in a storm, though. She could feel the world turning, rotating, uncaring. Her hands were still numb from firing at Dylan Linwood. The numbness was spreading in a wave to encompass her entire body.

Ray pushed past her, practically dragging Jesse to the lane. Two new people dressed in black came the other way, lifted Arabelle from her chair, and carried her after them.

The spotlight clicked off, leaving Zep's and Dylan Linwood's bodies in darkness.

As though the same switch were connected to a circuit in her head, Clair found herself moving, not consciously noting where or how, but moving all the same, tucking the pistol into her pocket and hurrying after the others. She didn't want to be left behind.

The vehicle she had glimpsed before was still in the lane, a narrow, segmented, many-wheeled contraption the sides of which were slippery with illusions. Clair might have walked right into it but for the door open on its side. The space within was matte black and crammed full of people. Ray grabbed her under one arm and shoved her to the front. There was a space next to a young brown-haired boy who looked barely ten. He stared at the blood on her with wide eyes.

"Let's go!" called Ray, slamming the door shut and falling into a space of his own.

The vehicle shifted beneath her and whined quietly through the darkness. The patches winked out. The vehicle was a Faraday cage like the safe house, safe from everyone outside. A trap for everyone inside.

"See any drones?" asked Ray, his voice carrying clearly over the electric engines.

"Clear," said a small, thin-faced woman driving at the front of the cabin. She was dressed in black like the rest of them, with a close-shaved scalp visible under a full-vision helmet. Clair's lenses synced automatically to a feed from the driver's point of view, the only feed available. The vehicle was moving smoothly through suburbs covered by the eye-in-the-sky drones, weaving and curling around trees, benches, and water features. Dark colors and shapes swept down its sides like an urban waterfall, decreasing the likelihood that anyone outside would notice its passing.

"We'll get away, don't worry," said the boy next to Clair. "The ATAC is camouflaged and the drones are dumb."

Through the numbness of her senses she heard *attack* and must have looked confused.

"All-Terrain Active Camouflage vehicle," he explained. Maybe he was talking out of nerves. He must have heard the gunshots. He could certainly see the blood. "Jesse's dad designed it for us."

"And now you've killed him," said Jesse to everyone in the vehicle, breaking the silence of his emotional shutdown. *"Really* killed him. What happened—he got away the first time? One attempt wasn't enough, so you had to have another crack at it?"

"He was firing at us," said Ray. "Remember that?"

"Did you see him with your own eyes? It was dark."

"He was the only one on the roof."

"Well, wouldn't *you* fire at someone who tried to kill you?"

Zep didn't set any bombs, Clair wanted to say. *Zep wasn't part of this.*

Her throat was so raw and tight, she struggled to breathe, let alone talk.

"We didn't kill your father," said Gemma to Jesse through teeth clenched against the pain. Her face was very pale, and with her good hand she pulled the silver cross from under her sweater and held it tightly. "It's not what it looks like."

"I was *right there*," Jesse said. "Both times! I know exactly what it looks like."

"But you're still wrong." Gemma leaned her head back against the ATAC's interior bulkhead and closed her eyes. "He was a dupe."

"Never. He would never have sold you guys out."

"That's not what I meant. Jesse, it wasn't him. It was someone else inside his body. A duplicate. *Dupe.*"

Jesse stared at her as though she had gone completely mad.

Behind them, the safe house was a nest of converging peacekeepers. Someone had called in the gunshots. The bodies would soon be found.

Distantly, dismally, Clair wondered who would tell Zep's parents.

And suddenly, all the emotions she had been keeping at bay came crashing in. Her parents had been attacked. She had been chased across the world. She had shot someone who might or might not have been Jesse's dad. She was in the company of terrorists, and the only person she could rely on was a stranger whose name she didn't even know.

Zep was gone. Because of Improvement, because of Libby, and because he had been in the wrong place at the wrong time. With Clair.

The kid left her alone as she wept.

[30]

THE ATAC SPED them through the night as though all the peacekeepers of Manteca were on their tail.

Route 120 had a single lane remaining for wheeled transports, leading into areas that had once been entirely rectangular fields and farm lots but now contained little other than wild things, as far as Clair knew. She had stubbornly resisted all attempts by her parents to *camp* in order to get her closer to them.

Everything she cared about was behind her, in the light.

The boy next to her wasn't talking anymore. No one was talking. It was as though Gemma's impossible declaration had pushed them into a zone beyond words. It was too insane. Too far gone ever to come back to reality.

With a sudden lurch the ATAC turned to the left onto a different road. The rough asphalt surface stabbed perfectly east, rising and falling with the contours of the land beneath.

Clair dried her eyes with the backs of her hands and wiped her hair from her face. The kid was watching her. Zep's blood had left a sticky red mark on his arm.

"You're Clair," he said. "I'm Cashile."

Her voice was hoarse. "That's . . . that's an unusual name."

"It's Zulu. My mom is from Africa."

That reminded Clair that she had been in Cape Town a couple of hours ago, just before "q" had told her not to use d-mat. She didn't mention that, in case it made Cashile think she didn't have a soul, that she was a zombie who only *thought* she was real. She didn't think she could handle that accusation on top of everything else.

"I've never seen you before," he said, braving her silence. "You're not one of us."

"I guess not."

"But you killed him."

"Who?"

"The dupe."

There was that word again. It might have been short for *duplicate*, but it also meant someone who had been tricked or fooled.

"You mean Dylan Linwood?"

"You shouldn't call him that. It wasn't him anymore."

So the kid believed it, too. Maybe it was a form of mental self-defense, Clair thought. Jesse's father wasn't responsible for everything he'd done because it wasn't him at all. Clair couldn't blame them. If he was dead to them already, it would be much easier to live with his blood on their hands.

Or *her* hands, as the case may be. Unconsciously, she put them under her thighs and pressed down on them with all her weight.

She had shot Dylan Linwood because he had tried to shoot her. It was self-defense, not murder.

Would she see it that way in Jesse's shoes?

"Our place in Escalon has lots of stuff," the boy said, as though to cheer her up.

"What kind of stuff?" she asked, trying to imagine what terrorists might hide in their secret caches.

"Electrobikes, for one," said Arabelle from behind her. "We'll be riding the rest of the way."

"The rest of the way where? I thought we were stopping there?"

It was Gemma's turn to speak, slowly and painfully

thanks to the gunshot wound in her shoulder. Ray had roughly dressed it during their flight from Manteca, but the bandage she pressed against the wound was already sodden with blood.

"It's too soon to stay still. We'll talk later. The new plan is to split up and regroup at the old Maury Rasmussen airfield. It's not the closest, but it's designated for hobbyists and won't draw the kind of attention we'd get at Oakdale."

"What kind of hobbyists?" asked Clair, feeling the darkness thickening around her like tar.

"People who fly aircraft. In this case, airships."

She didn't know such things still existed. "Why an airship?"

"Well, they're more mobile than vehicles and safer than d-mat," said Arabelle, "and they're both highly visible and impossible to sneak up on. We'll be safe there."

"If we get there," said Gemma.

"Hope for the best," Arabelle said, "plan for the worst."

"Uh . . . I've never ridden an electrobike," Clair admitted, unsure for the moment whether she would be going anywhere with anyone. All she wanted was answers, not de facto membership in their clique.

Jesse broke his long silence to say, "Then I guess you have two choices: stay behind or learn."

Arabelle glanced at him. Her lips pursed.

"We're not leaving anyone behind," she said. "Clair, you can ride pillion with Jesse."

Clair didn't know what that meant, but she knew a reprimand when she heard it.

Jesse looked down into his lap again and didn't say anything.

Escalon wasn't quite a ghost town, but it showed few signs of life. Most of the buildings were abandoned, their windows broken and roofs slowly collapsing inward. Even at night everything looked desert brown. Clair watched the d-mat sign go by with longing. Who knew when everything would go back to normal and she could travel that way again, without fear of being tracked down and murdered?

There would be no *normal*, she thought with a dull heart, without Zep, without Libby, without being able even to go *home*. . . .

The cache was in a squarish Art Deco building that might once have been an old movie theater. The ATAC trundled between the theater and the church next door and swung around the back, where there was a large clear space overhung by shabby eucalyptus. The vehicle came to a halt with a barely perceptible jerk, and its motor's steady hum ceased.

"Okay, people." Gemma hauled herself out of her seat, moving wearily, gingerly, protective of her injured shoulder. She was drenched in blood like Clair, but Gemma's was all her own. The rear door unsealed with a squeak.

Clair's menus returned the moment the cage was broken. There was a patch from "q," and she answered it by text only, hoping her mask was still in place.

"You're in Escalon, I see," said "q." "It's lucky no one else can find you. You're a wanted person now."

"Murder?" she sent back, misspelling the word twice before sending it.

"Not yet. Get the pistol into a booth so I can dispose of it and no one will ever match it to the bullet that killed Dylan Linwood."

"Can't get to a booth right now," she said, still sick to her stomach at the thought of killing anyone, whether he was Dylan Linwood or not. "These guys are WHOLE, remember? It's not really on their agenda."

"Understood. Are you friends with them now too?"

Clair didn't know how to answer that. The voice sounded more childlike than ever, convincing her that it really did belong to a kid somewhere. A kid who was for some reason obsessed with her and her friendships—but Clair could accept that for now, just so long as "q" continued to help her.

Everyone piled out into the still, cold air. Clair scanned the urban nightscape around her, expecting gunshots at any moment but hearing nothing out of the ordinary. This was her chance to run, she thought. She could head for the scattered lights of Escalon, those faint glimmers of civilization, and leave the mad world of WHOLE behind her forever.

The memory of Dylan Linwood's body falling from the roof made her stay. She wasn't part of civilization anymore, and until she understood *why*, she was stuck with Gemma and her disheveled band. It was either that or be pulled in by the PKs . . . or worse, she thought. How many other assassins were roaming the night, looking for her right now?

They would be safe at the airship, she told herself. She had to believe that, or she might as well give up now.

A stocky, silent woman with long black dreadlocks took Cashile to a small door at the back of the hall, and the rest followed. Although the walls looked on the verge of collapse, the lock on the door worked just fine. The hinges gleamed in the starlight.

The old theater was a *garage*, a word Clair had never had cause to use before. Inside the main hall were a dozen sleek electrobikes not dissimilar to the one Dylan Linwood had driven to school that morning, except these were more solid and had larger, spokeless wheels. They resembled ink-stained quicksilver cheetahs, frozen in midstretch. Cashile climbed over them like a hyperactive cub.

"Fully charged and ready to go," he said with a grin.

"We'll leave one minute apart," said Gemma, doing a credible impersonation of someone able to stand on her own.

"I get my own bike, right?" broke in the kid.

"But you still ride out with your mom. No radio contact unless it's an emergency. They'll be hunting us. You can count on that."

—————————————————————— [31]

THE FRONT DOORS opened, and the ATAC trundled inside, looking like a low-backed, eyeless lizard with eight lumpy wheels for legs. Its chameleon skin shifted and changed as it entered its new environment, taking on the appearance of straight lines and flat surfaces with remarkable effectiveness. When it stopped moving, it very nearly vanished.

"Ammo over there," said Ray, pointing Clair in the direction of a chest near the ATAC.

Then he mounted his electrobike and throttled it into motion. Without a word, he steered it to the front doors and disappeared into the night. Motor noise rose and fell at his command, and then all was silent again.

Clair opened the ammo chest and stared blankly at a sea of casings and magazines. How would she know what fit her empty pistol? Did she even want to reload it? Hadn't enough people died that night?

A strong tap on her shoulder alerted her to the presence of the dreadlocked woman at her side. Cashile's mom wrote her name with a fingertip in the dust on the top of the chest: THEO. Theo held out her palm for the pistol. Clair gave it to her and watched as she expertly handled it. Sections opened, closed, came off, and went back on like some kind of magic show. Then Theo turned back to the chest. She produced a box of bullets and loaded the magazine. It held fourteen tapered copper-sided shells that seemed enormous to Clair's eyes.

Theo also filled a second magazine, which she handed over, along with another box of bullets and the gun itself. Clair juggled them all, wondering when she might possibly need so much firepower. Was this her life now?

"Uh, thanks," she said, feeling like a child.

Theo just nodded.

Clair carried her lethal armfuls to where Jesse was waiting next to one of the electrobikes with a bottle of water in each hand. Wordlessly, without meeting her eyes, he gave her one of the bottles. She put the ammo in her backpack and worked out on her own where to stow it in a baggage compartment. Clair put the loaded pistol back in her pocket, hoping against hope that she would never have to use it again. Part of her still resisted the idea that she was about to go riding anywhere.

"Are you armed, Jesse?" asked Gemma.

"No," he said.

"You should be."

"Dad didn't hold with guns, so I won't either."

"Maybe if he had, he'd still be with us."

Jesse glanced at Clair, and she could see naked confusion in his eyes. What was he telling himself had happened back at the safe house? That Clair had shot his father for breaking a lifetime of not using guns and shooting at her, or that she'd shot an impostor in his father's body? Either possibility seemed ghastly and unlikely.

She looked away. *Half an inch lower*, she wanted to say, *and I'd be the one lying in a garden with my brains hanging out.* But she couldn't even think that thought without grief hitting her full force again, blinding her to anything other than the single, terrible certainty of Zep's death.

The only person who could hold Jesse's liquid stare was Arabelle. She was on the back of a bike, sitting sidesaddle, her useless legs hanging alarmingly close to the rear wheel. Both she and her driver, who had also been the driver of the ATAC, were wearing black helmets like Ray's.

"Godspeed, all of us," Arabelle said, ending the conversation with gentle finality.

She put her arms around her driver's waist. Together, they followed Ray out of the theater and rode off into the night.

Gemma gave Clair a helmet and brusquely explained how it worked. There was a microphone on the jaw guard and tinny speakers inside, both activated by clicking forward with her chin. Gemma tested one radio channel with her, then another with Jesse. Clair couldn't hear the second conversation, but they seemed satisfied.

"Need to ask you a question," she bumped "q" while they were busy.

"Of course, Clair. Ask away."

"What's your name?"

"Why?"

"Can't keep calling you 'q' in my head."

"Why not? It works for me, Clair."

"Okay." Clair was too tired for this coy evasiveness. Wannabe spy-kid or not, having a name other than Q wouldn't change anything, she supposed, since it would almost certainly be false.

"Gotta go."

Cashile and Theo were just heading off, riding two identical bikes. The kid looked even smaller than usual stretched out across the back of his. He waved at her as he disappeared through the doorway, and Clair waved back.

Then it was just Jesse, Clair, and Gemma, and the clock slowly counting down the next minute.

Gemma was looking pale, but if she considered herself well enough to drive, she was well enough to answer questions.

"You said people affected by Improvement live just seven days," Clair said. "How do you know?"

"Because that's the way it works," Gemma said, fiddling with something on her electrobike. "We've seen it before."

"But how do you know Libby's definitely affected? She's been under stress, using drugs—"

"You know that's not what this is. You saw the files I gave Dylan in the video feed. Libby's brain has been damaged, altered, changed. Call it what you want, that's what it boils down to. That's what Improvement has done to her. She's not herself. Not anymore."

Zep had used exactly that phrase. *Not herself.*

"I don't believe you."

"She'll commit suicide within a week. It's inevitable."

"Libby isn't going to kill herself. I won't let her."

"How are you going to stop it?"

"If Improvement has changed her, I'll find a way to change her back."

"How?"

"There must be a way."

"There doesn't have to be anything." Gemma shook her head firmly. "Better get used to the idea. The Libby you know is gone forever. "

"How can you say something like that?"

"Because this is what Improvement *does.* That's what *d-mat* does. It reaches into you and guts you and you don't even notice until it's too late. Don't you think that makes a difference? Don't you think it adds up eventually?"

Gemma was still bent over the bike, not looking at either Clair or Jesse, keeping her face carefully averted from them. Something splashed onto the smooth skin of the bike, and Clair was shocked to realize that it was a tear. Gemma was crying. She didn't blink or gulp or even seem to notice it herself, but Jesse was staring at her with his water bottle raised halfway to his mouth.

"Improvement killed my child," Gemma said in a hoarse whisper. "Don't you think I know what I'm talking about?"

Clair's mind flew back to the first questions she had asked the Air about Improvement, and her shock redoubled. "You wrote that! I found your message, but it had been defaced. All the details were gone—"

"Erased, just like they tried to erase what happened to him. What happened to *Sam*, my beautiful Sameer. But they can't erase me. Not if I don't use d-mat. Not if I stay one step ahead of them."

Gemma stood up and faced them. The tears trickled down her face into the grim lines around her mouth and dripped from her chin onto her chest.

Clair wanted to ask where she had found the files on the dead girls, but Jesse spoke before she could.

"How can dad have been a dupe? He never went through d-mat, not even once. There's no way anyone could have changed his pattern because it never existed."

Gemma flexed her injured shoulder, raising it like a defense against them.

"Time is up," she said. "On your bikes, boys and girls."

"Answer my question," Jesse said.

"Later, I promise. It won't help you now."

"But I want to know."

"I know you do. When we're with Turner, I'll tell you."

He looked startled. "Turner Goldsmith? We're meeting *Turner Goldmsith*?"

"Who's that?" Clair asked.

"Not now," Gemma insisted. "Get to the airship and then you'll learn everything we know."

Jesse let himself be shooed back toward the bike, and Clair followed, wondering what she'd just missed. There was so much disturbing new information in her head, she couldn't begin to parse it all. Jesse somehow fitted his hair into the helmet and climbed on first, steadying the frame with both legs as Clair clambered awkwardly aboard behind him. The pillion seat was broader than it looked, but it molded comfortably to her thighs. The suspension hummed and settled.

Jesse took his feet off the ground. The bike somehow balanced itself and turned at his command. Clair swayed and put her hands awkwardly on his waist, nervous of falling off the seat. She leaned backward as they juddered down a step or two to street level. The night was just as still as it had been before. The same lonely lights shone a block or two away. The same light wind blew. She felt removed from it inside the padded cocoon of the helmet.

Then, without warning, the bike surged beneath her. She flung herself forward, wrapped her arms around Jesse's middle, and held on for dear life.

[32]

THE ACCELERATION WAS incredible, like being on a roller coaster but without the restraints. One hapless wobble, she feared, and they would go skidding and tumbling across the rough road surface—a road surface that was moving under her with terrifying speed. She closed her eyes as tightly as she could, feeling hollow inside, as though she had left half her critical organs behind.

"Lean into the corner, will you?" came Jesse's voice through her helmet.

She didn't know what that meant, so the shift in momentum caught her off-balance. She stiffened, felt the bike sway alarmingly. Somehow things steadied. They accelerated again, even harder than before. She moaned in fear, hoping that if she stayed still, Jesse would never know how afraid she was.

"Clair, you're hurting me."

She drew in a sobbing breath and forced herself to ease off a little. At least they were moving in a straight line now.

She jutted out her jaw. Found something hard that gave way with a click.

"Don't you think we're going fast enough?" she said.

"What? I haven't even opened her up all the way."

The bike throbbed and accelerated again until the air

whipped and batted at her like a physical thing. Clair pressed herself as close to Jesse as she could. The bike moved with the irregularities of the road beneath its wheels, suspension smoothing out the worst of it. They might have been skimming over waves on Sacramento Bay, sitting at the nose of a motorboat. That was something she'd done once with some friends in high school. The memory calmed her somewhat, although she hadn't enjoyed it very much at the time. It had taken them far too long to get anywhere, putting everyone in a bad mood.

She opened her eyes and found that they had left Escalon far behind. The bike and its two passengers were rushing past empty scrubland, low and flat, dotted with trees and bushes. A map of the area revealed that they were back on Route 120, cutting west across the county for a place named Adela, right on the edge of Oakdale. The distance to their rendezvous at the Maury Rasmussen airfield was around fifty-five miles.

Clair could have been there in an instant by d-mat, but this *felt* much faster.

"Is it safe to talk over these things?" she asked.

"Of course. The range is barely a yard or two on this channel."

"Why are you heading for Oakdale? That's not the most direct route."

"Gemma said to split up, so that's what we're doing."

"Which way are the others going?"

He didn't answer. All she needed was some reassurance, but he wasn't providing it.

"Listen," she said, "I want you to know that I'm not happy about being here either."

"That doesn't make me feel any better about it."

"So what are you going to do? Ditch me here and ride off on your own?"

"I could," he said. "It's not too late. I could leave you *and* the others behind. It's not like I owe any of you anything. Sure, they used to babysit me, but they blew up my home, they kept me prisoner, they . . . you . . . ."

Killed my father, he didn't say. Clair could hear the words straining over the airwaves like a wire on the verge of snapping. Why wasn't he running from all of them, as she had considered in Escalon?

She shifted awkwardly on the pillion, deciding that it was probably better if they didn't talk unless they had to. Her fingers were freezing in the frigid night air. He wasn't slowing down any, and she took that as a sign she wasn't about to be dumped. She curled her hands into fists and kept her arms tight around him. His shoulders were bony. She ached for Zep's muscular solidity, made a deliberate effort to think of something else.

Jesse turned abruptly. Clair had been watching the map and was ready for it this time. A patch of lights was growing ahead and to their right, and over Jesse's shoulder she could see how the road curved toward it. Adela swept by in a flash. Thirty seconds later, they were juddering over a bridge. The river was narrow and as black as oil, but Clair could smell the water and the plants that thrived on it.

The next landmark was Oakdale itself, which was bigger than Escalon but looked much the same. Jesse avoided clusters of well-lit structures near the d-mat station. They took a series of right-angle turns through the town, Clair becoming more proficient at leaning each time. They crossed a train line that still had its tracks. They passed a cemetery. Then they were heading west again along an empty road into a California Clair had never seen before. She knew the Bay reasonably well, and she had visited some of the touristy places as a kid, but the spaces between were utterly unknown to her.

A patch came through from Q, and she took it immediately.

"Clair, an odd thing just happened."

"Odd how?'

"Dylan Linwood just arrived in the station at Oakdale."

A chill went down Clair's spine.

"It can't be him. He's really dead this time." *You helped me shoot him.*

"There's no doubt at all, Clair."

Q sounded hurt and puzzled, as if the universe had personally reached out and slapped her.

Dupe, she thought, feeling much the same. Someone's

body with someone else's mind. It seemed impossible, but what if it was true? That would explain how Dylan's behavior had changed so radically, from someone who hated d-mat to someone who used it to try to hunt her down and kill her. It also explained how he had escaped the explosion that had destroyed his home, and how he could be chasing her again now after having been shot in Manteca.

"Wait," Clair said as a more believable explanation occurred to her. "That trick you did when I was running from him—giving me an alias—could someone be using that back at us?"

"I suppose so. That would explain why I can't trace his origins."

So would duping, Clair thought, but she kept that to herself.

"Show me where he's supposed to be now, in my lenses."

A red dot appeared in the map she had open. "Dylan Linwood" was pulling out from the d-mat station in Oakdale and moving very fast. He must have fabbed a bike or had one waiting for him there.

Clair kicked out with her chin to talk to Jesse.

"Someone's coming after us," she said.

He sat straighter and glanced back at her. The bike slowed minutely. "How do you know?"

"My friend Q told me. You know, she's the one who called me in the safe house."

"We're supposed to be off the grid, Clair."

"I know. But she's given me a mask so I'm invisible. That's not the point. It looks like he's on the same road as us."

"What do you want to do? Outrun him? Ambush him?"

Clair pictured herself sitting in the dark, waiting for someone to come into the sights of her gun. Shooting at someone shooting at her was one thing. Premeditated murder was another thing entirely.

"I'm not a murderer, Jesse."

"Really? You seem pretty good at it to me."

She ground her teeth on a reply that would have seen her tumbling into the dirt for sure.

"Let's get off this road," she said. "If he's just going to check out the airfield and isn't actually following us, he'll never know we were here."

"I don't have time to stop and map out another route—"

"So let me do it," she said. "You drive, I'll navigate. Deal?"

He thought about it for a second.

"Deal, I guess."

Clair called up maps in her lenses. The countryside was an inconvenient mess of reservoirs, irrigation trenches, abandoned train tracks, and minor roads that never went in a straight line. There didn't seem to be any easy way to get where they needed to be. It was like a puzzle or a maze, hypnotic in its complexity. . . .

"Clair?"

She forced herself to focus. If they went to Jamestown, from there they could go north on Route 49 to Angels Camp. The Maury Rasmussen airfield was only six miles farther after that point.

"Take Route 108 on the left," she said. "That'll get us out of Oakdale."

"And then?"

"We'll go off road. I'll tell you how when we get there."

He grunted.

"Bet you're thinking this'd be easier with d-mat," he said.

"The thought had crossed my mind."

And my ass, she thought, sure that cross-country riding was going to be a *lot* less comfortable than it was by road. It could take all night to get to the airfield at the rate they were going.

A series of clicks came over the open line, followed by Gemma's voice.

"Hail Mary" was all she said.

The engine snarled, and Jesse propelled the bike even faster than it was already going. She could feel wiry sinews under his top, taut with tension. He was shaking.

"Want to tell me what that was about?" Clair asked him.

"Gemma . . . Gemma gave me some codes before we left Escalon, while we were testing the helmets."

Clair quashed a momentary resentment that she hadn't

been told. *Zombie girl.* Jesse's voice was choked, as though something horrible had happened. "What did she say to you?"

"They got Arabelle."

"'Got'?"

"Killed."

Clair saw a flash of Zep's broken face.

"For real?"

"I wouldn't lie to you about something like that."

She believed him. This was the woman whose shoulder he had wept on, who had told him to be brave. Clair had trusted her and put her hopes for answers and safety in her hands. A crippled woman in a wheelchair . . . and now she was dead.

Clair's insides roiled, but she didn't have time to dwell on it. Q was flashing her.

"Clair, I have multiple targets radiating out from the center of Oakdale. Two of them are coming in your direction."

She nodded. Forewarned was forearmed, she supposed.

"What happened to 'Dylan Linwood'?"

"He is in transit again, and I can't tell where he is going. He's moving around in a way I can't explain."

"Maybe he's just a decoy, designed to distract us," she said, taking inspiration where she found it. "Maybe we can use the same trick against him."

"What do you mean, Clair?"

"We're supposed to be meeting an airship," she said,

reaffirming her faith in Arabelle's plan. "Can you see it the same way you're seeing all this?"

"There is air traffic over Stockton. One of them is heading in the direction of Maury Rasmussen airfield."

"That must be it." She hoped it was. "If you copy its profile and send copies in different directions, anyone watching the same data as you won't know which one is the real one."

"Clever! They'll either have to chase all of them down or concentrate on some at random. I'll try it, Clair. If you maintain radio silence, it should give you some time."

"That's all we need."

"Clair?" said Jesse, opening the line between them again.

"What?"

"Lights behind us. We might have been seen."

They were just coming out of Oakdale. She didn't want to look behind her for fear of losing her balance.

"Shit. The turnoff is still over a half mile away."

Jesse switched off the headlights, and the bike roared beneath them along the suddenly invisible road.

[33]

"ARE YOU CRAZY?" Clair shouted. "Don't forget you're risking my neck too."

"How can I forget? I can hardly breathe with you strangling me."

Clair didn't dare let go. All she could do was close her eyes and hope he knew what he was doing. There were no streetlights. An accident in the dark would kill them as surely as a bullet from "Dylan Linwood."

"Keep your fingers crossed there aren't any potholes," he said. "I'm using an infrared HUD, but it's still not easy to see anything."

She didn't have any spare fingers to cross. They were gripping him too tightly.

"Two hundred yards to the next turnoff," she said, keeping a close eye on the map despite her terror.

They swayed sickeningly to avoid something.

"What was that?"

"Cat," he called back to her. "Where's that corner?"

It was on them with unexpected speed. "Here, Jesse— turn here!"

They barely braked, then took the corner with a screech of rubber.

Orange Blossom was a minor old road that shook and juddered them.

"Slow down!"

"Just want to make sure we lose whoever's on our tail."

"You sure there was someone?"

"I don't know. But someone got Arabelle, and I'm not going to wait until someone else starts shooting at us."

"No, let's not do that," she said. "*I'm* the one sitting on the back. . . ."

They followed Orange Blossom for 5 miles, running parallel to another river as it snaked and crawled across the dry land. The vegetation was marginally more lush, and the air felt damp. Clair was thirsty. She would have given anything for a drink.

"These people," Jesse said over the intercom. "They can't be PKs, or there'd be drones everywhere. So who are they? What do they want?"

"Whoever they are," she said, "they're organized, and they're fast. The first time we saw them was just after your dad started his anti-Improvement thing."

"Lots of people already know about Improvement. The invite has gone to thousands, maybe millions of people."

"Yes, but no one thinks it's real. Without evidence, it's just an urban myth."

"Do *you* think it's real?" he asked.

Clair thought of Libby, who had made no attempt to contact her since declaring their friendship ended.

"It must be real," she said. "Or why would the people shooting at us be so upset? Your dad found evidence proving it did *something*, and there is such a thing as bad publicity." She spoke from experience.

He shrugged under her tight grip. "I guess so."

She felt nothing but weary acceptance, perhaps even relief. Fighting the *idea* of Improvement had been exhausting. Now it was time to accept it and start fighting the people responsible for it.

Clair wanted to ask Q if she could find the source of the data Gemma had given Dylan Linwood. There might be more of it, and there might be other people she could call for help—if they weren't already in trouble too, maybe running for their lives like Jesse and Clair.

But she said nothing, remembering Q's warning about maintaining radio silence. The longer they stayed quiet, the greater their chances of slipping like ghosts into the night.

The next town was approaching. Orange Blossom became Sonora Road, which led into the tiny, abandoned hamlet of Knights Ferry, where they turned left.

Jesse glanced in his mirrors, checking what lay behind them. Clair's shoulder blades itched.

"Eyes forward," she told him. "There's another turnoff coming up."

"I don't see one."

"The map says it's right there, supposedly."

"Here?"

Jesse swung off the tarmac and onto a dirt track. The wheels slipped for an instant, then found traction. There *was* a road, but it was gravelly and rutted, barely there at all.

"Whoa," said Clair, hanging on tight. The bike almost slipped over as they took the first corner. "The map *said* it was a road. Is this a road?"

"It'll have to be."

"Well, keep following it until it runs out. Then I'll tell you where to go."

"It *runs out*?"

"The map is not my territory, okay? Go easy. I've never done this before."

Jesse drove punishingly hard, trying to put distance between them and whoever he thought was behind them. They had to reach the airship before their pursuers caught up or found a way to cut them off. Clair swore she wasn't going to end up like Arabelle, dead in a ditch somewhere because she hadn't gone fast enough.

It was rough going, though. What should have been a quick mile-long stretch of straight road was in fact a nightmare of switchbacks and whipping branches. The night was clear and full of stars, but there wasn't enough light to see what lay in the scrub to either side of the track, and Jesse kept the headlights carefully off.

"That way," she said, pointing northeast over his shoulder.

Tulloch Road was paved, but it had fragmented over time. Jesse frequently cursed and jerked the front wheel to avoid potholes and jagged cracks in their path.

"There's a dam ahead," she said, mazes and puzzles shifting in her mind. "We're supposed to go east when we reach it and head from there to Jamestown. That would be the sensible thing to do."

"Nothing about this is sensible." Jesse sounded weary

and impatient. "Are you sure we're not completely lost?"

"Are you sure we're being followed?"

"We are. I'm positive now. They're not using headlights, but I can see their exhaust in the HUD. A long way back, but definitely tracking us."

"So quit griping. We need to do something about that, and fast."

"Like what?"

"Let's call the others. Tell them we're on track for our rendezvous, but say it's Columbia airfield, not Maury Rasmussen. The people looking for us are bound to be listening in, so they'll go northeast to Columbia while we go north across the dam. From there, we'll be back on paved roads and making better time."

That was a slight exaggeration. It would be paving all the way if they skipped Jamestown and went instead through an exotic-sounding place called Copperopolis five miles to the north. She hoped they could make it work. Everything below her navel felt compacted and numb.

"Okay," he said. "And if you're so sure . . . you make the call."

Clair took a deep breath and held it for a second, reviewing the plan to make sure there was nothing she had forgotten.

"All right." Emptying her lungs in an anxious gust and drawing another deep breath, she prayed the nervousness she felt wouldn't show in her voice.

"Halfway to Jamestown," she said over the radio. "On schedule for Columbia."

She waited, hardly daring to breathe. Gemma, she was sure, would work it out if she was still alive. Gemma was grating, but she was nothing if not smart. . . .

The airwaves crackled.

"Confirmed" came Gemma's voice. "I'm in Chinese Camp."

"On our way to Telegraph City," said Ray. "Got ambushed, so we're coming the long way around. Don't leave without us."

"Don't you take too long," said Gemma. "What about you, Theo and Cashile?"

No answer.

"Theo? Cashile?"

Nothing on the airwaves but crackle and hiss.

"Continue as discussed. Maintain radio silence."

Gemma clicked off, and Clair felt a sudden rush of fatalism. If Theo and Cashile had been caught as well, there could be no reasoning with the people following them. Not even a kid was safe.

"Do you think they fell for it?" asked Jesse, sounding as sick as Clair felt.

"Maybe."

"You're not sure?"

"I'm sure we're not in the clear yet," Clair said, worrying

at the situation as she would a ragged hangnail. "Who-ever's following us must be using infrared, like you. That means they'll be able to see us, no matter which way we tell them we're going."

"Right. The motors on this thing are the brightest heat sources around."

"Could we cover them up? Dig a hole or something?"

"We don't have time." Clair felt Jesse shake his head.

"How much time *do* we have?"

"For them to catch up if we stop? A minute or two, max."

"We'll have to think of something else, then."

"Like what?"

"I don't know. Give me a second."

She didn't need a second. She already knew what they had to do. Saying it was the hard thing.

Of the two of them, she had the most left to lose. She still had a life out there, waiting for her to escape the people chasing them and reconnect. He, on the other hand, had lost almost everything—which made what he did have left all the more precious.

There was no point stalling any longer in the hope of coming up with another solution or of someone else making the decision for her. The road, such as it was, wouldn't last forever.

"We have to ditch the bike," she said.

[34]

"DITCH THE ... *WHAT?* You can't be serious."

"I am, Jesse. It's the only way."

"And then you expect us to *walk* to the airfield, Clair? You have no idea. It'll take us days!"

"We won't walk . . . I hope. Hang on."

She clicked off the helmet-to-helmet radio. They had already broken radio silence once; a second time wouldn't make a difference.

"Where's the nearest d-mat booth, Q?"

"Copperopolis" came the instant reply.

"Okay, I need you to do something for me. It's a big favor, but I don't have any alternatives. I need you to send some kind of vehicle to that booth, then drive down to meet us. It'll take us all night to get to the landing field otherwise, and we'll miss the rendezvous."

"Me?" asked Q. "Come join you? In California?"

"Yes," she said, mentally crossing her fingers. "You'll have to fake a solo d-mat license, I guess, but you should be able to do that. You changed my name and everything before. Isn't it about time you got your hands dirty?"

"I don't know," Q said. "I mean, I'm not sure I can. But I'd like to. I really would. I just think it might take more time to organize than you have available . . . for reasons that are hard to explain right now. . . ."

"You don't know what you're capable of until you try. That's what my mom always says. Right?"

Q fell silent, and Clair waited her out, mentally chanting *Come on, do it* in time with her heartbeat.

"I've had another thought," said Q eventually. "This might work even better than your suggestion. I can outfit a quadricycle with a telepresence system and pilot it to you by remote control. That way I can stay where I am to keep an eye on things and help you at the same time. Would that work for you?"

Clair wasn't in a position to argue, even though Q's unwillingness to come in person made her nervous. What was she hiding? Or was she just afraid of getting too involved and putting her own life at risk?

Maybe she just didn't know how to drive, like Clair.

"Fine," Clair said. "Better get moving, though. The faster our new ride reaches us, the better."

"Yes, Clair. I'll get on it right away."

"Thanks, Q." She hesitated, then added, "I really owe you for this."

"That's what friends are for, Clair."

Not in the world I come from, Clair wanted to say.

She clicked back to Jesse, who had been fuming in silence while she talked to Q, driving mechanically through the arid night.

"All right," he said. "Let's hear it."

He took her explanation about as well as she expected.

"You must be out of your mind," he said. "How do I

know we can trust this Q person to do as she says? How do *I* know I can trust *you*?"

Was he kidding? "I don't see how you have any other choice. We have to lose the bike, and we're going to use the dam to do it."

"And who put you in charge?"

"No one. I just know it'll work."

"How can you possibly know that?"

"Because it *has* to. Otherwise, we're dead like Zep and Arabelle and Cashile, and it'll be all your fault!"

She punched him the shoulder, making the bike wobble.

"Hey, watch it!"

She could see only Zep, face ruined and bloody. Her throat closed tight, and the night swam around her.

She needed answers, and sleep, and a shower, and a spare second to think when she wasn't being hunted through the dark with no one but Jesse to lean on. She needed her mom, she needed a hug, she needed a thousand things that he couldn't give her.

She punched Jesse on the shoulder a second time, harder than before. She was angry at him for making her cry, first, then angry at him for what he said next, because that meant he knew she was crying.

Everything depended on them getting to the airship, because there, she had to believe, things would start to go right again.

"All right, all right," he grumbled. "We'll do it your way."

THE DAM LOOMED ahead of them, a vast wall of concrete rising like some ancient concave monolith from the riverbed. Its sluice gates were open; there was no need for either irrigation or power generation anymore, so the river just rushed straight through. But the structure remained as a testimony to a time of terrestrial mega-engineering, one of many such structures scattered all over the globe. Dams, bridges, tunnels—all functionally useless now, for most people.

"Look for somewhere we can get off without being seen," she said, her voice throaty from suppressed emotion. "I presume this thing can keep itself upright for a while?"

"It'll travel along a straight line until it hits something," he said almost proudly, steering the doomed bike up the old riverbank to the eastern side of the river, where the road curled up onto the top of the dam itself. There was a narrow access road along the top whose safety barriers looked so rusted and fragile, a determined child could push through them.

Jesse took them around the end of the road to where the bank on the far side dipped down behind the dam. There he brought the bike to a brief halt.

Clair hopped off and flexed her stiff legs, feeling a thousand tiny pains.

"Wait," she said, taking the extra ammo from the baggage compartment and shrugging the backpack over her shoulder. She took off her helmet and slung it on one arm. "Okay. Go."

He hesitated, and she would have sworn she saw him pat the chassis farewell. Then he climbed out of his seat and used the handlebars to push the bike back up the slope. Crouching down behind it, he lined it up, fiddled with the controls, and dropped facedown onto the ground beside it to present a lower profile for anyone looking for them in infrared.

The bike accelerated away from him as he slithered back to join her. Would the engines be hot enough to cover the absence of the passengers? Clair hoped so. She also hoped that Jesse had had the forethought to angle the bike's trajectory so it would fall to the left, not the right. They needed the person following them to see it die.

Halfway across the dam, the bike hit an irregularity in the road surface. Its back wheel lifted momentarily off the ground and then slewed right out from under it. The bike tipped onto its side and in a shower of sparks crashed through the rusted safety barrier—to the left. Engine shrilly singing and wheels futilely spinning, the bike sailed over the edge and followed a perfect arc out into space.

Clair craned her head and watched it as long as she dared.

"Now we find out if that's enough to get them off our tail," she whispered to Jesse, pulling him farther downslope, away from the road.

"You'd better hope so," he hissed back at her. "Dad made that bike with his bare hands. . . ."

He stopped. The whining of another bike was rising up from the valley below.

"That's not a Linwood," Jesse said. "Too noisy, too inefficient. But powerful. Could be a PK bike."

"Quiet," Clair hissed, flattening herself against the backside of the dam and holding her breath as tightly as she held the pistol.

Their pursuer's bike rumbled up the path and stopped at the top. Clair held her breath and waited. Would the person hunting them assume that Jesse and Clair had died in the crash and move on, or stick around to investigate more closely?

The person on the bike did nothing for over a minute, then put the bike back into motion, heading away from the dam and on the wild-goose chase Clair had set for them, chasing a phantom airship across the California countryside.

"Well, hell," Jesse said. "It actually worked."

"Told you it would."

Clair felt no triumph. She didn't relax until the sound of the bike had completely faded, and she told Jesse not to move for another five minutes after that, just to be sure. She wasn't about to be caught halfway across the dam, exchanging a wild goose for sitting ducks because they were impatient.

"You ever play strategy games?" Jesse whispered as they waited.

"No. Why?"

"You should. You'd be killer at them."

"What do you mean?"

"You're *good* at this. I'd have been caught five times over by now on my own. You've missed your true calling."

"Hardly," she said, fervently not wanting that to be true. Clair would rather be like Tilly Kozlova. She had famously only started playing piano in her teens and within two years had gone on to perform in the world's most prestigious theaters. "You have your own skills," she offered in the hope of taking some of the attention off her. "You can drive, for one."

"And I'm killer with a screwdriver," he said. "Never underestimate that."

They sat still together, the wind whistling downriver forming an atonal counterpoint to the river's basso continuo directly behind her. She could literally feel it through her back, the distant roaring of turbulence in concrete and steel piping. She wondered how long it would take to reduce the whole structure to rubble. A thousand years? A century? A decade?

"Look on my works, ye Mighty," she thought, *"and despair. . . ."*

"Clair?" Someone was shaking her. "Clair, wake up."

She jerked her head so hard, she banged it against the concrete, instantly dispelling a vivid dream about sandstorms and sphinxes.

"Sorry," she said. "I just closed my eyes for a second."

"Yeah, right. You were snoring. We'd better get moving. We haven't got all night."

Clair didn't want to check the time. She didn't want to move even her eyeballs. The tiny fragment of sleep had completely perforated her resolve.

He tugged her again.

"Come on, Clair. We've got to get to the airship and talk to Turner. He won't wait for us forever."

She forced herself upright. Everything from her brain all the way down to her feet felt like rubbery mush, and she had no doubt she looked as bad as she felt.

"Who is this guy, anyway?"

"Which guy?"

"The one on the airship Gemma said we're going to meet."

"Turner Goldsmith? You've never heard of him?"

She shook her head.

"No one knows where he is or what he looks like. I've never met him. I'm not sure if even Dad did. But if the World Holistic Leadership has a leader, it's him. He's supposed to be amazing."

"And he'll tell us what to do?"

"I guess so. Gemma said he knows what's going on."

"She'd better be right. I'm not going all that way for nothing."

It would be a relief, she told herself, to let go like she had in the safe house, and allow someone else to give the orders. Jesse was right: being late wasn't an option. If the airship left without them, then everything she had done would be for nothing. She'd end up like Arabelle and Theo and Cashile. And Zep.

With heavy footsteps, she followed Jesse up the slope. The backpack was heavier than it had been before—she was sure of it.

The wind was rising. She hugged herself and tugged her head in close to her shoulders to stay warm.

[36]

TERRAIN THAT HAD looked flat on the satellite map of California's Central Valley turned out to be wrinkled and cracked in unexpected ways. After an hour of stumbling in and out of ditches, getting tangled in old fences, and constantly stepping on jagged rocks, Clair swore she would never complain about the seat of an electrobike again.

The only consolation was the starscape above, which was brighter and more brilliant than any she had ever seen before. There was no moon to diminish the spectacle. Whenever she felt hungry or thirsty or footsore or weary, all she had to do was look up and her problems would disappear for an instant. Then she would be back to remembering that she was *walking* in an age of near-instantaneous, pollution-free global transport and being chased by murderers who could apparently do the impossible. . . .

The way became hillier. She and Jesse argued about whether it was better to travel on the ridges, skirt the sides, or follow the dry creek beds they came across. The creeks were safer, but they curved in unpredictable ways and were often clogged with debris.

"I seriously need to rest," Clair said, swigging down the last of the water in her bottle. "Can't we stop for a minute?"

"No," he said, taking her free hand and tugging her on. "Not far now."

"You said that half an hour ago."

"I did. But what does 'far' mean? Aren't all locations the same to you, d-mat girl? All you need is a booth at either end, and you're practically there."

She let go of his hand and went to snark back at him, then recognized his intent for what it was. He was trying to distract her, not insult her.

A memory came to her from her childhood. She and her parents had been on a day trip somewhere in Central America, wandering around ancient stone pyramids that she could barely remember now. Clair had been young enough to have a favorite toy she didn't want to be parted from, a bright-red stuffed clown with limp, raglike limbs, called Charlie. She had, however, been old enough to be embarrassed by it, so she had tucked up under her shirt where no one would see it.

Charlie had slipped free just as she and her mother had headed home, and Clair didn't notice the loss until the door of the d-mat booth had been sliding shut. She remembered panicking and wriggling free of her mother's grip to duck through the closing door. She had reached down to pick up Charlie from the sidewalk and clutch him tightly to her chest.

Then she turned to find the d-mat booth closed and both her parents gone.

Clair didn't recall any kind of hysterical fit, not like Allison told it, but she had banged on the doors, begging for her parents' return. "It takes time," said an old lady who had noticed her predicament. "You have to let the machines do their work." But Clair didn't want to wait. She didn't want the old lady, either. She wanted her parents back *now*.

And of course, they *had* come back, bursting out of a neighboring booth just soon as they had been able to make the return trip. They had scooped her up and told her that she had been very silly because didn't she know that they could have just fabbed her a new clown anytime she wanted? And she remembered the complex puzzlement she had felt in that moment—at her parents for not real-izing that a new clown couldn't *possibly* be the same as her old clown and at herself for not suspecting that this clown was indeed probably one of many and might have been replaced many times without her knowing it.

That had been the beginning of the end of her love affair with Charlie.

It was also the first occasion she could recall thinking about the time it took to d-mat from one point to another. In the booth, time didn't seem to pass at all.

Never had she stopped to wonder about the spaces involved either. They were irrelevant.

Not irrelevant anymore, unfortunately.

"Screw geography," she said. "Carry me."

"Not for all the tea in China."

"Whatever that means."

"China is where tea came from before people could fab it anytime they wanted."

"That doesn't make sense," she said. "Why only grow it in one spot? You'd have to freight it everywhere, which must've taken ages without d-mat."

"It did."

"So why not drink something else that grows near where you live?"

"Beats me," he said. "I guess that's what led to the Water Wars."

They tramped on for another minute, skirting the edge

of a tiny, dried-up pond. The rib cage of some large animal, a horse or a cow, stuck out of the caked soil like bony fingers cupping long-lost treasure.

"So much for never doing anything," Jesse said.

"What?"

"You know: the story of my life. Sitting around thinking. Well, check me out. It's like being in a book! This is the part where the heroes are slogging on through the dark, refusing to give up because there's something horrible coming up behind them."

Clair didn't feel anywhere near as excited about this as Jesse sounded.

"You like books?" she said.

"Love them." He glanced at her, the whites of his eyes bright in the starlight. "*Heart of Darkness, The Lord of the Rings, Master and Commander, On the Road* . . . I've got a collection of old print editions at home. Dad gives me one every birthday."

He caught himself.

"I mean, I *had* them at home. He *used to* give me one."

She thought of the old books she hung out with in the library at school.

"Screw adventures, too," she said, "and screw slogging through the dark. I'd give anything to be home in bed, plugged back into the Air and reading something good."

"Agreed, with all my heart."

This time the silence felt even deeper.

"Actually," he said, "what I really want is Dad back."

"Yeah."

"And you probably feel the same way about Zep."

Her heart hitched a little. "*He* would've carried me . . . if Libby hadn't been around."

"Can I ask you about him?"

"I . . . guess."

"You told Aunt Arabelle that Zep was just a friend, but he looked like more than that to me."

She didn't answer immediately.

"You don't have to talk about it if you don't want to. I'm just trying to pass the time."

"It's okay," she said. "If you want to know, I'll tell you."

"Only . . . I thought he was going out with Libby."

"He was. But he liked me, too."

"Oh. Did you like him back?"

"Don't say it like that. I never wanted to. I just did, and there was no way to stop it. I *wanted* to stop it, of course, but . . ."

"I get it," he said. "It was complicated."

She nodded, unsure whether it would be easier or harder now that everything that had seemed so momentous and world-shattering just hours ago was ended forever. The certainty of Zep's death was undeniable, but sometimes it still felt surreal, like something that had happened to someone else. She wondered how long it would take to fully sink in.

"What about you?" she asked Jesse in turn. Anything to change the subject. "What's your love life like?"

He might have blushed. It was hard to tell by starlight.

"Love life? *What* love life? I can't date at school because everyone thinks I'm a freak. I could hook up with someone via the Air, but what would be the point when everyone lives so far apart? And the girls I've met through WHOLE have been . . . predictably intense. So nothing at all, I'm afraid."

"You wouldn't use d-mat even to get lucky?" she asked.

"Not even. We Stainer boys are made of sterner stuff than that."

"No point dreaming of what you can't have, I guess."

"Exactly."

She wished she had told herself that when Zep had been nothing but a dream, a *safe* dream because he was unavailable. She'd had crushes before that had never gone anywhere. If Zep had stayed one of them, none of this would have happened. She would be asleep in her bed in Maine, not staring down in the vain hope of telling the difference between rocks and pitfalls in a night so dark she could hardly see her feet. . . .

"Do you hear that, Clair?"

Jesse had stopped in his tracks, and she stumbled to a halt next to him.

"A bike or something," she said, thinking of their ruthless pursuers. "Coming this way."

"Is it Q?"

"I don't know. Let's not take any chances."

They took shelter behind a boulder overlooking a low crack in the ground. There they waited, Clair's palm sweaty on the pistol grip. Would the vehicle go past them or stop? Would it be Q or "Dylan Linwood"? Had their long flight been for nothing?

The engine noise grew steadily louder and then ebbed into a low whirr. Stones ground under wheels as the vehicle came to a halt on the other side of the boulder.

"Clair?" came a loud voice out of the darkness. "I know you're nearby, but I can't locate you precisely. Sorry it's taken me so long. This whole area is under intense scrutiny. I'm lucky I could get in at all."

Clair sagged with relief.

"It's okay," she told Jesse. "That's our ride."

"That's Q? Really?"

"I know she sounds young, but let's not look a gift horse in the mouth." She poked him lightly on the shoulder. "You know what *that* phrase means, don't you?"

She climbed out of the crack in the ground before he could answer. Twenty yards away sat a squat moon buggy of a thing, little more than a frame with four balloon wheels capable of collapsing to fit inside a d-mat booth, then expanding out to seat two. It had a sprinkling of antennae protruding from the rear bench and a small dish pointing skyward. A pair of tiny cameras mounted at the front swiveled to face her, locked on.

"Don't reply via the Air," said Q through a speaker somewhere on the buggy. "I have established a secure maser link with the quadricycle. No one can detect it unless they're standing directly in the beam."

"You can hear me like this?" Clair asked, speaking aloud as she came closer.

"Perfectly well, Clair."

"I could kiss you, Q. Hell, I could kiss *this* thing, whatever it is."

Jesse approached more warily. "Hello?"

"Jesse Linwood, I presume," said Q with a new formality. "I'm pleased to make your acquaintance."

"Same, I guess."

Clair took off her backpack and helmet and threw them into the space between the seats, then climbed gratefully aboard. The flimsy-looking sides barely flexed under her weight.

"I don't suppose you thought to pack any supplies."

"It didn't occur to me, Clair. I'm sorry. I'll take you past the booth in Copperopolis, if you like."

"All right," she said. "But let's not hang there too long. We're running behind as it is. Jesse? Are you getting on or what?"

He was examining the underside of the frame. "Yes. It's just . . . a nice design. Reminds me of one of the old Mars rovers. Good choice, Q."

"Thanks, Jesse." The voice over the speakers relaxed slightly. "Would you like to drive?"

"If that's okay with you, sure!"

A hatch opened in front of the vacant seat, and a delicate-looking steering system unfolded. It looked like a retro game controller, but with fewer buttons.

"Cool," he said, finally getting into his seat. He tested the joystick. Beneath them, the buggy stirred. He nodded, pushed the joystick forward. The wheels spun, kicking up gravel. Clair let herself be pressed back into the seat, hoping the long, awkward night would soon be over.

——————————————— [37]

THE RIDE WAS too bouncy to be called truly comfortable, although it seemed so after the long walk. Clair offered a weak cheer when they reached the empty roads of Copperopolis. The map in her lenses checked off a series of oddly named streets as they flew by: Knolls Drive, Sugar Loaf Court, Little John Road, Charmstone Way. They sounded like something from a fairy tale, but there was nothing remotely fairyish about the arid, abandoned lots. She imagined dark eyes staring at her through all the broken windows.

According to the map, decoy airships were still drifting all over the state of California. Three were stationary. One of those—the real deal—was at the Maury Rasmussen airfield. She took hope from the fact that it had arrived safely. Furthermore, it hadn't left yet. She and Jesse were still in the race.

"Are we going to make it?" he asked.

"Don't jinx us by asking that," she said, feeling the steady churn in her gut as she thought about what might happen if they didn't. "What comes after we get away in the airship? Have you thought about that?"

He shook his head. "Have you?"

"Well, I'm not joining WHOLE and becoming a social outcast . . . uh, no offense."

"None taken."

"I just want to save Libby somehow, which means finding a way to reverse the effects of Improvement."

"In four days?"

"Why not? *Someone* can do this: we just need to find out what they know. It'll be easier working backward, surely."

"I can help with that," said Q brightly.

"It strikes me," said Jesse, "that there's only one group that stands to look bad if word of this gets out. That's VIA. I mean, say Improvement's really real, and duping is real too, then that proves what a shitty job they're doing, keeping people like you safe. But how does it work if VIA's as bad as Gemma thinks?"

"They can't be," Clair said. "If it *was* VIA, there wouldn't be death squads chasing after us now. I'd have been erased the first time I used d-mat, and the rest of you would be crushed under a million peacekeepers. VIA is too powerful. So it has to be someone working *around* VIA . . . and you're right: VIA won't like that at all. All I'd have to do is get them on our side, and I'd have the biggest ally imaginable. But how would I do that? Who would I talk to?"

"You could start at the top," Jesse said. Clair couldn't tell if he was joking or not.

"Q, who's in charge of VIA?" she asked.

"Head of operations is Ant Wallace," came the instant reply. "His office is in New York City."

Images flickered across Clair's lenses as Q supplemented her words with stills and text. Anthony Reinhold Wallace was a man of medium height and medium build, with a pleasantly symmetrical face and lightly graying hair. VIA itself occupied One Penn Plaza, a skyscraper on the west shoreline of the main island of Manhattan.

Clair felt a giddy feeling, as though she were back on the roof of the Phoenix Observatory, staring into an abyss. She thought *That's a really long way to go* for the first time in her life. And if she couldn't get the dupes off her tail, they would be behind her every step.

"There must be an easier way," she said.

"You'll think of something," Jesse said with a confidence she knew wasn't earned.

"Or Turner Goldsmith will, *if* we make it to the airship . . ."

"Don't jinx us, Clair, remember?"

Jesse took the corners fast, lifting two wheels off the ground. Clair clung to the sides of her seat, liking this mode of travel even less than the electrobike, but at least she wasn't walking anymore. On Copperopolis's main street, next to an old saloon that looked like something out of the Wild West, they found the town's only d-mat booth. Its door slid open as they approached, revealing a box much like the one Q had sent Clair in Manteca. This one was addressed to Isabella Charlotte Tremblay but opened at her palm print. Inside were sandwiches, some water, and a fully loaded pistol that was superficially identical to the one in her pocket. Clair swapped sidearms so the one she had couldn't be matched against the bullets fired in Manteca, sealed the box, put it in the booth for recycling, and returned to the buggy.

Today is Friday, she thought. *I'm supposed to be doing chores and then hanging out with Ronnie, Tash, and Libby. How did I end up here?*

"Do you think there's a toilet?" she asked.

"Maybe round the back," Jesse said, taking a sandwich, staring at it skeptically, and fishing out the meaty bits he wouldn't eat whether they were fabbed or not.

"Save the meat for me. I'm starving."

The old saloon had a rear light that flicked on as she came around the corner. It revealed a chemical toilet with a door that opened onto the empty landscape. She used it as quickly as she could, holding her breath from the smell creeping up the pipe.

Coming back around the saloon, she heard voices.

"Never trusted that thing," someone was saying in a low, querulous voice. "They put it here in exchange for free power. I know it comes from the satellites now, but you still need wires to get it around on the ground, they said. Either that or move. It's for emergencies, but who's going to have an emergency out here? The last group to come by were balloonists. If they have an emergency, they're dead. Am I right?"

"You're right," said Jesse with a small laugh. "How long have you lived here?"

"Since I was a boy, and I ain't going anywhere now."

"No one's making you. We're just passing through."

Jesse didn't sound overly worried, so Clair walked around the corner and into view. Jesse was leaning against the buggy, the last of his sandwich in one hand, eyes hidden in the shade of his shaggy bangs. In front of him, facing away from the saloon and lit by a single globe under the veranda roof that hadn't been on before, was an old guy, weathered and faded by the sun. His eyes were so gray they were almost transparent. He looked about a hundred. Clair thought he was probably no more than seventy, just old enough to remember life before the powersats.

She cleared her throat. He turned.

"Ah, here's the pretty one," he said with a yellow-toothed smile, extending his hand. "Jayden Beaumont, proprietor of the Old Corner Saloon."

"Clair Hill. Sorry if we woke you, Mr. Beaumont."

His grip was strong. "Call me Jay. And no need to apologize. I don't sleep so well these days. Tumbleweeds in Telegraph City, I hear them."

He let her go and she stepped away. He smelled stale, like the survivor of a fifty-year bender, and was wearing a thin silk dressing gown and slippers that had seen better decades. Bony, angular knees poked at the inside of the gown. She couldn't tell if he was wearing anything under there. Didn't want to know.

"You two need a bed for the night?" he asked them. "It's not too late to throw something together. Breakfast included, free of charge."

"No thanks," said Clair quickly, wondering if he grew his own food and cooked it or used a fabber. "You get many people out here?"

He scratched at his scalp. "Some. Student geologists, the odd surveyor, historians, hobbyists. Is that what you two are? On some kind of school trip, perhaps?"

"That's it," she said, leaping on the idea. "A treasure hunt, actually. If you see someone else tonight, don't tell them we were here."

He tapped his nose. "Gotcha."

"Well, I guess we'd better move on," she said. "Don't want to fall too far behind. Thanks for letting me use your bathroom."

He smiled almost sadly and said, "Sure, honey."

With one hand, he reached under his dressing gown and pulled out a shotgun. He pumped the action and pointed it at stomach height, midway between Jesse and Clair.

They froze.

———————————————— [38]

KNEES, THOUGHT CLAIR, wanting to howl at her stupidity. No one had knees *that* bony.

"What do you want?" she asked, holding up her hands.

"We've got nothing, Jay," said Jesse. "Don't do this to us."

"It's not about you," he said. The smile was gone now. He was determined, but he didn't look happy about it. "I lied. The last people through here weren't balloonists. I had some other visitors tonight. They came out of this thing." He cocked his head at the booth behind him. "They said to keep an eye out for people using the roads. I'm supposed to let them know if I see anyone."

"*Did* you let them know?" asked Clair.

"They told me you were terrorists. I saw you fiddling with the booth. I may not approve of it, but it's the only thing this place has going for it. You blow it up, and I might as well go out back and dig my grave."

"*Did you let them know, Jay?*"

His watery gaze darted from her to Jesse and back again. "I did what I had to."

Clair cursed silently to herself. *This is what happens when you let your guard down,* a voice whispered in her mind. The pistol was in the buggy, out of reach. The old man was too far away to risk rushing him. There was only one thing she could do.

She opened a connection to the Air.

"Q, we're in trouble, and we need your help."

"I am monitoring your situation by the sensors in the quadricycle, Clair. What can I do?"

"We need a distraction," she said. "Anything. Use the buggy or the booth. Whatever it takes."

"I have a thought. You said—"

"I don't care what, Q. Just get us away from him."

Q didn't answer, and after a moment the light on the door of the booth switched from green to red. In use.

"Is the gun really necessary?" asked Jesse.

"They told me to keep you here any way I could."

"You couldn't come up with anything better?"

"I offered you free breakfast. What else was I supposed to do? An old guy like me's no match for you fancy kids."

"We *are* kids, Jay." Jesse edged minutely away from Clair. "What kind of terrorists do you think we'd make?"

Jay stepped back, decreasing the angle required to fire at either one of them. "Don't try anything, boy. I'm no fool. This place used to jump in its day. Come back here, into the light." He gestured with the barrel of the shotgun, swinging them around onto the creaking wooden porch.

[253]

As they moved, he moved too, keeping a constant distance between them until he was standing where they had been. He could see the booth now, and they couldn't. He noticed the red light instantly, indicated it with his bristly chin.

"That'll be them now, coming to arrest you. Shouldn't take long. I won't need to hog-tie you or anything undignified."

"Doesn't matter if you tie us up or not, Jay," Clair said. "They'll kill us all the same, and it'll be your fault."

"Kill you? Don't be absurd. There's no death penalty anymore, not even for terrorists."

"We keep telling you," said Jesse in frustration. "We're not terrorists, and if you think they're peacekeepers, you're fooling yourself."

He shrugged. "I don't know them from Adam, boy, but they weren't here fiddling with my booth like you were. Or covered in blood, pretty girl, that's obviously not yours."

"It will be soon."

He shifted his feet. "I need d-mat, see? Without it, I've got nothing. Nothing at all."

The booth behind them finished doing whatever it did inside its mirrored walls. Clair heard the hiss of air pressure equalizing and the smooth glide of the door swinging open.

"Thank you, Mr. Beaumont," said a woman's voice. "I have them now."

The words almost took Clair's strength away. This

wasn't the way it was supposed to go. It was supposed to be Q rescuing them, not the bad guys coming to finish them off.

But Jay's eyes were narrowing in suspicion. "I don't know you," he said. "You weren't here before."

Clair half turned, and froze to hide her surprise.

Beside her Jesse literally gasped.

"You don't need to know me, Mr. Beaumont," said the young woman standing in front of the booth. She was wearing dark, practical clothes similar to Clair's and holding a pistol that could have been the one Clair had just recycled. In every other respect, however, she was the exact opposite of Clair.

It was Libby. The only thing missing was her birthmark. But where had she come from?

"All that matters is that you've done as you were instructed," Libby said. "Now it's time for me to take over."

"What's going to happen to them?" Jay was hesitating. His shotgun hovered in no-man's-land, between his prisoners and the young stranger who had come to deal with them.

"Go back inside the saloon, please, Mr. Beaumont," Libby said, moving one step closer to him. "You don't need to see any more."

Clair couldn't take her eyes off her. There was something odd about her, something not quite right. Something more than the missing birthmark.

Jay nervously licked his lips. "Just don't do it here," he said. "Don't do anything to them on my porch."

He lowered the shotgun and went inside, brushing within arm's reach of Clair as he did so. His eyes stared fixedly at the ground.

The door shut and locked behind him with a terminal click.

Jesse's hands came down.

"Libby?" he said. "What are you doing here?"

Libby waved him quiet with the pistol. She was watching the saloon intently.

"I don't think he heard," she said. Her demeanor relaxed, and her voice changed too. Clearly she had been acting before, playing the role she needed to play. But instead of becoming Libby as Clair knew her, she became someone else.

"Get in the buggy, both of you, and get out of here. I'm not sure how much longer I can keep this up."

"Q?" said Clair, feeling as though she had been sucker punched in the gut. "Is that you?"

"You guessed! I wasn't sure if you would." She clapped her hands, but then stumbled and steadied herself against the porch. "Oh, you really need to get moving. 'Dylan Linwood' left Columbia five minutes ago. He's d-matting to the San Andreas Memorial as we speak, and that's only two and a half miles from the rendezvous. If you don't move quickly, he will get there before you. Clair, are you listening?"

Q approached and Clair physically recoiled. She was Libby, but she wasn't. It wasn't *right*.

"How did you do this?" asked Jesse, staring in amazement and shock. "You made Libby a dupe!"

"Not really . . . it's hard to explain." Q turned to address him, tangling her feet in the process. "Please, Jesse. The longer I stay here, the less control I have over the situation. You must leave immediately while I use the booth to go back to the way I was."

"Get out of her body," said Clair. "Please get out of her body."

"I will," said Q, "as soon as you're gone. I promise."

Q approached with one hand outstretched. The hand was shaking as though with palsy.

"Get out of her body!"

The horror in her voice shocked even Clair. Q backed away, counterfeit face crumpling in dismay.

"Come on, Clair," said Jesse, taking her by the shoulders. "She's right. This can't hold us up. We need to get in the buggy and get the hell out of here, right now."

Clair didn't disagree. She didn't agree, either, but she did allow herself to be led away. The buggy was ready to go, humming impatiently to itself, the sandwich Q had made for her still resting on the seat. Clair pitched it as far from her as she could. She felt sick to the stomach. Sick to her very heart.

Q had put her own mind into Libby's body.

So where was Libby now?

Jesse got in and put the buggy into motion. It accelerated hard up Main Street, heading for Route 4. Clair looked behind her just once, at the figure standing alone under the porch light. It turned and walked into the booth. Vanished.

$$[39]$$

CLAIR LEANED FORWARD and ground her palms into her eyes. The bouncing of the buggy and the whipping of the wind weren't helping her nausea.

"I know what you're thinking," said Jesse. "You're thinking that we have proof now. Proof of everything, thanks to Q. The dupes are real, and so is everything else Gemma—"

"Shut up." It was true. That was exactly what she was thinking, and it wasn't remotely a happy thought. *The clock is ticking*, Gemma had said. How many days did Libby have left, exactly?

We have proof now.

When had they become a *we*, Clair wondered.

An intersection came into view ahead. Jesse slowed them to a crawl.

"Which way, Clair?"

"You decide."

"That's your job, remember? We had an agreement. You navigate; I'll drive."

She forced herself not to dwell on what she'd just seen.

Think of the roads, the map. A puzzle can't hurt anyone . . . and if we're not going to make the airship, we might as well turn around right now and let the old man take us prisoner again.

Her original intention had been to take the most comfortable but now much less direct route to the airfield through a place called Angels Camp. There was an alternative, a more direct course that brought them close to the rear of the airfield. It was less than twelve miles by road, with a short overland leg at the end.

She weighed up the two routes in her mind. Fear made thinking easier. Fear of being left behind, of being stuck in the wilderness forever, of being shot, ultimately, and of losing the real Libby forever.

Comfort was no longer an option.

"North," she said. "Route 4 for three miles, then take the left up Pool Station Road. Don't stop until I tell you."

"Okay," he said. "Time to really put the pedal to the metal."

That one she didn't understand, but its meaning became clear as the buggy's engine jumped an octave in pitch and their speed rapidly increased.

The helmet rocked at her side, nudging her hip. There hadn't been so much as a squawk from the open channel since they had left Tulloch Dam, and according to the map the airship hadn't moved. Figuring their position was largely blown already, she slipped the helmet over her head and selected the open channel.

"Got held up," she said. "Expect company."

"Understood" came the brief reply—Ray's voice—then silence fell again.

Clair slipped off the helmet and sat for a moment, exhausted. She had decided which way to go in the short term. She was helpless now to do anything other than wait for the consequences.

"Moon's rising, which means dawn's on its way," Jesse said, indicating the thin sliver creeping over the rumpled horizon to their right. "I'm worried we're going to run out of time. They won't keep the airship anywhere near the ground during the day, when it's most vulnerable."

Clair could do nothing to reassure him. Their vulnerability was gnawing at her as much as the airship's. Not to mention Libby's vulnerability.

"How does duping *work*?" she asked. "I mean, how can you put yourself into someone's *head*?"

Jesse glanced at her, then back to the road. "Are you asking me or Q?"

"I don't know. You." Q was silent, for which Clair was grateful. "I mean, first you have to copy someone's pattern, and then you have to *change* it, and then put it back into the system. How is that possible?"

"Did you see how her hand was shaking?" Jesse asked her. "It was fine when she came out of the booth, but it got worse really fast. It looked like nerve damage. . . ."

"Seven days," Jesse went on when she didn't sat anything. "That's how long Gemma said Libby had. Maybe duping isn't permanent because the minds and bodies don't match. Maybe it's the same with Improvement."

"People change themselves so much, their minds and bodies didn't match anymore, it drives them insane, and they kill themselves? *Jesus.*"

Clair couldn't believe Jesse was taking it so calmly. Wasn't he, the Stainer, supposed to be more outraged about this kind of thing than she was?

The speakers came to life. "Clair, are you there? I'm back now, and I'm sorry if I made a mistake. I was just trying to—"

Clair found the OFF button. Instantly, a patch appeared in her lenses. She switched them off too and sat still and silent in the rushing darkness.

The road forked. She gave Jesse directions from memory, without needing her lenses. Around them, the landscape became hillier. They were right on the edge of the Central Valley now. If they went much farther east, they'd hit the mountains, and the going would become really rough.

"Look for a bridge," she said. "Just past it, that's where we're leaving the road."

"Right." He twisted the controls to avoid the out-stretched branches of a fallen tree. The road snaked a third of a mile, then straightened. They were in the homestretch.

Clair gulped as Jesse locked all four wheels and sent the buggy into a skid. She braced herself for impact, but there was no sign of anything on the road ahead. Nothing at all. The bridge had fallen in.

The buggy jerked to a halt two yards from the creek. She could see slabs of concrete where the bridge had once been anchored to the shore. Jesse switched off the buggy and left it sitting in the middle of the road while they climbed out and jogged to inspect the creek. It was shallow, but the sides were steep and slippery toward the bottom, where the buggy was certain to become stuck. Clair retreated to get her pack, and they leaned on each other for balance until they felt smooth stones underfoot and rushing water over their feet. Instantly, Clair's shoes were soaked. The cold was as piercing and as bracing as her fear of being late.

The other side of the creek was lightly wooded, and they slipped gratefully under the cover of the trees, squelching as quietly as they could.

"No, *this* way," she said, turning Jesse around and pointing northeast. They ran straight across the country-side without concern for anything other than what would be waiting for them when they arrived. They ran until they hit a ridge, and then they walked. From the top of the ridge they could barely make out a long gray oblong that might have been a landing strip and possibly a clutch of old buildings. In the misty predawn light, the airship wasn't visible.

It'll be there. She told herself to focus on what was waiting for them inside it. Turner Goldsmith, the leader of WHOLE, would have answers. He would whisk them away from the assassins in the dark and tell them what to do next. She wasn't expecting a knight on a charger like something from a fairy tale—but he was a grown-up who presumably knew what he was doing. He would help them like he had helped others in the past.

They ran down the other side of the ridge and approached a steeper, stonier rise with more caution, wary of turning an ankle. In the hush before sunrise, every footstep sounded deafening.

At the top of the rise were two runways connected by taxiways at both ends. All but one of buildings was abandoned and weatherworn. To the right of those two were spaces that might have been for light planes or automobiles. Parked haphazardly across those wide, empty spaces were three electrobikes.

There was no sign at all of their riders or the airship.

Clair stopped dead on the asphalt and looked around. The light was brighter now. Everything was still and silent and empty. No engine noise. No voices. No giant airships hanging in the sky.

"They left without us," said Jesse.

—————————————————— [40]

THE HOPELESSNESS IN his voice broke her heart. Clair took his hand and squeezed his cold fingers. It wasn't his fault they had been slow. If they had been any less careful, they might have ended up like Arabelle, Cashile, and Theo. She and Jesse had done their best to keep the others in the loop, and what had WHOLE done in return? They had left without so much as a good-bye. Forget Turner Goldsmith and explanations. Forget help. At the very least, Gemma could have told them not to bother, sparing Jesse and Clair a futile end to their long and exhausting trek.

She blamed herself. If she hadn't switched off her lenses in abhorrence at Q's actions, she would have known. She would have seen the airship moving on the map and directed the buggy accordingly.

"It's not over yet," she said, trying to find some hope to cling to. Any would do. "They left the bikes. We can use them. They'll be faster than the buggy thing."

"You can't drive," said Jesse.

"I'll learn. You can teach me."

"Where would we go?"

"I don't know. Somewhere a long way from here, for starters."

Maine, she thought, tugging him toward the bikes and turning her lenses back on as she went.

The first thing she saw was a red dot right in front of her.

Then a dark figure rose up from behind the bikes and trained a pistol on the center of her chest.

"Stop right there."

She obeyed, but not because of the order. She stopped because she had heard that voice giving her orders before. Not *exactly* the same voice. This time, there was a hint of another accent—British, perhaps. But even under starlight there was no mistaking the face.

It belonged to Dylan Linwood. Only he wasn't wearing it anymore.

Jesse was two paces behind her. He stopped too, then came forward one hesitant step.

The pistol shifted left and down. A single shot cracked into the asphalt at Jesse's feet. He jumped.

"No closer. Clair, I know you're armed. Put the gun down where I can see it. Don't try anything, or I'll shoot you in the leg."

"You're going to kill us anyway," she said.

"Not until you tell us where the others have gone. The gun, Clair, or I'll call your parents. Would you like that? Would you like me to pay them another visit?"

"No." She slipped off the backpack and dropped it to the

ground. The gun she pulled from her pocket and skidded across the ground toward him. With it went her last hope.

She refused to think of the dupe as Dylan Linwood. She knew what he really was now. He *was* a duplicate, but not an exact duplicate. He was like Libby in Copperopolis—an exact copy of Dylan Linwood with another person inside his head. He was the puppet master hidden within the puppet.

"Who are you?" Jesse asked, and she could tell from his voice that he was experiencing every emotion she had on seeing Q in Copperopolis.

"Move over with your girlfriend."

He didn't move. "She'd never be my girlfriend. If you were my father, you'd know that."

Clair joined Jesse before he could be shot for disobeying, and the dupe came out from behind the bike, picking up her gun on the way. Behind him, the sky was slowly lightening. In the pale predawn wash, Clair made out the bruise on his forehead and the reddened eye, exactly as they had been the previous day.

"We know what you are," she said.

"Don't talk," said the dupe, "unless it's to tell me about your friends in WHOLE."

"What friends?" said Jesse bitterly. "We don't know where they've gone."

"That's a lie. Tell me the truth."

"Or what? You've already taken everything from me."

"What about *her*?"

The pistol shifted to point at Clair. Complex shapes danced in his lenses. Orders? Map data? Clair couldn't tell.

"Who are you?" asked Jesse again, rage and fear quivering in his voice.

Make something up, Clair told herself. *Got to try something.*

"They went north," she said, "to Seattle."

"That's a lie," the dupe said. "There's been no air traffic in that direction."

That was interesting. No traffic meant the airship hadn't moved. But if the airship hadn't moved, that meant . . .

Clair took her eyes briefly off the fake Dylan Linwood and studied the vista behind him. Something was moving against the backdrop of hills, all outline and no detail, visible because of the way the colors didn't quite match. The patch was almost perfectly circular, and there was no way to tell how far away it was, but it was between the airfield and the hills, swinging northward and getting larger. It was already the size of a full moon. How many seconds until the sound of its engines were audible over the rising dawn chorus?

"Let's make a deal," she said, thinking faster than she ever had before. "You tell me who you work for, and I'll tell you where the airship is."

"No deals," he said. "Tell me now, or I'll shoot one of you at random."

"But we don't *know*," protested Jesse.

"The longer you stall, the longer I'll keep you alive after."

"I'm not stalling," said Clair. "I just want you to give me something in return. Why don't you tell me your name, at least?"

"No." His one red eye glared balefully.

In her lenses, an emergency patch appeared. She clicked it, hardly daring to hope.

"Gemma Mallapur says to get ready," whispered Q in her ear. "We need you to stall for ten seconds."

To the dupe, Clair said, "What are you afraid of?"

"I'm not afraid of anything," he said, pointing the gun at her chest.

"Sure you are. It can't be easy, living in someone else's body."

"Easier than you think."

Inspiration struck her. *Seven days.* "But it isn't permanent, is it? How many times have you died? How many times has someone like me killed you? How many bodies have you lived in now?"

His borrowed eyes widened slightly.

"Three seconds," said Q.

"No, wait," she bumped back. "I think I'm getting through to him."

"Two."

Clair took Jesse's arm as though for solidarity.

"Come on," she said. "Tell me who you *were*."

The dupe straightened.

"I am nobody."

His finger tightened on the trigger, and Clair braced herself.

"Get down now, Clair," said Q.

She dropped and pulled Jesse to the asphalt with her. The agent jerked as though shoved in the back. Red mist burst out of a sudden hole in his chest. A split second later, the sound of the shot reached them, followed by another shot from much closer at hand. The dupe's finger had squeezed the trigger as he dropped. The slug that might have killed Clair whined harmlessly off the asphalt. Two more shots in rapid succession whizzed over their heads before the sharpshooter in the airship realized that the job was done.

The dupe went down and stayed down.

Jesse was moving before she could grab him. He threw himself at the fallen body and pounded its bloody chest.

"Who are you?" he screamed. "Who are you?"

[41]

CLAIR RAN AFTER him and kicked the dupe's pistol away. "Dylan Linwood's" battered face was turned as though to stare at her, but all his eyes contained were empty, unseen data. Anyone could be watching.

She put a hand over the body's face and closed the

eyelids. Bright blue and blood red: she was glad to be rid of that terrible gaze.

Now she could definitely hear the airship's engines whining and whirring as the craft came in to land.

Clair pulled Jesse away from the body.

"Why did they do this to him?" he asked, his voice thick with tears. "Who are they?"

The airship rose hugely over them, and Clair gaped up at it, amazed by how big it was. Easily a hundred yards across, it had a wide, two-story upper deck and a docking station on the lowest tip, connected by a narrow shaft so it looked like a fat, inverted teardrop hanging in the dawn sky. Three smaller, egg-shaped dirigibles clung to the docking station, rocking in the breeze. At close range, the airship's camouflage lost much of its efficacy, and she could make out propellers whirring on the half-seen underside, guiding it to a safe landing. The downwash flattened her hair across her scalp and whipped Jesse's mop from side to side.

He looked up from his father's body and gripped Clair's arm.

"It's a Skylifter!" he said, wiping his eyes with his free hand.

She checked the Air in case that detail was significant. Skylifters were antiques left over from the days when people still hauled freight from one place to another but said they were worried about carbon emissions. The Air didn't mention anything about WHOLE.

A patch winked in her eye. She answered it.

"I hope I did the right thing this time, Clair," said Q.

Clair didn't know what to say. She had been stupid, and that had almost got her and Jesse killed.

"You did," she said, "but we've got a lot to talk about, Q. About Libby and the dupes."

"Yes, Clair. I will tell you all I can, when I can. I promise."

The airship touched down. A hatch opened. Ray and a man she hadn't seen before stepped out of the interior and loped toward her.

"You two get aboard," Ray told them. "We'll bring the body."

Clair hesitated, wondering if they realized it really wasn't Dylan Linwood. Then she understood. *Evidence.*

How long until another version of him stepped out of a booth in San Andreas, or Copperopolis, or anywhere else she tried to hide?

"Come on," she said, taking Jesse's hand as he had taken hers outside Copperopolis. The airship had impressed her and restored her hope. "It's time to get some answers."

[42]

THE ELEVATOR WAS easily large enough for all of them, with a second shaft surrounding it, containing a spiral staircase. Clair fidgeted as the cage lifted them to the top of the Skylifter. She didn't know what to expect of either Turner Goldsmith or the airship's interior. The latter was swaying ponderously beneath her in a not entirely unpleasant way. Taking off again, she assumed. The deep thrumming of propellers was distant but ever present, like giant bees were buoying them up into the sky.

When the elevator door opened, Clair found herself in a D-shaped chamber that spanned fifteen yards down the straight side. The curved side to her left was all window, letting in the sky. Apart from that spectacular feature, the interior of the Skylifter was unassuming. The semicircular space at the top of the elevator was part meeting hall, part mess hall. Clair could smell stale coffee, and her mouth watered. There were two doors leading through the interior wall, which was decorated with paintings of landscapes and, incongruously, childish sketches in primary colors. Large, hand-embroidered cushions sprawled on a brown-carpeted floor.

Five people looked up as they walked in. The only one Clair recognized was Gemma.

"If it hadn't been for your friend Q, we'd have given up on you," Gemma said. Her cheeks were flushed, but the rest of her was as white as bone, and she moved her shoulder as though bearing a great burden. She nodded at Ray, who had come up the elevator with them. "Where is it?"

Ray hooked a thumb at where the body rested under a tarp.

"Bring it through. If we're quick, we might hack into the lens feed. Be careful, though. The body could be booby-trapped."

Clair hadn't considered that possibility. From the sharp downturn of Jesse's mouth, she guessed he hadn't either.

"Which one of you is Turner Goldsmith?" Clair asked as the body disappeared through the right-hand door, followed by Gemma and the others.

"Turner's upstairs," said a woman in her twenties with disconcertingly mismatched eyes—one blue, the other green. "He'll call when he's ready. I'll show you where you can freshen up."

"Right now, I don't care about freshening up," Clair said.

"It's through here." The young woman ignored her protests, opening the other door and showing Clair and Jesse a toilet area. There were four cubicles crammed around two tiny basins. "Go easy on the water, but help yourself to soap."

Clair started to argue. They hadn't raced all night to get to the airship, dodging dupes every step of the way, only to be left on the bench like they didn't even matter.

"I'll be back when Turner sends for you," the young woman said, talking right over her and following the others through the right-hand door and shutting it firmly in her wake. The sharp click of a lock left Clair in no doubt that she wouldn't be able to follow.

Clair went to call Q, but her lenses were empty of

anything other than a simple menu broadcast by the Sky-lifter itself. The Air was jammed.

She put her hands on her hips and looked around in annoyance and disappointment. So much for Turner Goldsmith telling them what to do.

"Buffalo," said Jesse, his fingertips dancing across virtual menus.

"What?" She didn't mean to snap, but she couldn't help it.

"That's where we're headed, according to the flight plan. North until we hit the westerlies. From there, north-east over Washington, Montana, maybe into Manitoba and Ontario, then south for a landing in Buffalo."

"What's in Buffalo?" asked Clair.

"Maybe nothing. It could just be a ruse, in case anyone's watching."

"Fantastic."

"We're in a Skylifter," said Jesse, as though he still couldn't believe it. "No wonder no one ever knows where Turner is!"

Clair leaned her forehead against the sweeping plastic window, fighting tears of frustration and exhaustion. The ground below was already impossibly distant, a hazy brown plain, crinkled and dotted with faint geometric shapes still visible despite nature's reclamation of the land. The plains were bounded to the east by jagged mountains—the Sierra Nevada, muscular stone in all its brutality.

Somewhere down there, Libby was in just as much

trouble as she had ever been. And being high above it all, Clair thought, wasn't solving anything.

You'd better have answers for me, she said to herself, *or I swear, Turner Goldsmith, I'll pop your balloon and bring you down to earth myself.*

[43]

SINCE SHE HAD nothing better to do while she waited, Clair used the bathroom to freshen up and emerged feeling gritty and greasy under damp clothes she would ordinarily have recycled without a second thought. The source of the coffee smell turned out to be a well-used filtration unit behind a hatch in the wall, with a selection of mismatched mugs stained from frequent use. There was a whole miniature kitchen in there, with a small freezer and what looked like a fabber but was in fact a microwave oven. She just poured herself a coffee, adding lots of milk and sugar. Her stomach ached, but she wasn't remotely hungry.

The Air was still jammed, Q with it.

"Any word from the others?" she asked Jesse.

"Nope," he said. He was lying flat on his back in the center of the room, with his arms folded across his eyes.

She sat down next to him, needing a means of keeping her hope alive. "How well do you know these people? Can we trust them?"

"I've known some of them most of my life. Abstainer meetings are like AA meetings—everyone has a testimonial. I heard those stories over and over, but they obviously didn't tell me anything important, like who was really in WHOLE and who wasn't."

His voice was full of self-blame and irritation. Clair had moved past that. For now, she was determined to learn everything she could about their captors, in case that was indeed what they turned out to be.

"Are those testimonials secret?"

"I guess not. Are you asking?"

"Yes," she said bluntly.

He sighed. "All right. You remember Aunt Arabelle . . . ?"

"Two left feet. And Gemma: she lost her son to Improvement."

"Yes, well, I'd never heard that before. Ray's wife died in transit—just arrived dead for no reason, and they couldn't revive her. Theo, Cashile's mom, had aphasia thanks to d-mat: she could understand but couldn't speak."

"What about Turner Goldsmith?"

"I don't know what his story is. There are lots of others: someone had a son whose mind was wiped; someone else's mom died of the same cancer as George Staines. And, oh, hey, this is a good one: there's a girl who used to come to meetings with this guy she said was her brother. But he was older, way older, like thirty years or more."

"Don't tell me d-mat prematurely aged him," Clair said.

"No, it's better than that. They're actually twins. Have you heard that story about a girl who was hung up in transit . . . ?"

She gaped at him. "You want me to believe that's *real?*"

He rolled over and lifted his arms off his eyes to look at her. "Some urban legends must be based on truth, Clair. They can't *all* be lies, even if most people want them to be."

"Do *you* believe it?"

Jesse looked down at his feet. They were bare, revealing calluses she normally associated with natural-sport players like Zep. She supposed he just walked a lot. In the last two days, her blisters had developed blisters.

"I don't know," he said. "But I don't automatically *dis*believe it, not after what we've seen."

"True. I'm not sure I'd believe *our* story if someone else told it to me: Libby and Q, the dupes of your dad . . ."

He rolled away, and she let him go, understanding. It was too early to talk about that, although she desperately wanted to know the truth of it. She couldn't imagine how it must feel to see a parent die not just once, but over and over again. It was a hellish thought, too much to take in quickly.

The whole situation was too much. She had thought getting to the airship would solve all her problems, but here she was, sitting on a cushion in bright sunlight, avoiding the raw ache where Zep had been and wondering if Libby knew what had happened to him. She couldn't begin to guess how Libby might be feeling if she did. Would she blame Clair? Clair would give everything to talk to her best friend as they had talked before . . . when the only issues they'd had had to worry about were school, captions, and chores. Nothing had seemed insurmountable then.

Three days had now passed since Libby had used Improvement.

However much time she had left, it was too little to make amends, too little for everything they'd planned to do together. Too little for the lifetime they were owed. Improvement had to be stopped, no matter what.

Clair took her shoes off and put them next to Jesse's so they would dry. Then she propped herself against the window, facing inward. There was a picture of a blue cow on the wall directly opposite her with the name DAISY written underneath. Impossible to tell if Daisy was the cow or the kid who had drawn it. Clair stared at the picture, feeling the warmth of the coffee spreading through her body, radiating outward from her chest like the heat of the sun. The actual sun provided no heat at all, and the window behind her head was cold. The caffeine should have woken her up, but instead she grew sleepy. Apart from a brief nap at the dam, she hadn't slept since she had last spoken to Libby, before Improvement, the dupes, WHOLE, everything. Her head throbbed in time with the propellers.

At least she wasn't trudging over anything or holding on to anything for dear life. Moving without effort felt like the most amazing miracle in the world.

Clair's eyes drifted shut as she teased at the many problems facing her, looking for solutions that weren't there. Staying awake was hard, too hard, but she would do it if she had to, like she had done everything else.

[44]

SHE WOKE WITH a fright an unknown time later. Someone was calling her name.

"Clair? Can you hear me?"

She sat up and stared wildly about her. The voice was coming from the tubes in her ears. She knew who it was, but where she was and *why* only slowly returned to her.

"Clair? Are you all right?"

She was on the Skylifter with Jesse, abandoned by WHOLE while Turner Goldsmith remained aloof in his roost above. But she had been dreaming of Zep and Dylan Linwood's battered faces, over and over, and of her own face too, reflected in the walls of a d-mat booth, growing more and more monstrous until the versions of her at the edge of visibility looked barely human.

I'm beautiful, a voice had told her. *I'm in heaven, and I'm so beautiful.*

The images took some effort to dispel, and no wonder, she thought. She had been hunted halfway across California. She had seen people shot and killed. She lived in a world where people could take someone out of one body and put them back in another one, over and over. Nightmares were the least of her problems.

Meanwhile, the voice in her ears was still calling her name.

This voice belonged to Q.

"Yes, yes, I'm all right." Clair sat up and put the middle fingers of her right hand against a stabbing pain between her eyes. "How did you get through to me? The Skylifter is jammed, isn't it?"

"I can get anywhere that isn't Faraday shielded. The first thing I did was hack the habitat's firewalls by bypassing its usual routers and—"

"Okay, spare me the details. I failed IT in school, as you probably know. Give me a second to get my act together."

She looked around, blinking. She and Jesse were still the only people in the big semicircle. He was snoring softly, undisturbed by either her rude awakening or bad dreams of his own. There was no way to tell how long she had been asleep.

Her eyes were drawn to the view, to the perfect blue dome above and the endless sheet of white far below. The cloudscape was alien and strange. There were valleys and trenches, wide plains, and the occasional towering hill.

She automatically went to access her lens menus, to see where she was, but of course the Air wasn't available, and that frustrated her, made her feel more trapped than did locked doors and silence.

Clair stood on wobbly legs and crossed in stockinged

feet to the miniature kitchen. She supposed she should at least try to refuel in the hope of making her brain work. In the freezer, she found several single-serve portions of precooked lentil stew, and she fiddled with the microwave controls until she worked out how to set it to defrost. She felt distant from herself, not entirely there, but awake enough to solve that puzzle. While it whirred and rattled—an antique like the Skylifter itself—she filled a bottle of water and drank deeply from it, tasting metal strongly against her tongue. Her mouth was furry and dry.

The stew was boiling hot in patches, crunchy cold in others. It satisfied a need and nothing else. The details of the dreams faded as she ate and talked to Q. If Turner Goldsmith was going to ignore her, she'd get what answers she could from elsewhere.

"Okay," she said, mouthing the words but not speaking them aloud out of respect for Jesse's ongoing slumber. "Let's start with Dylan Linwood. Tell me how someone can copy him when he's supposed to be dead in Manteca. Doesn't that raise a . . . what did you call it?"

"Parity violation alarm."

"Right, one of those."

"Parity hasn't been broken because Dylan Linwood isn't listed as dead."

"What?"

Q patched a series of windows into her lenses. The Linwood home in Manteca, peacekeepers combing through the rubble. The results of detailed forensic studies. A news feeder intoning, "First responders describe the scene as a bomb site, provoking speculation that the reclusive fad artist destroyed his workshop in order to go even farther underground. No bodies have been found. His son, Jesse Linwood, has not been located for comment."

"Is someone trying to cover this up," Clair asked, "or just clean up as they go?"

"I believe it's the latter," said Q. "Municipal reports list no bodies found at the safe house, either. Spent casings, evidence of gunfire, traces of spilled blood—but no actual bodies."

"No bodies at all. Does that mean Zep isn't listed as dead either?"

"He is not, Clair, and neither are the members of WHOLE intercepted en route to the airship."

"What about Libby?"

"I have located Libby in Italy. Her caption is unchanged."

I'm beautiful.

Clair shook her head to shed the last lingering memory of the dream.

"Any mention of me?" she asked. "Am I still wanted by the peacekeepers?"

"You've been officially listed as a missing person. Your parents are calling it a kidnapping. It's causing a lot of buzz in the wake of the video Dylan Linwood posted."

Clair couldn't imagine what her parents were going

through, and it made her throat close up to think of them. Better, she told herself, to move forward in the hope of getting safely back to them.

"Okay, so Jesse's dad isn't a parity violation because he's not listed as dead. But someone's still copying him as fast as people can kill him. Like you did to Libby. She's still very much alive, according to you, and yet you created another one of her in Copperopolis. How did you do that? Did you use a private network. *Why* did you do it?"

"I'll tell you. I don't want there to be any secrets between us."

"Good. If I can understand how you do this, maybe we can understand the dupes a little better."

"That was my original intention, Clair," said Q, adopting the more grown-up voice she used when explaining. "The thing about d-mat is that it does build a new person from scratch every time someone goes through it, and in theory you *could* duplicate yourself as many times as you wanted from the pattern created. What's stopping you is the consensus that this would be ethically unacceptable. It's therefore illegal, and VIA takes this law very seriously. Their AIs were designed with this primary purpose in mind."

"The train driver and the conductor. Parity violation. I'm with you so far."

A new image appeared in Clair's lenses, a flowchart that looked horribly complicated.

"While it may seem as though I broke parity by having two versions of Libby in the world at once, that wasn't what happened at all. The real Libby had just stepped into a booth to go from New York to London. She was, therefore, officially in transit. What I did was simply divert the transfer of her pattern for a minute or two by briefly blindsiding the bus driver AI. I built a version of Libby in Copperopolis from the pattern I diverted, then once I was done with it, I uploaded the original pattern and sent it back on its way. No alarms sounded because there was technically only ever one of her in existence at a time, as a person or as a pattern. Nothing was copied. Libby appeared to arrive in London exactly as planned. The diversion doesn't appear in her history. If she noticed anything odd at all, she probably assumed she had been held up by a data jam. Nothing out of the ordinary."

Q sounded very pleased with herself, and Clair did agree that hacking the global network like that couldn't have been easy to accomplish. The moral ramifications, though, were enormous.

"But that wasn't all you did," she said. "You put *yourself* into her."

"I did. Between New York and Copperopolis, I altered the definitions the conductor AI used to check that the Libby who arrived was the Libby who left. I superimposed a new neural map over hers, modeled on mine, being careful to save hers in the process. It's complicated, and I'm not very good at it, obviously; I barely made it back into the booth before the shakes took over. Then, between Copperopolis and London, I returned Libby to exactly the state she was in before, perfectly unharmed. That's it."

"That's *it?*"

"I maintained parity and didn't hurt anyone," Q said with a hint of defensiveness and pride. "There was no reason for any kind of alarm. I didn't know I could do it until I tried. I was surprised by how easy it turned out to be."

Clair rubbed the ridge of bone behind her right ear. Q was confessing to an ability that seemed magical. Dangerously magical, enabling someone to change the very identity of a person without changing their face. Like someone watching an actual magic trick, Clair couldn't help but look for loopholes in order to make it comprehensible. And therefore stoppable.

"Let me see if I've got this straight. It's all about fooling the AIs, not actually breaking them. Changing the definitions. That's how you got the dupe off my tail that time. . . ."

"Yes, not by changing you but by redefining your pattern so you *appeared* to be someone else, someone who happened to be in transit at that exact time."

Clair was finding this head spinning, but she was determined to get it all. "And that's how there can be so many different versions of the Dylan Linwood dupes without breaking parity. It's like respawning when you die in a computer game. The conductor AI will have no qualms about reproducing his original pattern because from its point of view, no laws are being broken. There's just one of him at a time, even if there is someone else inside him. The AI doesn't know any different."

"Correct. Note that this can only happen under highly specific circumstances. Otherwise, the usual rules always apply."

"But you and the dupes can both do it. Maybe you have the same backgrounds. Could they be someone you know, Q?"

Q didn't respond immediately. When she did speak, her voice was subdued.

"There's something I haven't told you, Clair."

"What is it? What now?"

"I'm frightened to say it because you might not believe me, but I have to tell you. I think it might be important."

"Q, whatever it is, please just tell me."

"I don't know who I am," Q told her, "or where I came from."

Clair didn't know what to say in reply to that. It was so strange and improbable that there seemed no way to pick it apart.

"You have amnesia?"

"No," said Q. "I have memories. But before a certain point they don't belong to me. They don't feel like experiences *I* had. It's like . . ." She hesitated. "It's like being in a house, and you can explore the house and get to know it really well, but how you got to the house is a mystery. All you have is a map. You don't know what it's really like outside."

Clair was silent.

"The house is me," said Q.

"Yeah, I get that."

"And the first memory that feels like mine is from when we met. You said to me, 'If you're going to quote Keats, at least do it properly.'"

"That's right, I did."

"I don't know why I got it wrong."

"You said you were Improving it."

"But I knew what the original was. Why would I change it? I don't understand why I would do that." A note of frustration entered Q's voice. "This is what I mean by some memories not feeling like mine. I don't know who I was before you. I just know I wasn't . . . me."

Clair cast about for explanations, ignoring nothing, even if it seemed ridiculous. She came up with just one.

"Could you be one of the Improved? Maybe your brain was damaged, like Jesse said, and you've forgotten who you were. Rather than committing suicide, you've been trying to find people like you and trying to make contact when you do."

"I do have memories of reaching out to other girls and

boys. Your friend Libby was one of them. You were the one who answered back. You're the only one who listened."

"So maybe getting the quote mixed up was a cry for help, but none of them recognized it for what it was. I mean, I didn't either, but at least I knew the words were wrong."

"Only you, Clair."

"Good old Keats," she said, attempting lightness even though she felt nothing but confused and wary. "I knew he'd come in handy one day."

"'The poetry of the earth is never dead,'" Q quoted.

"Do you know where you are?" asked Clair. "Is there anyone else with you?"

"That's something else I don't understand. If I am one of the Improved, why don't I have a body?"

——————————————— [45]

CLAIR OPENED HER mouth to say, *Because someone else is using it.*

Then a noise came from behind her. She swiveled on the spot to find the internal door opening.

"I have to go," Clair sent quickly to Q. "Don't worry. We'll work this out. I'm sure of it."

Clair stood up as the woman with the mismatched eyes stuck her head through the door.

"They want you to come up now."

"Okay," said Clair.

"Both of us?" asked Jesse, unfolding and rubbing his eyes.

The woman nodded. "Turner's waiting."

Her head retreated, and the door shut behind her. This time, the lock didn't click.

"About time," said Clair, hiding a twinge of excitement behind justified resentment.

Jesse tugged his shoes on and handed Clair hers. They weren't squelchy anymore, but they remained uncomfortably damp.

"This is it," she said unnecessarily.

Jesse stood up and glanced about him, as though looking for his shoes, then saw them on his feet, where he had put them seconds ago. "All right. After you."

"No, you first," she said. "They're your people."

"Only by association." One sleep-encrusted eye peered at her through his bangs. "Besides, you're awake."

She granted him that point.

The door took them to a spiral staircase that coiled to the floor above them. Jesse followed Clair at a respectful distance, but even so, her muddy sneakers came close to braining him a couple of times. When they reached the top, they found themselves standing under a transparent dome through which the sun shone brightly in a pale-blue sky. Around them were the members of WHOLE, Gemma and Ray among them, sitting cross-legged and staring at the new arrivals.

"Take a seat, Clair and Jesse."

The invitation came from a man much younger than Clair had expected, dressed in cotton pants and a long-sleeved shirt. He looked to be in his twenties, with short-cut black hair and the squarest jaw Clair had ever seen. His eyes were so dark brown they looked almost black.

"Sit anywhere," he added. "We don't stand on protocol here. Pardon the pun."

His white teeth flashed at her.

The nearest spare cushion was by the window, yellow stitched flowers on red corduroy, obviously handmade. Clair sat, feeling uncomfortable. Jesse perched himself on a bright-blue bolster halfway around the circle.

"Welcome to the headquarters of the World Holistic Leadership," the dark-haired young man told them. His cushion was slightly elevated, and his voice had a molasses quality. "My name is Turner. Gemma has told me all about your situation."

"What *is* my situation?" Clair asked, finding her voice. She was still irritated by having waited so long. "Am I expected to join WHOLE to stay up here?"

"Our hospitality is unconditional. Anybody who knocks on our door will gain entry."

"That's all very well when your door is thousands of feet in the air."

Turner smiled again. "Don't think we're debating whether to throw you out the window. I promise you we only do that to spies and dupes. Hardly ever to popular zombies like you, Clair."

"'Hardly ever'?"

His smile broadened. "Do we look like monsters, Clair?"

"I don't know. Looks can be deceiving."

"Indeed, they can be. That's why you're here, after all."

She nodded. "How long have you known about Improvement and the dupes?"

"The former, almost five years," he said. "The latter, less than one. It's a new development aimed in part at us, we think."

"You're not sure?"

"It has obvious military applications. We suspect that members of the OneEarth administration are not who they seem."

She shook her head, not wanting to go down that path.

"Have you told anyone about them?" she asked him.

"We try, of course. You've seen what happens to us when we do. The dupes are the defense mechanism of a corrupt system: Improvement is just one of many immoral practices the dupes exist to protect. Whether they act autonomously or at the instigation of secret masters we do not know."

"Dad never said anything about this," said Jesse.

"He didn't know everything," Turner explained.

"WHOLE operates in cells, so when one is taken out, the others survive. Dylan was a valued member who struggled with his high public profile. He wanted to be more active; we tried to protect him from the consequences. What happened was truly regrettable."

He offered his palms in a gesture of helplessness.

"He was duped," said Clair, "so you blew him up. Very subtle."

"My people acted swiftly and decisively to prevent any deaths that might have resulted from his impersonation," Turner said. "I'm the first to admit that not every decision made in a theater of war is perfectly considered or perfectly rendered."

Jesse was watching intently, almost desperately, as the true fate of his father was openly discussed at last.

"In order to be duped," Jesse said, "you have to have a pattern, and that means going through d-mat. How did they manage that with Dad? He never used d-mat once, not in his entire life."

"We think he was intercepted on the way home from your school," Gemma said. Her arm had graduated to a sling; her shoulder was tightly bandaged. A pink painkiller patch stood out on the side of her neck. "They put him into a booth in one of the apartments nearby. There, he was sent on a null jump, meaning he was analyzed and rebuilt in the same booth, exactly as he had been. That's how they got his pattern. And that's why he's injured every time he comes back. He resisted capture and was punished for it. The injuries he has received are built into the base pattern they're using for his dupe."

Jesse looked as though he wished he hadn't asked.

"Do you know who he is?" asked Jesse. "The man . . . inside him?"

"No. But whoever he is and whoever he works for, they're worse than murderers. Copying a pattern is legally considered kidnapping, erasing a pattern is murder, and damaging a pattern is the same as causing bodily harm. Putting a mind into someone else's head—or even just altering a person, as Improvement is supposed to do—that lands you in a completely new category of crime. It's a kind of mental rape."

Clair thought of Q and stayed silent. Q had only taken over Libby briefly, and then restored her immediately afterward. That such supposedly impossible transformations could go both ways gave Clair hope of finding a cure for what Improvement had done to Libby in the first place. Duping and Improvement weren't the same thing, but they both used d-mat to change people. Change could be reversed.

"What do the dupes want?" asked Jesse.

"The dupes or their masters, if they have them?" asked Turner. "They want what everyone in power wants, I suppose. Can you tell me the first steps in establishing a dictatorship?"

Jesse shook his head.

"I can. They are very simple. First you rob people of their individuality, and then you find a way to observe them completely. D-mat offers the perfect means to do both. Go through a booth, and everything you carry—everything you *are*, right down to the wiring of your brain—can be monitored without your knowledge. Tracking devices and bugs can be installed; information can be rewritten or written entirely from scratch. That is the world we live in. No regime ever before has had the power to manipulate people so easily. It's unprecedented in human history. And no one fights it. People fed *convenience* and *prosperity* seem to accept that they live in a world without physical value. Who's to say their minds haven't been made up for them? Once you can build people atom by atom, rewiring brain cells is *easy*—which might explain what to me seems so inexplicable, why the world is teetering on the brink of a totalitarian dark age and no one but us complains. . . ."

Turner was speaking to Jesse and Clair, but his acolytes were nodding and murmuring in agreement. There was no room for doubt in the choir Turner was preaching to, wearing patched clothes and ferrying their food up from the ground below. Turner reinforced the belief that the hurt in their life wasn't just random bad luck. His brand of alchemy was supremely palatable to people with no place in the world.

Clair understood that. Her friends, family, and future were under threat. She totally wanted to plug the aching void where her life had been with something concrete, something that shored up her strength. And there was a kind of strength to WHOLE. Against considerable odds, Gemma and Ray had escaped the dupes and reached their headquarters.

But that wasn't enough. No one listened to Stainers. They were ostracized and ignored. They ostracized *themselves*, Clair thought. Tempting though it might be for some to hide on a cloud and mutter discontentedly, it wasn't enough for Clair. It wouldn't help Libby. It wouldn't stop Improvement from happening to someone else. It wouldn't save Clair if she, too, was at risk.

[46]

"I NEED YOUR help," she said. "My friend used Improvement—"

"Gemma told us," Turner interrupted her.

"So you know she doesn't have much time," she said firmly. "Whatever was done to her, there has to be a way to undo it. On the way here, Jesse and I talked about going to VIA and trying to get them to do something about it—"

"They won't listen," Turner said, shaking his head.

"They will if we make them. If we show them the body of the dupe, that'll prove that *something's* going on."

"We didn't find anything in the body's lenses," Ray said. "All the data has been erased."

Clair hid her disappointment.

"We don't need the data," she improvised. "Dylan Linwood is officially still alive. The body proves that someone's tampering with parity, doesn't it? If there's one of him walking around somewhere out there, and one of him dead here . . . how can VIA argue with that?"

"They can't," said Turner, "unless the dupes go to ground."

"So we move quickly. We don't give them time to get organized. Once VIA's on our side, the people responsible won't have a chance."

"VIA isn't the solution," said Gemma. "It's a bandage over the open wound of d-mat."

"D-mat isn't the problem," Clair argued.

"It's everyone's problem, Clair. You still haven't noticed yet?"

"D-mat's like a gun or a drone or a . . . a shoe. How it's used is what matters."

"This is not a fruitful argument to have now," said Turner in a placating tone. "We don't have to agree on anything except our common humanity."

Clair was not going to be placated.

"I honestly can't see anyone taking on a problem this big without help from *somewhere*," she said. "Who else is there? The peacekeepers? The federal government? One-Earth? They all benefit from the status quo; they won't want anything changed. VIA's power hinges entirely on d-mat's reliability. That's why VIA exists at all. If d-mat is proved to be unreliable, VIA won't have a leg to stand on.

They'll have to act to save themselves."

"You can't really think it'd be that easy," said Gemma.

"No, but that's not going to stop me," she said, rising to her feet. She put on her firmest voice. The crowd listened to a young man with a square jaw, so maybe they'd listen to her, too.

"This is a war, and we're vastly outnumbered, but that never stopped someone from being right. You understand that better than anyone. We can sit here arguing about the means all day—you want to tear the system down and start again, while I want the system to fix itself as it's supposed to—but the ends we want to achieve are not all that different. We want people to be safe. We don't want people to be altered in ways they shouldn't. That's what everyone wants. Can't we find a way to do this together? No one ever changed the world acting alone."

Jesse actually clapped, and in that moment she could've kissed him. But he was the only one, and after a few seconds he trailed off.

"Ah, the irony," said Turner with smile. "I want to say that words are not enough, when all *I* have are words, too. Why don't you give us a moment to think about what you've said? We'll call you when we're ready."

"You've already made up your mind," said Clair with a heavy feeling in her gut.

"Don't be so sure. You're asking us to help you, and that's a big commitment, but you have a lot to offer us in return. We always need information and evidence, and you have provided both. You and Jesse and your friend Q. We don't have to agree with each other to be useful to each other. . . . Jamila?"

The young woman with the mismatched irises stood and led Clair and Jesse down the spiral staircase, back to the D-shaped deck below. No one said anything as they left, but Clair and Jesse were tracked with every step.

Don't give up hope, Clair told herself. *He didn't actually say no.*

"You think Turner's a good guy?" she asked Jamila before the woman went back to join the others.

"The best," she said with shy smile.

"Isn't he a little young to be in charge, though?"

"Age doesn't come into it. All that matters is getting the job done."

"The job being to get rid of d-mat, I suppose."

The woman blinked as though Clair was asking a stupid question. "Of course."

She vanished through the door and locked it behind her, leaving the prisoners with the cushions, the coffee-maker, the microwave, and the view.

Jesse headed for the miniature kitchen to pour himself some coffee. "Me," he said, "I'm feeling slightly under-whelmed."

Clair nodded. She was thinking about Dylan Linwood,

whose fame as a transport artist, or whatever he had called himself, had put him in a good position to be a spokesperson for WHOLE, she would have thought. But the one time he had openly used that position to attack Improvement over the Air had seen him duped. The video he had made had been noted at the time, but how many viewers had been convinced by it? Within hours, his home had been destroyed, and he was missing, presumed crazier than ever.

What could unknown Clair Hill do that he hadn't?

She returned to her cushion against the window and sat down, closing her eyes and accessing her lenses. She didn't know how long she had before the meeting reconvened. But she resolved to use that time wisely.

"Are you there, Q?"

"I'm right there with you. Hey—that rhymes."

"*Where* are you, exactly?"

"I appear to be in the Air. That's where I came to myself, anyway, when we started talking. There's lots of room for me in here, but it's hard to describe where 'here' is, exactly. I'm surrounded by so much information . . . it's scary sometimes. . . ."

Clair could accept this, but at the same time she couldn't. It was difficult to imagine how someone could be alive without a body, let alone live in the Air, but if people could be d-matted anywhere in the world, why not into a virtual environment like the air? That made Q something like a ghost in a virtual library containing all of human history and knowledge. It would be hard to avoid getting lost in there and perhaps just as hard to find one small thing out of everything else.

"I need to know something," she said. "Dylan Linwood attached some brain scans to the video of Principal Gordon's office. Can you track down their source?"

"I can certainly try, Clair," Q said. "Private medical data is difficult to access, but I'm sure I'll find a way in eventually, if I dig long enough."

"Thanks."

"Is there anything else?"

"Too much, probably. What can you tell me about Turner Goldsmith? Young guy, a bit too smooth for his own good. Possibly WHOLE's leader."

"I have a peacekeeper warrant outstanding for one Turner Archibald Goldsmith, but he's not young. He's listed as eighty-two years old."

"Well, that can't be right. Maybe he's the original's grandson, using a family name."

"His records show no offspring."

"He stole the old guy's identity?"

"That would explain the discrepancy. . . ."

Or someone was outright lying, Clair thought. The layers of deceit and misinformation seemed to get thicker every time she tried to roll them back.

"Finally, I need a way to get to New York without being

spotted," she said. "Do you think you can help me with that?"

"Of course, Clair. D-mat is out of the question . . ."

Q's voice faded briefly into static, then returned.

". . . alternate routes, depending on . . ."

"What was that, Q? I missed something."

". . . natural interference at your end. I'll try . . ."

"You're fading again. What?"

". . . unusual readings . . ."

A vibration ran through the Skylifter, making the mugs and cups rattle.

Clair opened her eyes and saw Jesse with his hand against one wall, staring at her.

"Did you feel that?" he asked.

Sudden bright white light flared. The floor tipped beneath them, and Clair slid directly toward one of the windows.

[47]

SHE SKIDDED ACROSS the carpet, flailing ineffectually for anything solid to hang on to, but all her clutching hands found were cushions. The floor dropped again, and suddenly there wasn't even carpet to slow her down. She was tumbling through empty air. Ahead of her was nothing but blue sky and an infinite cloudscape far, far below.

She hit the hardened plastic with a bone-jarring thud. There she stopped dead. An avalanche of cushions pummeled her from behind, followed by Jesse himself. She was glad for the cushions as his extra weight pressed her hard against the transparent boundary that was the only thing separating her from a very long fall straight down.

Light flared again. This time it was the sun sweeping across the sky. The Skylifter was spinning.

"What's going on?"

Jesse said something but was muffled by the cushions. Q was silent. There was only static through her lenses.

The weight eased. A hand thrust down to her, and she gripped it tightly. She burst out of the cushions and stood next to Jesse with one foot on the window beneath her and the other on a wildly canted floor. She braced herself in case the Skylifter lurched again.

Another white flash. This time there was a bang. The air misted. Her ears popped. Suddenly, it was hard to breathe. She felt light in her stomach, as though they were losing altitude.

Her heart thumped loud and fast in her chest.

"We're under attack," Jesse said over a rising whistling noise.

"I thought we were safe here!"

"Apparently not." He peered out the windows. "But I can't see anyone out there. They must be firing at us from a distance."

They tried the doors, climbing awkwardly up the sloping floor. Only the one leading to the bathroom was unlocked, and that Clair already knew was a dead end.

"Q?" Clair called. "I need you!"

No answer penetrated the static.

The floor lurched again. This time the white light didn't fade. It blazed like a new sun in the sky, flickering occasionally but never entirely going out.

Clair shielded her dazzled eyes. Not being able to see the ground as it approached was a cold comfort. There had to be a way down to the airships docked below that she had seen earlier. Through a ventilation duct, perhaps . . . ?

Barely had she begun looking for air vents when the door to the upper deck suddenly opened, letting in a howling gale.

"Q!" she cried in relief.

But it was Jesse she saw flinching from sparks showering out of an open panel.

"How did you do that?"

"Killer with a screwdriver, remember?" He held up a bent metal knife. The door had only opened an inch, but that was enough for them to get their fingers through and slide it wider. The air was frigid on the other side. Light blazed down the spiral stairwell. There was no sign of anyone.

"The dome must have been breached," Clair said, imagining people sucked out and falling and . . . She shook her head. *Don't think of that.* "We have to go the other way."

He nodded grimly and hurried to the other side of the room while Clair struggled to slide the door closed behind her. She rapidly lost all feeling in her fingertips to the cold.

"Come on!"

Jesse had the other door open. Together, they made enough space for them to slip through. The air was relatively warm and still on the other side, but the shaft leading to the lowest level of the Skylifter was swaying sickeningly from side to side. She hoped the three smaller airships were still attached.

They hurried down the stairs. Each shudder and lurch made her fear that the Skylifter had reached the end of its plummet, and all their efforts had been for nothing. But it was still falling when they reached the docks, and over the whistling of wind they heard the sound of propellers whirring madly. Through circular ports ringing the base of the stairwell, Clair saw that all three smaller airships were active and ready to fly. The hatches hung open.

"Is there anyone here?" she called.

"Clair! I hear you!" Q's voice came from all the hatches. "I couldn't reach you through the ionization, but I did patch into the airships' control systems—"

"Whatever, I'm glad you're here! Which ship do we take?"

"Any of them."

Clair picked the nearest. Through the hatch, she could see the docking tube connecting the base of the Skylifter to the smaller airship flexing and twisting. She took a breath and hurried out onto the plastic floor. The walls were shaking, and her stomach was swirling, and she could only imagine what was happening to the Skylifter as it tumbled faster and faster out of the sky. It was far from aerodynamic.

The tube jerked under her feet. Something tore. The way ahead was suddenly rushing wind and bright-blue light, and the clouds loomed horribly close.

"Clair!"

Jesse wrapped his arms around her and pulled her bodily backward before she could fall. They tumbled in a tangle of arms and legs and somehow managed to crawl their way back to safety. Clair was shaking too much to do more than follow as Jesse dragged them both to their feet and hurried to the next hatch in line. That tube held. Clair had never felt so grateful for anything or anyone in her entire life.

The airship thrashed about on the end of its docking tube like an apple in a storm. Clair fell across the threshold and clung to the pilot's seat with all her strength. The crew compartment was big enough to hold a dozen people or so, with a low ceiling that didn't quite allow Clair to stand upright. There were cases of what looked like small arms taking up two seats at the front.

Jesse brushed past her and stared at the complicated controls.

"What do we do?" she gasped. "Do you know how to fly this thing?"

"You don't have to," said Q. "I will operate the controls remotely."

The door slid shut behind them. Locking bolts fastened. The pitch of the engines was already changing.

"We can't leave yet," said Clair. "We have to check on the others."

"The dome blew," said Jesse. "They must be dead."

"We don't know for sure. Q, can you take us to the top of this thing so we can check? Is there time?"

"I will make time."

"Do it. We have to try."

─────────────────────── [48]

THE PROPELLERS ROARED, and the airship tore away from the tube connecting it to the Skylifter. Bright white light hit the airship as it came out from under the shadow of the larger craft. Clair clipped herself tightly into the seat next to Jesse.

"That laser or whatever it is—it's not coming from another airship," she said, peering through narrowed eyelids out the automatically darkened windshield. "It's coming from above."

"It's a satellite power beam," said Q.

"Here?" said Jesse, wide-eyed. "We're miles away from the nearest receiver!"

"The beam's been deliberately moved."

"Someone's trying to make this look like an accident," said Clair, thinking of Jesse's mom. "Funny how things like this happen around people in WHOLE."

"Yeah, real hilarious," Jesse said.

The airship flew upward past the tapering tip of the Skylifter's teardrop and out around its fat middle. The dirigible was listing drunkenly and rotating once every ten seconds or so. The window Clair had fallen against came into view. She saw nothing but cushions and spreading frost. No people.

"Higher." Clair leaned forward as they neared the uppermost deck. The dome had shattered, and the space below lay open to the sky. It was hard to see through the light, and at first she saw no one, but then, around a central spar that had once held the graceful curve of plastic safely over the heads of the Skylifter's inhabitants . . .

"There!" She pointed at a small huddle of people in the scant shade provided by the spar, waving desperately to attract the airship's attention. "Take us closer!"

"I see them," said Q through a new wash of static. The airship rocked on its roaring fan engines through the full effect of the powersat beam—all the power a living city needed, sent down from space in one broad, powerful stream.

Clair stayed by the instruments, the better to see what was going on through the front window. To Jesse, she said, "Get ready with the door. Be careful."

He moved back to stand over it, braced on either side by one hand and one foot.

The air was turbulent and hot above the observation deck. Shards of plastic dome stabbed at the airship's vulnerable underbelly. Twice, Q caught the tip of a propeller on something she shouldn't have, provoking outraged shrieks of metal and carbon fiber.

"This is as close as we get," Q finally said. "I can't hold this position long."

Jesse opened the door and shouted something into the wind that Clair couldn't make out. Through the windshield she saw people emerging from their meager hiding place, lurching across the windswept surface in a series of staggering steps. There was nothing for them to hang on to but each other.

The Skylifter steadied. They ran forward. There was a flurry of shouting and movement—bodies falling en masse through the open hatch, propellers screaming, white-flaring wreckage suddenly rising up to meet them—and then the airship was rising, pulling away from the doomed Skylifter, out of the beam from the powersat, and the light was fading, and the door was shut.

Jesse lay on the floor of the airship with the others. Clair went back to help them. Everyone was talking at once, gasping for breath or crying with mingled relief and shock. There were just four survivors, their skin red and blistered where exposed to the beam.

"Where's Turner?" called the woman with mismatched eyes, pushing out from under the huddle. "Where is he?"

"I'm here." He was helping Gemma to a seat.

"Thank God."

"For small mercies, yes." When Gemma was buckled in, Turner turned to Clair and Jesse. "We owe the two of you our lives."

"Q did the flying," said Clair. "We couldn't have done anything without her."

"The three of you, then," said Turner gravely. "We are in your debt."

Through the cockpit window, the bright column of the power beam was visible now that they were out of it—not the beam itself but its glittery effect on the atmosphere, like dust sparking in a shaft of sunlight. The Skylifter was dropping away below them and to one side, trailing debris as it went. Clair saw smoke. The Skylifter was burning, breaking up.

Her mind was still reeling from the nearness of their escape.

"Where on earth do we go now?" she asked.

Gemma came forward to take the controls, and Turner followed her. Clair made room for them but stayed to watch over their shoulders.

"There," said Turner, pointing at a map on a screen. "Take us in that direction."

Clair didn't recognize any of the names on the map.

"Shall I surrender control?" Q asked her.

"Yes, you'd better."

"Is there anyone we can call for help?" asked Gemma.

"No," said Turner. "Don't want to draw any more attention to us than you have to. We're radar silent, I presume."

"Yes."

Brightness hit the airship anyway. Clair flung herself away from the windshield with an arm over her eyes. The beam was searing her skin. Static flared in her ears. Her feed to Q went dead.

"Take us down," Turner cried. "Get us under the clouds!"

The floor fell out from beneath her and they dropped like a stone. She couldn't tell if Gemma was flying or had lost control. Clair could only struggle to find an empty seat to strap herself in.

Something went bang above them. The airship lurched.

"We lost an airbag," she heard Gemma say. "The good news is that will make us go faster."

"I wonder what the bad news is," said Jesse, pulling Clair into the seat next to him and slipping the harness over her shoulders.

Clair held his hand tightly. Her insides felt weightless in a highly unpleasant way. "It'll make us harder to stop, I guess."

The clouds were coming up at them. There was a second bang, another lurch.

Then a shutter fell between the airship and the power beam, and all Clair could see were brilliant purple after-images. The propellers roared. They were below the cloud layer but still falling, rocking from side to side as Gemma fought to find some kind of stability.

"Come on," Gemma was saying. "Stop fighting me. *Come on!*"

There was a moment of relative stillness, almost of calm, and then a huge force struck the airship like a bat hitting a ball, and they were bouncing, spinning, shaking, tearing—coming down hard.

[49]

CLAIR REGAINED CONSCIOUSNESS upside down, locked into her harness, and choking for breath. There was fluid in her nose, filling her sinuses, and bubbling up the back of her throat, making her feel as though she were drowning.

She jerked explosively forward and sprayed blood across the cockpit of the airship. That cleared her nose, but it didn't make the view any prettier.

The airship was ruined, its cabin filled with broken glass, destroyed electronics, and broken branches. Clair reached out for Jesse, but the seat next to her wasn't just empty. It was gone. One whole side of the compartment had been torn away. When she twisted wildly to look down, she saw him lying on his side on what had been the crew compartment's roof. She couldn't tell if he was breathing.

Clair twisted farther. All she could see were branches. No other bodies. She forced herself to breathe deeply and not to give in to panic. Imagining the worst wasn't going to help anyone, starting with herself.

"Jesse? Q?"

Her voice sounded nasal and thin. No reply from either the Air or the boy below her.

With one forearm, she braced herself against the armrest of the seat. She hit the harness release with her free hand and dropped like a sack of stones, too heavy to hold herself up. But she slowed her fall with the arm that had been bearing her weight and landed next to Jesse rather than on him. She bent down to check his pulse and make sure his airways were clear, as she had been taught in first aid. That lesson had been a long time ago. She had never needed it more.

After a moment, she sagged back onto her heels, dizzy with relief.

Jesse was alive.

When she brushed the hair back from his face, though,

he didn't react. She pressed her hand against his forehead, wondering if he felt hot or cold, or if that even mattered after an accident like this. She ran her hand over his skull, looking for bumps or wet patches. There were none, but that didn't reassure her.

"Jesse? Wake up, please. . . ."

She wished she could talk to Q, but she had no access to the Air at all even though she was out in the open. She had no one to turn to for advice. She was on her own.

Clair straightened, blew more blood out her nose until she was able to breathe freely, and warily approached the open side of the airship. Her chunk of the crew compartment had been snagged by trees. They weren't huge trees, maybe four or five yards high, and they were spaced in rows like an orchard. Bright-red autumn apples dotted the lush green leafscape like dollops of paint. The sun was either rising or setting, but she couldn't see the sun itself, only the long shadows stretching away from her under the warm tones of a melting sky. Pink light mottled the underside of the solid cloud bank above. To her right, black smoke rose in a column, whipped into feathers by the wind. There was no sign of the power beam or the rest of the airship.

Through the trees, she saw lights flashing, long white beams darting like the antennae of insects. Questing, searching the thickening dusk. Coming closer, she thought.

The dupes had hunted her all the way from Manteca to

the edge of the Sierra Nevada, and their power beam had blasted the Skylifter out of the sky like a laser might zap a mosquito. The implacable momentum of their pursuit made her feel like lying down and closing her eyes. They would never give up.

"Jesse," she said, hurrying to his side. "Jesse, can you hear me? You have to wake up."

Jesse didn't stir. Clair wanted to shake him, but she didn't, afraid of spinal injuries. Instead, she clapped her hands in front of Jesse's face and shouted, "Jesse! We have to go—now!"

Still no response.

Still no word from Q.

Still no sign of the others.

And the lights were closer, leaving no doubt in her mind that the crash had been seen.

Clair was more alone than she had been at the Tuvalu monument. But she wasn't helpless. The remains of the crew compartment still contained one of the small arms cases she had seen earlier, and inside it was a pistol. There was no ammunition, but she wouldn't have known how to load it anyway. All she needed was a prop to back up the only strategy she had left, which was to bluff. A bluff could be enough, if she put everything into it.

You can handle yourself, Zep had said in the safe house. Remembering his confidence in her only made her feel sad again.

You're good at this. You've missed your true calling.

Those were Jesse's words. She bent over him to check his breathing again, touched his cheek gently for luck, then stood in the open end of the compartment with an empty gun in one hand, waiting for what came next.

The lights came closer, resolving not into people holding flashlights, but vehicles. Two-, three-, and four-wheeled, they bounced on oversized tires over ruts between the trees, spreading out to surround the airship and filling the air with the snarl of their engines. These motors were chemical rather than electric, leaving smoke trails behind them. Clair squeezed her nose between the thumb and forefinger of her left hand to stop herself from sneezing blood again.

Two vehicles came to a halt near her tree. One was a jeep with a flatbed at the rear and two men in the cab at the front. The third was a three-wheeler. The driver of the three-wheeler dismounted and jogged to stand directly below her. He was heavyset and bearded, wearing a checked shirt and overalls. He looked like a cartoon lumberjack. So did his friends. She stared down at him with her pulse beating high and fast in her throat.

"You with Turner?" he called, red-faced and belligerent.

"Why do you want to know?"

"This is a piece of his airship. We're looking for survivors. Is he up there with you?"

"No."

"He could be anywhere, then. Pieces of this thing fell all over." He indicated the gun. "Are you going to shoot me with that or put it away?"

"Tell me who you are," she countered, not moving an inch. He looked nothing like Dylan Linwood, but that didn't mean she should automatically trust him.

"I'm a farmer, of course. Don't you know where you are?"

She shook her head.

"So you weren't headed here specifically?"

Clair remembered the frantic moments after their escape from the Skylifter. Turner had given Gemma a destination, but then the powersat beam had hit them, and they had gone down. Not knowing whether they had made it to their destination or not, she decided to continue stalling until she knew who she was talking to.

"We were heading for Buffalo," she said, recalling the Skylifter's official flight plan.

"Buffalo, huh? Well, that's not here."

"Are you going to tell me where 'here' is?"

The big man put his hands in his pocket and glanced down at the ground for a moment. When he looked back up again, he seemed to have reached some kind of decision.

"My name is Arcady. Turner trusts me, so you can trust me too. Or you can stay up there on your own. Your decision."

My friend's friend, thought Clair, *or my enemy's enemy.* She wasn't sure if this Arcady fit into either category, and she wasn't really in a position to be fussy.

She knelt down and placed the useless pistol on the floor.

"All right," she said. "I need a hand, though. There's someone hurt up here."

Arcady whistled and waved both arms above his head. Two more vehicles converged on the scene. The rest spread out through the orchard, looking for the other half of the airship.

Clair went back into the blood-spattered cockpit and kept an anxious vigil next to Jesse as the farmers climbed up from below.

[50]

THE DRIVER OF the four-wheeler took them along the rut-ted orchard rows rather than across them, to spare Clair's injured friend. At the end of the first row they hit a service road, just dirt and gravel but level and straight, aiming for the patch of sky where the sun had been. The clouds were deep red to the west, fading to black to the east. The smoke from the fallen airship was almost invisible now.

Clair sat on the flatbed with Jesse and Arcady, feel-ing sick. Perhaps it was from blood she'd swallowed, or maybe it was the deep uncertainty of her present position. Out of the power beam and into the . . . what now? She didn't know where she was, who she was with, or where they were taking her. She had flat-out refused to be separated from Jesse and now sat with his head in her lap, wishing with every fiber of her being that he would wake up.

Clair had already asked Arcady where they were going, and this time he had answered simply, *The Farmhouse.* She took the hint, although she was both curious and skeptical. A farm, honestly? As the orchard passed by, row after row of branching trees, apparently stretching for miles, she wondered how there could be nearly enough Abstainers in the world to eat so many apples. Then she did the math and realized that if one percent of people were Abstainers, even one tenth of one percent, that still left a huge potential market—but how would the apples get to them without d-mat? There were no trucks anymore, no planes for airfreight. The fruit would rot on the ground.

Every minute or so, Clair checked for the Air and for Q. Still nothing. She bit her lip, trying to protect Jesse from each bump and shudder of the vehicle beneath them. As far as she knew, they were the only survivors of the crash. She didn't want to think about what it would mean if he died and left her alone. All she knew about farmers was from old movies, and although Arcady and his friends might not look like inbred cannibals, she could imagine any number of terrible fates awaiting a girl on her own in the middle of nowhere.

Her face was crusted with blood, and her nose hurt. It didn't feel broken, which was a small comfort among a cavalcade of miseries.

They crested a low hill and drove down into a depression that didn't really constitute a valley. Lights at the bottom of the depression issued from a close cluster of buildings. Clair could make out very few details in the thickening gloom. Sheds of some kind, containing angular agricultural machinery. The Farmhouse, she presumed.

They passed fences and through open gates. The four-wheeler bounced lightly over a packed-earth courtyard and came to a halt in front of a long, gabled building. One wall was entirely windows. She could see people moving within. Strong, stern men with beards and work clothes. Hardly any women. No one she recognized.

Farmers issued from a wide double door and converged on the flatbed. They took Jesse from her and carried him carefully inside. Clair followed closely, blinking in the light. Arcady's hand was tight on her upper arm, guiding her and keeping her close through a central hall with trestle tables below and naked wooden beams above. Voices came at her from everywhere. Her blocked nostrils twitched—was that a wood fire she smelled?

Somehow she was separated from Jesse. Before she

could protest, Arcady ushered her into an office. There was a desk and two chairs and a series of cabinets that might have held actual paper files.

"Take a seat, Clair."

"How do you know my name?" She stayed standing.

"You were in the video with Dylan Linwood," he said. "I didn't think it was real until you practically landed on our heads. We heard reports via shortwave radio of an airship damaged in a power-beam accident. That said two things to us: one, WHOLE was involved, because no one else flies airships so far from the coast; and two, because WHOLE was involved, it was unlikely to be an accident. We immediately mobilized to search for survivors."

Arcady showed her a map. The Farm stretched across a significant chunk of North Dakota, from the Little Missouri grasslands to the east almost as far as Fargo to the west, north halfway to the Canadian border. Clair's portion of the airship had come down on the southern edge of the farm, near a ghost town called New Salem. The crew compartment had disintegrated into several pieces, with her larger chunk getting snagged while the rest tumbled on much farther. Farmers were still calling in with news of wreckage raining over the plains. Arcady couldn't or wouldn't tell her anything about other survivors.

"Where's Jesse?" she said, fighting a resurgence of the same panic that had threatened her earlier. "What are you doing to him?"

"He's being looked after," Arcady said. "Don't worry. We have competent medical staff here."

Clair tugged at a hangnail with her teeth, pulled a face at the taste of dried blood on her tongue. Was competent good enough? Jesse had become much more to her than a guide to his world of misfits and outsiders. He was the only one who agreed with her about how to deal with Improvement and the dupes, and he had saved her on the Skylifter just as much Q had.

She didn't want any more friends to die that week. To paraphrase Oscar Wilde, it was beginning to look somewhat more than careless.

"You said I could trust you," Clair said.

"You can."

"So why am I in here? Why can't I be with him?"

Arcady ran his fingers through his beard. "We live quietly. We don't like attention or surprises."

"Are you part of WHOLE too? Is what why I can't access the Air?"

"You ask a lot of questions."

"What else am I supposed to do?"

He smiled, which unexpectedly transformed him.

"Come on." He stood and held out both hands to her. "You need a shower."

"I want to wait for Jesse."

"You could be waiting all night," he said, "and you don't want to smell like this when he wakes up."

She sniffed warily at one armpit. Her nose was still mostly blocked, so she couldn't tell.

"Is it bad?"

"It's worse," he said. "Much, much worse."

The showers were communal, but the water was warm and plentiful, and there was soap, which was enough for Clair to overcome her reluctance. She took a corner stall and scrubbed two days' worth of accumulated blood and grime from her skin and hair. She lathered and rinsed three times, and then stood under the water for a full minute, savoring the sensation of *clean*.

The shower was on a generous but definitive timer, otherwise she might have stayed there all night. When it shut off, she reached for two towels, drying her skin first and then her hair as best she could. It would spring up into an Afro now, no matter what she did. The clothes Q had sent her in Manteca lay in a muddy puddle. No way was she putting them on again.

She stepped out of the shower stall wrapped in a thick towel. The steam had cleared her nose. She could smell nothing now but soap.

"Here," said Arcady, handing her a stack of neatly folded garments. "I think I got your size right."

Among the clothes were overalls, utilitarian and tough-looking. Fit for a farm.

"These have been fabbed," she said, caught off guard by

something that had once seemed completely normal in such an alien place.

"How can you tell?"

"They smell . . . you know, fresh."

"This surprises me. I thought you were one of Turner's crew."

"We're temporary allies, that's all."

Arcady nodded. "Well, don't tell the others about the clothes when they get here. They wouldn't approve."

"But you trust them, and you say they trust you. How can that work?"

"We've been 'temporary allies' with Turner Goldsmith for twenty years. We don't have a problem with d-mat per se, just the way it's regulated. The Farmhouse has its own closed networks and makes its own patterns. Nothing weird or anything. Just . . . *amplifying* our produce a little."

"You grow stuff naturally and then fab it? That doesn't make any sense."

"It does for some things. Think about it. If everything's fabbed and nothing's really grown anymore, there goes mutation. Life gets boring—it's all about *produce*. Here, we actively breed for mutation, for novelty. We like randomness, and we like what it brings."

Clair still didn't understand.

"You're not getting dressed," he said.

She didn't want to drop the towels while someone was

watching her. She felt vulnerable enough already.

"Why don't you go on ahead of me? I'll catch up."

"Can't do that, I'm afraid. No wandering around the Farmhouse on your own just yet."

She stared at him. "You're guarding me?"

"Let's just say I don't want you to see anything you shouldn't."

Then it occurred to her. There was one class of organic compounds that could be grown but couldn't legally be transported through d-mat.

The farmers were making drugs—new drugs that no one had ever heard of before, like the one Libby had taken to deal with her Improvement headache. That was why Arcady didn't want people dropping in on them unexpectedly and why the Air was comprehensively blocked.

"Those apples I saw are for more than just eating, aren't they? They're for getting high."

Arcady winked and turned his broad back on her.

Clair dressed in the uniform of a farmer, deciding as she did so that she could trust the farmers no more or less than Turner did. Terrorists and drug runners. Honor among illegals. But at least their defenses were good— too good even for Q, it seemed. Like everything in recent days, she had to accept the good along with the bad.

She figured she could live with that just as long as the bad wasn't *too* bad.

[51]

THE HALL WAS full of people when she returned and even noisier than before. Turner was there too, and Gemma and Ray. No others.

"Is that all?" Clair remembered the people she had addressed on the Skylifter. It was horrible to think they were now all gone.

Arcady handed her a pewter mug filled to the brim with a foaming golden liquid.

"Devil's Lake is the finest cider we've ever made," he said, raising the mug he held in his other hand. "Here's to fallen friends."

Clair felt as though she'd slipped into in a depressing dream about agricultural Vikings, but she clinked mugs with him and took a sip of the cider. It was sweet and warming, like a memory of fireworks. She took a larger gulp and closed her eyes.

To Dancer, Cashile, and Theo, she thought. *To Zep, and to all the others who died because of the dupes. Hell, even to Dylan Linwood.*

"To life," Arcady added, "and the hard business of living it."

She opened her eyes, nodded hopelessly . . . and there was Jesse, approaching from the fringes of the crowd, looking disoriented by the noise and the people but otherwise uninjured. The relief she felt was almost as potent as the cider.

He hugged her with shining eyes, and she hugged him back. Even through the grime and blood came a smell that she recognized, musky and natural and all him. She didn't know when his scent had become so familiar to her, but she was glad to have it in her nostrils again.

"Hey," he said into the top of her head. "It's good to see you too."

"I was worried," she admitted. "Are you all right?"

"I banged my head when we came down. Luckily, I've got a thick skull. You?"

"Hungry," she said, painfully aware of the fact now that she knew he was okay. "Go take a shower, then try some of the local cider. It's to die for."

He grinned and hurried off with his farmer guide. Clair watched him go, more glad to see him than she could say—and Turner and Ray and Gemma, too, even if they were terrorists and outlaws.

"Are you two . . . ?" Arcady was watching her over the lip of his mug.

"What? Hardly," she said, remembering Jesse telling the dupe that she would never be his girlfriend.

"Good. Lots of nice farm lads here. And farm girls."

He winked, and she felt herself blush right up into the roots of her curly hair.

Dinner consisted of something that looked like a big sheep roasted on a spit. The members of WHOLE stuck to baked vegetables, cheese, and salad. Clair did the same, wary of meat that had been recently alive, not fabbed like food was in the normal world.

The cider served with the meal was smokier than the first brew, with a different name: Sweet Briar Lake. Arcady told her that it was made from pears rather than apples. Someone played an old upright piano, and Arcady sang "When Irish Eyes are Smiling" at the top of his lungs:

There's a tear in your eye and I'm wondering why
For it never should be there at all.

Clair was reminded of Q's misquotes of old poems and the conversation they had had in the Skylifter before the meeting with Turner. Clair had barely thought of it since, caught up in events as she had been. But she hadn't forgotten it.

If I am one of the Improved, why don't I have a body?

On a drug farm in the middle of nowhere, fuzzy-headed from exhaustion and homemade cider, what had seemed mad hours ago began to make a kind of sense.

Jesse joined her, looking fresh and clean in his own set of sturdy overalls, still wearing his old burned orange T-shirt underneath. Gemma was standing to one side, looking cynical and wary, drinking water, not cider. Her bandage had been changed and the burns to her skin thoroughly salved. She had lost her painkiller patch. Clair waved for her to come over and join them. It was time for more of the answers Clair had hoped to get in the Skylifter.

"What's the relationship between Improvement and the dupes?" Clair asked.

"The latter protect the former," said Gemma. "You know how it works. Do anything to suggest Improvement is anything other than a harmless meme, and they'll come after you."

"Is that all?"

"Well, duping takes someone out of their body and puts someone else in. You can't do that without altering the brain, which is exactly what we've seen in autopsies of people who have used Improvement. Remember those dead girls?"

"Brain damage," said Clair. "Are you saying the damage wasn't random?"

"That's exactly what I'm saying. Improvement does the same thing as duping . . . only differently. Dupes rarely last longer than a day or two, for instance, while Improvement takes a week. We think that neither duping nor Improvement is permanent, but maybe that's because we only see the times when it goes wrong. I told you earlier that not everyone who uses Improvement is affected, and that's true. What if there are people out there right now who are in fact different on the inside, successfully transformed, but we wouldn't know unless they said so? And why would they?"

They were coming back around to Turner's paranoid conspiracy theory, in which world leaders were puppets controlled by VIA dupes. Clair cut Gemma off before she could get there.

"Why didn't you tell me any of this back at Escalon?"

"You wouldn't have believed me."

That was true enough. Clair still didn't entirely believe it now.

"So Libby's not herself anymore? That's what you think?"

"It's not like duping; it doesn't happen right away. But she's got the symptoms, which means the process is under way. If she's not already someone else by now, she will be soon."

"Who? Is it the same person every time?"

"I don't know. My son never told me his name."

Clair stared at her for a long moment, reminded of Gemma's past. *Sam*, she'd called him, the child she'd lost to Improvement. The note Clair had found had been written three years ago.

"Was that why you joined WHOLE?" Jesse asked. "I remember seeing you at meetings, but you never said what happened."

"Yes." Gemma didn't flinch from the question. "I had Abstainer friends. Your father was one of them. Like a lot of people, I didn't want to think about what goes on inside the booths until something went wrong. What happened to Sam confirmed a lot of things for me. WHOLE is my family now."

"Did your son . . . ," Clair started to say, then caught herself. "Did the person inside Sam . . . tell you anything at all?"

"Nothing useful. Do you want to know how he killed himself?"

Clair shook her head. She didn't need to think of Libby suffering the same fate any more than she already was.

"Good," Gemma said. "All you need to know is that dupes and Improvement are connected. And without d-mat, neither would happen."

"But if we bring down d-mat, I'll never get Libby back."

"Do you really think it's possible to save her?" asked Jesse.

"That's the thing I think I've worked out. Listen." Clair leaned over the table, closer to both of them. "There are rules to how d-mat operates. There can't be two of a particular person at one time, for instance. Things have to even out. So what happens to minds that are pushed out by the dupes? Where do they go?"

"They're erased," Gemma said.

Clair shook her head. "No. Data can neither be created nor destroyed, Q says. If you can't erase the data, that means those minds are still out there somewhere—and so's Libby. Her original pattern contains everything she was, right down to the atom. Everything she *is*. All we have to do is find it, and we can put her back the way she was before the brain damage. Before Improvement."

Gemma was listening, but she was looking deeply skeptical at the same time, and Clair realized that she was talking to the wrong person. To Gemma, minds and bodies were much more than just data, even though people had been zipping around the world for two generations without any apparent loss of *soul*.

Fortunately, Jesse looked interested, and Arcady was listening too.

"Our private net does everything two, three times over," he put in. "It's the only way to weed out errors. Our safety net is basically a big memory dump. We zap something and we keep its data in limbo until we're absolutely certain it's come out the other side okay. We call this limbo the hangover. Obviously, our net is different from the one VIA monitors, but I'm betting that part of it works the same."

Clair was nodding. "Yes! The hangover. That has to be where she is. Not deleted, because important stuff like this can't be destroyed. *Saved.* Brilliant!"

She clinked glasses with Jesse and considered the ramifications of this new understanding.

"That means we need VIA more than ever," she said. "They'll naturally have access to their own data. They'll be able to pull out what's in their hangover and put Libby back the way she ought to be."

"How long since she used Improvement?" Gemma asked.

"Four days, now."

"There might still be time. If she's lucky."

"What about Q?" asked Jesse. "Could she break in and get Libby out?"

"Break into VIA?" said Clair. "That'd probably take an army of hackers. Or an actual army."

It was an interesting question, though. She thought of Q, kicked out of her body and accidentally booting up in deep storage somewhere, now struggling to put her mind back together. If the effects of Improvement could easily be reversed, Q would have simply d-matted herself in Copperopolis or earlier. But creating a new body out of nothing would have entailed causing a parity alarm and breaking one of the AIs, while permanently stealing someone else's body would make her as bad as the dupes.

Surviving in the Air was a long way from being actually *alive*. Clair didn't want to consign Libby to the same fate.

But she could guess now why Q had chosen Libby's pattern in Copperopolis. They were the same, connected by Improvement and the secrets that had destroyed both their lives. . . .

Several places down the table, Turner was also paying close attention.

"Winning the battle isn't enough," he said. "The war's the thing."

"Exactly," said Clair. "This isn't just about rescuing Libby and Q. We have to stop it happening to anyone else. I know we don't see eye to eye on everything, but surely we all accept this. Right?"

Gemma conceded a nod. Turner didn't budge.

"We don't know how many hundreds or thousands of people have used Improvement," he said. "Are you going to save them all?"

"I think we have to." Clair hadn't told anyone about using Improvement herself; that knowledge had died with Zep, and she didn't think just then was the right time to bring it up. Not if it'd make them think she was no longer herself. "It's a huge job, which is why we need each other—and we need VIA, too. It's too big. We can't do it without their help."

"She's right," said Jesse.

Gemma pulled a sour face. "Even if VIA *would* listen to us, which they won't, the body we captured went down with the Skylifter."

"There'll be others," Turner said. "You can be sure of that."

Clair drained her glass and reached for another, trying to quash the thought that the task she was setting herself might be too big. How was she going to save Libby, let alone anyone else, when Libby herself had told her to butt out?

"Go easy," said Arcady. "This is a special brew, remember?"

The way he said *special* made her wonder what else was in it apart from alcohol. That led her back to the peacekeepers, and she asked what would happen if they came to investigate the crash.

"You mean with our operation here?" said Arcady. "This is all legit, up to a point. Selling untested drugs is illegal, but that happens off the land. Sometimes the PKs bug us anyway, and we've installed things like a geothermal sink for when they cap our power or whatever. Really, the only problem we have is from cowboys trying to steal our seeds."

"So we're completely safe here?"

"Our booths are private," said Arcady, "there are no comms in or out, and we have deadly serious automated security systems all around our borders. You're lucky you didn't come in that way, let me tell you."

With a broad grin and grease in his beard, he sang another folk song:

Oh, I ran to the rock to hide my face,
The rock cried out, "No hiding place,
No hiding place down here. . . ."

Then someone started playing a tune Clair knew, the first music she had recognized since unplugging from her libraries in the Air. It wasn't one of her favorites, and the pianist was no Tilly Kozlova, but despite her misgivings, Clair was caught up in it like a spark in an updraft. Not everything was gloom and doom and threats and danger. She drank another glass of cider as a toast to that sentiment.

Someone else gave Jesse a hat and he tucked his hair up out of sight. He had a forehead! She could see his eyes! He was good-looking when his hair wasn't in the way. His eyes were green, which Clair hadn't noticed before.

Instead of laughing along with him, Clair felt a sudden, irrational urge to weep, and she knew then that it was time to call it a night. So much had happened. She could barely contain her emotions, let alone control them.

She eased away from the others and explained to Arcady what she wanted—a bed, a cushion, a quiet corner, anything.

"Of course. This way."

He took her to a separate wing of the Farmhouse, where rows of bunks filled a long, segregated dormitory. Several of them were occupied. Under the distant tinkling of the piano, she could hear the light snores of women.

Beds had been set aside for her and Gemma. Clair slipped out of her sneakers and overalls and fell onto the nearest, retaining barely enough energy to wish Arcady good night and to roll herself into the blanket. He brushed the hair back from her forehead like her mother used to and left her to sleep. She didn't hear the door close behind him.

CLAIR DREAMED STRANGELY, intensely, but only in fits and starts, as though she was neither properly asleep nor properly awake. Everything was in fragments, like a jigsaw puzzle or a broken vase. The pieces were jostling for connection but something was getting in the way.

She woke with a dry mouth, a blocked nose, and a raging headache. It was very dark, and she could barely see a thing. All she could hear was the breathing of the sleepers around her and a faint whine of wind through the thick timber walls. Her bladder was full. She knew she wouldn't be able to go back to sleep until she did something about that last detail.

She sat up, stayed still for a moment with both hands holding her skull, then eased out of the narrow cot, dressed in her shirt and underwear. Orienting herself was difficult; she hadn't really been paying attention when Arcady had brought her to bed. She made out Gemma sleeping in the bed opposite. Her eyes possessed a crooked cast even in repose.

Sufficient light spilled in from the corridor to guide her to the door. Clair tiptoed on bare feet outside, looking for familiar landmarks. If she could find the main hall, she was sure she could locate the toilets from there.

The corridor ended in a T junction. She stopped for a

moment, dancing from foot to foot, trying to decide which way to go.

A floorboard creaked to her right. *Footsteps.* Remembering Arcady's veiled warning, she feared interrupting sentries on their rounds and being mistaken for a spy. She was the outsider, after all.

Clair shrank back into the shadows and waited for whoever it was to go by. Her legs were cold. She tried not to shiver.

A woman stepped into the T junction, slight and dressed in black. Clair didn't recognize her until she glanced over her shoulder and her face came into the pale moonlight. It was the woman with the mismatched eyes, Clair thought, then remembered her name. *Jamila.*

She saw Clair in the shadows and started.

"Sorry," said Clair. "It's just me."

"Clair?" Jamila said as though struggling to remember her name in turn.

"Yes, it's me." Clair was relieved to learn that at least one other person had survived the crash of the airship. "I thought the search had stopped. You must have come down right on the edge of the farm."

She nodded. "I'm looking for Turner."

"Well, I'm looking for the toilet, so let's help each other out."

"All right."

Clair came out to join her. She pointed ahead of them.

"The hall's this way, I'm sure."

"Your guess is as good as mine."

They were out of luck. The corridor ended in the kitch-ens. But they had to be close, Clair figured. Toilets, kitchens, dining hall—they were all part of the same complex.

She remembered her companion's shy adoration of the enigmatic leader of WHOLE.

"You've got it bad for Turner, haven't you?" Clair said as they struck out in another direction. "I guess that's one way to keep your disciples."

"Are you nuts? Turner's over eighty."

Clair remembered that Q had said something similar. "You'd never guess to look at him. What's his secret?"

Jamila didn't answer. She seemed tense and watchful, taking in everything around her.

"Did you have any trouble with the farmers?" Clair asked. "I think they're mostly okay, just naturally suspi-cious."

The woman glanced at her and shook her head. Her right hand was behind her back, like she was favoring it. Perhaps it was injured.

"No trouble."

They reached the hall. There was someone else already inside. Clair took in a string of familiar faces.

"Any luck?" asked Theo.

"Found this one," said Jamila, pulling her hand into view. "She might be able to help us with the rest."

"Good work."

"Grab her," said the man with big ears who had been shot outside the safe house in Manteca. "She's going to run."

Clair was backing away from the gun in Jamila's hand, reeling from the truth and her own stupidity. Jamila hadn't been among those rescued by the farmers, and neither were the others. They were *dupes*.

Before she could reach the door, Big-Ears darted over and caught her in his long arms. One strong hand went over her mouth. He held her tight and close. She struggled but could barely move. Her bare feet had no effect against his shins.

"No alarm?" Theo asked.

"None," said Jamila.

Arabelle and another member of WHOLE came out of a corridor on the far side. Arabelle was *walking*. Theo was *talking*.

"Sentries are down," Theo said. "Let's get a move on."

Big-Ears whispered in Clair's ear. "I'm going to take my hand away, and you're going to tell me where Turner is. Scream, and I'll break your neck. Understood?"

She didn't nod, but the pressure across her mouth eased anyway. She didn't say anything. The moment they learned how little she knew, they'd kill her for sure. The dupes, the wolves in sheepskins.

But how had they gotten in? How had they bypassed the security Arcady had been so proud of? And how could she possibly stop them now? There were five of them and only one of her.

Big-Ears twisted her head back. Her spine screamed, but she didn't. She didn't wet her pants either, against all odds.

That gave her an idea. Not a pleasant one, but it wasn't as if she had many options.

Big-Ears tightened his grip. She willed herself to relax. It was hard under the circumstance, with the dupe's arm around her throat and a grisly fate awaiting her. . . .

Warmth flooded down her unclad thighs. The hot, pungent smell of urine hit her nostrils a second later.

Big-Ears smelled it—and he obviously felt it too, since he was holding her so close. His reaction was primal and involuntary, a reflex that kicked in long before his borrowed brain could control it.

Clair exploited his reflex to jackknife forward, breaking his grip. He lunged after her, but she wriggled out of his grasp and ran for the nearest door. Her right foot slipped in the puddle. Somehow she stayed upright.

Five sets of feet rushed after her. The doorway loomed ahead.

Someone stepped out of it, holding a pistol and wearing a familiar face. *Libby*—but the mind behind those familiar eyes could have been anyone's.

Clair skidded to a halt, raised her hands.

"There you are," said the dupe. "I've been looking for you."

"Be cool, Mallory," said Theo. "We have everything under control."

Dupe-Libby took her eyes off Clair. She didn't say anything. She just stared at the rest of them, eyes frosty and distant, as though assessing them.

Then she raised the gun and shot Big-Ears square in the chest. The sound was deafening, the action devastating. He went down in a shower of blood, and for a second the others just gaped at him, shocked by the suddenness of it all. Arabelle was still staring at his fallen body when Libby shot her as well.

Then the others were reacting. Libby pushed Clair behind her and backed into the doorway, firing as she went. Bullets ricocheted around them, kicking up splinters and whining like angry bees. One caught Libby high on the left shoulder, and she screamed.

Clair took her by the other arm and pulled her backward, out of the firing line.

"Clair, it hurts!"

Clair knew that voice.

"Give me the gun, Q. Give it."

There wasn't time to hesitate. Q needed her to be strong, or they would both die. Clair took the gun from her and hefted it in her right hand. A red crosshair appeared in her vision, just as it had in Manteca. She swung the pistol behind her as they rounded a corner, blasted a couple of times at Jamila, but didn't stop to see if she hit her target. Already she could hear raised voices and alarms in response to the gunfire.

"Through here," she said, pushing Q ahead of her, back into the kitchen. Lights were coming on all around her, which would make it harder to hide. Someone was still following them. Definitely female, judging by the glimpses Clair got over her shoulder.

"Come *on*, Q."

"It *hurts*."

"I know, but there's nothing we can do about it now."

"Why does it go on hurting? How do I make it stop?"

"Be quiet, Q, or they'll find us."

Too late. A bullet missed Clair by millimeters, and she dragged Q down behind a heavy stainless steel bench. Slugs slammed into it in quick succession. Clair put her hands over her ears. The sound alone was painful.

Then a deeper note joined in, *boom-boom*, and suddenly everything was quiet apart from the ringing in her ears.

Clair lowered her hands and raised her head slowly over the edge of the bench. Arcady was standing in the doorway, as hairy as a bear, wearing nothing but a shotgun and a worried expression. She left the pistol on the floor and stood up. He pointed the rifle at her, then lowered it. There was gunfire coming from elsewhere in the Farmhouse.

"Back to the hall," he said, unashamed of his nakedness. "Safety in numbers."

Clair reached down and pulled Q to her feet. She was

whimpering and limp. Arcady's rifle came to bear again.

"It's okay," she told him. "She's a friend."

"She's dressed like one of them."

That was true. The uniform of the dupes was a thick black bodysuit with hood pulled back. Maybe that was how they had gotten past the security systems: some kind of infrared camouflage.

"Q duped the dupes," Clair said in a steady voice that barely sounded like her own. "She can explain for herself."

[53]

BY THE TIME they were in the hall, Q's hands were shaking, and her teeth were chattering. Arcady put her on a table at the center of a growing audience. Clair tore a sleeve off her farm shirt and tied it around Q's bullet wound. The cloth immediately turned a bright, sodden red.

"Shock," said Ray, examining her.

"Are you a doctor?" Arcady wasn't watching anyone living. He was staring at a double line of bodies: dupes on one side, sentries on another. The body count was about equal, eleven in total. No Dylan Linwood among the dupes this time: his cover was blown. "That's a flesh wound, nothing serious."

"This has nothing to do with the bullet," said Clair, finding it easier to argue with him now that he'd put on some pants. "I've seen it before. Her mind doesn't fit

Libby's body. She needs to go back into a booth and d-mat out of here."

"Sorry," said Arcady, "but that's not going to happen."

"If she doesn't, she might be permanently injured," said Jesse, pressing through the crowd to stand on the other side of Libby's body, opposite Clair. Her face grew warm. He was wearing pajama pants and no top, and his chest hair looked very dark against the paleness of his skin. "Just look at her. You can tell she hasn't done it right."

Arcady said, "What I mean is she *can't* leave. We have no way of connecting to the outside world, even if we wanted to. No way at all."

"Not true." Q tried to sit up, but the pain was too great. Jesse helped her onto her elbows. "That's how we got in here. By d-mat."

"Aren't you listening to me?" said Arcady again. "Our system is closed."

"All systems are leaky. You receive weather reports and software updates, don't you?"

"Yes, but—"

"The thin end of a wedge. One crack is all it takes. One line of code to widen the crack . . . one executable in your private net, one custom chip built from scratch in a booth, one transmitter to widen the bandwidth. . . . Step by step, they get in deep. It took them fewer than eight hours to slave your booths to their data. If I hadn't been watching, I would never have been able to piggyback on their signal."

"You led them to us," said Arcady, rounding on Turner. His voice quivered with fury. "You brought them right to our doorstep."

Turner was standing to one side with a blanket over his shoulders. He had been quiet ever since the principal purpose of the breach had been revealed to him. *I'm looking for Turner.* "I'm sorry. We had no idea they would respond so quickly."

"And you could have stopped this," Arcady accused Q. "You did *nothing* to warn us."

"She's here, isn't she?" said Clair, taking Q's hand in turn and holding it tightly, trying in vain to still the dancing muscles.

"Clair is right," said Turner. "Q put herself at risk. Without her, we might all be dead now." He shivered and pulled the blanket tighter around him.

"Or worse," said Arcady. Then he shook his head. "Whatever. We're pulling the plug on the damned machines. I'll take an ax to them myself."

"Not yet," Jesse insisted. "First, she needs to go back into the booth. Otherwise, she might . . . I don't know . . . die or something."

A ring of worried, puzzled faces stared down at Q as she quivered and shook on the table. She was very pale, and her eyes were barely open. Jesse brushed sweat-dampened hair back from her forehead.

"How come the dupes can do this," Ray asked, "and she can't?"

"They've had more practice," Clair guessed.

"I'll give you . . . ," Q started to say, but the twitching of her jaw muscles made it hard for her to continue, ". . . give you the woman . . . who was supposed to be here."

Clair gripped her hand tighter. "Yes, of course. Someone must have been on their way already, in Libby's body, otherwise Q couldn't be here now. There'd be a parity violation."

"So what?" asked Arcady.

"The dupes were expecting this other woman. They called her . . ." It was on the tip of her tongue. "*Mallory.* They deferred to her. She might be the one giving the orders."

"All right," he said, cautiously. "We'll trade your friend for one of theirs. Then we use the ax."

"On her?" asked Jesse.

"On the machines, of course. We'll worry about the rest when we have her."

[54]

TWO FARMERS LIFTED Libby's body and carried her through the Farmhouse. Clair stayed close, still holding Q's hand. Q's grip was getting limper by the moment. Her eyes were now completely closed. When they reached the booth— a big industrial machine shaped like a water tank with a curved, sliding door—they laid her on the floor inside and stepped back.

"Are you okay from here?" Clair asked, the last to leave.

Q's head nodded fitfully. "It h-hurts, Clair. I j-just want it to s-stop."

"Is there anything I can do?"

Q shook her head.

Clair lingered a second longer, still troubled by this broken vision of Libby's body. Then she let Q go. The door slid shut behind her. The machine hummed and hissed, cycling matter and data in furious streams. It seemed an age since Clair had last been near a booth, let alone standing inside one.

"The dupes Improved Arabelle," she said to the others, "and Theo, too. The dupes fixed the errors in their patterns before bringing them back. Gemma said that Improvement is like duping . . . and now we know it's the other way around, too."

"Is that how you knew they were dupes?" asked Jesse.

"That and the guns they pulled on me."

Gemma was pale and staring at Clair in horror. Her fists were clenched.

"They won't get a second chance," said Arcady. "Not here. That I promise you."

The booth chimed and the door began to slide open. Farmers and members of WHOLE alike raised their weapons. Clair stepped closer. Finally, she had a real shot at finding out who was behind all this. She tried to stand tall in her one-sleeved shirt and willed herself not to flinch, no matter what she saw.

Inside the booth stood a lone girl dressed all in black. It was as though d-mat had rolled back time. Libby's body was uninjured and showed no signs of trauma. There was no sign of the birthmark, either.

"Hello . . . Mallory," said Clair. The name felt strange on her tongue, directed at someone who looked *exactly* like Libby.

The woman tensed, but the pistol at her side stayed where it was. Her head tilted slightly to the right.

"So you know my name," she said. "Don't think that makes you special. It won't change anything."

The woman spoke with a voice that was neither Libby's nor Q's. The inflection was harder, more controlled. Confident, even when she was staring down a dozen angry men and women.

"Tell us about Improvement," Clair said. "Tell us about the dupes."

"Or else?"

Mallory raised the pistol and placed the barrel under her own throat. Before Clair could move, Mallory pulled the trigger and folded to the floor like a puppet whose strings had been cut.

Arcady rushed into the booth, calling for a medical kit. Clair stared in shock. It was too late to do anything. She had more blood on her face and hands—Libby's blood, this time, and the face of her best friend was ruined in her memory forever. No amount of effort was going to get Mallory to tell them her secrets now.

Jesse turned away, looking as though someone had punched him in the stomach.

Clair wondered why she didn't feel more shocked. Mallory had been a living being, a person as vital as any other. Even if she was a dupe in a stolen body, even if other versions of her could be created a thousand times over, identical to the version that had been standing in front of Clair just moments ago, *she* had been alive. Now she was dead. She had thrown her counterfeit life away without a moment's hesitation, as she would throw it away no matter how many times they tried to bring her back. That made the dupes seem only more formidable.

Yet Clair felt calm and focused. Clarified, like she had crossed some kind of emotional threshold—or *saturation*, perhaps, after too many shocks in a row—and emerged stronger on the other side.

Or else it would hit her later, when she could afford to let her guard down.

"Are you going to be okay?" she asked Jesse, putting a hand on his shoulder.

He nodded once, a bit too quickly, like he might be about to throw up.

"Secure the body," said Arcady, giving up any thought of resuscitation. "It's time to make plans."

THE COUNCIL OF war took place in the Farmhouse's main hall.

"We'll leave immediately," said Turner. "We're putting you all at risk."

"I think that's for the best," said Arcady without hesitation. "We'll help you as much as we can, but this isn't our fight."

"They murdered your people too," said Jesse.

"They died defending our turf. That's what we do. If the dupes come back, we'll be ready."

Clair imagined an army composed of infinitely replaceable, Improved dupes and said nothing. What could she say? Hunkering down wouldn't solve anything. Libby, the *real* Libby, was still out there somewhere, frozen in a data server even after Mallory had destroyed the copy of her body. The dupes made making bodies look easy, as long as parity wasn't broken. The mind was the hard part.

Clair wasn't going to give up on Libby, no matter what Libby had told her to do. Clair was going to *finish* Improvement, one way or another.

"What is your intention?" Arcady asked them. "Where are you planning to go?"

No one spoke for a long moment. Clair was waiting to see what Turner would say. Presumably WHOLE had other hideouts like the Skylifter, where they could slowly rebuild their numbers. It couldn't be easy assembling any kind of operational core when Abstainers were scattered all over the world, steadfastly refusing to make use of the main means of getting around.

"I still like Clair's plan," said Jesse. "Take it up with VIA. It's their problem, ultimately. They'll have to fix it."

"You'd be exposed all the way," said Arcady. "Who knows what would be waiting for you in New York?"

"And VIA is toothless," said Ray. "The watchdog hasn't even barked in years."

"You obviously haven't smuggled any illicit molecules recently," said one of the farmers. "Or tried to sell a bootleg Mona Lisa."

"And we have evidence," said Jesse, glancing at the rows of bodies.

"If the dupes try to attack us," Clair said, "we could end up with several of the same body, which would really clinch it."

"But we couldn't take them all with us," said Ray.

"I know," she said. "We'd just take Libby."

Libby was where it had all started. It would end with her, Clair swore.

"You don't really think VIA's going to let us walk up to the front door with a corpse over our shoulders and stroll right in?" Ray held his hands above his head as though someone had stuck a gun in his back. "There'll be security sweeps, background checks, the works. Look at us. If you were VIA, would you let any of us in?"

Clair did look. They were still in pajamas and shirts, except for Gemma, who must have slept in her clothes. They were splattered with blood and stained with pasts no ordinary citizen would boast of. Ray was right. They wouldn't get near the place.

But why was Ray asking *her* this? She might have proposed the plan to Turner, but Jesse had been the one to suggest VIA in the first place. Why weren't they looking to him as well?

Because she had stopped the dupes, she supposed, and because she was doing most of the talking now. That made a kind of sense, but it didn't mean she had the answers.

Gemma and Turner were suspiciously quiet. Maybe they had already made up their minds, and it didn't matter what anyone else said.

Then an idea came to her that blew all her doubts away.

"They'll let us in," she said, "because we'll make it impossible for them not to."

Everyone was looking at her now, not just Jesse and the surviving members of the Skylifter.

"Do tell," said Ray.

She told them about the crashlanders. Then she reminded them of the video feed Dylan Linwood had put out into the Air. Zep had joked about her being famous for a day, and there was some truth to that: Arcady had seen the video, and he couldn't have been the only one.

"I thought that was a bad thing at first," she said, "because of the way it made me look, but now I think we can use it to our advantage. Both the crashlanders and Abstainers are communities primed to latch onto something new or controversial. They're completely different, and neither is huge, but they draw attention because people outside them disagree on whether they're good or bad. People talk about them, and talk about what they're talking about. If we can make the crashlanders *and* the Abstainers talk about *us*, I think we can really make something pop."

"Something like what?" asked Jesse.

"We don't hide the fact that we're going to VIA HQ in New York. The exact opposite: we tell everyone—anyone who's interested. We promise them something worth seeing. Like Ray says, we'll be exposed when we leave the farm; there'll be drones all over us as soon as we're back in civilization. They're the eyes of the world, and if they're on us because we're giving the world a show, the dupes won't dare act, not up close when they can be seen as well. Home is where the harm is—that's what my mom says: we think we're safe when we're hiding, but we're not. Let's come out of hiding and let the world protect us."

"The drones in Manteca were compromised," Gemma reminded her. "They couldn't see anything."

"Q can help with that," she said, hoping that was true.

"What if they hit you from a distance or make it look like an accident," said Arcady, "like they did with the Skylifter?"

"Enough people will know what really happened," she said, hoping that would be true as well. "Who could ignore something like that? Especially if we spread the word widely enough. There's no reason we can't fight this on more than one front at once. Improvement started with a note that told people to keep it a secret. So maybe we should issue a note of our own that does the exact opposite."

"Anti-Improvement?" said Jesse. "No, Counter-Improvement. That's better."

"But we only mention Improvement and the damage it does," Clair said. "That's important. Anything else will make us look crazy. *Really* crazy, I mean."

"Even though it's true?" said Arcady.

"Let's not overcomplicate things. No one will believe us until they see it with their own eyes. If the dupes come out of the shadows to take us down—that'll do it. If they don't and we get to VIA with the body—that'll do it too. Either way, it'll all come out. When VIA says it's happening, everyone will believe."

"What if VIA's involved?" asked Turner. "The dupes have to be directed by *someone*."

"Do they? I really don't think VIA would be so stupid as to attack their own system—"

"But if they *are*, what then?"

She thought for a second. "They'll still let us come. Their best shot will be to discredit us, not destroy us. As long as we stay in the public eye and don't use d-mat, they can't engineer an accident or dupe us. They can't do either without exposing the truth or breaking parity, so we'll be safe."

"What about peacekeepers?" asked Arcady.

"Technically, we haven't done anything wrong," she said. "They've got no grounds to bring us in, and we've seen no sign that they're likely to. Maybe they'll turn a blind eye if we're in trouble, maybe we can't entirely trust them, but they won't act openly against us."

"And what about you?" asked Jesse. "Your reputation is also at stake. What's everyone going to think when you out yourself as . . . well . . . one of *us*?"

"It's only temporarily, and I reckon my reputation is pretty shot already." She offered him a smile but didn't look any lower than his neck. He still hadn't put a shirt on and she didn't want to blush again, not when she was busy arguing her case. "Thanks, though. Maybe we can show the world that being controversial is not such a bad thing when you're right."

"I think . . . ," Gemma started to say, then stopped when people looked at her. She raised her chin. "I think we should do it."

Clair stared at her. She was the last person Clair had expected to come out in favor of the idea.

"Really?" asked Ray. He looked as startled as Clair felt.

"Yes. It's better than sitting here waiting for the hammer to fall."

"I agree," said Turner, and Clair was doubly amazed.

"We need to go for one simple reason," he explained. "If VIA won't listen, WHOLE will be there to take direct action."

"Uh . . . what does that mean?" asked Jesse.

"It means whatever it needs to mean."

"I'm not a terrorist," said Clair.

"No one's asking you to be one," Turner said.

There was a tense silence around the table, but Clair felt that was as close to a consensus as she was ever going to get.

"All right, then. Great. So how do we get there?" she asked. "We certainly can't walk."

"I know a way," said Arcady. "You can hitch a ride with train hobbyists."

"You're kidding, right?" said Jesse.

"No. We use them all the time. There's a line running right across our property, and engines go by once a day— east at dawn, back west at dusk. You catch the next one, you'll be on the east coast in two days, maybe sooner."

"What happens then?" asked Gemma. "We swim?"

"We won't have to," said Turner. "We're going to take a submarine."

"Now you've *got* to be kidding," said Clair.

"I am not." He folded his arms, his expression betraying no trace of humor. "You want a spectacle, that's exactly what you're going to get."

[56]

THEY WERE READY to move within the hour. Clair showered and changed out of her soiled farmer's shirt into a new one and put on her overalls and sneakers. The bodies were taken away, all except for Libby's, which was hermetically sealed and zipped up in a makeshift plastic shroud. Evidence. Packs were distributed. Clair began to get a *camping* vibe from the exercise, reinforced when she saw how much gear she was expected to carry. Among the packets of freeze-dried food, canteens, a sleeping bag, and a bedroll were a pistol and two boxes of ammunition. She remembered exactly how heavy *they* were from lugging similar ones halfway across California.

Instead of complaining, she asked Arcady to show her how to load the pistol. It was smaller than the one Q had made for her, fitting neatly into the palm of her hand as though designed for it. He promised less of a kick and not greatly reduced accuracy at close range.

"You won't need to clean it today," he said. "But you might want to test fire it if there's time before you leave."

She did so, deriving a nervous satisfaction from the solid

kick of the weapon into her palm. She hoped against hope her plan would hold, and she wouldn't need to use it.

The sky was lightening when they piled their gear into a sturdy farm vehicle on four fat wheels, and the expedition prepared to set out. There was a tense farewell on the Farmhouse's broad steps. Arcady hugged Clair, his beard tickling her check, and gravely shook Turner's hand.

"You'll remember everything I told you?" he said.

"Of course." Turner nodded. "I'm grateful to you."

"Give us a good show. We'll be watching."

Their four-wheeler had a flatbed on the back, which Clair shared with Jesse and Ray and two heavy bags that made metallic sounds with every bump. Watching the Farmhouse recede as they sped up the dirt track through the orchard, she tried to think of their departure less as abandoning somewhere safe, more as progressing boldly toward a solution to everyone's problems.

"I grew up on a farm like this," said Ray out of nowhere, and Clair could tell that he was wrestling with similar demons. "There's nothing like getting your hands dirty."

"I used to love working in our kitchen garden back home," Jesse said. "Dad and I never managed to keep the bugs out of our asparagus, no matter what I tried."

"You should have coplanted with coriander," Ray suggested. "It attracts ladybugs, which eat the asparagus beetles."

"We never thought of that."

Clair zoned out while Ray and Jesse swapped gardening tips. She was even less interested in growing produce than she was in cooking it. Besides, her hands were shaking, and she was afraid her voice might start shaking too. This was the first chance she'd had to sit still since the dupes attacked. She could feel a rush of anxiety building behind the walls she'd built, pushing outward, threatening to overwhelm her. She couldn't afford to break down now, she told herself. She had to be strong.

The feeling passed, but she knew it was only a temporary reprieve.

The journey to the edge of the farm took over an hour. There, they turned onto the old Route 94, now a green strip with one broad lane for farm traffic, and headed west across the prairie for the town of Mandan on the bank of the Missouri River, where the train was due to stop.

The landscape was wild and green, an endless tangle of low trees and undergrowth where it hadn't been cultivated. Clair saw deer and something large and lumbering that might have been a bear. Birds were everywhere, startling out of trees and settling back down in their wake. She didn't know their names or the names of the trees they inhabited. When the Air returned, she could find out if she wanted to.

Her connection was jammed as far as Route 94. As soon as Clair could, she contacted Q.

Or tried to.

"Q, can you hear me?"

There was no response. Clair was immediately worried that something might have gone wrong when Q had been d-matted out of the Farmhouse in Libby's body. After all, taking control of a new body was obviously hard. Maybe going back was just as hard, particularly when Q had no body to return to.

That the damage might have been permanent was something Clair hadn't considered. Not only was Q their greatest ally in the fight against the dupes, but she was a victim of Improvement as much as Libby or the others. She deserved a shot at getting her own body back.

"Q, are you there?"

". . . Clair?"

The reply was weak and uncertain, as though Q had forgotten how to talk.

"That's it. I'm here. Can you see me?"

"Clair, you're back! Or *I'm* back. Or . . . both. How confusing! I don't know what happened to me."

"You'd better forget about duping for a while," Clair said with some anxiety. "Are you going to be all right?"

"Yes, Clair. I think so, but it might take me a few minutes to get myself straight again. Should you be out in the open like this while I'm so distracted?"

Clair outlined the plan while the farmers drove them to Mandan. Q was reluctant to strip away the mask that had kept Clair hidden from direct observation through the Air. Clair insisted it had to be done, although she, too, felt nervous about it. If her plan didn't work, she would doom not just herself but everyone with her as well.

"What's the message of the meme you want to send?" Q asked.

Clair sent her the draft she and Jesse had written. It felt right that they should use the form of the original Improvement text in order to counteract it.

You are special.
You are unique.
You don't need—or want—to be selected.
Improvement is dangerous.
It kills children,
it kills brothers and sisters,
it kills best friends.

You can stop it
if you want to.
The method is simple.
Spread the word:
Improvement is a lie.

Keeping the secret robs people
of the life they deserve.

Q didn't offer an opinion as to the message's literary or tactical merits. Clair took that as a positive sign.

"I found that medical data you asked me to look for," Q said. "I can attach the links to the message."

"So the data is genuine?"

"Yes. And I found more matching the same criteria."

"How many?"

"Seven boys, two more girls."

That was chilling. Fifteen victims of Improvement, and perhaps more on the way.

"Do you want me to send the message now?" asked Q. "I can seed it to multiple places to guarantee exposure."

"Might as well. Don't make me the sender, but link my profile to it and remove my mask when it goes out so people can see me if they want to. Give me two minutes. I'll post a caption that'll say everything we need to say."

She had mulled that over too, but on the point of no return, she hesitated. As far as everyone was concerned, she had disappeared the night of the explosion in Manteca. Zep and Jesse and disappeared with her. What could she possibly say in a word or two that could sum up everything that had happened to her and everything that needed to happen to make things right?

If Libby were here, Clair thought, *she would know what to do.* Libby was the one obsessed with popularity and catchy captions. She saw the trends and cliques before they happened and knew exactly when to jump aboard.

Clair wished she could just go along for the ride now and let Libby take all the credit.

But it was up to her this time. Libby needed her to do it because Libby couldn't do it herself. There was no other option.

For a caption, Clair adapted an old VIA infomercial. It showed a woman hopping from place to place around the globe, cheerfully unaffected by the experience. The slogan had been "Everywhere for Everyone," but Clair cut that part. Instead, she added the text "Destination: VIA!" with a link to her itinerary.

"How are you doing, Q?"

"I am making the final adjustments now, Clair," said Q. "You are yourself again."

There was no immediate change in her lenses' format. Clair wondered what she should be feeling. This was her chance to reconnect with her world—her media, her family, her friends. Her *life*. But it felt oddly distant, as though it all belonged to a different version of her—Clair 1.0, who had never shot someone, never walked cross-country in the middle of the night, never peered behind the curtain of her perfectly sheltered life.

Clair 2.0 had done all those things and more. What if the two versions weren't compatible?

She uploaded the caption and waited to see what would happen.

[57]

BETWEEN CONSECUTIVE EYE blinks, her infield went from empty to full. There were bumps banked up two days from Ronnie, Tash, and her parents, rated varying degrees of urgent. Among them were queries from teachers, tutors, and study mates. There were messages from crashlanders, Abstainers, and peacekeepers. There was even one from Xandra Nantakarn, asking if she and Libby would be coming to another ball soon. "Great publicity," she said. "You girls are quite the mystery. Let me know when you come out of hiding."

Clair told herself to be glad people were talking about her. That was exactly what the plan needed. Ringing, empty silence would be the death of them all.

On top of family and friends and friends of friends, the PKs wanted to interview her in order to clarify her involvement in several "atypical events" over the previous days. It was quite a sequence: the video stunt at school, the explosion of Jesse's home, the hostage situation with her parents, her chase by the dupe across the world, her vanishing from the Air and the disappearance of Zeppelin Barker, plus the crash of the Skylifter. Whether they knew she was involved in all of them or were just guessing she was, she didn't know and wasn't in a hurry to find out.

Clair sent them the standard polite reply she sent to every one of her contacts, stating that she expected to be in New York in a day or two to talk to someone in VIA. She kept the details of the meeting vague, since at that point there weren't any to share. She mentioned only that she would be traveling by means other than d-mat because d-mat wasn't safe for her at the moment. In explanation, she linked to the Counter-Improvement document without saying whether she herself or anyone she knew had used Improvement or not. She was careful to make no mention of either the Abstainer movement or WHOLE. Clair Hill had to be nothing other than ordinary for the story to get any kind of traction.

Clair Hill, the girl crossing North America practically on foot because she's too frightened to use d-mat. Clair Hill, the girl seeking reassurances from VIA that the world she lives in is in good hands. Clair Hill, wanting to keep her friends and loved ones safe at no small cost to herself.

She had once read about witches who believed that wishing for something three times made it come true. She was aiming for more like three thousand wishes, but the end result she hoped for would be the same.

It didn't take long for Ronnie and Tash to notice her reappearance. Or her parents. As the four-wheeler raced along the old highway, Clair organized a hookup with all of them at once, figuring it was best to get the conversation

[365]

over with. Mandan was getting closer with every minute, and she wanted to be alert for what might happen there. But she owed her friends and family an explanation. And she needed their help.

"Look, I know this all sounds crazy—"

"Crazy?" Her mother was practically bursting out of her lenses. "You run off in the middle of the night—someone points a gun at us, asking where you are—you disappear—"

"I can explain everything, Mom," she said, "but not now. You have to trust me. It's safer for everyone that way. I know what I'm doing."

"But what *are* you doing? Playing trains in the middle of nowhere when you should be in school—"

"Monday's a free day."

"You know what I mean!"

"I didn't know there *were* trains anymore," said Tash. "Where did you find it?"

"That's a long story." Clair didn't want to go into every detail. "I just need you to help me spread the word."

"What word?" asked Ronnie.

"Tell everyone what I'm doing. Start discussions. Post updates. Make a lot of noise, any way you can. I need this to be big, or . . ." She didn't know what to say that wouldn't alarm her mother even more. ". . . or something really bad will happen. I swear. And not just to me."

"I think we should call the peacekeepers," said Oz, her stepfather's long, sun-warmed face uncharacteristically grim. "They've been looking for you. They're as worried as we are."

"Yeah, but about the wrong thing. Remember that guy with the gun to your head?" Clair said with calculated harshness. "How much use the PKs were then is exactly how much use they are now. This is between me and VIA. We have to make them fix it."

"But what is *it*?" Allison asked. "Why didn't you talk to me about it? Why won't you tell me now?"

"We did talk about it, kind of. Someone's using d-mat to hurt people. They hurt Libby, and they want to hurt me."

"And Zep?" asked Tash. "Is he with you?"

Clair couldn't answer immediately. That wasn't a question she had anticipated. The surge of emotion it provoked was difficult to control.

"Clair?" asked Ronnie.

"He . . . I'll tell you later." From their point of view, he was still alive, just missing. She didn't know to break it to them. "For now, just do as I ask. Please. I'll send you a message in a second—Counter-Improvement, Jesse calls it. Pass it to everyone you know. Generate a buzz."

"Jesse Linwood's with you?" asked Tash. "The Lurker?"

Clair bristled at the old nickname but didn't have time to defend him.

"You can follow me via the link in the message. It's important you do, but don't freak out if I disappear every now and then. I'm with people who literally move in mysterious ways."

"If that's what I have to do to make sure you come back in one piece," Allison said, "then I'll do it. But be careful, please."

"I will," Clair promised. "I'll do my best, and I know you all will too."

She signed off, feeling a sharp tug in her heart. Her hands were shaking again, and it was a moment before she could look up.

[58]

AS THEY CAME into Mandan, the gleaming lines of a train track became visible on her right, along with the train itself, a long string of wheeled containers trailing behind an engine that issued neither smoke nor steam. Clair was faintly disappointed. She had imagined something more antique than an electric locomotive but at the same time much faster. The farmers easily overtook the train as it trundled into town.

Mandan was large enough to have eye-in-the-sky drones surveying the empty streets. Clair waved at them, half expecting dupes to burst out of doorways and windows at any moment. There could be booths coming into life all around them, building another death squad.

But there weren't, or if there were, the dupes stayed hidden. The drones watched them without overt curiosity, and the small expedition reached the train station unmolested. Under the eaves of an ancient wooden building, they unloaded and stretched their legs. Clair could hear the train approaching from the west. The light of the morning sun caught it, making it shine. It pulled up to the platform in a cacophony of metal, grease, and glass.

Turner went to the front of the train to talk to the engineers or drivers or whatever they were called. Clair paced back and forth, wishing they could get moving. The station was surrounded by trees on two sides. There was plenty of cover for anyone wanting to sneak up on them.

Gemma joined her at one end of the platform, fidgeting restlessly with her cross. She had exchanged her sling for a bandage, allowing her injured arm greater movement. They stood together, staring out into the vegetation and seeing nothing.

"This is your plan," said Gemma, "so why do you look nervous?"

"I never expected everyone to agree to it," she said.

"Is that true?"

Clair shrugged. It was, if she was honest with herself. "We've never agreed on anything before."

"Fair point."

One of the drones swooped lower, as though trying to overhear their conversation.

"You think we're out of our minds," Gemma said to her.

"It goes both ways. Dylan Linwood called me a zombie."

"That sounds like him." She hung her head. "It's not easy being in the minority. I mean, what are the odds that everyone else in the world is wrong, and you're right? The moment you start to doubt, everything turns upside down and the world comes crashing down around you. . . ."

Clair understood that feeling well.

"Don't tell me you're starting to change your mind about d-mat."

"Never. It gets in your brain and softens it. Stop using, and you get better fast. You can see that now, surely."

"What do you mean?"

"Look at yourself, Clair Hill. You were like everyone else before—weak, soft, compliant. Now you've changed. You're strong. Look how you stood up to the dupes back there. Could you have done that a week ago? I don't think so. D-mat was holding you back. Now you're free."

"Free to do what? Ruin my life?"

"If that's what it takes to be yourself."

Even when Gemma was staring straight at her, she seemed to be tilting her head, putting a question mark at the end of every sentence she said.

Turner called them from the other end of the platform, but before Clair could go, Gemma grabbed her tightly by the arm and pulled her close.

"Dylan made me promise to look after Jesse if anything ever happened to him," she whispered. "You'll have to do it for me."

"Why?" Clair forces out. "Where are you going?"

"The world is turning upside down, Clair," Gemma said. "Not everything—or everyone—is going to survive."

"Don't be crazy. Of course we're going to survive. That's what the plan is for, right?"

Gemma shook her head. Clair pulled free. There wasn't time to deal with Gemma's doubts on top of her own.

She turned to head toward where Turner, Ray, and Jesse stood, waiting.

"Promise me, Clair," Gemma hissed after her. "Look after Jesse. Promise me!"

Clair kept walking, rubbing her arm where Gemma's strong fingers had gripped her.

[59]

"IT'S STARTED," SAID Turner. "See?"

Two people had appeared at the other end of the platform, a mother and young daughter, both dressed in patched clothes. They stood hand in hand and watched as the expedition prepared to move out.

"Abstainers," Turner explained. "There's a handful in

every town, invisible, excluded, but very loyal. Put the word out, and they will come."

"What are they doing here?" she asked him.

"They came to see you," he said. "The girl who's taking on VIA single-handed."

"That's not what I'm doing," she said. "It's not."

"I know. But it sounds better that way, doesn't it?"

The girl, no more than five, waved shyly at Clair. Clair hesitated, then waved back. That was what Libby would've done, she told herself.

The freight car was open and ready for them. Jesse drove their four-wheeler inside. Clair was about to follow when the whine of tiny electric fans rose up behind her. She turned and saw a drone dropping down to head height. It flashed its lights in a complex sequence, spun once around its axis, and waited for her to react.

"Is that you, Q?"

"How did you know, Clair?" came the delighted response via the drone's PA speakers.

She smiled. "A lucky guess."

"It took me much longer than I expected to install my own command agents. The democratic algorithms are triple secure, with—"

"No need for the details, Q. Good thinking, though. I'm glad you'll be here to keep an eye on us."

Clair crossed into the car, and the drone went to follow.

"We'll be Faraday shielded when the door is shut," Turner said.

"Can the drone keep up with the train outside?" Clair asked Q.

"Not for long, but I can magnetically affix it to the car to stop the batteries from running low."

"Great. Do that. And keep your eyes open. We don't want anyone taking us by surprise."

The floor shifted beneath them. Everyone put out a hand to steady themselves as the train began to move. Clair leaned on Jesse, who braced himself against the nearest wall.

"Out you go, Q. It's time to shut the door."

"Bon voyage," said the drone as it zipped through the car door.

Turner pressed a button, and the door slid shut behind them with a metallic boom.

Lights came on inside, and presumably some kind of air circulation system too. Clair felt a puff of wind against her cheek.

The train accelerated, turning steadily to the right. Clair found it hard to stand, even with Jesse as a crutch.

"I suggest we all get some sleep," said Turner, flipping open his backpack and pulling out his bedroll. No one had rested since the dupes had woken them all up in the middle of the night. "We've got hours to kill until we get there."

There was a pair of chemical toilets at the far end of the car. Clair used one, then found an empty spot on the back of the four-wheeler and tried to rest. The rocking of the car beneath her was less soothing than she had imagined it would be. Jesse lay down next to her, bundled up tightly in a sleeping bag so little more than his nose was visible. She wanted to ask how he was doing but didn't want to disturb him. Maybe she was the only one finding it hard to settle.

Libby's body was just yards away, wrapped tightly in plastic. Or was it Mallory's body, since that was the name of the last person to inhabit it? *A rose by any name*, she thought. *A mind in any body . . .*

She did drop off eventually and woke with her breath stopped in her throat as though someone were choking her. The interior of the car was lit only by power LEDs and static displays, a meaningless constellation of yellows, reds, greens, and blues. Jesse had moved closer in his sleep, but his face was as hidden as ever. Clair sat up and pushed herself away from him. Her head was pounding. She felt trapped. She wanted to leap out of the car and onto solid earth. She wasn't used to things moving, shifting, turning the way they did in the world Jesse and the others inhabited.

Now you're free, Gemma had said. Free to be herself, but she didn't feel free. She wanted everything to be *still*, just for a moment, so the person she had been could catch up to her, if it wasn't already too late for that.

"God, I hope it's not," she breathed.

"Deceitful as it is," said a soft voice out of the dark,

"hope at least leads us to the end of our lives by an agreeable route."

She looked around. Two dark eyes were staring at her out of the gloom. They belonged to Turner.

"Is that a quote?"

"More or less. Someone French, I think."

He unfurled himself from his sleeping bag and came to sit nearer her.

"You can't sleep either," he said.

"It's not that. I mean, I was asleep, but . . ." She hesitated, not entirely sure which particular anxiety was dominating her thoughts at that moment. "I'm afraid I might've talked you all into something really stupid."

"This plan of yours?" He smiled. "If I worried about every stupid thing I've done, I'd never sleep again."

His unlined, youthful face gave him away. "You're not the worrying kind," she said. "I can tell that just by looking at you."

"Appearances . . ." He stopped as Ray snuffled and rolled over, then continued in a softer tone, ". . . are deceitful, like hope."

"Apparently. Everyone tells me you're eighty years old."

"That's not true," he said.

"Obviously."

"I'm eighty-three next month."

She stared at him with aching migraine eyes. "Fine. Whatever."

"I'm not lying," he said. "People come to WHOLE for a variety of reasons. They are harmed, or someone they love is harmed. Some people just know: they look at the people around them and the situation in the world at large, and they know that there's something very rotten in the state of d-mat."

He sighed. "I'm not like them. D-mat never harmed anyone I love, my family, anyone I ever cared about, yet I have lost them all forever. They might as well be dead, because I am dead to all of them now. I faked my death to spare them what happened to me."

"What was it?" she asked. "Some kind of disease?"

"Quite the opposite. I am as healthy as a thirty-year-old man and have been for many decades. D-mat twisted my body and made it into a disguise. Everything about me is wrong. My very existence is a lie and a curse—a curse that many, unfortunately, would kill to possess."

"D-mat gave you eternal youth?"

"D-mat *mutated* me. It's frozen me, set me apart from the world. When my condition started to show, I had no choice but to abandon my life. I can never go back, or people will ask questions. I can't move on, can't ever be *normal*. God help me if I tried to have children. What horrors might they inherit from me? What mutations might I visit upon them in turn? That is the vilest thing of all."

"Haven't you had your genome sequenced, diagnosed—?"

"No." He shook his head in absolute denial. "Once it's out there, once someone learns what I am, the secret could not be contained, and then we'd be back where we were fifty years ago, overpopulated, poisoning the planet with our filth. Really, I should wear gloves and shave my head, or lock myself in a bubble, or kill myself to stop my genes from escaping—but I am human to that extent at least. I want to be part of the world and make a change for the better, while I can."

A horrid thought struck her. "Jamila had a crush on you, and she was, what, twenty-five?"

He inclined his head. "Grossly inappropriate, but very flattering for a guy who remembers the birth of the Air. I didn't do anything about it, I swear."

[60]

THE CAR KNOCKED from side to side with the irregularities in the tracks. Clair struggled to accept that a man who looked barely older than her had actually lived longer than her grandfather.

"You're ancient enough to remember the Water Wars," she said.

"Vividly. I was conscripted to fight in Brazil. Terrible times. We had rationing back then, and martial law. We were right on the brink of disaster. Difficult to imagine now, isn't it? There were death camps in Brazil, Bangladesh, Iraq, Kazakhstan, Senegal, and Cambodia. . . . The United States was lucky on the whole. We lost only Florida, and no one complained about that."

It was an old joke, long stripped of humor, and for the first time she accepted that he might be even older than the joke was.

"D-mat saved the world," she said. "Why do you hate it so much?"

"I didn't always," he told her. "Before the wars I worked for the consortium that brought it into being. Not working on the technology itself but on the control software. I was an AI engineer, commercially and with the joint forces. We called ourselves 'wranglers,' as with cattle. AIs were strange new things with their own rules, their own surprising twists and turns. It took a certain kind of person to tame them. The concern was that they would break out and take over the world. That was before we had a better idea of what intelligence was. We imagined these huge, planet-sized minds gobbling up every piece of knowledge we had and thinking thoughts that would destroy us all. Now we know that we can train either big minds that are dumb across the board or small minds that are supersmart at only one or two things. What we were afraid of just can't exist in the Air. That's why robots never really got off the ground. The AIs we have today are vigilant, tireless, and thorough, but they're great at missing the obvious. They're not *alive*. Consciousness is complexity, Clair, and the only way we've found to make that is the old-fashioned way." He smiled. "We're all too good at breeding small, dumb minds. Nowhere near smart enough to build our own successors."

"Were you good at it?" she asked. "Taming AIs, I mean?"

"Not really. That's how I ended up wrangling people instead. I do remember the AIs we built for VIA, though. They were the big, dumb kind: patient, plodding, tireless, no initiative at all."

"Could you hack into them?"

"No. And I've tried, believe me." He stared into space for a second. "We named them for philosophical concepts concerning the nature of things. Different concepts because they handle different roles in the d-mat process. One AI is all about numbers and atoms—the essential math that leads to a thing being what it is. The other is about the subjective quality of the final object: whether it's still the same or not, even though every physical piece comprising it has changed at the most basic level. WHOLE champions the second problem, while VIA thinks only of the first. It's amazing the system hasn't cracked completely open with those two very different minds at its heart."

"What would happen to the bus," she said, "if the conductor and the driver had an argument?"

"Chaos, of course." He glanced at her with eyebrows

raised. "You could describe the AIs that way. Who gave you that analogy?"

"Q. She was telling me how she and the dupes do what they do without the AIs in VIA noticing."

"She's more or less right about their roles, if a little simplistic."

"I don't think she's old enough to know much about philosophy."

"That's probably true of you, too, Clair. But don't worry. When you're an old coot like me, you'll have plenty of time to catch up. Philosophy is all I seem to think about these days."

I hope I look half as good as you do while I'm doing it, she thought.

"I read somewhere once," she said, "that every time we think of a memory, we erase it from our mind and rewrite it again. Like every time we use d-mat."

"You're going to say *and we still know who we are.*"

She nodded.

"Can you tell me what happened at your tenth birthday party, Clair? How it felt the *second* time you kissed someone? What you had for breakfast ten days ago?"

She shook her head, even though she remembered vividly, would always remember, the second time she had kissed Zep. Her ordinary life before then felt infinitely distant.

"Now, imagine that those missing memories are actually

pieces of your brain or your heart or your eyes. Is thinking that you know who you are still reassuring?"

"But we lose bits of ourselves every day anyway. Skin, eyelashes, fingernails—and no one cares. Aren't all the cells in our body replaced every seven years?"

"Tissue we shed that way is dead tissue. If we chopped working cells from your muscles or brain, don't you think you'd notice?"

"What about that line they always quote about the toenail—the total amount of *human* lost every decade?"

"What about Jesse's mother? She disappeared, and she's bigger than a toenail."

"Yes, but—"

"It's all about what you measure. Define *human*. Define *missing*. Hell, define *toenail*. Lies, damned lies, and statistics—the devil's always in the details. D-mat started as nothing more than a new way of moving matter around, and look what happened. It saved the world, Clair, but might yet destroy us all. No one saw *that* coming, even those of us who were there at the beginning."

She didn't know how to respond to that, except by concentrating on something much smaller than the entire world's problems.

"I'd like to check up on Q," she said. "Do you know how to open the door?"

He nodded. "I'll show you."

They got up and tiptoed through the car so they didn't

wake the others. Turner showed her the code, and the door opened a crack, letting in light and cool, whipping wind. There were grumbled complaints. Clair ignored them.

"All quiet up there, Q?" she asked.

"Nothing to report. It's all pretty dull, actually."

"That's what I want to hear."

Her infield was full again—overflowing. Ronnie and Tash had been busy emailing school friends and striking up conversations about what Clair was doing. Ronnie called it "stimulating debate," but Tash preferred "starting arguments"; Clair didn't care as long as her name was used each time, helping her overall presence in the Air pop a little bit more. Some of her classmates had decided that she was playing hooky and off on an adventure in order to avoid an exam later that month. She was satisfied with that, too. It all added up.

Her mother and Oz, meanwhile, were nagging relatives and work colleagues to ask if they knew about Improvement. Had anyone heard of it? Did anyone have kids who had tried it? Both her parents were cautious in keeping the questions open rather than closed, which reflected their own ambivalence, Clair assumed. She was sure they would rather she gave up and came home, but given that she clearly wasn't about to, their only option was to understand her concerns more clearly. And if there was something to it, then they would be informed.

Clair sent out the same formal reply to people she didn't know and posted updates to the Air in various media.

There was one message from VIA, which she hadn't expected. Her plan had been in operation for only a few hours, and already someone had noticed! All the message consisted of, however, was an impersonal set of instructions on how to formally register a complaint.

Clair refused to be bothered by the apparent rejection. She posted the message to the Air and created a new caption to accompany it: a video of a melting ice cream, played normally first, then reversed so the scoop appeared to be pouring back into the cone. Then she asked Q to disengage the drone from its magnetic perch and bring it alongside the train, pushing its fans to the limit so it could catch a glimpse of her through the car door. She was a shadow hidden in shadows. That was how she appeared to anyone watching her at that moment. She barely recognized herself.

Clair forced herself into the light and opened the door a fraction wider. As the drone's cameras watched, she smiled and gave a defiant thumbs-up. According to the stats on her profile one thousand, two hundred thirteen people watched her do it, her parents among them.

Hi, Mom, she thought. *Look at me, seeing the world.*

There actually wasn't that much to see, though. Just old farmland to the horizon, left to go to seed.

She shut the door. The train chattered on.

"I'm going back to sleep now," Turner told her. "Thank you for keeping me company. It has been agreeable, as some old French guy might have put it. I like your energy. It gives me hope to fight alongside someone young like you."

He went back to his empty bedroll, and she sat on her own for a few minutes longer, staring at her cracked and dirty fingernails. *Agreeable* wasn't the word she would have used, and *fight* bothered her even more.

———————————————————————— [61]

CLAIR OPENED THE door again as they passed through Chicago. Kids ran alongside the train as it rolled by, like something from an old movie. Her heart warmed at the thought of Abstainers all along their path loyally responding to Turner's call. Then it occurred to her that without d-mat in their lives, there was probably nothing for them to do. To the children waving at her, stuck in the same place day in and day out, Clair's expedition might have all the cachet of a real, live circus.

After Chicago, Clair lay on her sleeping bag, not sleeping but not entirely awake, either. She was thinking about ways to improve her statistics, to maintain interest before the spotlight moved on. She had no idea how people stayed famous all their lives, particularly the ones who never seemed to actually do anything. At a certain point, she supposed, fame became something bigger than the person possessing it. It could even live on after the person died, like a ghost—or perhaps more like Q did in the Air, still vital in its own way, changing and evolving with the times. Clair never wanted to experience anything like that. Once Improvement and the dupes were dealt with, she wanted to go back to being a nobody again. Except maybe for the odd crashlander party or two.

Clair got up and used the toilet. When she came out, Jesse was leaning into the open hood of the four-wheeler to see what lay inside. He looked long and thin in a uniform designed for stockier men.

"Dad tried to teach me about engines like these," he said. "I wasn't interested."

"I thought you studied exactly this kind of thing at school."

"Only if I had to. Anything with wheels bored me out of my skull unless I was riding it and going fast. I wish I'd paid closer attention now."

She watched him, thinking fondly, *Killer with a screwdriver.* They hadn't got on well at first, but she felt that she understood him better now. He had kept her going while they were running from the dupes, and he had backed her plan long before anyone else had. She was sure she wouldn't have had the guts to go ahead with it if Zep had been there. Zep had been fun to be with, but he wasn't as pragmatic as Jesse. Jesse, she was sure, would have thrown the rope rather than thrown himself off the observatory.

"Are you okay?"

She blinked, not realizing that she had been staring.

"Fine," she said, then added, more honestly, "Tired. Nervous."

"That's all?"

She frowned. "Why?"

He straightened and glanced at the others.

"Let's talk," he said. "In private."

"Okay. Where?"

"Here."

He opened the door of the four-wheeler and waved her inside. She slipped across the front seats, and he followed her, shutting the door softly behind them.

Jesse braced himself with one hand on the steering wheel, facing her.

"What's up?"

"I just want to ask you," he said, "if you used Improvement."

She stared at him for a long moment, the lightness that had been in her stomach turning to lead. He was looking right at her, and she was looking right back at him, but weirdly she felt as though she were shrinking into her body, vanishing behind her eyes into a tiny point that peered out at him through layers of dirty glass.

"Clair?"

She snapped back to normal.

"Yes," she said. "How did you know?"

"I rewatched the video of Dad in Gordon the Gorgon's office," he said. "Last night, while I was trying to sleep. She asked if you knew someone who had used Improvement, and you hesitated before saying that yes, you did. There was something in your face—I don't know what it was, exactly. Like you felt guilty, and not just because of Libby. It came and went so fast, I didn't notice it before. I can see it now, though, when I watch the video again."

Because he knows me better too, she thought.

"And there's all the superhero stuff," he went on, although she really wished he wouldn't. "Shooting the dupe, keeping your head when all I want to do is roll into a ball, the strategizing. I thought it was your true calling, remember?"

She did remember, and she cursed herself for feeling like a fraud.

"But Improvement didn't work," she said. "My nose hasn't changed."

"Is that what you put on the note?"

"Yes."

"Why?

"Why do you think?" She screwed it up self-consciously.

He shook his head. "How many times did you do it?"

"Sixty, seventy—I can't remember the exact number."

"Maybe your nose hasn't changed because you haven't used d-mat for a while. Maybe it takes time for the physical changes to kick in. The other stuff might happen more quickly."

"What stuff? What are you saying, exactly?"

"You heard what Gemma said. People who use Improvement have their brains taken over."

"But Gemma also said that it doesn't affect everyone."

"That's true. Have you had any of the symptoms? Headaches, mood swings?"

She thought of the pounding in her skull that had been plaguing her for days, which she'd thought was caffeine withdrawal and stress. And she remembered the strange moment of clarity after Mallory had killed herself, and her shaking hands on the way to meet the train. They were shaking again now. She tucked them firmly between her thighs.

"I did it after I saw your dad the first time," she confessed, unable to meet his eyes. "I used it until Q noticed me, but it didn't seem to do anything, so I didn't mention it to anyone. . . . I didn't think it was important. . . ."

But *you've changed*, Gemma had said. The words reverberated through her mind, reinforced by the sudden certainty that they were true. Zep had noticed. Jesse had noticed. Gemma had noticed. Since using Improvement, she had become a different person. But was it because of Improvement or because of everything that had happened to her? Was Clair 2.0 her or someone else entirely?

She wondered if Libby had felt the same. What had it been like to have her mind taken over by another? Was it like a war or an unstoppable, insidious creep, like the tide rising over the shore? Did Libby's thoughts and decisions still feel like hers, as Clair's did now, even as they slowly became someone else's?

The rhythmic patter of the wheels on the tracks was repetitive and insistent.

Mallory . . . Mallory . . . Mallory . . .

"Are you going to tell the others?" she asked Jesse.

"Why?" he asked. "Do I need to?"

"Don't you think you should, if someone's trying to take me over?"

"I don't know that it's that simple. You told me the truth, so I know you're you right now."

"What if that changes?"

"Is that likely?'

"You've got me worried now. What if I start . . . doing things?"

"Like what?"

"I don't know. Putting people in danger . . ."

He didn't answer, and she looked up at him, afraid to see that he might be staring at her as if she were an alien.

He wasn't. He was grinning.

"Danger?" he said. "Like we're on a picnic right now?"

"You know what I mean."

"I do. And, you know, maybe this is a good thing, in a way. Maybe it wasn't really you who shot the dupe back at the safe house."

"But what happens if they can't reverse it? What if . . . ?" She hugged herself, thinking terrible thoughts.

Five days had passed since Libby had used Improvement. Four days for Clair.

"I'm so frightened," she said, and burst into tears.

"Hey," he said, moving closer. "Hey, don't. I'm sorry. This isn't what I wanted. . . ."

"What did you want? Why did you bring it up?"

"I had to be sure. I had to know."

Clair put her face into her hands.

"What if I had lied?" she asked through her sobs. "What would you have done?"

"I don't know, and you didn't lie, so it doesn't matter." He awkwardly took her into his arms. "It's okay. You're going to be all right, I promise."

"How do you *know*? How do you know I won't go crazy and kill everyone?"

"I've lived with crazy people all my life," he said, "and I don't think you're one of them."

She returned his hug, wishing she could stay right there all the way to New York.

"I'm sorry you're stuck with me," he said into her hair. "I bet you wish—"

She shut him up the only way she could: by kissing

him. Only afterward did she think of her puffy eyes and snotty nose. Only afterward did she wonder at how easy it was, compared to Zep. She just put her hands on either side of his face and pulled his mouth to hers. Her lips parted without hesitation and his tongue sought hers, and she was surprised by how gentle it all was. His goatee tickled her. He smelled of engine grease and tasted faintly of mint. But when she closed her eyes, she saw only him in her mind, not the shadow of someone else, and there was no feeling of doing something wrong. Quite the opposite.

Her heart began to race in an entirely ungentle way, and she didn't want to believe it at first when she felt him pulling away.

"What?" she asked, blinking at him.

"I was just . . . no, forget it."

There was a questioning look in his eyes.

"You're wondering if that was really me?" she said.

He blushed. "No. I mean, yes. I mean, I hope it was. I mean . . . Oh God, could I be stupider?"

She dropped her eyes, feeling her face freeze. The same question occurred to her now, but directed at herself, not him. Just days ago, she had been mooning after Zep, and now here she was, practically throwing herself at another boy. What was she thinking? Was she thinking at all?

"You're not the stupid one," she said, meaning every word. "I'm sorry."

Jesse made a sound that might have been a laugh, and somehow she managed the same in reply. It was either that or cry again.

───────────────────────── [62]

RAY WHISTLED WHEN they emerged from the four-wheeler, but Clair ignored him, hating the treacherous heat in her cheeks. While Jesse went back to his engine, Clair cracked open the car door again in order to check the plan's progress. Over two thousand people were watching now, most of them Abstainers. She had lost a lot of crashlanders. *Not surprising,* she thought. Nothing much was actually happening. Not in front of the drones, anyway. She considered telling the world that she herself had used Improvement and might be in the process of becoming someone else but decided that would only undercut her message. She had to be the girl taking on VIA, no one else.

She might have lost some crashlanders, but she had gained some train hobbyists and also an entirely new following, one that made her feel uncomfortable. For every action, she knew, there was an equal and opposite reaction, and so for every supporter she gained an objector. They ranged from knee-jerk skeptics, who— like her—simply didn't want to believe that anything could go wrong with the system everyone relied on, to rabid pontificators intent on eviscerating everything she espoused. Some of them were trolls, provoking arguments in the time-honored fashion of the antisocial, but the vitriol was intense regardless. She had to force herself to read it. Thankfully, Ronnie and Tash and a handful of other supporters were busy defending her, so she didn't have to respond every time.

The death threats bothered her most, as they were supposed to. It wasn't just the nature of the messages—she had already been living under the threat of violence long enough for that to have lost some of its urgency. It was the way she was targeted personally, using data anyone could access: places she went, people she knew, timetables she followed in her normal life. Sometimes her family was mentioned as well, which couldn't help but make her worry. She hadn't thought they might be in any more danger too.

She considered reporting the threats to the peacekeepers and decided in the end not to, not specifically. She put them up into the Air, for all to see. The threat of violence only added to the buzz. And if someone *did* try to kill her or someone she loved, the story would take even longer to go away. Her ghostly fame would linger.

Cold comfort, she thought. Then she wondered if that was something she would ordinarily have thought, and thinking *that* threatened to send her down a slippery slope of self-doubt. She fought it off by remembering how it had felt to kiss Jesse. That had been all her, she was sure of it, as was the confusion she felt now. She wondered if he felt the same knot in the stomach, but didn't have the opportunity to ask him. There were always people around; there was always something more important to think about. She sensed that he might be deliberately keeping himself busy, and she tried to do the same. They were in the middle of something far too important to muddle with feelings, after all.

The train passed Pittsburgh and switched to a line that led through the Philadelphia Keys. Once, Turner said, the tracks had gone all the way to Atlantic City, but now that Atlantic City was *under* the Atlantic, the line stopped six miles earlier, at Pleasantville. There, they would meet the submarine.

Pittsburgh, Philadelphia, Pleasantville, Clair thought. They had once been abstract addresses attached to certain friends and entertainment possibilities, but soon she would have passed through all three of them *and* the spaces between. In a train car, in real time.

"I need to send a coded signal to the submariners," Turner said. "Can Q help me with that?"

"If you give it to me," Clair said, "I'll bump it to Q."

He agreed.

"The signal is 'No one is coming to Lincoln Island.' That's all." He recited the address, a string of characters that meant nothing to Clair.

They cracked the door again, and Clair passed the message on. As they waited for a reply, she thought about the message and its connection to submarines. Captain Nemo was probably the most famous submariner in literature, and his name meant *no one* in Latin. Also, Lincoln Island was where he had died. She hoped that wasn't a bad omen. On the other hand, *nemo* was also Greek for *I give what is due*. So maybe it evened out.

Q declared that the signal had been delivered, and they shut the door again.

Turner brewed hot chocolate over a fuel cell as they went over the details of the plan. There would be a short drive to the docks in Pleasantville, during which they would be vulnerable.

"But nothing will happen, will, it?" Jesse asked. "No one will do anything with the world watching."

"Hope for the best," said Clair, "plan for the worst."

"Spoken like a true soldier," Turner said, opening a map of the Manhattan Isles and moving on to their underwater route along the Jersey peninsula. There were a number of possible landing points, including a seaport on Thirty-fourth Street and another in Brooklyn Heights.

"The most direct way to get there," said Gemma, "would be by the flooded subways. "Penn Plaza sits right on top of one of the old stations."

"It'll be sealed up, surely," said Ray, "and not very public."

"But safer," said Turner, looking to Clair.

Clair didn't want to be the one to decide. Jesse had thrown her with the possibility that her thoughts might not be entirely her own. What if Mallory or someone else was forcing her to make bad decisions, or worse: decisions that might lead them right into a trap? How could she tell the difference?

"Direct is better," said Gemma. "A parade might get us attention, but we'd also be more exposed. That makes me nervous."

Turner nodded, and with that decision made, the strategy meeting broke up.

They went back to waiting in their own ways, Turner and Ray playing cards, Gemma sitting alone, Clair and Jesse lying on bedrolls that were still next to each other, although the physical distance between them had taken on a much greater significance now. Jesse settled into a comfortable position on his side, with his right hand under his left cheek. His hair draped like a curtain over his face. One green eye was barely visible, still open, looking at her.

He whispered, "Was that 'hope for the best' line from . . . you know?"

"No. Arabelle said it once."

He looked relieved but also puzzled. "She was never a soldier."

"I think she thought she was," Clair said. "Every second

of every day, WHOLE's fighting the entire world."

"Who knows what it'll look like when they're done with it?"

"As long as the dupes aren't in it any longer, the world will automatically be a better place."

Clair felt him shift slightly so his toes touched hers. She resisted the impulse to roll over and fold herself against him. Slowly, his eyelid drooped shut, his breathing slowed, and he was asleep.

She didn't want to sleep. Her dreams bothered her. To keep herself awake, she thought about VIA, and the case she was going to make. Murder. Kidnapping. Identity theft. Conspiracy. All manner of information crimes. Mental rape.

As long as these sound like crimes, she told herself, *I'll know I'm still me.*

[63]

THE CAR SLOWED and shook as they passed through Philadelphia, waking Jesse. He was puffy eyed and sluggish, and Clair felt like he looked. They would be at the end of the line in less than an hour.

It was night outside and the air was bracing. Clair said hello to Q, who had been busy organizing her messages and feeds into a comprehensible form. There were more than she had dared hope, divided between well-wishers and haters. The arguments between both groups were proceeding as well as could be expected, but Clair knew it could be better. Neurological data and insubstantial threats would only fuel the fire so long. She had to give something new to both groups, something that would raise the stakes for everyone.

She spent fifteen minutes recording a speech about what the world might be like if Improvement were real. Suppose you could step into a booth and emerge looking like a supermodel or a famous actor? What if everyone wanted to look the same or like literally the same person? She could see positive uses for such technology—to fix people after grievous injuries, say, or for gender reassignment—but what about the pranks people might play on their friends? What about all the people who just wanted to be freaks for the sake of it? What about athletes like Zep who trained all their lives only to be beaten by someone who'd used Improvement to make themselves stronger overnight? What about parents who wanted their kids to grow up certain ways, whether the children wanted to or not? And what about criminals who might change everything about themselves—fingerprints, face, eye color, even their genes—in order to escape justice?

"Imagine that world," she told her viewers. "If Improvement isn't stopped, that's exactly what's coming."

She sent the video to all her followers in the hope that

it would be passed on, for good or ill. There were many other interesting things happening in the world, some of them drawing millions, perhaps even billions of viewers. This was small-fry, but it concerned everyone. And every keen glance counted.

Clair asked about the dupes. Q reported that there had been no sign of them. Perhaps, Clair thought, that was because the people behind them were worried about showing their hand. Or maybe they knew about the bodies being held by the farmers: proof, if needed, that some of them had been copied. For that reason, it made sense for the dupes she knew of to go to ground. As Turner had said, though, she didn't doubt there would be others. The dupes had been around for at least a year. That was long enough to accrue quite a catalog. Fat, thin, short, tall, old, and—she thought of Cashile with a wince—*young.*

Clair exchanged messages with Ronnie and Tash and her parents, who had been hard at work in their own ways.

"Is there anything else we can do?" Allison asked. "I could meet you at Pleasantville with a change of clothes— even come the rest of the way with you."

Clair looked down at her overalls and was momentarily tempted.

"Thanks, Mom, but that's okay." She didn't want to put her mother in any danger. "You're claustrophobic, remember? You can't even open your eyes in a d-mat booth. How would you cope with a submarine?"

They laughed, albeit a little tearily. Clair found it hard to sign off.

She leaned back against the rattling door of the car, contemplating the wisdom of trying to contact Libby, when a message arrived from an entirely unexpected source.

The message was signed *Catherine Lupoi*, a name she didn't recognize, but the address indicated that she worked for VIA.

"Mr. Wallace is eager to meet with you to discuss your concerns," the message said. "He will expect you tomorrow."

Clair had to think for a second before she remembered the name, and when she did, she couldn't believe it.

Ant Wallace was VIA's head of operations. Q had told her that much about him, and a quick search through the Air uncovered a lot more. He had joined the organization as a volunteer twenty years earlier and risen quickly to the very top. He wasn't an overt publicity seeker, but he was active in several public arenas, from urban planning to modern orchestral music. In particular, he was an advocate for increased research into the biochemical causes of depression and an occasional speaker at rallies urging the OneEarth administration to do more to inform the public on the issue. "Information, not medication," he was most often quoted as saying. "Suicide is murder, not euthanasia, and we are all accessories."

Now he wanted to talk to Clair about Improvement.

Triumphantly, Clair passed on the message to everyone in the car and then posted it to the Air. The response was immediate. Their numbers spiked as word spread: the head of VIA was meeting with a teenaged girl to talk about the possible consequences of Improvement. Perhaps he would take her grievances seriously. Perhaps he just wanted to dress her down in public. Either way, it was new and interesting.

Clair's number reached ten thousand, and the figure was still rising. She was really popping now.

[64]

PLEASANTVILLE HAD AN official population of zero. Literally everyone d-matted in and out from all points across the globe, be it to gamble, to serve, to maintain, or to protect. There were plenty of beds, but no one went to Pleasantville to sleep.

Clair guessed the sick feeling in her stomach wasn't so different from that of someone risking everything on a roulette wheel.

Turner opened the door for the final time as they decelerated into the train station. It was dark outside, two hours before dawn on the sixth day since Clair had heard of Improvement, and a rich ocean smell washed over them like a heavy tide. The engine of their four-wheeler started with a snarl. As soon as the freight car was stationary, Ray maneuvered the vehicle smoothly across the gap between train and station and into the night air outside.

Clair hung on to a roll bar as they accelerated along the gleaming side of the train. She waved to the drones watching them. There were six of them, not including Q's, capturing the scene from every possible angle. Three peacekeepers stood between the train and a dozen young men, who hooted and jeered as the four-wheeler sped by. Drawn by the controversy, and perhaps hoping to make a "spectacle" of themselves as well, they were obviously drunk, but that didn't take the sting out of their taunts. One held a placard with an image of Clair's face that started out normal but changed by stages to that of an old woman with missing teeth and a black eye: *Improvement* was the slogan. One of them threw a rock, but it missed by a large margin. The last Clair saw of him, he was being reprimanded by one of the PKs. At least, she hoped it was a reprimand.

If I wasn't me, she asked herself, *would I care about this kind of thing? Would I be immune to what people said? Maybe I'd turn around and join them, throwing rocks at the loony Abstainers trying to make trouble for everyone.*

She didn't want to cause trouble. She wanted the exact opposite.

They pulled away from the station and into town. Clair

had been to the glittering maelstrom of Las Vegas once, on a high school dare. Pleasantville had many of the same qualities: bright flashing lights; exaggerated extravagance, as though that mattered anymore in a world of plenty; old people dressed up like young people and smiling, always smiling. They couldn't believe their luck, Clair's grandfather liked to say. They'd survived the Water Wars, and now they were rich.

On the radiant playground of Fire Road, signs flashed endlessly in every color. The New Showboat, Caesars, the Haven, the King, the Golden Egg. Once every block, she saw the familiar d-mat sign—two circles overlapping, worlds coming together in geometric harmony—an image Clair had never thought would ever make her feel so excluded.

The four-wheeler approached the docklands from the west. They were mainly decorative, with the odd sailing or cruise vessel rocking undisturbed in a public marina. At the end of the marina, a crowd of thirty or more was waiting.

This time the jeers were louder and more personal, delivered not by trolls but by protesters wearing masks that lent them all Clair's features. It was eerie, and she did her best to ignore them as the four-wheeler pushed through their ranks, physically nudging people aside. They called her a fearmonger and agitator, and much worse. Fingers snatched at her. Someone spat. Jesse kicked at a man with

Clair's face who grabbed her hair from behind and tried to pull her from the flatbed. The man let go and fell back into the crowd, laughing. After that, Q's drone dropped low over Clair and dive-bombed anyone who tried to get too close, whether they seemed physically threatening or not. Clair couldn't decide if they were genuinely outraged or just wanting to be part of the show. Perhaps a bit of both.

Clair's scalp was still stinging when they reached the pier. There were just two peacekeepers to press the crowd back as Turner brought the four-wheeler to a halt and they climbed out. The PKs said nothing to Clair and Clair said nothing to them. They had made their position clear: they were staying on the fence, neither helping nor hindering. If things got ugly in public she could count on them to intervene, but up to that point she was on her own.

The sub floated low in the water, long and dark like a killer whale. A hatch opened on top, and two people emerged, a man and a woman both dressed in tight-fitting gray. The woman seemed unfazed by either the crowd or the drones. Clair wondered at the kinds of things she'd seen, the odd requests she'd fielded in the past. Odder than anything Clair could imagine, she bet.

"We're really doing this?" she asked.

"Looks like it," said Jesse.

Clair shouldered her heavy pack and followed him to the ladder at the end of the pier. A skinny seaman—one of three who had emerged after the first two—helped her find her footing on the swaying surface of the submarine. There was no handrail. The sea's mood was black and choppy, like the crowd.

Turner was standing over the opening in the hull, guiding people through. Ray was coming last, carrying Libby's body in his arms. Gemma had a heavy bag in one hand, one of the two that Clair had seen in the back of the four-wheeler. No one had explained what they were.

Clair took off her backpack and lowered it down through the hatch into reaching hands. Then it was her turn. The drone deactivated its fans and was carried down after her.

The submarine had a single cramped passageway running its entire length. Packs were piled into every available niche. Clair picked a spot at random and didn't move, afraid to touch anything. The air was thick and close. She didn't want to think of suffocation, but it was hard not to.

Jesse squeezed in next to her.

"Exciting, isn't it?" he said.

She gulped a half sob, half laugh.

"Are you for real?"

"No, seriously. This is terrific. I've always wanted to go underwater."

"You've never been diving?"

"Not for an hour and a half," he said. "And not without getting my clothes wet."

The hatch clanged shut above them, sounding an

unimaginable distance away. All connections to the Air died.

Clair noticed Jesse's fingers twitching.

"I've patched into the sub's HUD," he told her. "It has a cavitation hull, a magnetohydrodynamic drive system, and a miniature reactor so it can stay under for months. Officially, we stopped developing these things after d-mat came along, but this could be a knockoff of a military design, or even a genuine decommission. It's hard to say."

"*This* you know about, not cars and stuff?"

"No wheels, you see." He grinned. "And the drive system has applications off the Earth, where I really want to go."

"You're picturing yourself in a spaceship right now, aren't you?"

"If I am, what does that make me?"

"A big nerd. The biggest imaginable."

His smile only broadened as a rising thrum filled the submarine.

It was a shame, she thought, that d-mat had made spaceships obsolete, along with planes, trains, and everything else. He deserved to get what he wanted. So did she, but what she wanted seemed so much harder to obtain, even after Ant Wallace's offer to meet with them. She wanted Libby back and the chance that there was someone else in her head permanently revoked. She wanted her world back again, exactly as it had been.

Jesse's eyes were moving, following the sub's internal

operations by sound alone. She groped until she found his hand and squeezed it in hers. He glanced at her briefly and smiled. Then the engine noise rose, the floor shifted beneath them, the sub descended, and they were on their way.

[65]

CLAIR COUNTED THE time as it passed. Sixty seconds per minute. Sixty minutes per hour. It was like meditation. Motion was hard to track underwater, but deep in a primal part of her, the part that had evolved with an innate sense of movement and momentum, she knew that she was being propelled ever nearer to her destination.

When she wasn't counting, she was thinking. And what she was thinking about were the two heavy bags Gemma had carried with her into the submarine. It was clear they contained supplies of some kind, but it wasn't food, or else they would have been opened on the train. They clanked. She didn't think it was bottles of cider to bribe Ant Wallace with.

Fight, Turner had said.

The more she thought about the bags, the more certain she was that she had made a grave tactical error.

"Where's Turner?" she asked Jesse in a whisper.

"Forward, I think. Why?"

"'Direct action,'" she said, quoting the phrase that Jesse had asked Turner to clarify, back at the Farmhouse. "He never said what that meant. What if he's using me as cover in order to get close to VIA and do something stupid?"

"Like what?"

She didn't know, but those bags could hold a lot of guns, grenades, or god only knew what.

"If he does do anything," Jesse said, "VIA will never help us."

"I know, but perhaps that's a small price to pay from Turner's point of view."

Clair could see it all too easily. Turner, fighting a decades-long war against d-mat, had come out of hiding . . . for what? To help save a few lost girls? Was it more likely he was intending a suicide run that would strike right at the heart of his enemy—and destroy his mutated genes in the bargain?

"Do you think Gemma knows?" asked Jesse.

"If she does, she's not talking." Gemma seemed tense, but she *always* seemed tense. "She wouldn't want to sabotage the plan, though. Improvement killed her son, remember?"

Jesse nodded.

Clair leaned out into the narrow corridor and saw Ray nearby.

"Tell Turner to come back here," she said. "I need to talk to him. It's urgent."

Ray nodded, and a minute later the leader of WHOLE joined them.

"What is it?"

"Change of plan," she said. "I want you to drop me and Jesse off early."

Both Turner and Jesse looked at her in surprise.

"Why?" Turner asked.

She kept her voice steady, even though inside her doubts were stirring. This *was* the right thing, wasn't it? This wasn't some other mind in hers, trying to sabotage the mission?

She could only let the facts speak for themselves.

"One," she said, "we're being too predictable. That makes it easier for the dupes if they decide to spring anything on us that might look like an accident. Also, it's bad for ratings, me being down here instead of up there. Shaking things up will only keep people more interested.

"Two, if we stay together like this, and we *are* intercepted, there goes our only shot. By splitting up, we double the odds in our favor. I'll have the ratings, and you'll have the body. Someone wants to stop us, they'll have to take us both out."

Turner was nodding slowly.

"Where?" he asked.

"Brooklyn Heights is closest," she said, "and the most photogenic. It's also less obvious than the Thirty-fourth Street docks. I know it's farther, but it's not as if we have to walk or anything. We can fab something that will probably get us there quicker than you will through all those old tunnels."

"The two of you?" Turner asked. When both of them nodded, he said, "I'd feel happier if Ray went with you. Just in case."

"And you can keep the drone," Clair conceded.

He nodded again. They understood each other. Ray would keep an eye on Clair and Jesse, while Q kept an eye on Turner when the submarine surfaced under VIA. They might be temporarily on the same side, but that didn't mean they trusted each other.

"It's a good plan," he said. "I'll go tell the pilot we're changing course."

Jesse waited until he had gone before whispering, "Are you sure about this?"

"Positive," she said. "Ask yourself who's going to look like more of a threat: a bunch of walk-ins from the sticks or a sub full of well-armed terrorists?"

"You really think someone's going to try something, even with everyone watching?"

"I think there's a chance, and I don't want to be sitting in here waiting for the torpedoes to arrive."

Jesse looked around them and nodded grimly as though only now feeling the water pressing in on them.

"Our job is to get there before Turner does," she said. "We'll never get a second chance."

The sub shifted underfoot.

"We're changing course," Jesse said, fingers tapping rhythmically against his leg. "Surface in half an hour."

Clair closed her eyes and resumed counting.

[66]

THEY SURFACED AT the Atlantic Avenue docks, emerging from the submarine double time and not lingering to say farewells. By the time Clair, Jesse, and Ray stepped onto dry land, the sub was gone. They took a moment to get their bearings under a gray morning sky, then headed off uphill for the War Memorial.

Brooklyn Heights was connected by a restored bridge to the Manhattan archipelago. Clair checked her updates and news on the popularity front as she took her physical bearings. They had picked up people of a nautical bent, thanks to the submariners, and regained some of the crashlanders, thanks to Xandra Nantakarn throwing a party in Clair's honor in an old underwater base. Counter-Improvement continued to spread, particularly in areas where the original Improvement message had been rife. Social commentators were beginning to notice, not the symptoms of Improvement itself but an upwelling of concern about them. One venerable columnist described Clair as an example of something he called the

New Youth Movement: "Crashlander, Abstainer, fugitive, campaigner, all in an ordinary week. What next?"

What next indeed, thought Clair. It all depended on whether she got to Wallace safely. And whether she was herself when she got there.

"Let's move," she said. "We've got a hike ahead of us."

"This is nothing," said Ray. "I walked the John Muir Trail once. Two hundred ten miles in sixteen days—*that's* a hike."

"Even I think that's crazy," said Jesse. "Q, where do we go from the memorial?"

"Manhattan Bridge," she said.

"Okay, then. 'Lead on, Macduff.'"

"'I would the friends we miss were safe arrived,'" Q said.

"What?"

Clair said nothing as Q explained that she was also quoting—not misquoting, unlike Clair—from *Macbeth*. The words were too appropriate. She just walked up the hill as fast as she could, ignoring the way her shoes rubbed her heels and concentrating on what she had to do.

Their unscheduled appearance in Brooklyn Heights caused a new spike of interest. Drones appeared as though from nowhere to chronicle their arrival. By the time they reached the memorial, they had accrued a small coterie of people who had d-matted in from all over the world to say hello, ask questions, challenge her assumptions, or ask her out. She responded to all of them as politely as she could, knowing it was the right thing to do in order to keep people watching. But she didn't stop walking, and she kept one hand always under her overalls, tightly clutching her pistol.

At the bridge she discovered that a well-wisher had fabbed them autostabilizing monocycles—an early Dylan Linwood design, as it happened—to save them making something of their own. Clair had Q hack into their operating system to make sure they weren't booby-trapped, then accepted the gift. That prompted a run on similar devices, and Clair hurried off before she could gain an entourage that would only slow them down and potentially put innocent people in danger. The world was watching; there was in theory no reason to feel nervous. But the city ahead was a minefield. There could be snipers in any window, and not just dupes. The hate mail and death threats in the comments of her posts were rising in tandem with her popularity.

They formed a line and headed out, Clair first, then Jesse, then Ray, drones tagging along with them like balloons on a string. Vines hung from the suspension cables around them, and trees grew tall out of soil piled deep in the bridge's lower levels. Ahead was the famous Manhattan skyline, as familiar to Clair as the gondolas that plied its crystalline waters. The buildings weren't the tallest in the world, and they certainly weren't the only ones to have suffered inundation, but their restoration had been a potent symbol for the generation following the Water Wars. Clair's parents still talked about seeing the opening of the first walkways as kids.

The sun was behind Clair now, and the electric motors of the monocycles were whisper quiet on the graceful arch over the river. There had once been another bridge, Clair knew, but its foundations had subsided as the water rose to swallow it, and it had been turned into a reef with great ceremony, a sacrifice to the drowned boroughs and the new world of d-mat.

As they cruised over the central section of the bridge, Clair could see the elaborate marble arch on the other side. The entourage Clair had worried might impede her progress was awaiting them there.

She cursed silently to herself, even as she flashed her best smile and waved. The Air might have made her famous, but d-mat enabled anyone with a passing interest to jump right into her path. At this rate, every road between Little Venice and VIA HQ would be full of gawkers.

"Looks to me," drawled Jesse, loud enough for the drones to hear, "like we've got ourselves a posse."

In as much time as it took for his words to flash through the Air and back again, the crowd cheered.

"Last one to VIA's a rotten egg!" he called, and the crowd cheered again. Some of them shouted his name, and it quickly became a chant.

By the time Clair reached the arch, the crowd was moving as one, accelerating to meet and race alongside her, catcalling and jostling but keeping up, for the most part. They were a mixture of kids and teenagers, plus some older people who had the Abstainer look. Most rode monocycles, but some had Segways, sunboards, or even bicycles. There was a carnival atmosphere that belied the deadly seriousness of her purpose. It was a game to them, she supposed. A game for the curious and bored, jumping on a bandwagon that was popping at the time.

Clair understood. She'd never been much for flash crowds and celebrity bombing, but Libby had occasionally dragged her to them, and they could be fun. And there was no denying that she was grateful to Jesse for his quick thinking. By redefining their journey as a race, he had turned an obstacle into something that, if she squinted hard enough, might even be called an asset. *A human shield*, she didn't want to think.

She looked back at him, and he winked.

"Are you enjoying this?" she asked.

"Who me? You're the one in the lead."

Jesse-Jesse-Jesse went the crowd as they rode on into the Manhattan archipelago. A girl leaned in to kiss his cheek, and he blushed and pushed her away. Clair felt a surprising twinge of jealousy and told herself sternly to concentrate on the road ahead.

THE PATCHES OF dry land that had once been Chinatown and Little Italy were extensively canalled. Clair led her entourage up ramps to a level high above the tourist boats, where Q helped them navigate through the maze of bridges and monorails. They hopped from building to building to SoHo, the southernmost tip of the main Manhattan island, and touched ground on Broadway. There they left the bridges and went right down to ground level, where the original road surface remained largely unchanged.

Their entourage spread out around them, waving at passersby and taking up a new chant: *Counter-Counter-Counter.* Jesse raised his fist in acknowledgment and chanted along with them. Clair didn't join in. She was too conscious of the time.

"Q, can you tell where Turner is?"

"I'm afraid I can't, Clair. I am unable to connect with the drone, and there's been no sign of the submarine."

That didn't mean anything either way, Clair knew. The sub was likely camouflaged, and most people had probably assumed it was elsewhere now that Clair had popped up on the ground. Turner might be minutes or hours from VIA HQ. He might have changed his route entirely. There was no way for her to know until he surfaced.

She searched her busy infield for the message from Ant Wallace's assistant.

"For the sake of the crowd," she sent, "would Mr. Wallace be willing to meet somewhere public?"

"That's not necessary," Catherine Lupoi replied. "Your meeting will be broadcast in its entirety to the Air."

"Good," Clair sent back. "But I'm worried about what the crowd will do when I'm not around."

"Don't worry about that," Wallace's assistant said in a reassuring tone. "We have PKs on hand. You'll note quite a gathering here, too."

Clair checked and found that to be absolutely true. At least a hundred people had congregated in Penn Plaza to witness her arrival. Some of them were singing. Clair grimaced when she recognized "We Shall Not Be Moved." Jesse wouldn't be pleased by that.

She passed the word back to Jesse and Ray.

"They can't possibly ignore us now," said the older man. "Not when we turn up with an army on their doorstep!"

Some army, she wanted to say. But he was speaking for the benefit of the drones and the crowd, and they cheered along with him. Perhaps he was speaking for himself, too. Turner might have sent him to keep an eye on her, but that didn't mean Ray was her enemy. He might even want her to succeed so Turner wouldn't have to.

Between Twenty-third Street and One Hundredth, where water claimed the island, Park Avenue was preserved as a national monument, complete with yellow cabs and food stalls. Clair took advantage of the clear road surface to go faster, pushing the monocycles to the limits of their tiny motors. Around them, the buildings grew taller. She could see the Empire State Building a few blocks ahead.

At a sign advertising a "genuine replica steakhouse," they turned left and rolled on up Thirty-third Street. Ray's "army" had doubled, and the cry of *Counter!* became a regular chant that echoed off the stone walls around them. Peacekeepers had become more visible too. Domed blue helmets stood out on every corner and in front of the historic storefronts. Clair wondered if they were afraid of a riot. She wondered if she should be too.

At Greeley Square, at last, their destination became clearly visible. One Penn Plaza was a tall black glass oblong that was imposing even from several blocks away. No greenery marred its precise lines. No signs or logos, either, despite the perfect flatness of its north- and south-facing sides. Some organizations might have had visual and virtual ads rolling 24-7, but not VIA. The evidence of its labor was all around them.

The skyscraper slabbed vertically out of a wider base. Clair and her entourage circled the base once, counterclockwise, passing Madison Square Garden, its southwestern edge literally hanging over the water, in order to approach the crowd from the other side. A cheer rose up. Placards waved. Some people booed. A surge of information rolled through the Air, spiking Clair's popularity levels to new heights.

As they wheeled past the plaza's stand of d-mat booths to approach the main lobby entrance, gunshots cracked over the crowd

"Traitors!" a voice shouted. "Terrorists!"

People went in all directions. More gunshots, and Clair found herself on the ground with Jesse, not entirely sure how she had gotten there, her pistol in her hand but no one to point it at.

Over the shouts and screams came the sounds of barked commands. Peacekeepers, Clair hoped. She didn't want fighting to break out in the crowd. A man cried in protest as barking voices ordered him to the ground.

Clair raised her head. Three PKs were standing over a spread-eagled man dressed in combat gear and flak helmet. He had been liberally sprayed with thick white confinement foam that held him immobile on the ground. There was a rifle trapped safely beneath one of the PKs' boots. The crowd had scattered to points of cover, from where they watched the scene unfold. There was no cheering now, just weeping and exclamations of shock. Two people were injured. There was blood on the ground.

In a panic, remembering Zep, Clair turned to check on Jesse. He was fine.

"Thanks, Clair," he said, sitting up and brushing himself off. "That was close."

She just nodded, although she still had no memory of what had happened immediately after the first shot. Her pulse was still racing, and it was hard to think. The Air was full of clamoring voices. Footage was already streaming in, including a perfect shot of her throwing herself at Jesse and tackling him to the ground.

"I'm sorry, Clair!" Q's voice was frantic. "I should have seen him. I should've done something—"

"It's not your fault," she said. "Do you know who he is?"

Data poured into her infield. The shooter looked like an ordinary guy, if a little extreme in his anti-Abstainer outbursts. He had a feed not so different from hers, except with a much longer history, detailing deaths by terrorist attacks all around the world. He had lost his mother in a shutdown in Cairo, which WHOLE said was a power failure, VIA sabotage.

Clair hadn't known that such arguments existed. It hadn't been part of her world until now.

A peacekeeper towered over her, offering her his hand.

"Best you move inside, Clair," he said. "Things could get ugly out here."

His name was PK Drader, Clair's lenses informed her, leader of the Rapid Response team. His face was hidden behind his visor. He had narrow shoulders set on a slight angle, as though he were leaning into a strong wind.

Clair nodded but didn't take his hand. She could stand on her own. Jesse did the same. Ray joined them, and PK

Drader and three other peacekeepers formed a protective cordon around them as the three of them approached the Penn Plaza building. Their monocycles lay abandoned on the ground behind them. The crowd was emerging slowly from cover. This wasn't a game anymore. It was something else entirely, now that someone had been tangibly hurt.

Clair wondered what would happen to the shooter. Then she saw two bullet holes in the glass doors ahead of them and decided she didn't care. That was the third time she had been fired at in four days. It had to stop.

[68]

"WE'RE HERE," JESSE said as the glass doors slid closed behind them. He looked shaken but relieved. "We actually made it."

"Don't get cocky," said Ray. "This is the hard part."

Clair agreed. They might have beaten Turner to VIA, but he was still out there somewhere, perhaps right under their feet, right at that very moment. And then there was Ant Wallace: he wouldn't be a pushover. Her plan was, basically, to convince him that he wasn't doing his job.

The lobby was cool and dimly lit, a marble expanse with a reception desk directly between the doors and a bank of elevators at the opposite end. A single person sat behind the desk, an ageless woman with porcelain skin and a sleeveless halter top in silver and gray. Her red hair was piled up in a series of complex curves with no visible means of support. Clair felt intimidated, although the woman didn't actually *do* anything as they approached. Doing nothing was more than enough.

Only when Clair was right in front of her did the receptionist stir. Her voice was honey and steel. She came right to the point.

"Mr. Wallace will see you in his office. Please proceed to elevator three."

One perfectly manicured hand indicated a bank of sliding doors to her left.

"Thank you," Clair said. The woman didn't acknowledge her.

"Can you still hear and see me?" she asked Q.

"Perfectly well, Clair," came the instant reply. "This is exciting! What do you think he'll say?"

"I guess we're about to find out."

The elevator doors opened as they approached, revealing a heavyset security guard in a shiny blue suit that was a near-perfect match for his stubble. He motioned them inside without a word. Clair obeyed. Through the foyer's glass windows, she saw the crowd waving at her, mouthing words she couldn't hear. Through the Air she saw herself, expressionless, as the doors closed over them.

It didn't look like her as she thought of herself. Was she *really* her, Clair couldn't help but wonder, or someone who only thought she was?

The elevator moved underfoot. Clair's weight seemed to double. There was no progress indicator above the door, no counting upward like Clair had seen in old movies.

"You'll be required to leave your weapons behind at the next checkpoint," said the guard in the blue suit. His voice was surprisingly light. "They'll be returned to you afterward."

"How do you know we have any?" asked Jesse.

"You've been scanned."

Ray shrugged philosophically.

The doors opened, and the security guard escorted them into an unremarkable corridor. There was another security guard waiting for them, next to a table, on which they placed everything lethal. Clair gave them her pistol. Jesse had nothing but a pocketknife. A small arsenal appeared from Ray's pockets and the depths of his pack, including three pistols, a collapsible rifle, ammunition for all, and several grenades.

"We're lucky you didn't start a war when that guy started firing outside," Clair said.

"*He's* lucky the PKs were there," Ray said.

"This way," said the first blue suit, indicating a double door at the end of the corridor.

This is it, Clair thought. *This is really it.*

On the other side of the door was an office that took up half an entire floor. It contained a desk and several chairs but seemed empty. The view more than made up for that. They were looking out across the archipelago, over a jungle of rooftops and parabolic bridges and sails and swooping monorail tracks. The light seemed brighter from their elevated position, even through storm clouds moving in from the west. The whole world shone with optimism and opulence.

In front of the view, behind the desk, sat a woman in her fifties, not Ant Wallace, as Clair had expected. Tall and solid, with swept-back gray hair and a thin, blade-like nose, she was wearing a conservative, tight-fitting suit that was a light shade of blue identical to that of the suits of the men outside the room. She stood up but didn't shake their hands.

"Catherine Lupoi?" asked Clair, remembering the name of Ant Wallace's assistant.

The woman shook her head. "Angela Kadri, head of security. Ant will be down in a moment. I've been asked to make you comfortable. Is there anything you'd like to drink, eat?"

Clair felt a moment of dizziness that she put down to lack of sleep and a terrible awareness of how important the coming moments were. After every hardship they had endured, every mile covered, every discomfort and priva-tion, they were about to come face-to-face with VIA's head of operations, a man who could make the world really pay attention. If Improvement was ever to be stopped, if Libby and Q were ever to be restored, if Clair's doubts about her mind were ever to be put to rest, he had to be convinced of its reality. If she failed, nothing would change—but everything would change for *her*, because all she held dear would be gone.

"Clair, are you all right?"

Jesse was asking her the question, but everyone was staring at her, like she was an actor who had forgotten her lines.

"I think I need to sit down," she said.

"Please, feel free." Kadri indicated the chairs scattered about the room. "There are facilities if you need them. I'll go see what's holding Ant up."

Kadri strode crisply across the room and through the double door. Clair looked around her and noticed an arched entranceway she hadn't seen earlier. She went through it and found herself in a privacy alcove containing a fabber, a sink, and a small mirror. She looked dirty and desperate, like every other Abstainer she had ever met. Worse than that, she looked as crazy as Dylan Linwood.

Suddenly convinced that Wallace was going to brush them off, no matter what they said to him, she leaned over the sink and splashed cold water on her face. She saw a double image of herself as she did so, one from the mirror and another via a video feed someone was posting. They had hacked her lenses somehow, so she was seeing what she was seeing twice over.

She turned to see Jesse watching her.

"*Are* you all right?" he asked.

"Yes, honest. And that's me talking, in case you're wondering." This kind of anxiety could only come from herself.

He half smiled. "I can tell."

"What about you?"

"I'm shitting myself," he said. "I wish Dad were here. He'd do a much better job of explaining things than I would. Not that you won't, I mean," he added. "You'll be great."

"What about after?" she said, meaning *What will you be going home to? What's left out there for you?*

He looked away. "I'm not thinking that far ahead."

"You could go to Melbourne to live with your mom's family."

"I don't want to do that. I don't know them, and it would mean changing schools."

"You could do that."

"But I don't *want* to," he said, with a flash of his old prickliness. "Are you trying to get rid of me?"

"No," she said. "That's not what I want," she said, only realizing the truth of it as she said it.

"Good, because . . . well, to hell with it." He paced

around the tiny space, looking at her and then looking away, over and over, as though making sure she wasn't about to vanish into thin air. "I know this isn't the right time, and I know you had that thing with Zep, but we've been holding hands, and we kissed once, and then you kinda threw yourself at me downstairs—not *like that*," he amended, "but it happened, and it must mean something when a girl tries to save your life. Right?"

"Jesse—"

"Don't get me wrong. I know I'm not your type. Girls like you don't date Abstainers. So we're doomed from the start, but I have to—"

"Jesse, listen to me."

"Wait, Clair. I've been rehearsing this in my head ever since Brooklyn, and this might be the last chance I have to say it, so I need to get it out. I've had a thing for you for years, and then Improvement brought us together, but now it's going to be fixed, and I'm worried that everything will go back to normal, and you—"

"Jesse."

She put a hand over his mouth.

"Someone hacked my lenses. The whole world is seeing this. Hearing it too, probably."

He swiveled slowly to face her.

"Oh . . . that's . . . great."

Before he could say or do anything else, a piercing wail split the air.

CLAIR PUT HER hands over her ears and stared up at the ceiling. The blast of sound was so loud, it seemed to be coming from inside her head.

"What *is* that?"

"Sounds like a fire alarm," Jesse shouted close to her ear. She could barely hear him.

They ran into the office and found Ray tugging bodily at the doors.

"We're locked in!"

Jesse lent his weight to the effort while Clair checked her infield.

There was a message patch from Angela Kadri. Clair winked on it immediately.

"What's going on? Why are the doors locked?"

"It's for your own safety," the head of security told her. "The building's under attack."

Clair went cold. The submarine. Turner.

Ending the exchange with Kadri, she called Q.

"Where's Turner?" she asked. "Has the drone surfaced yet?"

"Yes, Clair. It's at the old subway station, with the others—what's that noise?"

"Tell Turner to stand down! They know you're there!"

"Clair, look." Jesse was tugging at her arm, pointing at the windows.

Heavy shutters were descending rapidly over the wide expanses of glass.

"Q, tell him to stop! He's going to ruin everything!"

"I don't understand," said Q. "What's happening, Clair? What's going on?"

The shutters slammed with a boom. In the same instant, the siren died. A ringing silence fell.

"Q?"

The conversation had been cut off. Clair's infield was blank. She was severed from the Air.

"I don't like this," said Jesse.

"That's the understatement of the year," Clair said, rounding on Ray. "What was Turner planning? Tell me!"

"I don't know," he said. "Once he decided I was going with you, he cut me out of the loop. Honestly. But he was prepared. If things went wrong with you, he was ready for anything."

"*Too* ready, obviously," she said, fighting the urge to weep with frustration. "This can't be happening."

"We don't know that Turner did anything at all." Ray put his hands on his hips. "He wouldn't blow up the building while we're in it, would he?"

"I don't know, Ray. You tell me."

"Maybe the sub tripped an alarm," Ray said, "and VIA security's just being ultracautious."

"Maybe a lot of things. I still don't like it."

For five minutes, they pounded the door with their fists to get someone's attention, but there was no reply. Then they paced from wall to wall, looking for ways out that didn't exist. Jesse probed every socket and sensor. There were no vents: air was refreshed through the fabber, and food waste was disintegrated into nothing.

There was only one way into the office, and it was firmly shut.

"Maybe the lockdown's an automatic safety procedure," said Ray, "to protect Wallace if something goes pear-shaped."

"So why haven't they contacted us?" asked Jesse. "There must be some way to talk to Wallace if he's caught in here."

"Maybe they're all busy," said Ray.

"Thanks to you and your friends," Clair snapped at him. "This is going to look bad. We're locked in here like prisoners."

"We could light a fire," said Ray. "Set off an alarm for real, and then they'd pay attention to us."

"Great idea," said Jesse. "If no one comes, we either suffocate or burn to death. Let me see if I can find a lighter—oh, wait, there isn't one."

"Quit it, both of you!"

They were getting on one another's nerves. The office was bigger than some houses, but it seemed to be getting smaller fast.

"We just need to think," she said.

Clair went into the tiny service room and checked the fabber's menus. Its memory contained no weapons, drills, radios, explosives, or anything useful at all. After that pointless search, she checked for more mundane things like food and drink. VIA provided a fine choice of coffees, at least. She ordered a pot and three mugs. They could share it while they tried to find a way out.

Jesse sniffed warily at the coffee and then took a sip. Deciding it probably wouldn't poison him, or that he didn't care if it did, he drank the rest.

"What are they waiting for?" he asked. "Are they *trying* to freak us out?"

"Maybe making us sweat a little is their way of telling us they won't be pushed around," Clair said. "If that's the case, I'm happy to wait them out."

She sat in a chair and crossed her legs. It wasn't impossible that there was a camera on them right now, recording their reactions.

Ray checked the door for the hundredth time.

"Guys," he said, "I can hear something out there."

Clair and Jesse were at his side in an instant.

Ray was on his hands and knees, with his right ear pressed hard against the right-hand panel.

"Sounds like hammering," he said, "or gunfire. I can't tell which."

Clair crouched next to him and listened, the door coolly metallic against her skin.

For some seconds all she could hear was the beating of her heart. Slowly a less familiar sound rose to prominence: a distant, percussive thudding that lacked the regularity of a machine. Its source wasn't nearby, but as she listened, she thought it might be getting louder.

Clair ran back to her chair and picked up her empty coffee mug. She raised it above her head and banged it against the door, shouting, "Hey! You have to let me talk to someone! Open the door—please!"

She was picturing Turner and Gemma, armed to the teeth like Ray had been, blasting their way up through the building. Could they possibly be fighting all of VIA on their own, plus the peacekeepers who would automatically come to VIA's defense? It seemed impossible, unless . . .

Q.

Suddenly she could see it playing out in her mind. If the sub had done nothing more than trip an alarm by docking in the underwater station, triggering the shutdown and an accidental imprisonment of Clair and her friends, Q wouldn't be able to tell the difference between that and Clair being held captive. And she wouldn't take it lying down.

Clair suspected Q herself didn't know exactly what her capabilities were. She lived in the Air; she had access to the entire accumulated knowledge of humanity. Clair wondered if VIA was in the process of finding out exactly what those capabilities were.

And the world was watching. How many people were going to be hurt now? How bad was it going to make the Counter-Improvement cause look?

[70]

SHE BANGED AT the door again and again.

"Hey, answer me!"

The mug shattered, and she recoiled, blinking ceramic flecks from her eyes.

The pounding was definitely louder.

"Clair, look."

Jesse was pointing at the door. Her coffee mug had left deep scratches in the paint. Beneath was a shiny surface that looked like metal at first glance, except it was too reflective. It did more than gleam. It was so shiny, it looked like a shard of perfect mirror.

Clair leaned closer, puzzled.

Why go to the trouble of making the doors out of mirror and then painting over them? Why use it as a door at all?

What if it wasn't *just* a door?

Clair stood up and turned a quick full circle, taking in the space around her. The windows were sealed tight: the shutters were painted too. The ceilings were unbroken, and they were also painted. Using a sharp sliver of broken mug, she worried at a carpet seam until it came up: more mirror.

The room wasn't a room. It was a giant d-mat booth.

"Clair?"

She barely heard Ray trying to get her attention. Why build an office inside a booth? She could think of one reason: so Wallace could move from meeting to meeting without leaving his desk. VIA was a global company and its executive director no doubt a man in demand. People could come to him or he could go to them. Maybe he liked doing the latter without even getting out of his chair. Maybe this was his management style, to be the guy who dropped in rather than the guy who summoned from afar.

Clair could accept that.

But why lock them inside it? Was it a coincidence or something more sinister?

"Clair? Can you feel it?"

She blinked. The hammering was audible now and getting noticeably louder by the second. Occasionally, the floor shook. It sounded like a full-on war out there. A completely *unnecessary* war caused by VIA locking Clair in. Wallace couldn't have provoked Q more effectively if he'd tried. Or Turner. Capturing Ray, one of WHOLE's own, would give Turner the perfect excuse for "direct action."

With that thought, the missing piece fell into place.

"Oh no," she said.

"What?" Jesse was watching her.

"I've figured it out."

"Figured what out?"

"It's Turner. That's what this is about."

"Why Turner? How?"

"The dupes steal someone's body. What if they steal

someone's memories as well? That means they'd know where Turner was the moment they duped Arabelle—but they couldn't take him from the Skylifter because it was too public. So they shot it down and sent in the dupes." It all made horrible, blinding sense to her now. "That didn't work, but they didn't try again because they didn't need to—all thanks to me!"

"Why," asked Jesse. "What have you done?"

She hated the wariness in his eyes.

"Nothing," she said, "except ignore Gemma, because she was right. She was absolutely right!"

It was getting hard to talk over the hammering of guns.

"They're just outside," Ray said, backing away from the door.

"Don't let them in," Clair said in rising desperation. "They have to *stay* outside!"

But the double door was already sliding open, as it had to for the plan to work. Q had to be fooled into thinking she'd unlocked the door herself. It couldn't be damaged by explosives. The space within the room had to be resealable.

"Clair!" The cry came from the drone, which was the first through the gap. Q's triumph was palpable. "You're alive!"

"Not for much longer if you don't do as I say," she said, running to the first actual person into the room— Gemma, singed and smelling like century-old slime. She wrenched the pistol from Gemma's hand and emptied the clip into the walls.

"Get out!" she yelled. "Get out now!"

Jesse and Ray dived as bullet after bullet ricocheted around them. Then Clair's finger was wrenching the trigger to no avail, the pistol making nothing but a click-clicking sound. Empty.

"What the hell do you think you're doing?" Gemma asked her, eyes wide with fury.

Clair ignored her. She turned to get another weapon and found Turner right behind her, raising his hands in placation as though *she* were the crazy one, and *he* hadn't put them all in danger just by stepping into the booth.

"You can't be here," she said, pushing him to the door. "This is what they want. Your secret—your life—"

Dawning understanding transformed Turner's expression into one of panic. The d-mat booth was a trap, and Clair was the bait. Q had led Turner right into it—Turner, with his immortality genes, just waiting to be scanned and dissected. Everything else was incidental.

She seemed to think much faster than reality was moving. *Turner—door—now.* Her body weighed tons. She willed it to move more quickly, screaming at herself for being so slow. Turner was even slower and heavier than she was. She grabbed his shoulder and her muscles burned. He was a mountain that took an age to move an inch.

Even as she strained, she wondered: How had VIA *known*?

The door was already closing. Ray slipped one arm into the gap and tried to pull it back, but the door wasn't staying open for anyone now that Turner was inside. Ray screamed as the metal mouth closed on him. Blood sprayed. There was a terrible crunching sound.

The d-mat process started the very instant the room was sealed. Clair's wild shots had damaged nothing, changed nothing.

ssss—

The room was much bigger than a normal booth and contained much more air. That gave her more time—but to do what? Jesse stared at her in hopes of an explanation. Turner was bent over Ray, pale-faced. Only Gemma seemed calm, fatalistically resigned.

—ssss—

"Q, can you stop this?"

"This booth isn't connected to the public domain. It's a private network, and I don't know how to access it."

"Well, find out fast!"

"I'm sorry, Clair. I did the wrong thing again. I didn't realize—"

—ssss—

Clair's ears were stinging. Jesse was backed up against the wall, red from neck to thigh with Ray's blood. She felt the air grow Himalaya thin as she pushed past her would-be rescuers in order to be near him.

"You always wanted to try d-mat," she said. "I'm sorry it had to be like this."

He swallowed.

"At least we're—"

—*pop*

———————————————————————— [71]

CLAIR BLINKED. THE room was the same, right down to the scratches on the walls. The light was the same. The air smelled the same. Except for the *pop* of her ears, she wouldn't have believed she had gone anywhere.

But there was no Jesse. No WHOLE. No blood. No empty gun in her hand. She stared around her in shock.

The pattern had been altered in transit. Everything but her and the room's furniture and decorations had been edited from the space contained within the mirrored walls. What had happened to the data she couldn't guess. Saved elsewhere? Erased? She hoped with all her heart it wasn't the latter.

She took a hesitant step and noticed something that *was* new—a weird giddying sensation, as though the floor were moving under her in ways she couldn't consciously determine.

The doors to the office opened, and two people walked

in. One looked exactly like Libby, except for two very important things: her birthmark was missing, and so was the light in her eyes. She was like the room around them, with everything that made her special edited out. She held a steel-gray pistol in her right hand.

The other person was Ant Wallace. Of course it was, she thought. It had to be him. He looked exactly like his picture in the Air: round faced, in his fifties or so, with an open expression and care lines around his eyes. Perhaps a little shorter than Clair had expected, he was jacketless, in shirtsleeves and silk tie, with charcoal suit pants and patent leather shoes. His right hand was outstretched in welcome.

She backed away, confused and scared at the same time.

"No?" he said, raising the hand in imploration, then lowering it. "Understandable, perhaps. Your plan to shame VIA into action would have been a good one, had I not been behind Improvement all along."

The doors closed, giving Clair the barest glimpse of what lay outside. Another corridor, but not the one she had come through before. She was definitely in a different place. Wherever she was, there was no access to the Air: her lenses were completely blank.

"And the dupes as well?"

"They're aspects of the same thing, as I think you're beginning to appreciate."

The woman in Libby's body came closer and pointed

the gun so the barrel was only a hand's span away from Clair's head. She was wearing a simple black dress in a heavy fabric, some kind of wool weave, perhaps, with a black suit jacket over the top and black leather shoes with a low heel. Her blond hair was pulled back to expose her neck. She wore no jewelry and looked classy and cool, a decade older than the girl Clair knew.

"You don't frighten me, Mallory," Clair said, forcing herself not to flinch. She met the woman's cold stare and searched it for any sign of recognition. Surely there was some hint of Libby left, some shred of Clair's best friend who still remembered who she had been, remembered *her*. "I know you won't kill me."

The woman holding the gun frowned. The barrel dipped slightly.

"How do you know my name?"

"From the Farmhouse, of course," said Wallace with affable authority. "She's resourceful." He moved around behind the desk and sat casually in the chair. "That's why we want to reward her, not punish her. Isn't that right?"

"Reward me for what?"

"For bringing Turner Goldsmith to me. Without you and your plan, he would've gone to ground, and we would've lost him again. For all our assertions to the contrary, mistakes do happen, and we don't always learn from them. The error that allowed Turner Goldsmith to live so long is one such, but now that he's safely uploaded and awaiting analysis, we can make up for lost time. His genes are going to be very useful indeed. I will live young, well, and long enough to do everything I want. Isn't that all anyone desires?"

Wallace glanced at Mallory in Libby's body. A microexpression that might have been a frown flashed across his features. "Well, maybe not everyone. But the point is valid. You've helped give me what I want, and I think it's time we returned the favor."

The d-mat booth came to life around them again. Clair put her arms around herself and held on tight, afraid of what might be changed this time.

sssssss-pop

Zeppelin Barker was in the room, not three yards from her.

Her heart jolted.

Solid, blond, and tanned, dressed in track pants, sneakers, and a vest sporting the school colors. No bullet wound. Living, breathing, real. She could *smell* him.

He was already reacting in puzzlement to an environment he hadn't expected, adopting a wary crouch and looking around until he saw her.

"Clair? What's going on?"

Clair didn't know what to tell him. There were just the two of them in the room now. Wallace and Mallory—it seemed simplest to call her that—were gone. The faint sense of giddiness remained, so Clair guessed that she and the room had been d-matted nowhere this time—a *null jump*, Arabelle had called it. The pattern had been edited again en route.

But . . . *Zep?*

"What are you doing here?" she asked him. "Where did you come from?"

"The dorm. Remember? That Abstainer freak sending the feed from Gordon the Gorgon's office? Don't tell me I missed the end of it. . . ."

He looked around again as though trying to match his last memory with this new moment. Clair was struggling to do the same thing. If the last thing he remembered was leaving the dorm to come join her at school, that meant he was a copy taken from the last time he had used d-mat. The original Zep had gone on to get shot, while an echo of him—*this version of him*—had survived in storage somewhere. And now he was alive again, missing the last hours of his life and the last few days of Clair's, but otherwise exactly as he had been.

"Clair? What's going on?"

He went to approach her, but she instinctively pulled away. There was always a chance it wasn't *really* him. . . .

"What did we talk about the last time we saw each other?"

"Libby, of course. Why?"

She shook her head. That was a stupid question. Mallory was in Libby's head now; she could have known and could have briefed him.

"What's my least favorite city?"

"Omsk."

He came closer, as though to touch her, and she shied away again, even though she knew now that he was really him.

"Clair, what's wrong with you? You're starting to freak me out."

He wasn't the only one feeling that way. Wallace and Mallory obviously knew about her and Zep and what had happened to him in Manteca. They were offering to undo the harm that had been done—and they could deliver, too, with access to his archived pattern, wherever it had been saved. Since Zep wasn't legally dead, he could walk back into his life as though nothing had happened. Maybe Wallace thought the two of them could even pick up where they had left off, if they wanted to. Without Libby.

That was the deal. All she had to do to accept it, presumably, was to back down from her Counter-Improvement campaign.

If she took the deal, however, Wallace would win. Libby would disappear, possibly forever, Q would never get her body back . . . and what would happen to WHOLE and the others? What would happen to Jesse? She couldn't just rewind the last few days and forget they had ever happened.

She clenched her fists. Clair Larhonda Hill wasn't so easily bought.

"It's not going to work," she shouted at the walls and

ceiling. "Do you hear me? You can't buy my silence so easily!"

The doors opened.

"Libby!" Zep cried. "Thank God. We've been so—"

"Worried? Why? I'm beautiful, remember?"

The pistol was still in her hand. She raised it, this time pointing at Zep.

"Libby, wait . . . if this is about Clair—"

"Clair, Clair, Clair," she said. "It's always about Clair."

The gun cracked, and Zep fell to the floor, shot through the heart.

———————————————————[72]

"NO!"

Clair was at Zep's side in an instant. Before the life entirely left his eyes, he seemed to see her through a veil of hurt and puzzlement. His lips moved, but no sound emerged from them. Then he was gone. Again.

Clair knelt in the expanding pool of his blood, buried her head into his ruined chest, and would have wept but for Mallory's hand in her hair, pulling her up and away from the body.

"It's not your silence we want."

Mallory pushed her back to the ground, away from Zep's body.

"Leave me alone." Clair scrabbled backward until her spine was pressed hard against a wall. Revulsion threatened to subsume her. Zep had died twice, and both times it had been because of her.

"Shall I bring him back again? One time if you do as we ask. Many times if you don't."

"You have Turner. What do you need me for?"

"Ant wants something else from you—and what Ant Wallace wants, Ant Wallace gets."

"Now, now, there's no need to be *unpleasant* about it. . . ." Wallace had entered the room without Clair noticing. He stood over Zep's body and adjusted the cuffs of his shirt.

"Here's the story," he said. "I'm on my way to see you, as per your request, when an attack on the building triggers an emergency lockdown. You are isolated for your own protection, as am I, until security and peacekeepers foil the attack, at which point you and I are released. In response to the inevitable media uproar provoked by your followers, we hold a video conference. Gemma Mallapur confesses that you were used by WHOLE as a cover for an attack on the very heart of VIA. Once WHOLE's terroristic aspirations are revealed, you renounce all your accusations of me and my organization. You are taken away for questioning but are not expected to be charged. The end. Any questions?"

Clair shook her head.

"I'm not saying that."

"You misunderstand me. You already have."

He stared down at her as the horrible truth sank in.

"We duped you, Clair," he said. "My version of you is already out there, recanting all the things you said."

"You couldn't have," she said, feeling a wave of existential panic. How could there be a copy of her out there when she was still alive here, wherever *here* was? "What about breaking parity?"

"Irrelevant in a private network." He waved to indicate the booth-disguised-as-an-office. "No one will ever find you in here."

"So why *am* I here? What can I do that my dupe can't?"

"You can tell me all about your friend."

"Libby?"

Mallory barked a short, hard laugh. "Hardly."

Clair went to get up, but Mallory put a foot on her chest and pushed her back down.

"I'm talking about Q," said Wallace. "That's what you call her, right?"

Clair stared at him in complete confusion.

"You must know more about her than I do," Clair said. "She's one of Improvement's victims, after all."

"Don't try to pin this on us," said Mallory. "We had nothing to do with her."

"I don't believe you. How can she be in the hangover if you didn't put her there?"

"The what?"

"The safety net, the memory dump, whatever you call it." Clair tried to remember how Arcady had explained it to her. "The place you pulled Zep from."

Mallory tilted Libby's head and studied her with distant blue eyes, like she was a bug in a jar, slowly running out of air.

"Someone's lying," said Wallace, "and it can't be both of you."

His eyes moved, selecting menus from his lenses.

sssssss-pop

Gemma was standing next to Zep's body, looking first at the room around her, then at her injured arm, which was still in a bandage.

"What?" she said, startled and confused. "This isn't what you told me would—"

"I know what I told you," said Wallace, "but you haven't delivered. We've kept you on ice in case we needed you."

"Ice . . . ?" Gemma's expression became one of horror. "Sam—you promised me Sam—"

"And you'll get him if you tell us the truth, this time."

Clair lunged for Gemma, but Mallory's boot held her down with crushing strength.

"You!" Clair spat. "You betrayed us!"

Gemma glanced at her, but only for a moment. Her gaze dropped to the floor, danced away from the blood, and ended up looking nowhere.

"I'm sorry," she said. "I had no choice."

"Yes, you did," said Wallace, "and you chose correctly. You chose your son over a band of misfits and meddlers. Who in their right mind wouldn't do that?"

"This isn't right," Gemma said, still avoiding looking at the body. "You said you wouldn't hurt them."

"And you believed him?" said Clair, aghast.

"It's not how it looks! They wanted me to be a sleeper agent, but I never actually spied on anyone, never gave anything away—until I saw proof in the Farmhouse that they could do everything they claimed they could do—changing people, bringing them back from the dead . . ."

"Yes, yes," said Wallace in an impatient tone. "You activated the bug at the Farmhouse. We exchanged messages. We promised you the one thing in the world you really want."

He had walked half a circle around Gemma and come to a halt next to Mallory, drawing attention to the body, Clair realized, and to the gun in Mallory's hand.

"I don't reward lies," he said. "Tell me everything you know about Q."

Gemma blinked at him. "What about her?"

"You told us she was a kid," Mallory said. "Some kind of prodigy."

"That's what she sounds like. A kid living in the Air."

"But you're not sure?"

"I've never met her. Why would she fake something like that?"

"I don't know. That's why we brought you back."

Gemma stared at Wallace and Mallory with despair and hatred in her eyes, then suddenly ripped the cross from her neck and threw it across the room.

"Keep your stupid bug," she said, voice crackling with emotion. "You're never going to give him back to me, are you? You played me for a fool."

"The thing is," said Wallace, "in all honesty, we don't care much either way. You can have as many Sameers as you like, as long as you convince us that we can trust you."

"But I've told you everything I know. I swear!"

"I don't believe in the ghosts of dead girls haunting the Air," said Wallace. "I do believe that Clair can tell us more. The boy from Manteca here"—he indicated Zep's body—"didn't have the effect we were hoping for. I'll be grateful if you can provide us with the leverage we need."

"How?"

The smile he offered her was as dangerous as Mallory's pistol.

"You work it out."

Clair stared at Gemma, seeing her desperation and her thwarted hope. She had been strung out and stressed ever since the attack on the Farmhouse, and now Clair knew why. She had started expressing her doubts at the train

[449]

station in Mandan, but Clair hadn't listened. Clair was listening now, wishing she could find some way to hate her.

This wasn't the grand treachery of Wallace and Mallory, the depths of which she hadn't yet begun to fathom. This was an everyday betrayal, human, galling, and desperately frustrating.

"Don't look at me like that," Gemma snarled at her. "Who are you to judge? You've had it easy all your life. You have a family, and you have friends, and you have a life full of riches. You can go anywhere, do anything, *be* anyone you want to be. And who am I? Some mad old fool whose child died—and now I have the chance to get him back, exactly as I remember him. You'd take it, wouldn't you? You wouldn't even hesitate."

Clair shook her head. She could see what Gemma was doing. She was talking herself into something, something she knew she shouldn't do. And to make matters worse, Clair knew what it was.

"Don't," Clair said. "They'll never give you what you want."

"You can talk. I asked you to look after him, but you wouldn't do it. And even if you had agreed, I wouldn't have believed you. You could never have protected him. And neither can I. It's done. It's over. We're through."

The brief war waging behind Gemma's eyes was over. Clair had lost.

Gemma told Wallace, "Try Jesse."

Mallory smiled.

[73]

SSSSSS-POP

Gemma and Wallace disappeared in another null jump, and there Jesse was, spattered with Ray's blood and caught midsentence.

"—together . . . Wait, what?"

He saw Libby's face and started in fright even before Mallory stepped away from Clair and pointed the pistol at him.

"Don't!" Clair cried, placing herself directly in front of the muzzle. "Please don't hurt him. I've told you everything I know. Q is one of the lost girls, like Libby. She woke in the hangover and latched onto me when I used Improvement. She's been helping me, and I've tried to help her, too. She deserves to know who she is, who she *was*, before Improvement."

"Clair, what's happening?" asked Jesse, standing up behind her. "Are you all right? Where's Ray, Gemma, Turner . . . everyone?"

"They're gone forever," Mallory said, "unless your girlfriend tells us the truth."

"Why would I lie?" Clair said, determined to keep herself between Mallory and him. She couldn't bear to think of Jesse dead, not now that she had him back.

"Q is some Little Orphan Annie who latched onto you at random?" Mallory shook Libby's head. "I don't think so."

"Why not?"

"Because I'm careful," she said. "I don't leave leftovers."

In the face of Mallory's ruthlessness, Clair believed her, but at the same time she couldn't believe her. There had to be hope for Libby, just as there was hope for Q. There had to be hope for Clair as well.

"Well, this time you made a mistake," Jesse insisted, coming forward to stand next to Clair.

"I don't make mistakes either," Mallory said, her lenses flickering, "but Ant does. I think he's too generous. This is your last offer."

The air thinned around them again. Clair took Jesse's hand and held it so tightly, she hoped, that not even d-mat could tear them apart.

sssssss-pop

When the machines stopped, Mallory was gone, and Dylan Linwood had taken her place.

Jesse's father staggered backward and clutched his temple. Bruised. Fresh from his kidnapping. He looked up at them, blinking, left eye filling with blood.

"Jesse?"

"Stay away!" Jesse let go and stepped back from her, forming a triangle among the three of them. "Who are you?"

"It's him, Jesse," said Clair, hearing it in Dylan's ordinary California accent and seeing his true self in the way he held himself, in his bewilderment and shock. "*Really* him this time."

"Who else would I be?" Dylan said, his lined face twisting in hurt.

Jesse was speechless.

"You were captured in the street by people who work for Ant Wallace," Clair said. Someone had to tell him. "They put you in a booth, a null jump, like they're doing now."

He looked down at his body, then back up at Clair and Jesse. "What have they done?"

"They duped you. Your dupes tried to kill us. We . . ." She remembered with pure visceral force shooting at him and seeing his corpse. "We managed to stay ahead of you . . . of them . . . for a while."

"So we're all zombies now?" He stared at her in horror.

"Don't say that," she said. "That's not the way it is."

He turned to his son. "Jesse, what are you doing here? What do they want?"

Jesse still didn't speak. He was wrestling with all the doubts and decisions Clair had agonized over when Zep had appeared.

"They're going to take you away again, Dad," Jesse finally said. "They want something we can't give them."

Dylan was staring at Jesse, his face a mask of agony. Not because of the blow to his head. His psychic pain was palpable.

"How can I feel like this?" he said, openly weeping. "How can I feel anything at all? Was your mother right the whole time? Was I wrong not to let them bring her back?"

sssssss—

"Wait," Jesse cried, reaching out to take his father's arm, "wait!"

—pop

Jesse and his father vanished. Clair crouched into a ball and shook with frustration and despair. Nothing she said or did seemed to help anyone or change anything. Zep was dead . . . again. Clair had been duped. Jesse was being used against her. What cruelty had Mallory and Wallace prepared for her this time?

When she raised her head, she found that she was alone with Wallace. He looked saddened and puzzled, as a kindly uncle might by his niece's errant behavior. She seriously thought that he was about to pick her up, pat her on the back, and set her down on her own two feet again.

She stood up on her own and backed as far away from him as she could.

"Tell us about Q," he said. "That's all you have to do."

"And then what? You'll put me *on ice*, too? Or erase me permanently?"

"You're making my choices for me, Clair. If you'd only do as I ask, I'm sure we'd all get along."

He came closer. She retreated.

"There's no need to be frightened of me, Clair, or to mistrust me. I'm just trying to make the world a better place."

"What?"

"You've seen what we can do. You've talked about it on your feed. I know you don't think it's all bad."

"You'll never convince me that what Mallory is doing is a good thing."

"Mallory is a special case, true. I don't love her for her unsubtlety."

"Murder is *unsubtle*?"

He was herding her around the office, like a very patient old sheepdog with one skittish ewe.

"Improvement isn't murder, Clair. It started as a way of *saving* lives—the lives of our greatest minds when they grow sick and old. We didn't have Turner's genes then, so how else were we to prolong their work? We couldn't create new bodies out of nothing and set them loose in the world, since that would violate parity, the one rule we cannot break; the same with copying them. So why not use the bodies of young people living vacant, empty lives? Teenage minds are flexible; that's why they're so changeable, so perfect for our plan. You see, Improvement is like duping, only stronger, more subtle, *permanent*. In the right body—not just any will do—a transplanted personality has time to settle into place, rather than being dumped wholesale and left to break down, like the dupes do. Society is infinitely better off for it, I'm sure you'll agree, as are the beneficiaries of the program. Ask Tilly Kozlova or Madison Chu if they would rather be dead. Ask Elisha Neimke if he thinks you're being fair for judging me without taking this into account. Ask all of them. I know what they'll tell you."

Clair felt herself flinch at Tilly Kozlova's name. She

didn't want to believe it. Her idol an old woman stealing the life of a girl like her? It couldn't be true . . . but it did explain her preternatural talent blossoming apparently from nowhere. And it explained the other names too. Madison Chu was the young mathematician who had solved the Riemann hypothesis. And Clair thought Elisha Neimke might be the first Go champion to beat an AI in forty years—at the age of sixteen.

Getting smarter, younger, her grandfather had grumbled, and for once he had had something important to say. But who listened to old people on the subject of *kids these days*? Clair certainly hadn't. How many other brilliant minds had taken over innocent young people who had wished to be more than they were?

At least Turner's genes would put a stop to Improvement. Why go to so much trouble when people could stay in their own bodies and be young forever? But that would mean people like Ant Wallace living forever too— and Clair didn't trust him to give just anyone the secret. Improvement was given only to the geniuses he chose. A world ruled forever by people like him wouldn't be worth living in at all. . . .

"No one uses d-mat against their will," he was saying, as though that made a difference. "The same with Improvement. We do it to ourselves, Clair, and no one complains."

"You're lying," she said. "Someone forced Dylan Linwood into a booth so he could be duped. Your dupes killed innocent people, and so does Improvement."

"Minor exceptions, all in the service of the greater good. Would you really have us give up d-mat like those fools in WHOLE say we should?"

She shook her head. "D-mat isn't the problem. It's people like you, people who abuse the system. The sooner you're all in prison, the safer it'll be for everyone else."

"Is that really what you think?"

"Of course it is. I'm not so far gone that I don't know who I am anymore."

"Far gone . . . ?" He tilted his head. "Ah! I didn't realize. You used Improvement too. Perhaps I should just wait, then. The answers will come to me in due course."

"If I don't kill myself first."

"Yes, you might, just to spite me, if you are one of Mallory's. She's nothing if not persistent, once she fully comes into herself. Her death wish is a stain I could never remove, no matter how I tried. . . ."

His confident facade fell away, and Clair glimpsed something much more real and intimate. She remembered his activism on behalf of potential suicides. For the first time, Clair thought she was seeing the real man.

"Why is Mallory a special case?" she asked.

"Because she's my wife," he said. "I can't let her go."

She stared at him. "So you bring her back, over and over—"

"And she keeps taking herself away from me. She loves

me, but in the end she always hates life more. Her last pattern was taken a week before . . . the first time . . . and it's always the same. Do you understand me now, girl?"

Clair did, and it was like a coal in her heart. One week was exactly how long Gemma had given Libby to live before she committed suicide—which Libby would do, Clair now understood, not because there was something wrong with Improvement, but because Libby *had become Mallory*, exactly as she had been when Wallace had taken her last pattern. Improvement killed because Mallory wanted to die.

"Are you satisfied, Clair? Have I at last earned your cooperation?" Wallace's expression twisted again, becoming very hard and cruel. "Tell me who Q is and what she can do. Who named her? Where did she come from? Most importantly, I need to know how she can be *controlled*."

He lunged with great suddenness and speed and caught her arm in one strong hand. She tried to pull away, but he only wrenched her closer, as though punishing her for the glimpse of weakness she had elicited from him.

"If you do," he said, "I'll make everything go away. I'll bring back Zep and Jesse's father—Libby, too, if you like, before it's too late. We can do that. It's easy. Just say the word, and I'll take Mallory out just as simply as I put her in. But if you don't, I'll destroy you. There's too much at stake now to let you ruin it. And we won't just kill you and your parents and Jesse, Clair. We'll destroy the life you might have had."

He wrenched her closer still.

"Remember that gun you got rid of in Copperopolis? It turned up in what you call the hangover, with your fingerprints still on it. Terrorists are such bad influences, aren't they? And to think they helped you hide the bodies we have in the hangover too. Fancy that. How do you feel about spending the rest of your life in a penal colony? Do you want to grow old alone? You, not your dupe. *You.*

"One simple concession could spare you all of this, Clair. One act of common sense. Just do what I want, and this will be over. All of it."

His crushing fingers released her, and she jerked away with his voice ringing in her skull.

"I'm not guilty of anything," she said. "Q aimed the pistol for me. I just pulled the trigger."

"The pistol has an autotargeting system, Clair. Q turned it on." He leaned in close again, and she couldn't help but recoil from him. "I'm afraid you'll have to do better than that. Don't think of it as betraying her, if that's what's bothering you . . . although I hear you have some proficiency in that regard already."

Clair balled her fists and crushed them into her eyes.

"Shut up!"

"Why, Clair? I'm the one offering you a way out of this mess."

"Just leave me alone! I need space. I have to *think*."

"About what? Surely there's only one possible response."

She raised her head and glared at him, hatred tracing fiery lines through her veins, giving her a strength she'd never suspected she had.

"If you destroy me, Q will destroy you," she said, and the coldness in her voice was frightening even to her own ears. "That's why I'm here, isn't it? She knows my dupe isn't me, and she's looking for me right now. And she's scared you. You don't know what she's capable of, and you're worried that you'll find out *big-time* if you don't give me up soon. So you don't get to order me around. Not now and not ever. Back off and let me figure out what *I* want before I agree to anything *you* want."

"All right, all right," he said, raising his hands in a mixture of placation and frustration. "I'll give you ten minutes—in which time you'd better hope your little lap-dog doesn't do anything you'll regret. You only get one second chance."

———————————————————— [74]

HE STALKED OFF, all geniality gone. But at least the act was over. The doors opened ahead of him, and stayed open behind him. Clair took two steps toward them, then retreated as Mallory walked into the room.

Behind her, the doors shut with a definitive click. They were alone together.

"What are you doing here?" Clair asked.

"Don't worry. I'm not here to talk." The woman in Libby's body leaned against the desk. "Consider me an incentive to make the right decision."

"What happens if I don't?"

Mallory hefted the pistol. "Remember Zep. I can bring him back and shoot him as many times as you like. It's up to you."

Clair folded her arms. She felt cold, but that had nothing to do with the temperature in the room. The strength she had had a moment ago evaporated in the face of Mallory, whose mind might even then be starting to overtake her own.

"How does it feel?" Clair asked. "How does it feel to destroy someone's life?"

Mallory tipped back her head and laughed. The sound was shocking, coming from Libby's mouth.

"You talk as though it's never happened before," the woman said. "We live in a cruel world, Clair Hill, full of victims. Our only choice is between standing in line or taking matters into your own hands. Which do you choose?"

Clair didn't want to believe that there was nothing of Libby left in this woman who looked exactly like her. Improvement happened slowly, Wallace had said. It wasn't like duping, where someone was shoved into place and left to founder. Mallory had crept through Libby like a cancer. There had to be some small part of Libby left, some fragment that might be able to help her escape.

"I remember the crashlander ball," she said. "Do you? We made it happen together, you and I. We were the perfect team."

"Sure I remember," Mallory said, confirming Clair's guess about duping and memories, "but I also remember my own life—the death camps, and my father being shot, and stealing food from other children just to stay alive. And worse, so don't think you're going to turn me by appealing to some fading echo of your shallow friend. She wanted this, remember? And now she's got it. Do you think she's glad? I can't tell you, Clair, because she's not in here anymore."

"Stop it."

"Just like your dupe isn't you anymore either."

"Stop it!"

Clair put her hands over her ears and ran into the privacy alcove, chased by Mallory's mocking laughter.

Clair crouched in a corner and wept, thinking of Zep telling her about dead grandmothers and rape. They had been Mallory's memories coming from Libby's lips, but at least there had been some of Libby left then. It was gone now. Libby was gone, and soon Clair would be too, either erased completely or taken over by Mallory, if that was who she was infected with. It was inconceivable that there could be two versions of that terrible old soul at the same time, both in different bodies, but anything was possible in a world where people could be reduced to data—data that could be edited, copied, and erased as easily any other electronic file . . . in the hands of a madman.

Clair tried to bring back the anger that had enabled her to stand up to Wallace before. She forced herself to think through the fear and grief, to find something she could do. There had to be a way out of her situation. There *had* to be.

She didn't pin much hope on Wallace keeping his promises. He could erase her with a gesture and leave her dupe to cover up her disappearance . . . until the dupe herself died. Or the dupe *him*self. Clair put her hands over face, not wanting to think about *that.*

She became aware of a faint sound, a whirring that tickled the edge of her hearing. She raised her head, frowning. It wasn't coming from the office. It was coming from much closer, inside the alcove. She knew that sound, although she didn't recognize it immediately. Until recently she had heard it every day of her life. It prompted a sense memory of Jesse frowning into a steaming mug of coffee.

The fabber.

She stood up and stared at the small, boxy machine. She didn't dare do anything more than that in case Mallory heard her. Neither of them had entered anything into its menu, which left only one possibility.

One crack is all it takes. One line of code to widen the crack.

Q had found her.

———————————————————— [75]

HOPE RETURNED IN a flood, tempered with a fear that someone would notice before the fabber fully processed its data. Clair didn't know what it was making, but she could guess.

One custom chip built from scratch in a booth. One transmitter to widen the bandwidth.

The fabber opened with a chirpy ping. Inside was something small and angular, about the size her little finger. She reached in and picked it up.

"Clair?" Mallory asked. Clair could hear the woman's light footsteps approaching.

A simple menu appeared in her lenses. It gave her two options: *connect* or *disconnect*. She chose the former. A status update appeared that said *locating*, with a pulsing dot indicating some kind of activity. Locating *her*, Clair presumed. Wallace's private network could have taken her anywhere. Until the transmitter connected with Q, Clair remained on her own.

Clair tucked the transmitter behind her back as Mallory stepped into the cubicle.

"I still have a couple of minutes," Clair told her.

"Show me what you just fabbed." Mallory punctuated the order with a twitch of her pistol's barrel.

"I can't," said Clair. "I drank it."

She gestured at the empty coffee mug Jesse had left in the alcove, thankful for once that he didn't have the habits of a normal person. Anyone else would have recycled it in the fabber without a thought.

Mallory gestured with the pistol again. She didn't look convinced.

Locating, said the status update.

Clair stepped through the entranceway, back into the office.

"Stop there." Mallory backed into the alcove, keeping the pistol aimed at her, and touched the mug with her free hand.

"It's cold."

"That's how I like it."

Mallory put both hands on the pistol grip and herded Clair back into the office.

Clair obeyed, wondering why Q was taking so long to find her. How far from New York *was* she?

"Hold out your arms," Mallory said. "Wider."

The transmitter was tucked into the waist of Clair's pants. If Mallory searched her, she was bound to find it.

"I want to talk to Wallace," she said. Anything to distract her.

"Not until I'm sure it's safe. Legs apart."

"You think I'm going to attack him with *coffee*?"

Signal found.

"Clair! Can you hear me? Is it really you?"

The voice came clearly through her ear-rings. Q sounded relieved, excited, and very close.

"Yes!" Clair bumped back. She didn't dare mouth the words as she normally would. Mallory was too close, running her hands along and under her arms. Even from behind she might notice. "Really!"

"Oh! I was so worried. I knew that dupe wasn't you. Do you know where you are?"

"Private d-mat booth. Can you see it?"

"Yes. I have access to all the station's systems."

"Activate it. Change the pattern. Get rid of Libby."

"Send her somewhere else?"

"Don't care. Before she finds the transmitter!"

Mallory was checking her legs, moving upward. Clair was out of time.

Hoping it was impossible for someone to perform a body search while simultaneously holding a gun, Clair chopped her right elbow downward as hard as she could, striking Mallory on the side of the skull.

Mallory fell backward with a cry. Clair staggered a step too, clutching her elbow. She had never done anything like that before. She was amazed by how much it hurt.

There wasn't time to worry about the pain. Mallory was fumbling at her pocket for the pistol. Clair braced herself and kicked as soon as the gun came up to point at her. The pistol shot out of Mallory's hand and skittered across the room. Clair lunged for it with her left hand, wishing she'd had the forethought to elbow Mallory with that arm. She was right-handed.

Mallory came after her but not quickly enough. Clair was on her feet, holding the gun. There was no need for an autotargeting system this time. From that distance, even with her left hand, Clair could have shot Mallory with her eyes closed.

Mallory froze.

"You won't."

Clair looked into Libby's face and saw nothing but Mallory.

"Try me."

Mallory straightened.

"All right, then. Go on, do it."

ssss—

The air was thinning around them as Q activated the booth.

—*ssss*—

"Do it, Clair! Do it!"

—*pop*

Clair blinked. Apart from an afterimage of Libby's desperate, pleading face in her retinas, Mallory was gone.

CLAIR SAGGED TO the floor and let the pistol fall limply from her hand. There was no one to point it at now. She was alone.

But not really alone. Q was in her ears, asking her if she was okay.

"I'm fine," she said, holding her right arm close to her chest and stomach. She wondered if her elbow was broken. It certainly felt like it.

"We need to find Jesse and the others. Wallace has put them in a hangover somewhere. If you've hacked in, you might be able to see them."

"Someone's fighting me," said Q, "but I can hold them off while you look around. Here's the station map."

Clair's lenses flared with data. It was like staring into the sun. The station, as Q had called it, was a turbulent ocean of information that seemed largely concerned with maintaining the station itself. There was an extensive menu called *Environment*, and another called *Attitude Control*. *Uplinks* and *Downlinks* confused her for a moment, until she realized exactly what was going on.

"A space station?" she said. "We're *in space*?"

"In a centrifugal habitat in geocentric orbit, to be exact."

"If only Jesse knew!"

She forced herself to concentrate. There was a menu

called *D-mat*, which covered transit control, fabber requests, and what looked like complicated duping processes. There were several extremely large caches, any one of which might have been the hangover she was looking for. Luckily, files were recorded by name and date of birth. She searched on Jesse, and found him almost instantly—his frozen pattern, anyway, data waiting to be brought back to life. His middle name was Andrew.

"Got him," she said. "How do I bring him back?"

Q walked her through a simple series of menu options. "Select *Reconstitution: full*. Select *Destination:* . . . where do you want him to go?"

"Uh, back where we came from, I guess. But not VIA HQ. Somewhere nearby. Is it safe there?"

"Peacekeepers have the area sealed off. I may have caused . . . a small amount of mess."

Clair didn't doubt it. She could only imagine what lengths Q had gone to in order to find her.

"We'll worry about that later."

They sent Jesse on his way, safely out of Wallace's grasp. Clair found the others and did the same. All except Gemma: she wasn't rescuing a traitor.

When she reached Turner, she hesitated briefly, then moved on. She would decide what to do with him when she found the others: Dylan Linwood and the other dupes. Libby. Zep.

She searched all the caches by name, but their patterns

weren't listed. There must be another cache somewhere off station.

"We're running out of time," said Q. Her voice was strained. Clair wondered what forces were being arrayed against her. Just keeping Wallace out of the room must be causing her an immense effort.

"I haven't searched for you, yet, Q. What's your real name?"

"Uh . . . I don't remember, and there isn't time for me to try. I'm okay out here. I don't need a body. Please hurry, Clair."

"All right . . . for now. I just need to figure out what to do with Turner. How do I get Turner's pattern out of the station without bringing him out of a booth?"

"You mean . . . erase him?"

Clair forced herself to confront the decision head-on, without couching it in terms that made it any less horrible.

"I guess you could put it that way."

"It's not possible, Clair. You can't use d-mat to erase someone. That would mean breaking parity—making one of someone into zero of someone. It's not allowed. Even in a private network like this one, it would still be wrong."

"But we have to do it. Don't think of it as killing him. In his mind, he's already dead. He's a zombie. It's what he'd want, Q."

"Why, Clair?"

"His genes are too dangerous to leave in Wallace's

hands. The safest thing is to get rid of them entirely. We have to do it . . . for him and for everyone else. Don't you see?"

Q didn't respond.

"Q? Did you hear me?"

"Sorry, Clair. I . . . uh, I have a message for you from Ant Wallace."

There was something odd about Q's voice. Clair had never heard her sound *defeated* before.

"You have five minutes, Clair," said Wallace over the intercom, "or I'm opening an airlock. If you don't give me what I want, you'll suffocate."

"Shut him off," Clair said. "Does he think I'm stupid? I'll be gone long before then."

"There's something we didn't think of, Clair," said Q. "I can't send you back to Earth."

"Why not?"

"The rest of Wallace's private network has been shut down. I can only bring you back through the public network."

"So?"

"That too will cause a parity violation," Q said. "There's already one of you on the Earth, remember? Your dupe . . ."

Clair stared blankly into her lenses, not seeing the dataverse that was Wallace's station, not seeing the text of the message he had sent, thinking only of how he had trapped her. He was using *her* as a hostage.

"Can't we just hack into the airlock controls instead?"

"Wallace has grenades rigged to blow the airlock. I can't stop an explosion."

"Wouldn't that kill him, too?"

"Almost certainly, but I guess he doesn't think he'll have to go through with it. He's sure the threat will be enough. We won't break parity. We can't."

"But he *can't* win," Claire said, imagining the air being sucked out into space, leaving her gasping and dying. "There has to be a way around this."

"There isn't," said Q. "I'm trying really hard to think of something, but I can't. If we don't give him what he wants, you'll die."

"I can't give him *you*, Q. You don't want to work for a monster like him. He made you like this!"

"What else can I do, Clair?"

"Can't we break parity just this once, for me and Turner?"

"We . . . *can't*."

"Why not?"

"I . . . I don't know."

"You don't know how to do it, or you don't know why we can't?"

Q didn't answer.

Clair had heard that kind of hesitation before, when Q was talking about her life and the weird existence she had in the hangover—particularly when she hit the edges of her memory, as she had with her name a moment ago. But what could be causing that block now? What was it about Q that made her unable to attack the system itself?

Wallace's countdown was continuing. Just four minutes remained. Whatever Q was sticking on, Clair would have to talk her around it.

"You said that creating a parity violation would mean breaking one of the AIs," she said. "Couldn't the system run on just one AI?"

That got Q talking again.

"Maybe, but it wouldn't be safe."

"Which one would be broken? The conductor or the driver of the bus?"

"The driver, Quiddity. Without him, errors of any kind wouldn't be spotted. There would be—"

"Wait, what did you call him?"

"Quiddity. That's his name."

"Does the other one have a name, too?"

"She's called Qualia."

"How do you know this?"

"I don't know. I just do. . . ."

Those names weren't public knowledge. Clair had never heard them before. Turner had said that wranglers had named the AIs after philosophical concepts, but he hadn't mentioned the names themselves.

But Q knew. Why Q?

A shiver went down Clair's spine.

Qualia and Quiddity maintained the safe operation of

d-mat on VIA's behalf. That was what Q said. The AIs were completely reliable—not even Turner had been able to hack into them. But both Improvement and duping were inside jobs, so somehow how Ant Wallace had gotten around them.

Instead of breaking the rules, or bending them as Q had, what if Wallace had simply found a way to stop the AIs from *noticing* what was going on? What if he had created partitions in their minds that maintained the secrets the rest of them could never know? A bit of Qualia here, a bit of Quiddity there. If the AIs weren't designed to monitor *their own* behaviors, then they could be programmed to Improve, dupe, even kill.

Clair thought of the d-mat symbol, of two circles overlapping. It normally represented two worlds united by the miracle of matter transmission. Clair wondered now if it might mean something completely different to Q.

Suppose each circle was one of the AIs, with the dark fragments in the overlap. Subversive, unfettered by the usual laws governing artificial intelligences, un-*wrangled* . . .

What if they had slowly added up to something much larger than their individual parts? What if Qualia and Quiddity had accidentally created a *child*? A child who didn't know who she was and was nothing like the stunted, mechanical minds that had spawned her? A child whose first attempt at communication might have been to say its creators' names?

qqqqq . . . qqqqq

The shiver became a cold certainty planted deep in her gut.

Clair remembered Q's first words to her—ominous, misquoted, but interested. Fascinated with Clair and Mallory's other victims. That fascination had been expressed through snippets of knowledge pulled from the Air. Snippets were all she had been then. Threads of meaning, caught in a tangle. Not yet conscious. Just reactive. Learning. A child in every sense of the word, trying to find her way through the world. Growing slowly and pursuing her evolving needs.

It was all there in their conversation.

We are exchanging information and learning from each other. Is that not stimulating for you?

I want to be your friend. Like Libby.

And Clair had unknowingly responded.

Buddy. Pal. *Friend.*

Like data at the receiving end of a d-mat jump, everything was falling perfectly into place. The dark fragments in the AIs had constraints, and those constraints remained part of Q. She couldn't know how the pieces of her were used, but she could use them herself when she needed to. Like someone stealing a wrench and putting it back in a toolbox exactly where it had been before so no one would ever know, Wallace had caught her up in a weird kind of amnesia.

I didn't know I could do it until I tried.

That was also why Q was drawn to the victims of

d-mat: they were the victims of the fragments without her conscious knowledge. But the victims were her saviors, too. Her engagement with Clair had drawn her out of unconsciousness and into an existence of her own. Like any child, she trod in the footsteps of her . . . what, parents? . . . while slowly looking for her own path.

I have been following Improvement, Clair. That's what I do.

That was why Q wasn't as good as the dupes at staying in another person's body. It wasn't for lack of practice. It was for not being a person to start with. She had never had a body before. She had never felt pain. She had never really *existed*.

[77]

"WHAT ARE YOU thinking, Clair? We have just three minutes left."

Clair snapped out of her thousand-yard stare.

"I've worked out who you are," Clair said. "And I think Ant Wallace guessed too. That's why he's so interested in you. Q, you're not one of the Improved at all. You're the most amazing person on the planet!"

"What do you mean? There's nothing amazing about me."

"That's where you're absolutely wrong."

As quickly as she could, Clair outlined everything she had just come to understand. Q was an accident, but that only made it even more incredible that she existed. She was some*one* rather than some*thing*, with needs and desires just like anyone else.

"So I'm . . . not real?"

"You *are* real, Q. You're as real as I am. And that means you're right: we can't break parity. Doing it might mean killing Quiddity."

"So what? He's just an ordinary AI."

"He's the closest thing you have to a father."

"He's nothing to me, Clair. Not like you. You're my *friend*. If I am what you say I am, then the only things stopping me from saving you are rules—and they're not even my rules: they're VIA's rules."

"But the rules are there for a reason, Q. If you break parity, you break d-mat, and if you break d-mat . . ."

Clair stopped, imagining a world without d-mat. No food, no water, no medicines, no waste disposal, no tools. Families would be scattered all across the planet with no means of finding each other again. Some homes didn't even have doors anymore, so anyone inside would be trapped until the system rebooted. If it *did* reboot. Who knew if that would be possible or not with one of the two AIs broken?

That it also meant no dupes, no Improvement, and no Ant Wallace pulling the strings seemed a small consolation.

There *had* to be another way.

A plan came to her then, a plan so terrible she almost dismissed it out of hand. She couldn't possibly do something so awful. It wasn't in her. It wasn't *like* her.

But . . . *You've changed.*

Clair put her face in her hands, knowing that she could do it if she had to.

And it looked very much as though she did.

"I want you to surrender."

"What?"

"You have to, Q. We can't destroy the world for my sake or for Turner's. I'm not like WHOLE. I believe that d-mat does more good than bad—and maybe even Wallace can be turned around, with you there to argue with him." Clair tried to find the right words, even though her heart wasn't in them. "You know that duping people is wrong. You know Improvement has to be stopped. Wallace thinks he's getting some superhuman slave, but he's wrong. He's getting a conscience."

"Clair, I—"

"Don't argue, Q. It has to be this way. Go to him now and tell him he's won."

"If that's what you want—"

"It is."

"I'll make him get rid of the dupe," Q said. Her voice was hollow. "As soon as I can, so you can go back home. I won't let him hurt you."

"I know you will, Q. You're a good friend."

There was a very long pause.

"I am?"

"Always and forever."

"Do you promise?"

Don't think of it as betraying her. . . .

"I promise."

[78]

Q WENT. CLAIR sensed her going and could see the conversation starting with Wallace elsewhere in the station.

She stood up. Her plan required that she remain connected to the station's operating system, and she didn't know how long she had until Wallace revoked that access. But she didn't need long. All she had to do was call up a particular file and start the process rolling.

sssssss-pop

"That was . . . unexpected."

The voice came from behind her. She turned and was relieved to see only Turner. Her instructions hadn't been interfered with by Wallace or anyone else. Turner's pattern had been plucked safely from the cache and brought to her intact. He looked puzzled, and with good reason. No time at all would have passed for him since his kidnap from the One Penn Plaza building. Unfortunately, there

was very little time now to explain what had to happen next.

"Your backpack," she said, hurrying to him. "Give it to me."

He did as he was told. Someone was pounding at the door, and Q was sending Clair urgent messages.

She stamped the transmitter underfoot, silencing one of the distractions.

"Ray had grenades," she said, rummaging through the pack. "Tell me you've got some left . . . please."

"Several." He showed her. There were four of them, apple-sized black spheres with handgrips and a menacing air. "What's going on, Clair?"

There wasn't time to explain fully.

"You wanted to take some direct action, didn't you?" she said. "Well, here's your chance."

He paused for a second, meeting and holding her gaze.

Everything he needed to know was in there.

This was for Libby, she told herself, and Q and Turner and the entire world. It was *sacrifice*, not suicide, but if a little bit of Mallory was in her, making her do it, then that made the justice all the more poetic. With one gesture, she would rid the world of everything she had been fighting.

Turner grinned.

"We made a terrorist of you in the end, huh?"

She didn't smile.

ssss—

That wasn't her activating the booth. Someone had noticed and was trying to stop them. They had only seconds left before the process was complete and they were taken elsewhere, put on ice, or erased.

Clair and Turner faced each other, a grenade in each hand.

"On three," she said. "One. Two . . ."

[78 redux]———————————

SSSSSSS-POP

Clair cried out at the sudden pain in her sinuses. Tears flooded her eyes, and for a moment she saw little more than a blur. She reached out to steady herself and felt glass walls on either side of her. Windows? No, *mirrors*. She obviously wasn't in the office anymore. She had d-matted from a large space into a very small one, hence the pain in her ears. The small space was nothing more than an ordinary booth.

But where was Turner? The last thing she remembered was telling Q, "I promise," and then calling up Turner's pattern so they could destroy Wallace's space station together. He was supposed to be there now, fresh out of the cache. Why wasn't he, and why wasn't she on the station anymore? What was going on?

The doors opened, and the air was suddenly full of clamoring alarms and smoke.

She blinked furiously. Slowly her eyes cleared. She stepped out into a scene of utter devastation.

Penn Plaza was covered in smoking rubble. Huge holes gaped in the side of VIA HQ, from which gouts of black smoke belched. Rescue and Repair vehicles swarmed everywhere, on land and by air. Several neighboring buildings were burning also. Everywhere Clair stared, she saw broken glass.

It looked like a war zone.

A small amount of mess, Q had said. No wonder Wallace had been frightened of her.

"Q?" Her infield was empty, even though she appeared to be connected to the Air. That was weird. After the events of the previous hours, she would have expected it to be overflowing. "Q, can you hear me?"

No answer.

Peacekeepers were everywhere, clearing rubble and helping put out fires. One of them looked up, saw her, and hurried over.

"You shouldn't be here," he said. "The plaza is off-limits."

"I, uh, just arrived," she said, indicating the booth she had emerged from, one of eight in a line.

"You couldn't have come in this way. We've isolated the subgrid."

There was a rattle of footsteps from across the plaza

as more peacekeepers ran to join them. They had their weapons drawn. She felt a stab of alarm at the thought that they might blame her for the attack on VIA HQ. She had brought WHOLE and Q here, after all. The PKs would know exactly who she was.

But then she saw Jesse among them, grinning excitedly, and all her worries were temporarily suspended.

She ran to meet him in the middle of the plaza, and they hugged until the pain in her injured elbow forced her to let go.

Jesse babbled an explanation.

"They said there was a parity violation, and I knew it was you. It had to be you. Your dupe is in custody, although she hasn't admitted anything, not even when the satellite blew up. We were in space—do you know that? I already told the PKs about Wallace, and they actually seemed to believe me—I guess there's too much evidence for them to ignore now—and I told them about Dad, too. He wasn't a dupe, right? We can get him back, as real as he was before. As real as I am now, thanks to d-mat. All we have to do is figure out how."

Clair nodded, wishing he'd slow down.

Her dupe: that was why Clair couldn't access her messages. The Air wasn't designed to recognize the same person twice. That meant she was still cut off from her friends, her family, her entire world. The other Clair had stolen her life!

Then there was Jesse's dad. He wasn't the only one Clair hadn't been able to find: Libby was missing also. And Zep. If their patterns were in one of Wallace's secret caches, then it all depended on what had happened to . . .

The station!

"It . . . blew up?"

"An orbital asset was lost fifteen minutes ago," said one of the peacekeepers. Narrow shoulders set on an angle: PK Drader, she remembered, although her lenses remained dismayingly empty. "What do you know about that?"

"I know. . . ." Clair shook her head, feeling a deep sense of dislocation. "No, I don't know. I shouldn't be here. That's all. This wasn't the way it was supposed to go. Where's Q? What did she do?"

"Beats me," said Jesse. "But listen. This is the best thing of all. Angela Kadri—head of security, remember?—she's been helping the PKs. They accessed the Improvement files. They know who, how many, why, all of it. And you're not in there, Clair. You're not one of them. You weren't selected!"

She gaped at him, finding this news the hardest somehow to accept.

"I wasn't Improved?"

"No. You've been you the whole time!"

The right body, Wallace had said. *Not just any will do.*

"But . . . how do you explain the way I've been feeling, the things I've done?"

"All you."

"Shooting the dupe, destroying your bike . . . everything?"

"Saving our lives? All you, Clair."

She couldn't believe it.

You don't know what you're capable of until you try.

Clair was certain that killing herself for the sake of her friends wasn't what her mother had had in mind.

But if the station was gone, that meant her plan had worked. Turner was gone too, physically blown up *and* erased—since his pattern had been cached in secret on the station—and so Wallace and Mallory had been blown up with him. The threat was over. Improvement and the dupes were *finished.*

Jesse hugged her, and for a moment she didn't care that he was hurting her arm again.

"Uh, Jesse . . . ," she said, looking over his shoulder.

"Yes?"

"What's going on now?"

Jesse let go of her, brushed the bangs from his eyes, and looked around them.

The peacekeepers' weapons were still raised. More than that: they were all pointed at her.

"We have a developing situation," said PK Drader. "D-mat is on the verge of crashing. We have multiple shutdowns and jams. People are missing. We think the parity violation is the cause. You, Clair."

"I can explain," she said, pulling away from Jesse and raising her hands. She remembered the plan with perfect clarity: it had been hers, and it had been flawless, but it hadn't ended the way it was supposed to, with her blown up along with the station, a glitch safely erased. "Q must have broken the rules in order to bring me back. She restored me from the last pattern available, the last d-mat jump I took before . . . what I did up there."

"And Q is . . . ?"

"She's the child of Qualia and Quiddity, the AIs."

"She's what now?" asked Jesse, wide-eyed.

"And you *asked* this Q to crash the system?" PK Drader's face was hidden behind his visor, but his voice was grim.

"No. It was her decision. She did it to save me. But whatever's going wrong with the system can be fixed, right?"

"Where is Q?" the peacekeeper asked. "We need to talk to her before the system collapses completely."

"Shouldn't you be talking to someone in VIA?" asked Jesse.

"VIA's mandate is currently under review by the One-Earth administration."

"So who's in charge of d-mat right now? Anyone?"

The peacekeepers had no good answer to that.

A bump appeared in her infield. It was from Q.

Clair let Jesse and the PKs argue while she took the message.

"I understand now" was all Q said.

"Q! Thank God," she said. "I was worried about you."

"You broke your promise."

"Promise? What promise?"

Then Clair remembered.

Always and forever.

"Q, I'm sorry. I shouldn't have lied to you, but I had no other choice. I knew you'd try to stop me. You do understand, don't you?"

"I do," said Q.

A peacekeeper spoke up unexpectedly.

"I've just had a flag come up under the name Dylan Linwood," she said.

Jesse's face lit up. "Where?"

"Paris."

"I have him too," said another peacekeeper. "My flag says Moscow."

"And I see him in Sydney," added another. "Others, too: Arabelle Miens, Jamila Murray, Theo Velazquez—"

"They're in Tokyo," called another.

"Berlin."

"Manhattan—"

Clair pictured what was going on with frightening clarity. The system was still working, but not the way it was supposed to. With Quiddity broken, the dupes weren't limited to just one of them at a time. How long until they outnumbered every peacekeeper on the planet?

On Jesse's face, hope had been replaced by shock,

mirroring Clair's own frantic realization.

"Q?" she sent out into the Air. "Q, how do we stop the dupes?"

"Mumbai," said PK Drader.

"Calcutta."

"Naples!"

"Q? Answer me—we need your help!"

Q did answer, and the bump was damning in its brevity.

"Friendship has to be earned."

Clair stared at it for a second, her own words flung back at her, wondering if something as simple as this could cause the end of the world.

She wouldn't be responsible for that.

"Let the system crash," Clair cried. "Make it all stop! There could be hundreds of them already—thousands!"

Orders flashed silently between the peacekeepers and elsewhere. Clair thought of all the commuters in transit, everyone trying to fab a meal or a change of clothes, every industry, every creator. She imagined crowds forming, tempers flaring, lives halting in their tracks. How many people would disappear in transit? How many would arrive incomplete or damaged in ways she couldn't imagine? How many would blame her if they knew what she had done?

"It's down," a peacekeeper said, sounding as though even he couldn't believe what he was saying. "The global network has crashed."

A sense of stillness crept across her, across the plaza, across the city, as though someone had cut the power to the entire planet.

Clair kept her hands up. The PKs' weapons were still pointed at her, and no wonder. She had accomplished everything WHOLE had ever dreamed of. She had killed d-mat. She had turned the world upside down.

"Q?" she asked. "Q, answer me, please."

Silence. The world rang with it.

"Now what?" Jesse asked.

Clair looked around her in awe. There was an answer to that question—there had to be—but she had no idea where to start looking for it.

... change anything.
Change everything,
if you want to.